"Valdes-Rodriguez brings savvy and sometimes savage humor to chick lit."   —*Daily News* (New York)

"Once again, without resorting to didacticism, [Valdes-Rodriguez's] novel becomes a subtle vehicle for demonstrating the rich diversity of Latina culture."   —*Library Journal*

"The three amigas—a television actress, a single mother, and a manager of musicians—each has her own distinct lifestyle, quirks, and notions of romance, yet each manages to help her friends find balance, along with loads of good times."   —*The Sacramento Bee*

"Entertaining."   —*Entertainment Weekly*

"Humor abounds in Valdes-Rodriguez's new novel . . . women of all ethnicities will identify with the real-life trials of this novel's three friends."   —*Romantic Times BookReviews*

The Dirty Girls Social Club

"The feel of a night out with the girls . . . charming . . . undeniably fun."   —*The Miami Herald*

"A compulsive beach read . . . smart, brassy, and messy enough to make you pause mid–sunscreen slathering."   —*Entertainment Weekly*

"Delivers on the promise of its title . . . a fun, irresistible debut."   —*Publishers Weekly*

"Laugh-out-loud read . . . with no-holds-barred humor."   —*The Dallas Morning News*

"Wonderful writing, delicious humor, biting sarcasm, and impressive intelligence."   —*Detroit Free Press*

"Alisa Valdes-Rodriguez's writing style is raunchy yet refined . . . but in the end, it's the complex, finely drawn characters who make the book work."   —*Rocky Mountain News*

Make Him Look Good

Make Him Look Good

Alisa Valdes-Rodriguez

St. Martin's Griffin

New York

www.stmartins.com

Library of Congress Cataloging-in-Publication Data

Valdes-Rodriguez, Alisa.
    Make him look good / Alisa Valdes-Rodriguez.—1st ed.
        p.   cm.
    ISBN-13: 978-0-312-34980-6
    ISBN-10: 0-312-34980-7
    1. Hispanic American women—Fiction.   2. Man-woman relationships—Fiction.   3. Miami (Fla.)—Fiction.   I. Title.

PS36223A425M36   2006
813'.6—dc22

                                                                2005044806

First St. Martin's Griffin Edition: February 2007

10 9 8 7 6 5 4 3 2 1

To my mother, Maxine Conant, for teaching me to love words. To my dad, Nelson Valdés, for giving me the guts to put them on paper. To Patrick, the babydaddy, for giving me time to write. To K. C. Porter, for music. To J. N., for the inside celebrity scoop. And to Alexander Patrick Rodriguez, for continuing to be the best minuscule muse a mommy could ask for.

acknowledgments

Thanks to Leslie Daniels, the best agent (and friend) a nervous (neurotic?) and superstitious (psycho?) writer could have. Thanks also to Elizabeth Beier, my fabulous editor and the only person I know who can actually use "fabulous" in a spoken sentence without sounding weird—*Oops, we did it again, ooh baby bay-buh!* Hugs and thanks to Matthew Shear, cheery master of the paperback universe; Matthew Baldacci, sickeningly fit master of the marketing universe; and John Murphy, cynical king of the hell that is the public relations universe. Thanks to artmaster Michael Storrings for the sexy, savvy covers that put books in hands. Finally, *un montón de* thanks to Sally Richardson, brilliant and benevolent queen of the entire wacky (in a *good* way, honest!) universe according to Saint Martin. Thanks too to the Albuquerque Fire Department girls, for letting me hang around the station. You ladies rock!

Make Him Look Good

Prologue

Fabulous, sweetie.

I'm wearing *super*-tight Rock & Republic jeans with heels—expensive heels, okay? We're talking Dolce & Gabbana, with a sparkly gold bikini top, and I feel *fabulous*. From my bleached, blown-out hair to my perfectly white manicured toenails (and coco-brown tanned feet) fa-bu-lous, or, as we say here in Miami, Spanglish capital of the world: *requete, pero requete fabulosa*.

The dance mix is pumped up, and everyone is feeling good. By "everyone," I mean all two hundred guests invited to this, my private engagement party at Amika—only the *best* dance club in Miami. I'm surrounded by my girlfriends, each cuter and tipsier than the next. We've got our drinks on—Cristal, *chica*—the bass is bumping, and I no longer have back fat. Do you know how good it feels to rid yourself of back fat once and for all? *Te lo juro*, sweetie, it's incredible. I don't miss the back-fat jiggle. No one needs boobs on their back, do they? I don't, not anymore. Anyway, my feet move to the music, and I am no longer uncoordinated, either. I am not fat. And I am graceful. *Chévere*. I didn't know I could dance like this. Did you?

Oh, I am *also* calling you *sweetie*, which I bet you didn't expect. You thought I was shy and nervous. When you feel this fabulous, "sweetie" just pours out of your mouth, kind of like the Cristal pouring into my glass. No, pardon *me*. My *flute*. Fabulous, fat-free girls like me don't drink out of glasses, sweetie. Please. We *flute* it, all the way. I like how you're getting into the groove with the rest of us girls, kicking back, letting the world know we *rock*. Did you notice the room smells like coconut oil and mango butter? Love that.

Look at this place. The colorful striped walls, retro yet chic. The big white chairs. The striped booth seats. The shiny wooden floors. The deco lighting. The gorgeous bartender dudes with the sculpted bodies and the chiseled faces. This is heaven. That's what this place is. So stylish it almost hurts, the way great sex is so good it almost hurts. And don't get me started on the sex thing. Ricky and I did it before we got here, and we're going to do it again later. He's the best lover I've ever had. He's, how shall I put this? He's simply fabulous.

So *fabulous*. I know. It's not a word I have ever used to describe myself, until now. Yes, it's a word I thought only really belonged on *Queer Eye*, but now that I'm, you know, fabulous *too*, now that Ricky Biscayne has fallen in *love* with me, it works. Let me repeat that last part, in case you didn't catch it. Ricky Biscayne has fallen in *love*. With. Me.

I look up, still moving my amazingly toned new body to the beat, and see Ricky Biscayne, the hottest Latin pop singer on earth, standing with his manager and friends across the room. There is no straight woman on earth who does not recognize his supreme perfection. My heart stops for a minute. I die a little looking at him. He is so exquisite you just sort of convulse inside, like a sneeze, and your heart stops the way it does when you sneeze, too. Ricky is godly.

To my mainstream friends, I'd say Ricky looks like a younger, sexier, less greasy Antonio Banderas. To those of the Latin American persuasion, I'd say he looks like a tougher, rock-and-roll version of Chayanne, or a taller, buffer Luis Fonsi. He's wearing a lime green guayabera and white linen pants, and you can see just a hint of exactly how well-endowed he is. And he is. Trust me.

Ricky winks at me with one big, honey-brown eye, and blows a kiss with his pouty pink lips. He grins and the dimples pop out.

Damn, girl. *Pero Dios mío.* What good deed did I do to *deserve* this? Ricky, that superstar stud over there, the one every woman in the room wants, is my future *husband.*

"Pinch me," I tell my tall, elegant sister, Geneva.

"Gladly," she says. She chugs her Champagne, then she actually pinches my arm. And twists the flesh like a radio dial.

"Ow! Not so hard!"

"Hey, you *asked* me to," she says. "Don't get all pissy."

Geneva enjoys pinching me, because she's my big sister and has always loved torturing me in small ways. But she's happy for me, too. And she *knows* why I need a pinch. It's because I can't believe all those prayers to La Caridad del Cobre, the patron saint of Cuba, worked. I've prayed for years to *la virgen* that she would let me meet and marry Ricky Biscayne. And she came through. Look. It's a literal miracle that I'm here.

So you *know*, this is the third time I've asked Geneva to pinch me since we rolled up beneath the fat green palm trees in Ricky's white stretch limo an hour ago. I asked her again when *Entertainment Tonight* interviewed me half an hour ago. My arm is going to be so black and blue tomorrow people will start to gossip that Ricky, the gentlest, smartest man you could ever meet, is, like, a *wife* beater. I can't imagine anything more absurd. Honestly. Ricky is sensitive, handsome, and mine.

I still feel fabulous, though, bruises and all. My geeky friends from the book club look like they belong here, with all the celebrities and models. I look around at the smiling faces and moving bodies, and realize *everyone* knows: That I'm as fabulous as my sister, times *ten.* That I *got* him. Me. Milan Gotay, former laxative publicist. Former nobody. Former dull girl from Coral Gables. Former tub-o-chub, former klutz, former slacker living at home in her childhood bedroom. A celebrity fiancée, about to marry the man whose posters I've had taped to my closet door for a decade.

Everyone is here, the media, celebrities, and *you* people, my crazy, drunk, happy, stupidly glamorous *girlfriends*, because Ricky, a sensitive songwriter and genius artist, looked out at the audience at an intimate concert at a club in South Beach, and he plucked *me* out of the crowd to sing to onstage. He held my hand that night, and never let go. I went back to his hotel room with him that night, and the lovemaking was so intense, and so perfect, I wept for joy.

I know, it sounds like a cheesy romance novel. But these things happen. No, really. I've loved Ricky since I was a teenager. You could even say I have been obsessed with him. So you can only imagine, this whole thing is a dream come true for me.

"Time to get up," says one of my friends. I look at her funny and she laughs. I turn away and look at Ricky again. That's all I want to do, stare at him, from now until the end of time. I remember why he proposed to me, and it feels like tiny spiders crawl inside my ribcage.

Ricky fell for me because of a certain special something in my eyes, he said. Something special he'd never seen in another woman. He divorced his supermodel wife for me. Me! A lowly fan. I've been like Julia Roberts in *Pretty Woman* ever since, shopping on Ricky's card, jetting around the world with him, staying in his mansions and penthouses. Just last week I took a group of my book club girlfriends for a cruise on Ricky's yacht. We were out on the deck in all white, sunning ourselves like lizards, sipping up the tart, minty-sweet *mojitos* made fresh for us by Ricky's chef, who came along.

It's amazing, really.

Have I mentioned I feel fabulous? What? Only four thousand times? Sorry.

"Milan?" asks another of my friends, in a voice surprisingly like my mother's. "Are you awake? Get up. You're going to miss Ricky's performance."

I turn away again, move my hips to the beat of the music, smile at a male movie star I've admired for a long time. Eduardo Verastegui? That's his name. I can't believe he's here! Wow. See, life has ways of amazing you, changing you, changing the way people treat you. All you have to do is focus on what you want. Some people pray. Some people work hard. I did *both,* and here I am, with the bass thrumming my heart in my chest, and my jeans fitting better than ever.

I mean, *look* at how the women here are looking at me. I'm not competitive or insecure or anything, and I love my female friends to death, but there *is* a certain *rush* I get from all these women pretending *not* to be jealous of me. I can see how they really feel, though. Like they don't want their men to get too *close.*

Love makes you beautiful; how else to explain that I'm the ugly duckling who became the swan? I truly believe this. They see I'm in love, and that my happiness might lure their boys away. That's okay. I don't blame them. I used to have that feeling about other women, too—my man-stealing sister in particular, but that's another story for another day. Right now, my sister—the most glamorous girl to ever come out of Coral Gables—is standing here with me, swaying to the hard groove, and I don't think anyone can decide who's hotter, me or Geneva. When you're this fabulous, like me and G, people just gravitate toward you, and by "people" I mean *men.* I wouldn't take their men, though. I have Ricky. I already took *him* from his wife. I don't need anything, or anyone, else.

I can't tell you why I always knew this would happen, but I did. And here I am. It's happening. Ricky Biscayne wants to marry me. It's amazing what a little prayer can do, when it's focused right. A little prayer can make your dreams come true. Look at me. I mean, it doesn't get more fabulous than this.

"Get up," says Geneva, pinching me again. "The show's going to start soon."

"Ow, quit it!"

"Get *up.*"

"What? Up? Up where?"

"Your sister's here, and you're still asleep," she says. I have no idea what she's talking about.

I look around the club, at the dancers, the revelers, and try to figure it out. One by one, they stop dancing, and stare at me. The music starts to fade. The DJ looks sad, and starts to pack his things. No!

Don't go! Come back! I hear my own voice, distant and forlorn, "Late? Late for *what*?" We ladies of leisure don't have to be anywhere, especially not now, not here, at my engagement party.

"For Ricky's performance, *hija*," she says, only now her voice has changed, and it sounds pinched, nasal, and neurotic, like my *mother's*. The music fades, and in its place I hear a new sound—the anemic wheezing of the air conditioner in my childhood bedroom.

I open my eyelids, sticky because I fell asleep after work this evening, before even eating dinner, and neglected to remove my eye makeup and contacts. My cheek is stuck in a glue of drool to a page of *People* magazine, which I now recall reading before I passed out. I peel the paper off, and see the story. A celebrity party photo page, including a party at Amika. Ah. Now I remember. I'm *not* fabulous. I'm Milan, drool-cheeked and crusty-eyed. I blink up at the ceiling of my room. Six Ricky Biscayne photos are taped up there, and my favorite one has started to come unglued. I turn to the Hello Kitty clock on my bedside table. Almost eleven at night? How is that possible?

I turn my head and see my mother standing next to the bed, frowning, holding a glass of water in one hand, her other hand poised and ready to pinch me again, with gleaming-red devil nails. I wonder if she planned to give me the water to drink, or to toss it in my face if I didn't get up. She pinches me.

"Ow!" I cry when she does. I sit up and feel the back fat jiggle. Still there. "Why must you *do* that?"

"Because you're lazy," says my mother. She looks at her watch. "You told me to wake you if you fell asleep before your Mister Ricky was on *The Tonight Show*, so here I am, doing as you asked. But if you want the truth, I think you should channel all this Ricky discipline into discipline on your job. Your uncle says you're not doing what you should. What is wrong with you, Milan? You want to get fired?"

I don't answer her, because the answer is *yes*. I *do* want to get fired. I don't want to be here, Milan the chubby laxative publicist. I want to go back to sleep and live in the fabulous life I created for myself there. I pull the thin, floral sheet over my head and roll away from my mother, begging the dream to return. I decide in this moment that I will meet Ricky for real, and I will follow my dream.

"What is wrong with you?" my mother demands, pinching me again, through the sheet. "If you don't want to get up, fine. But your sister's here, and you invited her to watch with you. She drove all the way from Miami Beach, and you, you can't get out of bed. What is wrong with you, eh?"

Again, I say nothing. I know the answer. Everything's wrong with me. I wouldn't know where to begin. Actually, I do know where to begin. I begin by peeling the bits of paper from my face, and trying not to notice how disgusted my mother looks.

Oh, and by the way? Welcome to my life in Coral Gables.

The First Trimester

thursday, february 14

So, welcome to my frilly yellow bedroom. Girly, immature. Teddy bears. And not just that, but *Care* Bears. Pitiful. I know. How *sad* is it to be twenty-four years old and still living at home with your mom and dad (*and* grandparents)? How sad is it that I'm still here, in this white-brick home in Coral Gables, near Blue Road and Alhambra Circle, on my once-canopied twin bed, silly ducky slippers hanging off my pudgy feet, a pink terry-cloth robe cinched around my waist, my greasy flat nothing brownish hair pulled up in two slightly sad, droopy-bunny ponytails?

"*So* sad."

Yeah, well, *thanks*. That's my sister Geneva speaking, as she stands in my doorway with an amused, superior look on her face. Geneva holds her Yorkie, Belle, under her arm like a football. The dog pants, making the red bow between her ears bob up and down like the comb on a nervous rooster. I am not what you'd call a dog person. There's nothing worse than the hot, rotten smell of dog mouth, and I can smell it from here. Yorkie mouth from here. I detest the dog, and I detest Geneva.

You know, *Geneva*. My tall, thin, financially successful thirty-year-old sister? The one who looks like a slightly darker, slightly prettier Penélope Cruz? The one who is five-eight and got an MBA from

Harvard—compared to the five-four University of Miami graduate that is me? The one who has a group of female friends just as perfect as she is and no shortage of men she likes to call "sex toys"? The one whose feline body and long legs turn jeans into an art form? The one who has stolen exactly three boyfriends from me in the past ten years, during which time I only had four boyfriends, even though she claims it wasn't her *fault* that they left me for her? She said it was my fault, for not putting more effort into my appearance, my clothes, my studies, my job, my life. She then tried to act like she'd done me a favor by offering fashion tips and career advice. Right. *Her.*

Geneva has just walked into my room without knocking, wearing her "work" clothes—a spaghetti-strap black silk tunic that would make any other woman look six months pregnant but which, combined with skinny jeans, a sparkly tan, and strappy black sandals, makes Geneva look like a haughty, leggy Spanish princess. Her long black hair is twisted back in a tight knot, exposing the small yet scary dragon tattoo on her left shoulder blade, and she's got a black and white scarf wrapped around her head. Anyone else with a scarf twisted around like that would look like Aunt Jemima's nanny. Geneva? Royalty.

I do not make eye contact. You know, it's not advisable, with her being the devil and so on. I try to seem distracted and unconcerned. I type on the VAIO laptop between my extremely pale legs on the bed. The "n" key is worn off from all my loser online activities; these include commenting on people's blogs, doing chats, and posting fake profiles of myself on personals sites, just to see what kinds of responses I get in different cities. I pretend like I don't know that with that one little word, "sad," Geneva is talking about the loser that is me, the state of my hair, my body, my clothes, my bed, my room.

I feel her frowning at my robe. "How long have you had that thing, Milan? God. I remember it from when I left for Harvard." Geneva always mentions Harvard, and she always mentions the Portofino Towers, where she recently bought a condo. She's a name-dropper. She picks up my phone from my dresser. "Hello Kitty. Milan? Sad."

I ignore her, focus on the computer. She puts Belle from Hell on the floor, and sits next to me on the bed and peeks at the screen. I turn it away from her. I hear Belle doing the scratch-and-sniff under my bed. What has she found there? I can smell Geneva's perfume, something musky and dark. Something expensive and very grown-up. I am aware that after a full day working in Overtown as a laxative publicist for my uncle's "pharmaceutical" company (don't ask), I smell like a goat. But it's been so long since I smelled a goat I can't be sure. The last time was at a petting zoo in Kendall when I was ten. I tried to mask today's goatness with Sunflowers perfume I got on discount at Ross earlier because I was too lazy to take a shower.

"What ya doing?" Geneva asks, stretching her neck to see the screen. For the record, my sister would not be caught dead in a Ross, or any other store with the slogan "dress for less." That, for Geneva, would defeat the purpose of dressing at all.

"Just trying to set up a chat room." I scowl at the screen to make myself seem smarter and more ambitious than I am. To make it seem like Geneva's criticisms mean nothing to me. To seem like I'm happy here, in this room, in this house, in my life.

"You guys have wireless now?"

"Yes," I say. I set it up, but I let my dad think he did it. Our parents think I am a dutiful, passive Cuban daughter to have remained living at home, where I do things like wipe my grandmother's bottom (she's too stiff with arthritis) and fold my dad's undershirts (his Y chromosome makes housework impossible for him). To our Cuban-exile parents and tens of thousands just like them all over South Florida, girls like me—chubby, unmarried, overlooked—stay home until we're (best-case scenario) married or (worst-case scenario) hauled away to the convent. Geneva and I know the truth about me, however. I'm not dutiful or traditional. I'm not even a virgin (but don't tell my parents, please). Rather, I'm a purebred American slacker. I'll have a life one of these days, when I get around to it.

Other things you need to know about me: I would be pretty by normal standards, but because I live in Miami, a city where pretty must be nipped, tucked, and liposuctioned into uniformity and submission to qualify, I am plain by association. I have a pleasant round and very white face, with freckles. People stop to ask me for directions. I have been told I look "nice," but I am selfish and wild in my head.

Geneva lifts a foot and rotates the strappy sandal, cracking her ankle. It sounds like grasshoppers in a blender. I hate that sound. She used to dance ballet, and developed this disgusting habit of cracking everything all the time, especially her ankles, with no regard for those around her. She has double-jointed arms, but doesn't show off about it anymore, thank God. "A chat room?" she asks, unaware that her joint popping has made me want to throw up. "For what?"

"My Yahoo group."

"Las Ricky Chickies?" Geneva says the name of my group with a hint of scorn. Or is it mockery? With her, I can never tell. It *could* be derision. She says it as if Las Ricky Chickies, an Internet forum in honor of sexy male pop star Ricky Biscayne, were the dumbest thing in the world. To her, it probably is. After all, she throws parties for the rich and famous, and gets paid very well for it, so well that she makes hundreds of thousands of dollars a year and gets to name-drop at the same time—like anyone really cares that Fat Joe ordered massive amounts of caviar or something for a tacky rap-star party. She recently bought herself a new BMW, in white. I myself drive a fabulous puke-green Neon. She has no need, as do we mere mortals, to connect with our idols in other, more pedestrian ways.

For the record, Ricky Biscayne is a Latin-pop singer from Miami, half Mexican-American and half Cuban-American, and he is my obsession. I *love* him. I have loved him since he began as a salsa singer, and I have loved him as he recorded Grammy-winning albums in the Latin-pop genre. I love him now, as he prepares to cross over to the mainstream English-language pop realm. I love him so much I am the secretary of Las Ricky Chickies, the unofficial Ricky Biscayne online fan club. In addition to this club, I am also a member of a Coral Gables book club, Las Loquitas del Libro (the crazy book girls), that meets weekly at Books & Books. You might say I'm a joiner. That's the big difference between me and Geneva. She carves her own way and expects everyone to follow. The sucky part is, they usually do.

Geneva flops backward on the bed and picks up one of my Care Bears to throw it into the air, only to punch it violently on the descent. Then, as if trying to tell me something, she tosses the bear at the poster of Ricky Biscayne taped to my closet door.

"If you must know," I say, "we're going to have a live chat during Ricky's *Tonight Show* performance."

I look at the pink Hello Kitty clock on my nightstand, then at the TV on the sagging metal stand in the corner. It has cable. It doesn't look like it, but it does. My dad, who owns a shipping and export business and whose expensive ties are always crooked, jerry-rigged it somehow. Cuban ingenuity, I suppose. We never throw anything away, even though we're far from poor. My dad just tries to fix everything, or make a new invention out of it. This house is full of junk. Junk and birds. Canaries. We have four birdcages scattered around the house, and among my many unsavory chores is that of cleaning them.

"You think Ricky's gonna do well in English, Milan?" Geneva asks, with a tone that tells me she already knows the answer, and her answer is *no*. She rolls onto her belly and tries again to look at the screen. "He's so corny. I don't see how an American audience could deal."

"Ricky does well at everything he tries," I say. I stop myself from correcting her misuse of the term "American" to mean only English-speaking U.S. citizens. I'm an American. So is Ricky. So are most of Ricky's millions of fans. "He's perfect."

Geneva snorts a laugh and starts picking at her short, bitten, mangled fingernails—the only imperfect thing about her. The ankle cracking is bad, but the fingernail thing is worse. It makes a little clicking sound like a car that won't start. Click, *click*. Click, *click*. "Isn't it a little juvenile to be obsessed with a pop singer at your age, Milan?" she asks. "I mean, no disrespect, but . . ."

"*Stop* with the fingernails," I say.

"Sorry," she says. But she does it again, this time very close to my ear.

"Don't you have your own house to go to or something?" I ask as I push her hands away. "God."

"Condo," she corrects me. "In the Portofino." Right. How could I forget that Geneva, president of a multimillion-dollar party-planning company favored by rappers and Latin American soap stars, just bought a very expensive condo for herself in one of the most expensive buildings on Miami Beach. Enrique Iglesias is her neighbor. She has joked about taking him away from his Russian tennis-babe wife. I did not find the joke amusing, for obvious reasons.

"Why are you here?" I ask. Belle has emerged from beneath the bed with one of my flat, comfortable sandals and is trying to either kill it or hump it. "It's late. Go home. And take that rat with you, please."

"Mom asked me to hang out for a while to help her prepare for a show," says Geneva. Amazingly, she takes the sandal away from the dog. "What, I can't hang out here? You want me to leave?"

I'm about to say yes when our mother, Violeta, an AM talk-radio host, sashays into the room carrying a tray with milk and cookies, like some housewife mom from a fifties TV show. She stops when she sees the two of us about to fight, me crouching away from Geneva, and Geneva leaning in for the kill. Mom knows us very well, and it shows on her face—or what's left of her face. She's had so much plastic surgery the last few years I hardly recognize her anymore. She looks like a tightly pulled lizard with Julie Stav hair.

"What's going on here?" she asks. She leans into her hip. Like Geneva, our mother is thin and tidy, and she does the hip-lean thing to give her the appearance of *caderas*. For the record, I got all the *caderas*—hips—my mom and sister lack. I'm shaped like a pear. I'm overweight, slightly, in large part because of an addiction to guava and cheese *pastelitos* from Don Pan, but I still have a tiny waist. A certain kind of man likes that shape, but in general it is not the kind of man I like. I am told I look like my mulatta grandmother, even though I am the whitest member of our family. We run the spectrum, we Gotays, from black to white and back again, even though no one but Geneva seems to admit that we have any African in us.

My mom and Geneva look alike, or they used to before our mother started to look like Joan Rivers with a platinum-blond bob. Mom wears high-waisted beige dress slacks, probably Liz Claiborne, her favorite brand, with a short-sleeved silk sweater, black. The whole obsession with black is something she shares with Geneva. Mom's breasts were recently remodeled, and they seem to have moved into their perkier bras quite happily. Did you know that when you get a boob lift they put something like a golf tee under your tits, attached to your ribs, to hold them up? Gross. Besides, it's just wrong to have a mother with perkier boobs than you, isn't it?

"Everything okay here?" asks Mom.

Geneva and I sort of shrug.

Mom purses her lips. They used to be smaller than they are now, those lips. They've been blown up somehow, like tiny pink bicycle tubes. "Something's going on," she says. She sets the tray down on my Holly Hobby dresser, next to the porcelain statuette of La Caridad del Cobre. She taps her red manicured nails on the dresser top and scowls at us. I think that's what the face is, anyway. I'm learning to read her body language, like she's a cat now and can only express feelings with the arch of her back or something. Mom would be well served to have a tail these days.

"I think Milan wants me to leave," says Geneva. "Mom, she's so unfriendly."

Before I have time to lie in protest, our mother sighs and does the thing where she makes us both feel so guilty, we are paralyzed. I want to save her. I want to make her happy. I hate myself for being a disappointment. Mom says, "You two. In Cuba, you'd never act like this."

Geneva stands up and walks to the tray of cookies. "May I?" she asks our mother. Mom does her hand in a circle in the air to tell Geneva to eat, but she continues to frown at me.

"If this is about the thing with the boys," she says. "*Tú tienes que olvidar de todo ésto, Milán.*"

I look at the television and ignore the fact that she just told me, in Spanish, that I have to forget about Geneva stealing all my men. Jay Leno appears to be winding up his zoo-animal segment, having petted a baby lion for the past few minutes. Ricky will be on next. I unmute the volume and study the screen. "Shh," I say. "Ricky's coming on. Everybody be quiet, please."

"Blood is thicker than water," says our mother, pacing the room. She rarely stays still, our mother. She is high strung, wired, and motivated, just like Geneva. Mom sidesteps Belle—we share a dislike of dogs, my mother and I—and picks up a stack of magazines on my nightstand, all of them with Ricky on the cover. She sighs and clicks her tongue at me. "Ricky, Ricky, Ricky," says my mother as she drops the magazines one by one, as if Ricky made her tired. "I am *sick* of this *Ricky.*"

"Sit down, Mom," Geneva tells her through a mouthful of coconut ball. "This'll be fun. I just want to see him make an ass of himself on national television." Geneva brings the tray to the bed and sets it down next to me. She herself sits on the floor, with a great crackling of misused joints. Belle climbs into Geneva's lap and licks a fleck of grated coconut off Geneva's chin. Geneva doesn't seem to mind. "Milan? Cookie?"

I take a coconut cookie ball, and bite. They are sweet enough to make you squint, chewy, made of nothing but sugar, vanilla extract, and grated coconut in heavy syrup. It's the taste of my childhood, sugar and coconut. Cubans eat sugar like Americans eat bread, and I don't even want to think about what my pancreas looks like. As I munch it I log in to the chat room and greet the twenty-one other Ricky Biscayne fans who are there. I know all of them by screen name. My mother and Geneva look at me, and look at each other with raised brows and smirky, pretty mouths. Fine. I know. They think I'm pathetic. A geek.

"Chew at least twenty times, Milan," says Mom. "You're not a snake. You're getting crumbs everywhere on your shirt."

"Nightgown," I correct her.

"With you it's hard to tell," says my sister.

"Shh," I say. "Leave me alone. I'm trying to focus on Ricky."

"This hair," says Geneva. She reaches up and touches my ponytail. Belle snaps at my lifeless strands and I daydream of punting her across the room. "You'd look so good if you got some highlights. Please let me do a makeover on you, Milan? Please?"

"Highlights would look beautiful," says my mother.

"Shh," I say.

"You should let your sister fix your hair," says our mother.

"Shh," I tell them as I type my hellos to Las Ricky Chickies. "Leave me alone."

"How's your face, Mom?" Geneva asks. Mom recently had a face-lift, which explains why she has bangs cut into her bob at the moment.

"Oh, I feel great, better than ever," says Mom. Her cheeriness is almost unfathomable.

"Shh," I say.

"Did it hurt?" asks Geneva.

"Not at all," says Mom. No matter how many surgeries and other enhancements she has, our mother always says she feels great afterward. I glance at her. I can't tell if she is smiling or not. I *think* she is. She sips a bit of milk and looks surprised as she nibbles a coconut ball through her rubbery lips. I know enough to know she is not actually surprised. Not much surprises her.

On the TV screen, Jay Leno holds a CD up for the camera. It's the same photo as the poster on my closet door. The closet itself is full of cheap linen work clothes from the Dress Barn. Sad, I know. I decorate like a high school girl and dress like a middle-aged secretary. But I have plans. Once I'm out of here. I'll get real furniture and real paintings or something. I'll get real clothes once I lose twenty pounds. Until then, it doesn't seem worth the expense. Seriously. If you saw what

I was up against, all the implants and high heels prancing up and down the Miracle Mile, their perfect little bodies ducking in and out of the Starbucks just to be seen, you'd realize that unless you have the spectacular *cuerpazo* of a *Sábado Gigante* model, it's almost better to hide yourself. This is a city where the entire concept of pretty is impossible, where paunchy men in khakis and belts stare, and women spend hours a day and many fortunes making themselves stare-ready. I don't have that kind of time. Or if I do, I don't have that kind of patience. And as a laxative publicist I certainly don't have that kind of *money*. Don't judge me. I get enough of that at home.

Leno glances at the glossy photo of Ricky's perfectly bronzed six-pack and appears to suddenly have a mouth full of lime juice.

"Oh, jeez," he whines. "Put on a shirt!" The crowd laughs. The host grins and says, "Don't hold the abs against him. He's a great guy, really. Ladies and gentlemen, please help me welcome the newest Latin crossover sensation, Ricky Biscayne!"

"Oh, Ricky," cries my sister, making fun of me. "You're so dreamy!" Belle yaps her approval.

I sit up and hold my breath. Suddenly, everything else is too loud. Mom's pinched breathing through her five-year-old nose job. Belle's hyperpanting. The cool baritone hum of the air-conditioning vents, droning in concert with the twittering night song of cicadas and tree frogs in the backyard. Even with the window closed, the creatures are loud. At night, Miami swarms with things like this, things with slime or sheen on their backs, shiny-eyed things with suction cups on their big, goblin feet. This is why I prefer to stay inside at night, by the way. By day, Miami is one of the most beautiful cities on earth. By night, it's Mars.

Geneva's cracking ankles and clicking fingernails. I grab the remote from the bed, and tap, tap, tap it up. I don't want to miss Ricky's big moment.

With an energetic bang of trumpets and congas, the upbeat song begins, and Ricky starts to dance. "Dance" is actually too sissy of a word for what he does. It's more like making love to the air, grinding, pulsating, shimmying. Oh, *baby*. He's a graceful, masculine dancer. That's what people notice most about him. His hips, his tiny thrusts and gyrations, all with that happy, naughty grin and those shiny white teeth. Movie star teeth. Not an ounce of fat on him, either, just pure sculpted grace. He has the kind of rear end you want to grab and sink your fingernails into. Or teeth.

The camera pans across his band and focuses for a moment on a balding, redheaded man who plays the guitar with one hand and the keyboard with the other. He's got a microphone attached to his keyboard and sings into it with tremendous passion.

"That guy looks like a tiny Conan O'Brien," says Geneva.

"Shh," I say. The little Conan looks into the camera and I feel a strange pang in my gut; he's got none of Ricky's looks, but this guy has a certain appeal. Eh. Maybe not. Maybe I'm just like a groupie who will do any guy in the band just to get a shot at the leader.

Go back to Ricky, I think. Why is the camera focused on this guy? Who cares about the backup musicians when Ricky Biscayne is on-stage? Honestly. The camera zooms back to Ricky, and every woman on earth recognizes his supreme maleness, even my mother, who, I notice, has let her tight jaw go slack at the sight of his wiggling. Is that drool I see in the corner of her mouth? *Asquerosa*. Maybe she can't feel her lips anymore? She told me that for her boob lift they actually had to remove her nipples and put them back in a different place. Sick.

"I'd marry him," I say out loud, grabbing another coconut ball from the pink plastic plate. "In a minute."

"*No serías feliz*," says my mother, meaning, You wouldn't be happy. I think my mother must tell me at least once I day I won't be happy doing something I want to do.

Happy? With Ricky? Eh. Maybe not. But who needs *happy* when you could have a body like *that* in your bed? I'd cry the entire freakin' *day*, filling wads of tissue with my tears and snot, if it meant spending the night thrashing with Ricky Biscayne.

I take a peek at Geneva, and to my surprise she appears to be enraptured by Ricky. She looks embarrassed. I don't think I've ever seen her look embarrassed before.

"See?" I tell her. "He's *not* making an ass of himself."

Geneva lifts her brows and looks around the room, then at me. "No," she says. "Actually, he's pretty good. I'm surprised."

"He's gonna be huge," I say.

"He might," says Geneva. "You might be right."

"I told you," I say. "You should have believed me. I mean, you usually like my taste in men."

Geneva ignores the jab and starts digging through her weird little fringy purse with the big tacky DIOR on the side, looking for her phone. She opens it and dials someone and starts talking in a loud voice about how she thinks she wants to get Ricky Biscayne as an investor in her newest business venture, Club G, a South Beach nightclub she plans to open later this year. "I know," she says. "I thought he was all about the neck chains and the mullet, too. But not anymore. He's totally hot. I think he's got it, star quality. It's what I'm looking for. Get me in touch with his people."

"Shhh," I say. Geneva scoops up her demon dog and takes her call into the hallway. Thank God. I don't need her in here.

"I'm going to bring your *abuelito* in," says my mom, rising from the bed. She stands in front of me, blocking my view with her flat Liz Claiborne–pants butt. They're like mom jeans, only they're pants. She means that she's going to bring my grandfather in from the front porch, where he likes to sit "on the lookout" for communists.

"Move!" I say, trying to duck around her for a view of Ricky.

"You need a hobby," says my mother, in Spanish. She tries to pinch my arm. When we were little, she used to pinch us to get us to pay attention to her. I swat her hand away, and she says, "This thing with Biscayne, it's ridiculous. You're not a little girl."

Then stop pinching me. "You need to move," I say, pushing her. I consider mentioning that I know all about *her* grown-up "hobby" up in La Broward, but, you know. It wouldn't be polite to tell your mom you know she's screwing a Jewish plastic surgeon on the side. I followed her one time, and spied on them. He's pretty muscular, for an old guy, like that one dude, Jack LaLanne. He's got a weird orange tan and big thick veins like blue worms in his neck. Dad's been schtupping bimbos—his secretaries and whatnot—on the side for decades, so it's only fair. And you wonder why I'm still single?

She sighs and leaves the room. I happily lose myself in Ricky's performance. I've lusted after him since his first hit on WRTO Salsa, ten years ago, and continue to lust in pulsing, throbbing ways that shame me. There must be some defect in the genes of the women in this family, I swear. We're like a bunch of loser nymphos, especially Geneva the man-stealing whore. Oops. I didn't say that.

The camera focuses on Ricky, in his form-fitting, fashionable jeans and tight-fitting, nearly transparent dark blue tank top, his tanned arms sculpted in rounded waves of muscle. My mouth falls open as I stare into his hypnotic eyes. He's like an evil witch doctor, taking over my soul. I know. He's only looking at the camera. But I can't help it, I have this overwhelming sense that he's looking right into my soul. The lyrics are meant for me. They speak of a man's love for a plain yet complex and underestimated woman. No other man sings about average women with reverence. Seriously. I mean, not that I'm average. I am just average in Miami. And, for once, there's a man in the world who appreciates that a woman like me might be wild, passionate, lusty, interesting.

The chorus ends, and a *timbale* solo comes up. Ricky begins to dance again, with backup dancers, all of them female. And when he begins to do a sexy little salsa step, one masculine hand over his belly, right in that spot where men have hair creeping up in a sinful little line, his other hand held up as if holding my hot little fingers, I quite nearly choke on the last of the coconut balls. One minute he grins like the boy next door, dimples, full lips, cute; the next, he frowns with intensity, jaw determined and heroic, his eyes burning with dark lust and power. His body's motions send shock waves through my nervous system, and goose bumps rise on my skin. Ricky Biscayne is, without question, the sexiest man on earth. His hips thrust forward and back, and I correct myself. He is the sexiest man in the *galaxy*.

As he opens his mouth to sing the last chorus, I begin to speak a prayer to my statuette of La Caridad del Cobre. The peaceful virgin watches me with sympathy from her post on the white Holly Hobby dresser, ceramic blue waves lapping in curls at her feet. God only knows she's seen me do a lot of kinky, lonely stuff in this room, some of it involving innocent victims like hairbrush handles and tubes of eye-makeup remover. Don't ask. Anyway, I'm surprised she even tolerates me, actually. I'm surprised she hasn't struck me with lightning for my raging slacker libido.

"Holy Virgin," I say. "Please help me meet this man. I'll do anything."

Anything? the virgin seems to ask.

"Anything," I repeat.

Man, I'm sore. It was another slow day at the fire station yesterday, just a couple of calls from the regulars—a lonely diabetic and an older homeless guy who knows exactly what to say when he calls to get the paramedics out. *I'm having chest pains. I can't breathe. I'm dizzy. I can't feel my arm.* So, in between playing counselor to the lonely and desperate of South Florida, I lifted, big-time, in the station's weight room. Me and Tommy, competing like we do to see who could squat heavier—and me winning. Yep, that's right, I told them, the "girl" is strong. They still can't believe I'm smoking them on the physical exams, but they're coming around.

I'm not huge or anything, just solid, tall, and lean—like a professional volleyball player, which I might have been if I hadn't had a baby when I was still in high school. I rocked at volleyball. I've always been athletic, and I'm careful about what I eat. Not that I don't eat, I just eat a lot of protein and vegetables. A typical lunch for me might be a can of tuna, eaten with a fork, and a bag of grilled vegetables with a rice cake. Boring, but it does the trick. When I first started in the department five years ago, I was the first female on the team at Station 42. There was a lot of doubt about a woman firefighter. Not anymore.

Or at least most of the guys don't have a problem with it. L'Roy still seems miffed, but that's probably just because I never gave him any, and he's lusted after me from day one.

I'm home now, in my green stucco tract house in Homestead, about to start my four days off. That's our schedule, two full days on, four off. I am beat, and I'd like to sleep, but I've got my feverish thirteen-year-old daughter resting her head in my lap. She's sniffling, struggling with the flu. I feel the tickle of the illness creeping into my throat, but as any single mother knows, I won't be able to actually be sick. I'll have to guzzle DayQuil and coffee and muddle through. Single moms don't get to be sick; we get to be *drugged*. The good news is that with four solid days off, I might get a chance to chill. *Might.* I said *might*.

I might get a chance to see my new man again, too. Did I say man? Preceded by the word "my"? Wow. (Grin, grin!) I guess I did. I am not in *love* or anything, but I have a playmate. I haven't told my daughter, or my mother, or anyone. Haven't told them what, you ask? This: I've had a few secret lunch dates with a local divorced cop named Jim Landry. He's tall, which is good because at five-foot-ten I'm not short. He's six-three at least, with dirty blond hair cut short just the way I like it. Like me, he's fit and takes his job protecting the public very seriously.

The only thing I really don't like about Jim Landry is that he's a born-again Christian and likes to talk about God all the time. He goes to church on Tuesday nights. He has a fish on his car. I mean, I respect it, but I don't dig it. I grew up Catholic, Irish Catholic, and I like to read Joseph Campbell and think about world religions and what they mean to everyone, so basically I don't need anyone shoving Jesus-this and Jesus-that down my throat all the time. But at the same time, men aren't exactly falling off trees at my feet, especially not cute, available ones, so I'll see if I can adjust to Jim's God-o-rama in exchange for a little nookie.

I see him at fire scenes now and then, and he surprised me by asking me to lunch last month. We've had three lunches, and even though it sounds shallow, we have very good chemistry and smell compatibility—even when he eats onions. He's the only man I've known who doesn't stink after onions. We had sex for the first time just yesterday, at his house, nothing earth-shattering, but pleasant. It was the first time I've done it in many years. So, you know, other than the flu, I feel young and sexy again just thinking about him. It's nice to have a reason to shave my legs again. I'm feeling good.

I stroke Sophia's wavy, dark brown hair, and try not to think about the sleep I won't be getting tonight. I replay yesterday's romp, Jim's dark brown eyes and the pheromone man-smell of his neck. I'd forgotten the animalistic sense of peace you get, as a woman, sniffing the musk of a man's neck.

My daughter and I lay atop the light goose-down comforter with the pale lavender Restoration Hardware duvet cover. The bedding was too expensive for me, but I fell in love with it and bought it. I am an excellent window-shopper, and sometimes I give in and use my credit cards. I'm usually not that impulsive, but I figured if you have to be single in your bed you might as well be comfortable. My bedroom is my oasis, a creamy, purple retreat. Sophia sighs, and I want to make her better instantly. If only we moms had that power.

I had her when I was fourteen, almost fifteen. Just a year older than she is now. I didn't feel as young then as I think she is now, but I realize now I was just a baby, too. I raised her alone, and made up for my long guilty hours at work, first as a waitress and grocery clerk, and for the past five years as a firefighter, by sharing a bed with her in a studio apartment. Maybe it was selfish, me wanting Sophia's warmth and reassuring breath by my side. When she was ten, Sophia said she wanted her own room like all her friends had, and I bought this little house through a HUD program. I don't want to live in Homestead, but my income restricts my choices. I like to drive through Coral Gables and Coconut Grove, looking at homes. If I won the lottery, that's where I'd live, in one of those old cities with big trees and lots of shade. Homestead is too bright, too hot.

I kiss her forehead. People say teenagers can't be good mothers, but

I *was.* I was a damn good mom, and still am. I knew what I needed to do to be a good mother, because it was just the *opposite* of everything my parents had done. Don't smoke, don't drink, don't do drugs, don't collect welfare, don't beat your child, don't beat your partner in front of your child, don't be homeless, don't live in your car, don't sell your car for food, don't forget to brush your child's teeth for, like, years, don't leave your child unattended most of the time. It was easy to know the rules. She's turning out good, too. Soccer star, good grades, friends, chorus. A good kid. I hate to see my daughter ill, but I'll tell you, I love having my baby back, if only for a little while.

Sophia looks up at me with big, honey-brown eyes, the skin over her high cheekbones red from the flu. People who don't know us usually mistake us for friends rather than mother and daughter. Sophia is tall, like me, and looks older than she is. And people can't believe we're related because of the differences in our coloring. I'm a natural blonde, with blue eyes, tanned skin, and a squarish face. My short hair juts out in ragged peaks. I look good with long or short hair, but I keep it like this because when you're rushing into a fire scene you don't need to be worrying about tucking your hair up into your helmet. Some of the guys at the station say I remind them of a younger Meg Ryan. Others say Jenna Jameson, but I think that's mostly just to try to piss me off. I don't get pissed. I laugh right along with them; it's the best defense.

Sophia, in contrast, has skin the color of a roasted cashew. She's already nearly my height, and will likely be taller when she grows up. She's a big, strong girl. Her dark, wavy hair falls to the middle of her back, wild in a way that reminds me of women from Arthurian legends. Guinivere or something. Sophia isn't heavy, but her hips and thighs are thicker than mine, and already she wears a larger size in pants. I'm a ten; Sophia's a twelve. Sometimes, I can't believe my child is this big already. It truly feels like less than a week since she was born. Our mouths and noses are very much alike, and once we tell people we're mother and daughter, they see it.

"Try to sleep," I say. Is that too much to ask? That she sleep so I

can, too? But just as Sophia settles her head onto the pillow, a soft
knock comes on the thin wood of the bedroom door. The doors are
hollow and splinter easily. That's a sign of a cheap house. I want a
better house someday. And I'll get there. You'll see. When I make
lieutenant, and then captain. But this will do for now.

My mom, Alice, now forty-six, pokes her head in and smiles sarcastically as she pushes large brown plastic eyeglasses higher on her
narrow stab of a nose. Since my penniless alcoholic father's death five
years ago, Alice, the ultimate codependent enabler with nowhere to
go, has lived with us, sleeping on the pull-out sofa. Alice smokes cigarettes in the front yard, in a housedress. I won't let her smoke inside.
She still hangs out with her biker-bar friends, an unsavory bunch of
Confederate-flag-waving yokels I've hated for decades. Some things
never change. Alice most of all. I hate living with her, but I don't
have the heart to kick her out. Abandonment is her specialty, not
mine. I've stretched far the other direction, toward compassion and
generosity.

"I thought you might want to see who's on the *Tonight Show*, getting rich," whispers Alice. I don't call her Mom because I think that's
a title you have to earn. The slight odor of fresh cat discharge wafts
in; I need to change the litter box in the tiny laundry room off the
small garage. The granules of litter spray across the floor and seem to
get tracked all over the house. I have to run the vacuum, too. There is
never enough time, it seems, to do everything that needs to be done.
You'd think Alice might help out, but no. That would be too consid-
erate of her.

As Alice waddles back down the hall in her cheap leggings and
Lynyrd Skynyrd T-shirt, she mutters, "No-good Messican son of a
bitch." I know instantly who she must be talking about.

With my heart racing, I grab the universal television remote from
my unfinished-maple nightstand, hold the batteries in with my
fingers—I lost the back to the thing years ago and have lost faith in
the duct-tape method—and aim it at the small white TV on my un-
finished dresser. Sure enough, there's my high school sweetheart, Ri-

cardo Batista, or, as the world now knows him, Ricky Biscayne, singing his heart out. He looks so normal and harmless on television. On television, he almost looks like a nice guy.

"Who's that, Mommy?" asks Sophia. She sits up, rubs her eyes. I think she might have pinkeye. We'll have to go to the pediatrician.

I look at Ricardo's wavy dark brown hair, his high cheek red from singing. I look at his big, honey-brown eyes, and the pain of his unexpected abandonment washes through my body as forcefully as if it had happened minutes, not years, before.

"He's a boy I used to go to school with back in Fort Lauderdale," I tell her, with a false smile and a stabbing memory of the first time I ever really felt loved, long ago. Fourteen years ago, to be exact. "You get some sleep, baby."

orty miles north, in Bal Harbour, Jill Sanchez watches Ricky Biscayne sing on a fifty-inch Sony plasma television that, when a button is pressed, whirs down out of the ceiling of her home gym. The television is as thick as a slice of bread. Jill, who believes carbs were invented by Satan, has not eaten bread in five years. This is her second workout session of the day, the first having been at four this morning. She wears a pink and gray Nina Bucci sports bra, and sexy matching stretch pants that ride low on the hips and have holes cut out along the sides of the legs. Jill Sanchez has her own line of workout wear that makes loads of money for her, but, being a woman of discriminating tastes, she refuses to wear her line herself, knowing that her clothes are cheaply made. She has a Nike endorsement and finds the shoes suitable and convenient; they come every month, free, in the mail, a dozen or so pairs. This morning, she wore baby-blue Lululemon yoga pants with a matching tank; they make outstanding workout wear. And Jill knows workouts. A trained jazz dancer, on average she exercises three hours per day.

As she pumps her legs on a stair-climber, she remembers the last time she herself performed on *The Tonight Show*, two years ago. Or was it four? Five? God, no. Really? She frowns at the passage of time, as if frowning might stop it. It can't have been that long ago. Jill pumps her legs harder, hoping to keep her thirties at bay, even though she is already thirty-seven. As a policy, she does not consider the fact that she will soon enter her forties, even as she has her hair colored every five or six days to make sure no one ever sees the graying roots. The forties are unthinkable to Jill Sanchez, who still believes she belongs on MTV's *Total Request Live* alongside teenaged singers with their black, bitten fingernails and angst. The harder she pumps, the faster her long, straightened brown ponytail with the highlights swings back and forth, just brushing the top of her mighty, spherical, and famously famous rear end.

Six years ago, she was the first woman to simultaneously have a top-rated movie, album, and perfume in a single week. She'd gone on the *Late Show*, singing and dancing in those scandalous nude-colored pants that some people thought rode just a wee bit too low, revealing by design the tiniest hint of well-coiffed, short-short, sweet-smelling pubic hair, but also being interviewed about her new movie and clothing line. The clothing line, for the record, then brought in more than $175 million a year, worldwide, because—and wasn't it obvious?—women everywhere wanted to dress like Jill Sanchez, and men everywhere *wanted* them to.

Some people in the press liked to say her star was fading these days, just because she'd had a messy couple of divorces and other assorted and generally well-timed and professionally calculated "scandals," including this newest one about the fur. PETA is a group of whiners, in her opinion. How many of them wore leather? Huh? How could anyone complain about fur and wear leather? Whiny losers and hypocrites. They should try being her, Jill Sanchez, for a day or two. They'd know about brutality then. Was it *her* fault the media vultures circled her carcass day and night? Was it *her* fault the vile press descended upon every scrap of Jill-ness she threw their way? Who were "the press" anyway, except a bunch of wannabe stars, envious sagging hags and ugly pockmarked men she'd never even give the time of day?

Everyone in the press had bucked teeth or buggy eyes. She did not doubt that the very men who wrote horrible things about her whacked off to her image in their private moments. They picked on her because she was a woman, and a powerful one at that. Lots of *men* in Hollywood had botched love lives and bombed movies, but the press was easy on them. Just look at that skeezy George Clooney. Or that other one, the superboring guy who always sounded like he was sleeping or stoned—Kevin *Costner*. The media went easy on them. But not on her, Jill Sanchez. Jill Sanchez, they *crucified*. Hollywood had such double standards for women, and Latina women in particular. Just look at Paula Abdul. The cute-as-a-button *American Idol* judge had been divorced *three times*. But did the media crucify her or call her a whore? No. She'd run over someone on the freeway in her Mercedes, and then she'd slept with that one *Idol* contestant, but no one hated her for it. Did the media call *her* heartless, ruthless, all the words they had called her, Jill Sanchez? No. They reserved *that* venom for Jill.

But Jill Sanchez had not gotten to be Jill Sanchez by sitting idly by while the world happened to her. She made the world happen, just how she liked it, and her slick, highly produced upcoming comeback movie and album would prove it. And once she'd taken care of all that, Jill would be free to find love, real love, once and for all, and maybe pop out a baby or two. And maybe, just maybe, her father would forgive her for not being the docile Puerto Rican daughter he'd always wanted. Maybe then she'd actually learn how to make the *arroz con pollo* she always ordered out for on those rare occasions when her mother was able to talk her father into visiting.

As it is, Jill's father, a plumber by trade and odor, says he is too ashamed of her "*puta* ass-shaking" videos to set foot in her home or her life. He tells her he has never watched one of her videos all the way through, and seems to favor her oldest sister, a homely school-teacher who can do no wrong. His loss.

Jill's mother, for her part, reminds her that just because the public thinks Jill is in her late twenties does not mean that her *ovaries* believe likewise. Her mother has long been intensely critical of Jill, her middle and flashiest daughter, and in a way this criticism has subconsciously driven Jill to overachieve in every aspect of her life, in the hope that her mother will finally be pleased with her.

Jill has never gone to therapy and doesn't understand her conscious—much less subconscious—motivations for success. She will never go to therapy, mostly because Jill Sanchez is convinced that there is nothing *wrong* with Jill Sanchez and that fault, when it must be assigned, always falls elsewhere. In the meantime, she likes looking at herself and believes others do, too. It doesn't get much deeper than that.

Jill watches Ricky Biscayne sing his guts out, and smiles to herself. What he lacks in the penis department he more than makes up for with that gigantic vibrating sweep of voice. No one sings like Ricky Biscayne. When he left this house yesterday to fly to Los Angeles with his stupid sorry-ass wife, Ricky had been giddy with nerves, and Jill had tried to reassure him by fucking his brains out. The host of *The Tonight Show* was nice, she'd told him, and would make Ricky feel comfortable.

Jill and Ricky *tried* to be "just friends" but slipped up and made love—twice. Once in the kitchen, and once on the slick black tiles of the pool-house floor. He had agonized over it, as usual, complaining of his lack of control and his need for a personality overhaul, of his love for Jasminka Uskokovic, the pathetic Serbian stick-figure "supermodel" he'd married. He'd even talked about Jasminka's dog as if the dog would feel betrayed by him. Jill had reassured him it was the last time, knowing as she did it that it was a lie. Actors were good at lying. Ricky had been wounded from a life without a father, and from having been molested by a male neighbor who'd pretended to be a father figure when Ricky was about sixteen—both issues he'd rather not talk about but that she had been able to draw out of him in their moments of quiet postcoital intimacy, as he rested his head on her belly and his tears filled her navel. Jill, like most predators, understood weaknesses, and used them to her advantage.

After sex yesterday, she and Ricky had gone to her enormous and well-appointed in-home recording studio, and he'd gamely listened to some tracks from her upcoming album, *Born Again*. The album cover would feature a photo of a nearly naked Jill, sexily, sweatily suffering, tied and nailed to the cross. If *that* didn't get attention, she figured, nothing would. Ricky had suggested harmonies that blew Jill's mind. He was a much better singer than she was, but a little computerized pitch control could fix that. Besides, he wasn't as smart about business, which was one of the reasons she'd broken up with him the first time, six years ago. He was damn stupid about business, in fact. That and the fact that he'd boned her younger horse-faced sister, Natalia— but he'd been high, Natalia was a two-horse-faced whore, and that was all behind them now.

Still, they have so much in common that she regrets the breakup at least once a day. They are both Miami Latinos. Jill is Puerto Rican and has the diamond flag necklaces, Hector Lavoe albums, and *boricua* thong panties to prove it. Ricky is Cuban from his dad and Mexican from his mom. They both started out in humble homes, he in Fort Lauderdale, she in Wynwood, Miami's most Puerto Rican neighborhood. Through hard work and discipline they had moved themselves to places of power and prestige—meaning South Beach waterfront homes, hers five times the size and price of his, but whatever. They both sing and act, though she *knows* she is ten times the actor he is and feels no guilt in telling him so; sadly for Ricky, there is no actor's equivalent of pitch control.

They both love fashion, though Jill is sure that her taste, which leans toward fur, leather, Versace, and other assorted dead things, and diamonds, is much better than his, which tends toward the sorts of items a member of Kid 'n Play might have liked: stone-washed jeans with too-big patches on the front, long knitted scarves, and those weird square-toed biker boots. He dresses like a member of Menudo, in Jill's opinion, before they started calling the band MDO. Happily, there is pitch control for poorly dressed men: it is called *Jill*.

Both Jill and Ricky want children someday, and plan to pierce their daughter's ears during infancy, something Jill's current fiancé, the boyishly handsome and patently non-Hispanic white actor and screenwriter Jack Ingroff, finds barbaric. Jill is forever having to translate the culture of her life for Jack, and it is exhausting.

With Ricky, Jill never has to explain herself. It is too bad he is married, really. She'd been relieved at first, to be rid of him. He was much more in love with her than she was with him, and even though he swore he had quit doing coke, she wasn't convinced. She'd had a crush on him at the start, that was all, but when she realized how tiny his penis was she'd had a hard time keeping up the excitement, no pun intended. If he'd been better endowed, she might have stuck it out with him back then.

But as it was, the thing with the drugs and the dick, you know, it made sense to just be *over* it already. She had decided to move on with Jack, who was famous, mostly sober, and had the ample, ready loins of a Brahman donkey.

This did *not* mean she stopped thinking about Ricky. Now that Ricky's star was crossing over to the mainstream, and now that Jack was turning out to be a bit of a literal whoremonger, Jill believed Ricky might finally be able to hang with her without feeling threatened the way so many of these guys did. Jill works hard. She needs her men to do so as well. Otherwise, it won't last. If she's learned anything from her failed marriages—one to an awkwardly effeminate bartender and the other to a carnally talented gymnast from Cirque du Soleil—it is that a successful woman has to marry her equal, or not marry at all.

Oh, and the bonus? Jack is deathly jealous of Ricky, whom he sees as a threat because of his shared ethnic background with Jill. Jack knows that even though Jill is strong and powerful, part of her wants a *machista* asshole to put her in her place now and then, someone she can claw, a real man who would grab her wrists to keep her in check. She longs for this type of passion and drama. Because of his crunchy granola New England upbringing, Jack will never be that kind of guy, no matter how desperately he wants to in order to please the un-pleasable and unspeakably perfect Jill Sanchez.

She-man habit aside, Jack, thanks to his poet mother with the Birkenstocks, hairy armpits, and New England pedigree, will now and forever be something of a wuss.

Jill opens her mouth as her new trainer, a big Austrian named Rigor, squirts in a stream of cool, clear, bottled water. His nervous as-sistant wipes the sweat from her face with a pink monogrammed Egyptian cotton towel. The press ridicules her preference for high-thread-count towels and linens, but that only shows you how desper-ate they are for news and how inexperienced they are personally with high thread counts. Anyone who's experienced a thick towel does not want to go back, and Jill sees this as something of a metaphor for her own life and career. She is not going back. Ever.

Rigor informs her that she has fifteen more minutes of cardio be-fore they begin the sculpting session. Jill looks at herself in the mir-rored wall and wonders if all this sweating with Rigor isn't shaving a little too much off her famed backside. She isn't that starving bag of bones, Renée Zellweger. She certainly doesn't want to look like it, ei-ther. "I'm known for this," she says, slapping a manicured hand against her bootylicious rump. "And I don't want to lose it. I do, and you're fired."

Rigor nods, and Jill relaxes a bit. She had to fire the last trainer af-ter he leaked a story to a tabloid about Jack's alleged occasional bouts with transvestite prostitutes. They denied it all to the public, of course, but Jill knows it was true. Jack is her equal, but he is getting too complicated.

On the screen, Ricky's face tenses with passion, and Jill gets a se-cret thrill remembering the last time she saw that expression, as he pressed her body against the cool stainless steel of her Sub-Zero freezer. He mostly made up for size with motion and focus on the woman's parts, and she'd gotten used to it. No one knows they are still in love. Now isn't the right time, strategically, to let it be known, either. Jill and Jack are costarring in a romantic comedy that opens in two months, adorably titled *Came Tumbling After,* and she has to wait at least until then to make a big move. Pretend to be happily engaged. Giggle through a Diane Sawyer interview or something. After her Oscar nomination—if she doesn't get it for this role, she doesn't know what she'll get it for—Jill will be free to do whom and what she pleases.

No, no one knows about Jill and Ricky and the happy reunion looming on the horizon. But they will. Jill has a plan, and she's never seen a plan of hers fall through. She looks again at her reflection and smiles. Yes, sir. Jill Sanchez has plans. It does not matter that Ricky is married. He settled for Jaṣminka when he couldn't have Jill, and really, honestly, was there a marriage anywhere on earth that could withstand the interference of a booty like this? She didn't think so.

M y name is Jasminka Uskokovic, and I am not dead.

I am twenty-six years old, and right now I hold hands with my husband, Ricky Biscayne. His hand is cold. Mine is hot. In the middle is moisture, from his nerves. His palms sweat with anxiety often. We sit on overstuffed creamy beige sofa in living room of a luxurious suite at the Beverly Hills Hotel. My fat brown dog, Mishko, snores at our feet as we watch broadcast of Ricky's performance on *The Tonight Show.* It was taped earlier in day. I can see our reflection in big gilded mirror across the room, and we are beautiful couple. We'd make such pretty baby. I'd like that, very much.

I take deep breath and try to place the mild astringent scent of air in the room. Pine? Yes, but with something else, something delicious that clears the head. Mint? I think is pine and mint. I wonder how the room carries this scent. No candles burn, and no obvious air freshener. Could it be the cleaning solution they use, or detergent for washing towels and sheets? I am very scent-centered, and I recall scents the way other people recall conversations. I make soaps in free time and try to reproduce the scents of my life in them. When we return to our home in Miami, I will make soap of pine and mint, to remember this moment.

My long, dark brown hair is pulled back in ponytail. My eyes feel sticky and tired. This man is very special. I look again at the mirror and see us. I swell up inside that this man chose me for his own. I wear no makeup because I don't need it. I have soft, clear skin, broad, high cheekbones, a long nose, full lips, green eyes, and an Eastern Europe-an symmetry that has given me a profitable career in modeling. I be-gan to be model at fifteen, and by sixteen *Vogue* and *Vanity Fair* both said I was newest "supermodel" from Eastern Europe. I don't want so much to be model anymore. I want now to be Ricky's wife and mother of his children.

Many people find modeling glamorous. Not me. I associate it with death. I was fifteen when my family's cottage home in the fertile, hilly green town of Slunj was dynamited by Croatian forces, with entire family (other than me) inside. I had been making out with my boyfriend that day, Croatian boy from sympathetic family. We were hidden in a cool green pocket of pine trees near one of the larger wa-terfalls outside town. The shelling and exploding began, and we stayed hidden, afraid, until the sound of explosions stopped and night came. The boy begged me not to go home, to come with him, to pre-tend to be Croatian. He said his family would care for me. But I wanted to find my family. To know they were okay. I wanted to be with them. I'd run home past stone walls and majestic pines, smelling burned flesh, gunpowder, and tar in air, stunned by the glowing orange embers everywhere, the smoke and chaos. When drunk Croatian sol-diers asked me to name my ethnicity, I had lied and said Croatian. It wasn't entirely lie, actually. I have, had, Croatian grandmother. I speak the language fluently. The soldiers each kissed me on lips and moved on. This was victory for them.

When I returned to the once tidy cottage house with the flowers in boxes along the front walk, the home in which I had grown up, there was nothing left but smoldering red and black pile of debris. All along path to my house I'd come across decapitated bodies of old men I'd known. The Croatian soldiers had singled out the old men. To this day I have never fully understood the issues between Serbs and Croatians; to me, it was all stupid, men trying to come up with ways to kill other men, ways to rape women. Both sides were equally vile to each other. My own family had not been political at all, and my mother and father both believed the recent "tensions" had been orchestrated by United States after fall of Soviet Union, in hopes of smashing any other country that might try to become communist stronghold—Yugoslavia included.

For *this*, I thought then, staring into the milky, frozen eyes of the dead. For *this* the old men lay chopped to bits in the streets. Twice I'd had to stop to throw up walking to the cottage. All along the way, I found young women and others wandering in my same daze, unable to comprehend what had come to pass, the soundtrack endless wail of thousands sobbing, and people limping blindly toward what had been, in injury and disorientation, like ants whose hill has been stomped to nothing, searching for entrance, for safety. I sat by rubble of my home and waited hours, unable to believe what had happened. I called out names of my family members. But no one came. They were gone. I could not cry at first, because the mind and heart were not designed for such enormous loads of grief. A human being faced with this weight of emotion simply stops feeling, the breaths coming fast and shallow. I knew they'd all been home. In instant, my mother, father, grandparents, and four siblings had vanished. The entire neighborhood had been blown to oily splinters.

I had been surprised to find one lone survivor: my tiny brown mutt puppy, Mishko, a gift from my father, limping and with bloody eye, but alive nonetheless, with her tail wagging at sight of me, impervious to her own injuries and still able to lick my hands and face with affection and optimism. The feel of dog kisses kept me from killing myself. Mishko saved my life. I scooped Mishko up and began to wander. I heard from those who wandered streets that Serbians like us were being forced from the land, and that we were all walking out of the town. And so I joined other people along road, surrounded by livestock, tractors, old cars, and whatever scraps we could salvage from our lives. It's like dream now. Later I would learn that refugees from Krajina that day had numbered three hundred thousand. The dead civilians had numbered fourteen thousand.

It was at that moment, walking out of my hometown with no one left in world to love me but a one-eyed dog, that I began my long relationship with starvation, a drawn-out flirtation with death. I had been plump and round. But when I realized I had survived massacre because of my womanly lust for a Croatian boy, I wanted to get rid of my hips and breasts. I wanted to waste away. I did not deserve to live. I hated myself for surviving.

Weeks later, as Mishko and I spent numb days in stunned silence on cot at a refugee camp in Serbia, a tall, elegant man in gray striped suit had walked up and down the rows between cots, staring through eyeglasses into faces of the girls he found there as if he were looking for someone he knew. In truth, he was scout for ruthless, successful international modeling agency in Paris, searching for someone exactly like me: a beautiful, unfortunate girl whose face might be used to sell perfume in fashion magazines. In all, he went home to France with twenty-two Serbian girls and one puppy. I lived in apartment with four other girls and Mishko, the dog having gotten quite fat eating all the food the girls were forbidden. I quickly became the most successful of us all, as my empty eyes and sunken features were at once scarily symmetrical and otherworldly. I believe I looked like pretty, fragile, empty, hollowed-out corpse doll.

The years that followed since have all run together, and there are times I wake up and do not know where I am. There are times I take a knife to the flesh on insides of my arms and legs, cutting until I feel *something*, anything. It takes that much sometimes for me to feel at all. I have webs of scabs across my body that have to be airbrushed out of photos. If I didn't cut, I wouldn't feel connected to world of living.

Meeting and marrying Ricky was the first action I had taken that made me start to feel alive again, as he tenderly coaxed me from shell, as he sang to me and I felt love again. I had not expected to marry, but he had asked, and that meant family, didn't it? And family meant finally moving on. It meant eating, no more cutting. Soon.

I had been starving myself almost as habit to remain, at five-foot-eleven, a skeletal size two. I was used to burning in my gut. It comforted me. Cigarettes had become my substitute for food, but I didn't like what they did to skin or nerves and I would quit soon. I trembled often. I wanted to eat again. To quit smoking. To have children. To stay home and not model anymore. To start family and try to root myself in the world again.

Ricky likes me thin. When we go out in public together, to a party or a concert of his, my emaciated body is source of pride for Ricky. He, like many men who choose to date only models, tells me the sweet, acetone scent of my breath, a by-product of the body digesting itself, turns him on.

I don't like how mean Ricky gets when he drinks. But we anyhow share a bottle of Dom Perignon Champagne, a gift from the hotel manager. On my empty stomach, the alcohol goes directly to my head, making me woozy, sad, and sleepy. We wear cheerful, matching pale green silk pajamas I picked up for us on Rodeo Drive yesterday, in color close to that of my eyes. I watch him closely. His beauty is so great it makes me ache. His tanned skin, dark mess of hair, and inspired, almost madmanlike light brown eyes seemed, when I first met him, warm like home was warm, and I felt instinct to protect him and please him all at once. He was one of those people who seemed to be boy and man at the same time, the kind of man who could get away with saying or doing the wrong thing because his smile, the dimples of it, the sincerity and beauty of it, made people forget his faults. He had smooth sort of skin, creamy-looking, without much body hair, the kind of skin you wanted to bite. I was hungry for Ricky as surely as I was hungry for food, and yet I never felt him connect with me, the way man and wife should be together. His mind always seemed elsewhere.

I don't know right now whether intensity in Ricky's eyes indicates anger or pleasure. In interviews, he is laid-back, the kind of guy you might want to have over for barbecue. At home, he is different, his own toughest critic, obsessed with making himself better. His perfectionism amazes me. I myself have stumbled through life making every mistake you could make and never bothering to correct them.

In my eleven-year modeling career I have met many rich and famous people. But I have never known more focused human being than Ricky Biscayne. He smells of cigarettes and woodsy cologne. His smell reminds me of Slunj. Home. He is always trying to be better, at everything he does, from singing to cooking to making love. If I have one orgasm with him is not enough in his opinion. He will push me to go again, two, sometimes three times, even when I insist I am satisfied and ready to go to sleep. He doesn't do this to please *me*. He does it because Ricky is always performing. Proving something to someone, to God. I wonder when, exactly, Ricky will be good enough to make Ricky happy. He makes me feel awe.

I look from screen to his real face, trying to register what he might be thinking or feeling. We have only been married one year, since meeting at fashion show in Paris where I was model and he was musical guest. I still have a difficult time reading him. He does not exactly keep secrets from me, but he seems to keep storms of self-doubt from me, bottled-up anxiety and rage I do not understand. If I had his kinds of gifts, I would be happy all the time.

"Is *so* good your wonderful performing," I say, aware of my lingering Serbian accent. I overemphasized the "so." I don't think I'll ever be able to pronounce "Thursday," which comes out of my mouth "tours-day."

Ricky doesn't answer me. Rather, he pushes my hand away, leans forward, elbows on his knees, and studies himself. He sniffs and scratches at his reddened nose with back of his hand. Is he sick? The stress is getting to him. He seems sick all the time, sniffling sniffling sniffling. I reach out and begin to massage his shoulders, planting small kisses on the back of his neck. He shrugs me off of him, and concentrates on the screen.

Quickly, Ricky is up, sprinting across the room to the desk, where he sits and uses his laptop to log on to check his CDnow.com ranking again. He is obsessed with this number. Since the segment began, he tells me, it has dropped by 480,000. Nearly half a million spots in two minutes? Amazing.

"Padrísimo," he says, finally breaking a small smile, using the Spanish slang he uses when he's either very happy or very angry. His moods change as quickly as weather in Miami, cloudy and foreboding one moment, sunny and sharp the next. Success makes him crazy with happiness, but only for a while. He runs back to the sofa, takes powerful leap over the back of it, right into my lap, with rippling, masculine grace.

Ricky is skilled, wonderful dancer; in fact, that is a big part of his success as singer. His stage shows are exactly that, shows—choreographed, exciting, with Ricky at the center, shimmying and strutting. He was a track and soccer star when he was younger, in high school, and his mother, Alma, still has his old bedroom filled with trophies. Ricky works out like an athlete, even if he enjoys an occasional cigarette. His abs are hard, and at this moment they aren't the only part.

"I love you, Jasminka," he says, his eyes locked on mine.

We embrace, and kiss. Ricky scoops me off sofa and begins to carry me toward bedroom, singing.

"Hey," I say. "What you are doing me, huh?"

"Let's make a baby," he says.

I have been asking for children since we married, but Ricky has always asked me to wait until his career was better, because, he said, he wanted to be hands-on father, unlike his own absentee dad. Besides which, he said it would be mistake for someone in his position to have children too young, because his career thrived on his appearance of youth, and young men weren't supposed to have children, especially not if they wanted their female fans to maintain the illusion that they might someday be his lovers. I'd wondered, silently of course, how he could keep that illusion if he were married, but I never asked.

"You are serious? You are ready?" I ask him, tears of joy forming in my eyes as he lowers me gently onto the bed.

He looks deeply into my eyes, and answers simply. "Yes. Are you ready to give up modeling for a while?"

I answer my husband with kiss. I am ready to give up modeling forever. I am ready to come back to life. Happiness tickles my body like sunlight on cold skin. I close my eyes and thank God for finally making Ricky happy.

friday, march 22

Well, hello there. Welcome to the job from hell. I'm Milan Gotay. I'll be your escort. If you feel happy, uplifted, or optimistic, come over here to my workplace for a while. We'll fix you right up. We'll make you dread your next breath. We'll make you call Dr. Kevorkian. It doesn't help that I'm dressed like a bag lady in yet another ankle-length, baggy linen dress suit from Ross, beige, complete with huge round plastic buttons, the kind that shatter in the washer like SweeTarts on molars. I know better. I really do. But I can't bring myself to spend real money on clothes for this job. I mean, no one sees me. Other than my uncle, who is my employer. What's the point?

I should mention here that I'm dressed extra-baggy because I am scheduled to leave tomorrow morning on a weekend cruise with my mother and sister and I therefore want to hide today. For this same reason, I have a greasy white paper bag full of guava and cheese *pastelitos* on my desk, and a massive iced coffee. Yummy junk makes the day go faster.

The cruise is my mother's great idea to get me and Geneva to trust each other again. It's actually called a Rebuilding Trust Cruise, and it's some genius new-age guru's scam to get a bunch of sad, angry people to pay money to do things like fall backward into each other's arms.

Me? I think it's a really, really bad plan. I mean, get a bunch of people who hate each other to go out on the high seas for two days and one night of bonding? Hello? What is this guru chick smoking? I wonder if they do a complete head count. I bet the cruise comes back missing one or two people every time. I'm going to do my best not to push Geneva overboard, but I make no promises. Not only has she taken my boyfriends with alarming regularity, but she continues to make wardrobe suggestions in the form of her leftover accessories, which she leaves for me in slightly wrinkled white paper Neiman Marcus bags. I hate her, almost as much as I hate this job.

I stare at the grim gray wall of my cubicle and contemplate quitting—for the seventy-sixth time today. I kick off the tight gray Payless pumps under my desk and rub my feet together in their runny hose. It makes a scratchy noise inside my legs. Yuck.

"No, I *know Miami Style* magazine doesn't *usually* run stories on regularity aids," I say, as sweetly as possible, into the phone.

"You mean laxatives?" asks the reporter on the other end.

"We say 'regularity aids.'"

The reporter chuckles. I hate when they do that. I look around, find solace in the new photo of Ricky Biscayne I found in *People* magazine, which, to my great joy, just named him a "sexiest man alive." No argument there. If only to fall into his eyes instead of being . . . here.

"Regularity aids," repeats the reporter, laughing. "Oh, shit. Er, no pun intended."

I search the photo and notice that same redheaded musician in the background, staring right into the camera. Again I feel that weird pang in my heart. Like I've met him, or know him, something very eerie about him. He reminds me of a ghost for some reason, but a cute ghost—cute and mysterious. When I was little I used to think I saw ghosts. Maybe one of them looked like this guy.

I look up at the round white clock on the wall in the hallway. It is the same plain kind of clock they used to have in my grade-school classrooms, with big black numbers, and it moves just as slowly. Two? How could it only be two? I glance down at the coffee-stained script on my metal desk. I mean, do I really need a script for this? Shouldn't it go more like: *Hello, I'm Milan and I'm here to try to sell you on the dumbest thing you've ever heard of?* Whatever happened to honesty in business? Oh, wait. This is Miami. We never had that.

I'm bored. By my life. It's a fine life. I know that. But it is damn boring.

Just three more hours. Then I can go home and get ready for the book club, where tonight we will be analyzing the Kyra Davis novel *Sex, Murder and a Double Latte*. I *love* my book club. I love this book. Okay, muscle through it, Milan. Do it.

I read the script out loud, as required by my uncle, "Because, you see, E-Z Go is *more* than just a regularity aid. It's a *lifestyle*. From celebs to the pres, everyone has to go. And if you gotta go, why not E-Z Go?"

I don't mean to sound like a freakin' droid, but come *on*. The script is awful. But my boss and uncle, Tío Jesús, wrote it himself. Have I mentioned he has the writing ability of a fifth-grader? He thinks he's a good writer, though. He also thinks no one can tell that the hair on his forehead actually originates on the back of his head and is combed forward like a dead thing squished on the road. I have to read this script this exact way, every day. I'm also supposed to be pitching Tío's crapper drug for pregnant women, but I'm not all that sure it's, like, safe for fetuses. I don't want that kind of responsibility.

As usual, I'm met with eerie silence, ghost-town, tumbleweed-blowing silence. There's nothing to ease the pain but the sickly motorized buzz of the window-unit air conditioner. Tío is too cheap for central air. Cheap bastard. Did the reporter hang up on me? It wouldn't have been the first time, certainly. My heart sinks. "Hello?" I call into the phone, as if yelling to the bottom of a well. "Hello?"

Finally, the reporter speaks. "Uh, is this, like, a *joke*? Did my boyfriend tell you to call?"

"No," I say. Well, actually, my career *is* a joke. But that is obvious. At least it is obvious to everyone but my parents, who still, like, pretend to be proud that their little Milan is helping Tío Jesús with his shit business.

"Sorry. I thought it might be a joke."

"That's okay," I say. I am a joke.

I have to think of something, quick. I have to land a story, or I'm in trouble. I haven't landed a story in weeks. I flip through the *People* magazine in front of me, and stop on a golden, glowing photo of Jill Sanchez, the beautiful Puerto Rican movie star and singer, posing on a red carpet for the release of her latest line of exercise wear, her head turned sharply over her shoulder so that her rear end and big white smile are both aimed directly at the photographer. I feel a rush of small joy that a woman of ample tush might be a star in America. But as instantly as I feel pleasure at this thought, I feel sick that this woman looks as flexible and heartless as a panther. Jill has no back fat, just a lean little crease where the ribs begin. Like millions of other people, I hate Jill Sanchez because I'm *not* Jill Sanchez and will never *be* Jill Sanchez.

"Uh, we might get Jill Sanchez as a spokesperson," I blurt, like an idiot. Oops! It was a complete lie, of course. From what little I know of her, Jill eats plenty of fiber and so would likely be quite regular all on her own. I feel guilty and weird for even picturing Jill Sanchez pooping, and silently ask La Caridad to forgive me.

The reporter laughs even louder. "You picked the actress with the biggest ass in Hollywood? Oh, my God. Jill Sanchez, queen of the crapper. That's hilarious, dog." Reporters should not call publicists "dog." There's something very wrong with that.

Laughter. Click. Dead space. Dial tone. Sinking feeling I might have just landed my beloved uncle a massive lawsuit. I place the black plastic receiver back in the cradle, tug at a strand of my flat, unstyled light brown hair, drop my head onto the stink-ass desk, and begin to cry. Because *Cosmopolitan* says you're never supposed to let anyone see you cry at work, I stop. I live my life by magazines, just so you know. It's retarded, but I can't help it. I have no other barometer of what normal life is supposed to look like for normal American women. My favorite is *InStyle*, probably because I am utterly Out of Style. I look at the clock again. It is *still* two. What the hell? How is it possible that time moves backward here? I, of all people, work in the Twilight Zone. How nice.

I hear Tío clear his throat in the next cubicle. Then, there he is. Uncle Jesús, or rather, Uncle Jesús's balding brown head, rising above the partition, followed by his thick round eyeglasses. He looks like a nearsighted thumb. I can almost hear the scary music playing, like the monster is coming. He was listening to me, of course. That's what he does. Eavesdrops on me all day long, and because I am family, he has no problem instantly critiquing my performances. Other employees get twice-yearly performance evaluations. Me? Twice an hour, if I'm lucky.

"I know," I say. I can't look up at that combover. I'll cry again. Anyway, I know what he's going to say. I put my hands over my ears but hear him anyway.

"You weren't aggressive enough," he says, in Spanish.

"I know."

"You can't lie to reporters. It's not smart."

"I know."

"Why did you do that? Are you stupid?" He taps me on the back of the head with a piece of paper. I should file for abuse.

"I don't know," I say. Thinking, Yes, for taking this job.

"You better call back and tell them you lied."

"I know."

"If you don't make quota, we'll, uh, have to talk," he says.

"I know."

"I mean *talk*."

"I know."

"I don't want to have to fire you. My own niece."

"I know." Wouldn't be the worst thing in the world, now would it? Tío coughs. "My favorite niece."

"I know," I say, but I know he's lying.

Tío Jesús, like everyone else on planet Earth, prefers Geneva.

————

can't believe I, Geneva Gotay, a woman who prides herself on being alternative and cutting edge, am sitting outside on the patio at Larios in South Beach like a SoBe tourist. Belle is here, too, peeking up out of her little black carrier, and she's no more impressed with the place than I am. But this is where Ricky wanted to meet, so here I am, waiting for the sexy singer and his new manager, Ron DiMeola. If he'd said, *Geneva, you pick the spot,* I would never in a million years have chosen this. Too commercial. Too predictable. If it had been up to me, and if we'd had to stick to South Beach, I would have suggested China Grill, or Pao. Something elegant and cool. I love Asian food, and around here, you know, there's nothing exotic or particularly interesting about Cuban food—or Gloria Estefan, for that matter. Ricky picked Gloria's beachfront restaurant. You can take the neck chains off the boy, but . . .

It has been a little more than a month since I saw Ricky on *The Tonight Show*. I can hardly believe how quickly everything has come together in setting up this meeting and getting him interested in my club. I shouldn't say that. I'm not surprised. I know how to get things done. I'm just excited. People always ask me how I "do it," meaning how successful I am at business, at nearly everything I try. The answer is simple. No fear. If I fail, I try again. And if I fail, I do it again. That's all. Again and again. There are two things I don't believe in: luck and failure. Setbacks only make me work harder. That, by the way, is also a Cuban thing. A recent piece in the *Herald* talked about how the Cubans who came to Miami twenty years ago in the Mariel Boatlift, penniless at the time, are now almost all middle class, making more money and finding more success in just one generation than did most Floridians who were native to the area. So, it goes without saying that I had no fear in calling Ricky directly and asking. And here I am.

I'm wearing MaxMara, my favorite brand of the moment, a flirty ruffled miniskirt made of distressed pale cream and mustard floral silk, a tailored linen jacket with a Chinese collar, and strappy brown Giuseppe Zanotti sandals with a scorpion buckle. I've stacked each of my wrists in cream and kumquat chunky bangles, and my eyes are hidden behind a sexy pair of Salvatore Ferragamo sunglasses with creamy white rims that I picked up just this morning at the Bal Harbour shops. You might say I have a shopping fetish.

My long black hair is flat-ironed into obedience. I wrapped a black and cream silk patterned scarf around my head this morning, like a gypsy headdress. I'm thinking this is my new look. The turban. I'm planning an exotic, mystical atmosphere for Club G, and figure I ought to live its essence every moment, embody the product I am selling, become one with my vision. My makeup is done in peach and gold tones that seem at once natural and luxurious, and slightly Eastern. Feeling, overall, pretty damn fabulous.

I've already chatted with the Colombian valet, the Uruguayan hostess, and the Chilean busboy, because you never knew who you might need. The busboy? *Pobrecito.* He asked me if I was a *novela* star. Said he recognized me from somewhere. This happens. Very sweet.

The waiter brings me the glass of mineral water I ordered for me, and the bowl of bottled water for Belle. I thank him in Spanish. Never assume anyone in this town speaks English. Always assume they speak Spanish. I compliment his hands and leave him blushing. That's what I do. Position myself on top, the one making judgments, the one in charge, but in a roundabout way that makes others feel self-consciously happy. There is so much power in this method. Trust me. If you can get people to fall in love with you, you can accomplish anything.

I look around at the city I grew up in and realize how much different it looks after being in Boston for a few years. Sometimes, you have to leave a place to understand it. I now realize that Miami wasn't a big deal until all the Cubans moved here in the late 1950s and early 1960s. Before us, it was a mosquito town. At the start of the twentieth century, there were only about a thousand people living in Miami. In the '60s, more than six hundred thousand Cuban exiles came here, fleeing communism. Hurricanes destroyed this city over and over, and nobody but us, apparently, had the tenacity, or stupidity, or mob connections, or all of the above, to keep rebuilding this place. Most of us either already had money or we had the education and desire to make money.

Now, Miami is the largest Hispanic-majority city in the United States; as a group, Cuban-Americans have done better than pretty much any other immigrant group in the nation, which is amazing. Cuban-American women, as a subgroup, have higher levels of eduation and income than any other women in the United States. No, I didn't say any other *Hispanic* women; I said any other *women*. We succeed at higher rates than all other women here. I attribute our success to our tendency to never give up and to fight with anyone and anything that gets in our way. We Cubans are a nation of pugilists, and we've turned Miami into a city of pugilists. Don't believe me? Go to any Cuban restaurant and stand near the outdoor coffee window, with all the men in guayaberas, and just listen to them. Fight, fight, fight. That's what Cubans do best. Fight, and eat.

I'm not trying to insult my own people here. It's just that, as the Elián González and the Posada Carriles debacles showed, a tolerant bunch we are not. Once you leave Miami, you understand just how crazy we look to everyone else. We look like Nazis *con sabor*. That's what we look like. Don't let me get into this discussion with my father, though. Oh, man. It all ends there. He, like many of my countrymen, tolerates dissent and free speech as well as he might tolerate arsenic. There's a reason the highest suicide rates in the Americas are among Cuban women in Cuba, and Cuban-American males in the United States. Men lord it over women in Cuba, and once we women get here and get a taste of freedom, we love it. The men hate us for it in Miami, trust me.

I check my watch. I walked here from my condo, but I'm ten minutes early. I hadn't meant to walk that fast. What to do? The worst thing is to do nothing, to sit and be stared at like a zoo animal. Especially here. I hope I don't see anyone I know. I hate zoos, the whole animal sense of having nothing to do but wait to be fed, ogled, or die. That awful feeling of never-ending, dependent pause. I never go to movies alone, either.

Blissfully, my cell phone rings. I look at the caller ID. Ignacio, the black Cuban ballet dancer I've been dating—one of the *Marielitos* I told you about who's done well here. I answer the phone and speak sweetly to him. I really *do* feel a certain excitement when he calls, even though I never intended this to be a relationship; I intended it to be occasional sex. I've had a few black sex partners; I have a thing for black guys, especially if they wear baseball caps backward and "wife beater" tank tops. But Ignacio is different. He's very well educated, talented, funny, and smart, and I fear I'm starting to really like him.

He asks me to attend a book reading with him later tonight. Uh-oh. We've, you know, never been on a real, official *date* before. I'm also not the poetry-reading type. Why would a person sit and listen to a poem if you could read it? And another question: Do you go on a date with your sex toy? Would that ruin everything? Would we have anything to talk about for that long? Would I see someone I know?

He rattles off the details—it's an exile poet he knew back in Cuba. Safe. No one in my crowd would attend something like that. I say yes. I don't want to be out too late tonight, since I have to get up early and go on the Trust Cruise my mom bought for me and Milan. Mom seems to think my sister and I have deep-seated issues, that we don't trust each other. The sad truth is that Milan is so dull it is impossible to have issues with her; I don't think about Milan often enough or with enough energy to make it worthwhile to trust or not trust her. She's a big blank in my life. We don't have much in common, we don't have much to talk about, and I leave it at that. I do not mistrust my sister. To mistrust someone, you have to actually care deeply about what they think.

I rummage through my Luella Carmen "biker bag" and remove my Shiseido lip base, liner, color, and gloss, and apply them in the four steps. Afterward, I wish I had a newspaper to read, or my BlackBerry to check e-mail; I left the latter in the car. I take a pen from the bag and start writing key words I want people to associate with Club G on the drinks menu, which I've removed from its holder. Nothing helps

you focus more than writing things down. I write everything down.
All the time.

*Theme and vibe. Colorful. Rich. Eastern influences. Gold, red, or-
ange. The colors of the sun on your eyelids. Cardamom. Green
mango. Bedouin tents. Draping silk. Sahara. Soft floors. Oasis. Belly-
dance. Koi. Nutmeg. Musk. Huge red pillows. Tiny round mirrors.
Tassels. Secluded tentlike corners for making out. Folds of cloth on
every surface. Womblike. Warm. Tropical but not in a Miami sense.
Tropical in a sweepingly dry Moroccan sense. Throbbing. Sexual.
Female staff dressed in see-through harem garb. Lots of abs.
G-strings. Male staff shirtless with harem pants. Genies. Magical.
The colors of curry. Soft, sexy lighting. Sex. Money. Harem. Sex,
everywhere. Nude portraits. Graphic yet tasteful sex photos, hard to
tell what they are unless looking very hard or very drunk. Sex.
Money. Oil. Power. Sin. Pleasure. Genghis Khan. Pleasure dome.
Power did decree.*

I look up and see Ricky Biscayne pull up to the curb in a black
BMW 5 series. I have a white one. We have matching cars. That's
kind of cool, anyway. At least he has good taste in vehicles.

He is alone. I fold the menu and stash it in my handbag with the
pen. He gets out, hands the keys to the valet, and I see his faded jeans
with the big patch on the knee, yellow silk guayabera, and dress shoes.
He looks good, but sort of clothing-clueless. I call out to him and
wave. He smiles and joins me at the table, as most of the diners stare
in awe. They all seem to recognize him, which is exactly as I hoped it
would be. Why bother to get a nobody to invest in your club? You
need star power if you want to get anywhere in the club business in
this town. That, and a theme that sets you apart.

"Hi, Ricky. I'm Geneva Gotay. It's really great to meet you."

I stand up and hold my hand out to shake his, but he pulls me in
for a strong embrace, kissing me on both cheeks, the Miami way. He

smells of lettuce and tobacco, and his skin feels cool and slightly clammy.

"¡*Coño!* You're prettier than I expected, *morenita*," he says, flirting. Even Ricky recognizes that I look black. But my own parents? Forget it. They think we're white. In Boston, everyone assumed I was black. He glances down at Belle, who pants up at him. "Cute dog," he says.

"Thanks," I say.

He sits across from me at the square, beige granite table and takes off his sunglasses. I am still turned on from imagining what Club G would mean to amorous drunk people, so I instantly want to jump him, lame jeans and all. He'd probably be an incredible sex toy. You can just tell which guys get it and which guys don't. His eyes are his best feature, almost amber yellow, with green and brown flecks, intelligent and angry as hell. I hadn't realized the anger bit when I saw him on television. On TV, the anger comes across as lust. There's a fine line between the two, really, if you think about it. He's got that proverbial bad-boy thing. He's dangerous, that's what he is. Danger, of the nature that women crave like chocolate.

"Yeah, girl," he says, in a joking manner, doing his hands like a gang member. I would like to say it's unnatural, but it's not. He's steeped in it. "Harvard Business School. I just think something different when I think that. You don't look Harvard. Dang, girl. Hey." He sits up straighter, leans down to pet Belle, winning points with me. "Is it true your mom is Violeta, with the radio show?"

"Yeah."

"Cool! My moms loves that show. She listens to it every day." He fingers a crucifix around his neck.

"Really? That's funny."

"Your mom be talking about some crazy things," he says. "She's all *puñeta y pinga y to' eso*, man."

On second thought, maybe I wouldn't do him, even if he asked. I like my dangerous men to at the very least have safe grammar. I smile with my nose, a snooty little prep-girl smile, to let him know that I'll humor him but don't find him all that charming. All those years at Ransom Everglades School made me a first-class snob, when I need to be. He gets it, and looks away, shifts in his seat.

"Nah, you know." He scans the crowd and tries not to look hurt. "You really do look better than I thought." He leans back in his seat, hands clasped behind his head, and licks his lips at me. "You got plans tonight?"

"Yes, thanks," I say. "Poetry reading."

His brows shoot up and he laughs. "Okay, girl, I'm scared of *you* now. Check you out." Why is he speaking Ebonics?

I decide to do the all-business approach. I look at my watch. "So, Ricky. Where's your manager? I thought he was coming, too?"

Ricky shrugs. "Ron? Nah. That *mamabicho* ain't coming. He got business in the Cayman Islands. I don't think I need him for this. I trust you."

Business in the Cayman Islands? That's not good, is it? Only dealers and money launderers have business in the Cayman Islands. "But you just met me," I say. "How can you trust me?"

"You got Harvard, you look awesome, you're a Miami homegirl." Ricky sniffles and rubs his nose with the back of his hand. He clears his throat and places a cool, clammy hand on top of mine. "So, beautiful, where do I sign up?"

"You're joking, right?" It can't be this easy.

"Not at all," he says.

Someone should counsel this man, I think. He could very well sign his life away to a pretty girl. Is he really this stupid? I'm stunned. Someone should save him from himself. But not me. Not now. I caught him, and I'm not letting go. I smile sweetly, and remove a contract and silver Tiffany pen from my briefcase.

I wonder if there's room for Ricky on the Trust Cruise.

———

atthew Baker sits in the recording studio in his usual work clothes—black jeans and a faded Green Day T-shirt, with a warped and well-loved Marlins baseball cap to protect the prematurely bald spot on the top of his head. He is twenty-eight and has been losing his hair steadily for the past seven years.

For this and several other reasons, Matthew Baker is incapable of recognizing that many women find him mysteriously attractive. Most attractive about him are his smallish, dark brown eyes, which turn slightly downward at the outer edges, the heavy-hooded eyes of a thinker, affecting eyes that make women want to find out what's on his mind.

But Matthew *knows* none of this, even when told. In his heart, he knows only that he is *pathetic*. Every morning, he counts on finding a mess of short red hairs tangled in the shower drain, and every morning, as he wipes them up, flicks them from his fingertips, and flushes them, he feels a little less attractive to the entirety of womankind. Given that his hair had been *bright red* to begin with, he feels that the powers of the universe were particularly unkind to him when doling out the details in his "appearance" column. He doesn't see any godly reason why he should have to be balding, redheaded, freckled, chubby, *and* short. What, did God hate him? Five-foot-nine, unlikely. That, in a nutshell, is how Matthew Baker perceives himself: short, bald, and unlikely. Unlikely to ever get another date, now that he's been dumped, for the third time, by the same plain yet brilliant and passionate woman.

Matthew presses the button on the computer and the song he's been working on all day starts to play through the speakers. It is almost finished. It's a ballad about strolling in Milan, Italy, with a soulful woman, called "The Last Supper." He's been laying down the keyboards, the drums, and the background vocals for a single on the upcoming new Ricky Biscayne Spanish-language song. Bored, he's gone ahead and recorded the lead track as well. Ricky's English crossover, which mostly features Matthew's singing, truth be told, is slammin', burning up the charts. Ricky wanted to do nothing but English from now on, but Matthew has persuaded him not to give up his original core Spanish audience, the ones who will, Matthew figures, still love him after America's love affair with the hot-new-Latin-sensation crap peters out. Didn't Ricky understand yet that the American media could not make room for a Latino star for more than a season or two? It doesn't matter how talented the star is. Latin seems to mean trendy and disposable to mainstream America. Every six or seven years, it seems like, the country announces the arrival of "Latino chic," only to let it die out again the following year, every new wave of it seeming to have been the first ever. Ridiculous.

Matthew closes his eyes and listens to the melody and lyrics, both of which he's written. As he focuses, a new harmony line comes to him. He writes it down, fighting the urge to go back into the studio and record it. Damn. The song sounds fucking *great*. Once he learns the song, Ricky will have another hit record. All those years of song-writing classes at Berklee College of Music are finally paying off for Matthew, as the craft gets easier, and more exciting. Sort of paying off, anyway. Ricky makes mad money these days, and Matthew knows he ought to be entitled, by virtue of creative input, to a big cut of it. But Ricky has him on a yearly salary. It isn't the best setup. But Matthew has not been raised to associate art and creativity with money. He has never really been in music for the money. People who look like Ricky might go into the business for money. But guys who look like Matthew are usually musicians because they love music, period. Matthew knows he's a dipshit about the money. He'll have a talk with Ricky one of these days, and see if there isn't something they can do, an arrangement they can come to, that would be a little more fair. Matthew's mother and father might not have taught him the importance of business sense and money, but they had taught him the value of karma and justice.

"Time to go," he says to himself, though even as he says it he realizes there is no reason to rush back to his apartment. There is no one waiting for him, and nothing much for him to do once he gets home. But the principle of the thing makes him leave work. That's what people do, right? Normal people. Normal, twenty-something people. They leave work at the end of the day, even if they love their art so much they would gladly stay up all night working. They go home and have lives. Matthew has a home, or at least an apartment. The life thing, however, continues to elude him, particularly here in Miami, where he never has, and probably never will, fit in.

For years, growing up in San Francisco and elsewhere, Matthew had looked at the shiny men's dress shoes in department stores and wondered just who the *hell* wore the kinds with tassels or black-and-white cowhide. He'd wondered the same thing of belts. Now he knew. Men in Miami wear those things. He'd never met a bigger bunch of preppy pretty boys than the Latino dudes in this city, all of them walking around in a fog of Gucci cologne with the kind of jeans you could buy only in Europe. You wouldn't think any real men would wear something like yellow moccasins until you moved here, and he isn't just talking about sissy men, either. Macho men wear soft leather fancy shoes here, and they never seem to skip a day of shaving. The men in Miami seem to moisturize. He's never seen anything like it. A slob at heart and in appearance, Matthew despises Miami for its lack of hippies, hairy-pit women, and messy artistic-looking men. Men like him. This city, in the humble opinion of Matthew Baker, is too fucking slick, so slick it's greasy.

Matthew locks up the recording studio at Ricky Biscayne's house, waves good-bye to Jasminka, who lies mournfully by the pool like a dried-out piece of model jerky. In another time and place, she would have floored him with her beauty. But around here, she is common. The women who get your attention in Miami Beach are the fat ones, because they are rare. Beautiful women? Everywhere you look. This is why Matthew often feels like a starving man at a banquet, forbidden to eat. So many amazing women, and not a single one interested in him.

She raises a weak-looking bone of an arm and waves back, like something dragged from a concentration camp. She has all these red marks on her arms. Matthew has asked Ricky about it and now knows that Jasminka cuts herself. What kind of crap is that? Matthew feels sorry for her, but even more than that he finds her creepy. She is impossibly skinny, like an alien. It is sick to be that skinny. And then the cutting. People have issues. He doesn't care how rich, famous, or pretty you are, you have shit you want to hide from other people and that is all there is to it. People are weird and complicated and, at the moment, he is sick of feeling sorry for them, especially Jasminka. Matthew wants to feed her all the time. Ricky never seems to notice how sad his wife is, or how needy, how chopped up. Ricky doesn't get it.

Matthew walks to the side yard to unchain his Trek bicycle from the trellis. He doesn't know where Ricky is, and he feels oddly liberated by Mr. Super Stud's absence. There was a time, almost ten years ago, after meeting as insecure students at Berklee, when he and Ricky had been dorm mates and, he thought, good friends, talking music until late in the night, hitting clubs, laughing over pizza and Celtics games. Back then, they joked about how ungodly, stupidly fucking *pretty* Ricky was, and how ridiculously, volcanically rich Matthew's "Barry White voice" seemed for his skin tone and size. Matthew thought Ricky looked like a soap-opera actor, and Ricky thought Matthew looked like a baby that might have been produced by a union between Ren and Stimpy. Both guys could sing in those days. Matthew thought Ricky sounded like Luis Miguel or something. Ricky thought Matthew sounded like Bono, which he probably did back then, having been very into Bono at the time.

Back then, they had joked about how Ricky, the "Latino" from Miami, spoke worse Spanish than Matthew, the "gringo" from San Francisco. In truth, Matthew's hippie parents had been Baha'i missionaries in Panama and Bolivia for much of his childhood, and he'd grown up in weirdly scratchy homemade pants tied on with string, often shoeless, living between small towns in Latin America and the family's small bungalow house in a shady part of Oakland. And by shady he meant drive-bys, not trees.

Matthew begins to pedal home—a one-bedroom SoBe condo with

futon furniture, a dead houseplant, and not a whole lot else. Matthew can afford more. Ricky pays him about eighty thousand a year. Not bad in Miami. But the truth is, Matthew doesn't know how to decorate, or shop. Those things don't matter much to him. What he lacks in furniture, he makes up for in musical equipment. He has more than twenty guitars, many keyboards, computers, drums, all manner of instruments. His apartment looks like a pawnshop.

He thinks about Ricky as he rides. Ricky seems to be getting progressively less mature as time goes on, and these days he goes to a lot of beachy hotel parties without Matthew, seeming to prefer his shiny new crowd of lame-ass wannabe models and stars. What sucks even bigger-time is that Ricky seems like he can't sing as well now as he could five years ago. Like he got a throat disease or something. He coughs and hacks and sniffles, like he's got tuberculosis or a hairball. He seems like he can't focus to save his life. Matthew has a feeling that the decline in singing ability has to do with the increasing frequency with which Ricky indulges his curiosity about tobacco and cocaine, but he has no proof of the latter, other than the red nose. He knows better than to ask about it, because Ricky doesn't like to talk about weaknesses. No, he takes that back. Ricky likes to talk about *other* people's weakness, just not his own.

Just the other day, when Ricky was introducing Matthew to some of his new management-team members, he'd joked that Matthew was "the Baha'i Rick Astley," which stung like a motherfucker. Fuck Rick Astley. Okay? If you were a redheaded male singer, you did *not* want that comparison, okay? Matthew knows he himself isn't heartthrob material like Ricky, and he knows he'll never make any man-of-the-year lists, other than "most sunburned." But Matthew has musical talent, and a powerful singing voice that he uses more and more to bolster Ricky's weakening one. That deserves respect, as does the fact that most of Ricky's songs have been written or at least cowritten by Matthew, even if he rarely gets official credit because he is way too nice, because somehow his role was grandfathered in, from the days before success, and never updated.

Matthew whistles the latest melody he's come up with as he leaves for home, and congratulates himself for actually riding his bike to work today. He's put on a few pounds in the past couple of years. Lonely, he's substituted eating for company. He wants to lose weight, but he doesn't want to have to stop eating to do it.

He slips the round white plastic earpieces from his iPod into his ears and begins to pump his short, bowed legs. The ride from Ricky's house to Matthew's small apartment takes about ten minutes, and by the time he gets there he is exhausted. Not physically exhausted, but emotionally exhausted.

Matthew has once again made the mistake of spending the entire bike ride thinking about Eydis, the ghostly, somewhat plain Icelandic singer he fell for at Berklee. She has a voice that reminds him of the aurora borealis, just like he wrote in the song no one knew was his love letter to her. And a sense of humor that catches everyone off guard. She also speaks six languages and hopes to live one day in Milan, Italy. He's never met anyone as amazing as Eydis. She also happens to have a wonderfully full bottom, a butt like an upside-down valentine, and Matthew is a butt man. Anyway, he has her favorite playlist of dreary ECM artists programmed into his iPod, that's what exhausted his ass. Listening to Eydis's favorite songs. The sickeningly sweet memory of that horrible, wonderful woman.

They met in music history and dated for five years. She is taller than he is but told him his height didn't matter. She told him he had the most penetrating and intelligent gaze she'd ever seen. She was the only woman he'd ever known who thought he was better-looking than Ricky. She'd performed amazing, biteless oral sex, lodging a vibrator against her cheek as she sucked him, delivering a most unnerving and amazing sensation. They shared a passion for Thai food and Monty Python. He loved her, both the pure and the raunchy bits. He wanted to marry her. Then she dumped him for some hairy-assed, hairy-backed, hairy-eared Israeli drummer in the cruise-ship band she had taken up with. Dude looked like a really handsome Wookie. Eydis is stupid about men. She falls for them all.

This last dumping of Matthew happened about six months ago. Matthew was blindsided by it, but Ricky, during a late-night session involving two six-packs of Fat Tire, had sagely pointed out that it should not have come as a surprise, given that Eydis had cheated on and dumped Matthew Baker on exactly three previous occasions, always returning like a pigeon when the new relationship petered out, cooing for him to take her back. Matthew realizes he is Eydis's stocky security blanket, and part of him hopes she will one day outgrow her infidelities and finally settle down with him. Unlike Ricky, who claims to detest children, Matthew loves them. During his years with his parents in Bolivia and Panama, it was the children who were the most forgiving, the most hopeful. Children *rocked*.

For his love of children and Eydis, Ricky calls Matthew a pussy, and Matthew is not sure Ricky has it wrong on the Eydis portion. In fact, if Eydis were to show up at his door tonight, begging him to take her back again, he would. There's a chance. She's in town. He knows her schedule, and he knows her ship leaves tomorrow. If she were to trip up the stairs and beg, he'd take her back. That might just have been another list to which the unlikely Matthew could imagine himself topping—biggest dumb-ass pussy of the year. Sounds about right to him. He thinks for a moment about heading down to the docks to try to talk to her before her ship sets off again. He knows more or less what time she'd get there. He might casually bump into her, and casually beg her to come back to him. It could work.

The whole reason Matthew moved to Miami—aside from working with Ricky—was to be able to see Eydis on her days off, when her Carnival ship docked and she came ashore to love him. Six months since the latest dump, and he still hasn't gotten over it, or dated anyone. When you look like Matthew Baker, in Matthew Baker's opinion, you don't just go up to women and ask them out, because you risk nine times out of ten having them laugh at you in front of their friends. He figures he'll never date again, unless the thing with the hairy Israeli doesn't work out, of course, and then, there he'd be, pussy boy, begging.

Friday night in South Beach. Oh, man. It is going to be a crazy one, he can tell. His gay neighbors have told him that South Beach is only 10 percent gay these days, that all the hip gays have moved on to Belle Meade or Shorecrest. Still, Matthew feels like his neighborhood is *full* of gay guys because, having grown up mostly in South America, where no one talks about homosexuality, he still cannot get used to the feeling of men's eyes on him. The Saint Patrick's Day spring-break stupidity would be going on tonight, and there would be drunk tourists and other weirdos puking green beer all over, girls sucking Jell-O shots out of each other's navels, and the like. The only place he could imagine that would be crazier than South Beach was Rio. Maybe Gomorrah, Sodom, one of those. He'd have to get upstairs and hole himself in.

Matthew observes the crowd of cars already clogging the street, feels depressed. There are beer-faced frat boys, fat tourists in pastel shirts, models, golden girls with Ann Richards hair, rowdy groups of big-nose girls from Brazil and Japan who look pretty from only the chin down, drag queens, and insecure middle-aged men who drive penis cars and rev the engines at intersections. He really doesn't fit in in Miami, but even less so around *here*. Somewhere, there must be a place where he'd actually fit in. The closest he's come is San Francisco, the thought of which makes him even gloomier. You can't make a living as a pop musician in San Francisco. You just can't. The city is too damn laid-back for hard-hitting pop music of the kind that Matthew likes to make.

Speaking of which, a car drives past now, blasting Ricky's English hit song. It is surreal. The male driver sings along, and looks at Matthew like he's scum, like the driver is much cooler than Matthew for listening to a hip Latin singer, and the driver has no clue that Matthew not only wrote the song but is the main voice on the recording, too. Life is too weird sometimes.

All his life, ever since he was a little boy listening to crackly radios in homes and shops in Latin America, ever since he got his first guitar when he was four years old, Matthew has written songs. It came naturally to him, so naturally that he never really considered it a talent. Talent seemed like something that had to be at least a little bit challenging. Music was fun, and easy. By the time he was ten, Matthew was a master guitarist, and he'd composed more than a hundred songs. That's just the way he is and has always been. When he was about twelve, he decided that he wanted to grow up to hear one of his songs on the radio. Now, with four years of working with (for?) Ricky Biscayne, Matthew has heard exactly eleven of his songs on the radio in Miami. It is fucking amazing, as Ricky would say. But this one, the English-crossover tune, his song for Eydis, is the first one that has hit hard in the mainstream market, and since *The Tonight Show* performance it has steadily climbed the charts and seems to be headed where none of Matthew's work has gone before: The Billboard Hot 100.

Matthew is so happy, he even waves at the guys in frayed Daisy Dukes who whistle at him across the street. They know it bugs the crap out of him when they do that—the shorts and the harassment. They have told him they wanted to "queer eye" him, meaning make him over. Shudder. Women. He likes women, thank you very much. Every size of woman, every color. He loves them all. Even the pregnant ones are sexy and sensual to Matthew, who thinks women rule the universe with life-giving powers.

The only women he sees regularly are Ricky's wife and her model friends, them and the various skeezer bitches who work for Ricky and blow him whenever he asks; but they are not appealing, quite the opposite. He does not, under any circumstances, want his dick in a mouth that once held Ricky's dick. He of all people knows the countless orifices into which Ricky has dipped himself. No thanks. Also unappealing are Ricky's assorted groupies, who actually offer with some regularity to do Matthew if he'll introduce them to Ricky. The thought is as appealing to Matthew Baker as electrodes to the nuts.

In desperation, Matthew signed up for an online dating service a month ago, but has yet to actually ask anyone out. The women on there scare him, with those weirdly fishbowl-looking gray photos it looks like they took of themselves next to their computers with digital cameras. They must be very lonely to have to take their own photos like that, with the extended arm showing and the nose too big because of the weird angle. So far, he's heard from only one woman, whose profile talks mostly about her childhood sexual abuse and trust issues. He did not take her up on an offer to get togther at a tattoo parlor. They have to be as desperate as he is, and that isn't good.

Matthew climbs the three flights of stairs to his apartment, wades through the shrapnel of his life, chords and keyboards, guitars and take-out trash, and opens the freezer. Ice cream. Chunky Monkey. A DiGiorno pizza. In the fridge, he finds a couple of Sam Adams bottles. Those, and a couple of hours of channel surfing, and he'll be all set. Yup, all set. The way Matthew sees it, going out is expensive and pointless, and he's earned the calories and mindless television.

B
ulls tapdance on my cranium. The headache has as a backdrop a sore lower back and an aching belly, all foretelling the arrival of yet another glorious period in the barren land of Milan. I would like to take the Pill, like Geneva, but I wouldn't want my dad to find the pills and flip out on me. He thinks I'm a virgin, and for some stupid reason this is very important to him.

As the decrepit ice maker in the office kitchen down the hall plops out its latest frigid offerings with a harsh *thunk thunk thunk*, I gather my belongings, consisting of a purse and a purple vinyl lunch bag probably intended for children. I rush past the sound of Tío Jesús bellowing into the phone to one of his suppliers, and hurry out the door of the glorified trailer that is the E-Z Go offices, into the muggy gray light of Overtown, by many estimates the most miserable and cockroached neighborhood in Miami. I instantly hear sirens, emergency vehicles rushing somewhere in crisis. Welcome to Overtown.

My breasts bounce a little as I trot to my car, tender and lifeless with the PMS stupidity. I need to shorten the straps on my bra. I'm too lazy to remember to do that. I can feel myself bloating, swelling up like Harry Potter's evil aunt in that movie. I need an elastic waistband. And more pastries. Oh, and coffee. Mmm, coffee. A good book wouldn't hurt. Thank God it's Friday—book-club night with Las Loquitas del Libro! I can't wait to see the girls and listen to them laugh as their spoons click comfortingly against the porcelain of their coffee cups. Best sounds in the world.

I hear something rustle in the bushes, probably something delightfully Overtown, like a rat snacking on a pigeon carcass. Miami is wonderful, yes, if you are in the right places. In the wrong places, it is disgusting, with things that never rot in trash cans, things that just mold and puff up and ooze—kind of like me at the moment, come to think of it. I feel disgusting. I need a shower. I push aside the food wrappers and old mail in the driver's seat of my Neon, and dump my tired body into it. I engage the door locks and the air-conditioning, which somehow comes out smelling like dirty feet and tuna fish (time to change the filter?). I drive as quickly as possible through the neighborhood and onto the freeway. There are always stories in the *Herald* about carjackings and rapes, and, you know, I don't really want to be that kind of story. Or any kind of story, unless it involves marrying, or at the very least screwing, Ricky Biscayne. Which I'd do, in a second. Even if he's married. If Ricky Biscayne had a harem, I'd happily join it.

Once I'm zipping along—or as close to zipping as one can get in a Dodge Neon—I turn the dial to my mother's AM radio talk show, *El Show de Violeta*. It started as a local show, initially aimed at the Cuban-exile community, women in particular, but now, as Miami's Hispanic demographics have grown more diverse, Mom's show is aimed at Spanish-speaking women in general. Violeta has been doing the daily show for twenty years, and has never been paid for it, which Geneva and I agree is just plain wrong. Bear in mind that Geneva and I rarely agree on anything, and I am telling you right now that the Trust Cruise tomorrow is not going to change a single thing. I will never, repeat *never*, trust my sister. But we don't tell Mom anything. She's the one who likes giving advice, much of it hypocritical, particularly the stuff about fidelity and marriage, two subjects neither of my parents seems to know anything about.

"Hoooollllaaaaa, Miami," cries my mother in her trademark greeting, through the crackling speakers I long ago blew with loud Ricky. Jesus God! She sounds like a macaw. She belongs at Parrot Jungle, pecking seeds out of children's hands. She continues in Spanish, "Happy Friday! Welcome to *The Violeta Show*! Today we have sexologist Miriam Delgado joining us from Mercy Hospital, to talk about an issue that affects many marriages, but which many in our community don't feel comfortable talking about. I'm talking about the clitoris."

I search the car for something to throw up in. The *clitoris*? Really? My mom's going to spend the next hour talking about *that*? You don't even like to think your mom *has* one, let alone listen to her talk about it for a whole damn hour. God. It's a good thing my dad doesn't ever listen to the show. He thinks it's silly, figures she talks about cooking and cleaning, and I don't think he's heard a single one in ten years. I don't know how he'd handle *this* topic. He's a bit *machista*. I doubt he knows what the clitoris is, much less where. Eew? Can I please not be having these thoughts? Is this not a form of child abuse?

Mom pauses for emphasis, and I can almost see her serious frown. Then, dramatic as someone doing a dying scene in a Shakespeare play, Mom drops her voice and says, "Dr. Delgado, welcome to the show."

"Thank you, Violeta," says Dr. Delgado, without a hint of humor. She sounds really old, like an antique piano being pried open. "It's a real pleasure to be here with you today, talking about marriage and the female clitoris."

Ralph. No, seriously, I'm going to be sick. And traffic is hardly moving. Is there a *male* clitoris? Please tell me I didn't miss that chapter in the Kama Sutra.

Suddenly, my headache gets worse, and I feel something sticky and primordial splooge out of me. Great. Nothing like blood oozing into the stained seat of your Neon.

Have I mentioned I'd like a new life? Yeah. And a new car, too. A white Mercedes, to compete with Geneva's white Beemer.

My dream car.

My name is Jasminka, and I'm still alive.

The bloodlike, saline scent of ocean swirls around us, blowing in off beach a block away. Ricky holds my hand as we walk past paparazzi and gawking tourists toward door of Tides South Beach hotel. I wear bright blue cotton robe, with sandals, thong sandals. Ricky is dressed in jeans and trench coat, I don't know why. He looks like detective from bad movie. He acts like one, too.

I'm here for a photo shoot, for a spread on the top swimsuit models in Miami, to appear in *Maxim,* and Ricky said he had to come with me. I used to be able to go to shoots alone, but recently Ricky seems very possessive, afraid I might cheat on him. He talks about it all the time, as if I would do such thing. I have never considered the possibility. Besides which, I'm feeling sick today. Why would I be looking for men to cheat on my husband with? Poor Ricky. I wonder what's troubling him. I hope he's not projecting.

Some of the photographers shout his name, and mine. They snap photos of us. Ricky holds hand up in front of one of the cameras and tells man to leave us alone. I'm not the only model here today. There are ten of us. A nice, round number. And the media are out in swarms.

We enter hotel lobby and people turn to stare. I breathe in the cool vanilla scents of lobby as they whisper through it. It's a fashionable crowd, self-conscious as they tend to be at these hotels. I don't know why social life of Miami must revolve around hotels, especially for people who actually live here, but that's how it is. Hotels are more than just places to stay here. They are places to go to be seen. Ricky loves it, I can tell by way he carries himself, like one of those male pigeons that chases the female ones around, cocky and proud. It's so soothing here, cool and white.

Almost as soon as we enter, young woman with black cat-eye glasses and a flippy pink shoulder-length hairdo rushes over to us with walkie-talkie in her hand. She wears all black. I assume she is publicist or assistant. This is their uniform, and they almost never laugh. I wonder, if you tickled her, would she even smile? She smells of men's cologne, of lime and salt, like a margarita.

"Jasminka," she says, very serious. I nod behind my large sunglasses and do my best to smile. I feel like I have hangover, except I haven't been drinking. I grab on to Ricky for balance. I'm hungry, but sick. The woman grumbles something I can't understand into her walkie-talkie, puts it on her ear to listen for a response. "They'll be right over to get you," she says. I realize now that she has British accent. I am getting better at telling different accents apart. Everybody speaking English used to sound the same to me. Maybe her perfume is English.

Ricky pulls me in and kisses me dramatically, as if he has something to prove to everyone here. "I love you," he says. I taste tobacco on his lips, the secret smoke he tries to keep from his fans. I see lights from flashbulbs popping off and realize there are lots of photographers here, too. I don't understand why they care so much about the lives of two strangers. We're not even very interesting if you think about it—at least I'm not.

Soon, two large men with shaved heads appear at my side. With them is short, thin man with unmistakably gay hand gestures, wearing leopard-print shirt that is far too tight and short. I don't like to see man's nipples through shirt. He introduces himself as fashion director for magazine, and after we all shake hands and they all tell me how fabulous I look, they whisk us off to bar. The shoot is going to take place here, in the 1220 Bar, the director tells me, though I assumed as much from army of technicians in the place. Lighting, hair, makeup, wardrobe, nails, you name it. Everyone has staked out their own little corner of bar and started to set up.

I see four of other models huddled at table, sipping iced tea or water. It smells of grilled steaks and balsamic vinegar in here, pepper too, and I think we must be close to a kitchen for one of restaurants. I wave and smile, but the thought of tea makes me faint.

"I need to sit down," I tell Ricky. He scans the room and settles on spot at the shiny, thick blue-glass bar. A spot far from everyone else. I wonder why he never seems to want to socialize with others when I'm around. An assistant rushes over and tells us not to dirty the glass because photos are going to be shot at the bar. Ricky nods, hostile. He doesn't like being out of his element. This is my element, and he doesn't like that I have advantage. He likes to be in control.

"I want this to be last one for a while," I say.

"The last what, baby?" he asks me.

"Shoot."

"Yeah?" His eyes wander room, and he doesn't seem to be listening to me. I want to quit modeling, but I don't think this is right time to talk about it. I am sad he isn't listening, and sadder that he hasn't noticed I am ill.

"Ricky, get me some soda water please?" I ask him.

"Huh? Oh, sure."

He leaves me at counter and heads for the catering table. I still don't know why they cater these things. Surely the fruits and pastries aren't for models. They must be for the photographers and assistants and magazine people. Ricky returns with regular Coke. I feel sad again, and my forehead has small beads of sweat on it, even though I feel cold.

"I can't drink this," I tell him.

"Why not?" He's looking around room, at all the models who are stringing in. Right in front of me, he stares like fox with its tongue hanging out. Like I'm not here.

"I am trying to stop caffeine, I told you," I say. I think I might be pregnant, so I've stopped all things that might harm baby. I took home pregnancy test last night, and even though I'm not supposed to take it for another few days, it looked positive to me. The cross in the results window meant pregnant, and even though the two pink lines were pale, they were *there*. I'm sure. Ricky doesn't believe I'm pregnant because sometimes I have irregular periods from not eating enough, but I feel sick and think it's a sign. Ricky thinks I'm sick because I quit smoking and started eating broccoli and taking prenatal vitamins from the drugstore. "Plus, all that sugar. I can't."

Ricky rolls his eyes as if I've done something to annoy him, mutters "*pendejo*," and starts back toward catering table. I reach out to stop him. "No," I say, "it's okay. I'm fine. Don't worry about it."

As soon as last model arrives, and, no surprise, it's a Canadian girl, French Canadian, that everyone is raving about, a young girl with a drug problem who is notoriously late for everything and will likely burn out soon, the fashion director claps his hands to get our attention. He calls us "girls," and tells us that we're going to be at bar, in bikinis, holding but not sipping colorful drinks, that overall "effect" he wants is of "lifeless, frozen girls, you are *sexy cadavers*, girls, got that? You are rigor *mortis* on these cold metal seats with your legs spread and your breasts hanging out blue and cold, like you're waiting for the man of your dreams to come and warm you up and bring you back to life with his big, hot *uhhhh*." As he grunts last word, he thrusts his girlie hips forward and back, and I feel even sicker.

There's something very sick about this business, I think. Some of these girls aren't even eighteen yet, but that's how they talk to us all the time.

We models are corralled toward the wardrobe section of the room, and I suddenly wish Ricky would leave. He's only husband here, and all of us are about to strip and put on bathing suits. I don't really want him looking at all these other women naked and bending over. But he's sitting, in chair now, watching it all with a strange smile on his face. I remove my clothes, and my breasts feel very tender out of the bra, like they felt when they were first growing when I was eleven. I feel sort of sick, and a little bloated. I'm used to being naked in front of people, it's just part of the business, but the thought that I might be pregnant makes me feel very exposed, as if I want to hide away in cave.

The wardrobe director chooses white and orange Onda de Mar bikini for me, sporty and psychedelic. I love it, the way it hugs my breasts to chest, keeps them safe and snug, and want to keep it. The bottom is roomy, not thong, and I'm thankful for that. I am in no mood to be exposed too much right now. I can't. I hope they let me keep bathing suit. I mean, after you wear bikini, you know. It gets personal.

I try not to look too much at the other girls as they bend and stuff themselves into their suits. There's so much competition. I have to remind myself all the time that I am as good as others, and that they are as good as me, that we are all equal. But it's hard not to look at their thighs to see if they're touching, or not to feel a little bit proud that someone else might have a dimple of cellulite in a place where I don't. I don't like being this way. I am not proud of what modeling has done to me. I size up other women all the time.

We head over to the hair station, and the stylists start to come up with their creations. I glance at Ricky and try to see through his pants with X-ray vision to see if anything has occurred that shouldn't have, from him looking at all these naked, beautiful women. He's staring at young black model who is bent over, mooning him. How can he do that to me? He shouldn't be here. I don't like that he's here. I am tired of it. Modeling, Ricky. The whole thing. I love him. But I'm just tired right now. I just want to sleep, alone, without anyone touching me.

In the end, my hair is braided on either side of my face, like Native American princess, and I am topped with big, white floppy hat, the kind that star Ricky used to date, Jill Sanchez, might wear. The stylist tells me he's going for modern Joni Mitchell look on me. I don't know who he's talking about.

I'm brought next to the makeup station, take a seat in the black canvas chair, and the artists open their large black suitcases full of colors and pigments. They start to pat, smear, and rub me. The dry scent of flesh-toned powder fills my nose. I am nothing more than a canvas for these people. They forget after a while that we are people. Or they never realized it in first place. I close my eyes and try to think of other things. I'm chilled. I listen to conversations happening all around me. The artists chat. *So I told him there's no way I'm doing that again. Uh-uh. No way. What does he think I am? His own personal whore?* And models talking to each other. *Laxatives? Me too! I used to use them all the time, but it's sort of a problem once you're on a shoot, like, if you have to go right there? One time I had an accident, actually . . .* I try to think of other things, but death is foremost on my mind. The scent of makeup and metal. I imagine this is what funeral parlor smells like.

Soon enough, we're all ready to be placed on our seats. Somewhere, someone puts a CD on. Björk. Fitting. The shoot director hops here and there, adjusting us. There are plants on bar. He demands they be removed. No life, he says. No life anywhere here. Assistants bring fashionable martini and other glasses full of colorful liquid and set them along bar near us. I look at other girls and see that they, like I, have gray and black makeup. We are all made to look beautiful, but lifeless and bruised. Even our bodies have been smeared gray and blue. The director approaches me with his head tilted to one side. "Spread," he says, pushing my knees apart. He adjusts crotch of the suit to cover me just right. "Just like that. Good, perfect. Beautiful." I smile at him in thanks, and he scowls. "No," he says. He smells of sweat and semen. "No smiles. You are dead, girl, you hear me? Dead. No smiling."

His words stab me. Make me want to run away. I look at Ricky to see if he has heard and if he is as outraged as I am. He is busy staring at Canadian girl. I hate this, all of this. It's absurd, the whole thing. I don't want to be dead girl. I have *seen* dead girls. I wonder if this man, this fashion director, has ever, in his life, seen dead girl. I want to ask him. To slap him. I want to scream about all this. I want to curl in a nest and protect my baby. I know I'm pregnant. I feel so emotional right now. I can't cry. It will ruin my makeup. My dead-girl makeup. But I don't know what else to do.

I stare at cool, blue glass of the bar, and think of swimming pool at home. Our home. The only home I've had since my childhood disappeared. I love my home, the safety I feel there. I imagine I am there, in backyard, only place in the world that soothes me.

This is my last shoot, I tell myself. This is the last time I model. I have a name. I have a past. I am my mother's daughter.

And this is last time in my life I ever play a dead girl.

've turned off my mother's show, and, blasting yet another Ricky Biscayne CD, I pull the now-bloody Neon into the half-circle driveway of my parents' house. I'm not quite sure how I'm going to walk into the house like this, a mess, but I will try to face everyone head on, and slink along the walls or something. I get out of the car and scoot past my grandfather, who is dozing on the porch in his chair. I open the front door to the comforting olive-oil smell of my grandmother's cooking. Another exciting Friday night with the old folks. Smells like *vaca frita*, which means "fried cow" in Spanish but is actually a delicious dish of shredded beef sautéed in tangy lime and garlic sauce. There will be white rice, and a side salad. Maybe some plantains. I'm starving. My stomach rumbles. It should be another hour until Violeta the clit-master gets home from the Hialeah radio station, and dinner will be served. I don't think I'll ask Mom about the show tonight. I don't really want to hear it.

After dinner, I'll head to Blockbuster to get a movie everyone might like; I'll make them popcorn and then try to disappear quietly to go to my book club—this time with a tampon firmly in place.

My dad, Eliseo, is home from work and still in his blue suit and red tie. He sits reading *El Nuevo Herald* in his plaid recliner in the living room, and notices my long face immediately. No, I think. Don't look at me. Don't see the blood on my dress. Please don't. There's nothing worse than your Cuban dad realizing that the person he wants to be forever a girl is actually a hairy, bloody, grown woman. It's very creepy. Look away! Look away!

"Sit," he declares. He takes off his reading glasses and sits forward, listening. "Talk."

"Papi, just give me a chance to use the bathroom, I'll be right back."

"Okay, but then you talk. I can tell something's bothering you."

I slip down the hall, watching for errant family members who might invade my privacy. Whew! No one. I get to the bathroom and duck inside, locking the door behind me. I turn my back to the mirror and swivel my head in a poor imitation of the *People* magazine photo of Jill Sanchez, craning my neck to see how bad the damage is. A dark red spot, about the size and shape of a lime. Not as bad as I thought. But still not good. I take off my clothes and hop into the shower. I wash quickly, hop out, towel off, and stick a deodorant tampon where you stick them. I wrap myself in a towel, scurry to my room, put on a pair of old sweats and a large T-shirt, and return to the living room, my hair wrapped up in a towel.

Dad eyes me suspiciously. "A shower? What have you been up to?" Why must he always seem to be implying that every woman on earth, if not being watched hawkishly by a man somewhere, is a whore? Even me, who he thinks a virgin?

"Nothing, Papi. I'm tired. I needed the water to wake me up."

"Wake you up? In the evening?" Even more suspicious.

"Book club," I say. "Las Loquitas del Libro. Remember?"

"Oh, the knitting club," he says with a satisfied smile. Dismissive. Fine. He has no idea how racy the stuff we read is. God forbid he ever read *Going Down*, by Jennifer Belle—one of my all-time favorites. He'd have a heart attack. He thinks I get together with a bunch of spinsters to knit baby booties. I don't care. Let him think what he wants. He will anyway, no matter what the evidence to the contrary is. Dad is weird like that. He creates his own reality, often in direct contrast to the real world around him. To him, he is in charge. To us, he is to be tolerated.

The living room is separated from the rest of the hall and family room by elevation—up a step—and by a low wrought-iron fence. You actually have to go through a little gate to get to the living room. I grew up thinking it was normal to have a fence indoors. I enter the living room yard and sit on the sofa. Dad looks at me and sighs.

"Spit it out," he says. "What's going on."

"It's nothing."

"Talk."

I sigh and weigh my options. I hear the quick, dry flutter of the canaries fussing in their iron cage on the enclosed back porch, and I relate to them. Trapped. No matter what I tell him, he won't believe I have a problem. He believes my life is perfect, and does not endure complainers well. "I don't think I like my job all that much, Papi," I say, tears forming in my eyes. Geneva's right. I am a wimp. I didn't expect to react so strongly, but *Cosmo* said nothing about crying in front of your father, and, you know, period hormones and all. I guess it's okay.

He shrugs and purses his lips in that dad-sign-language meant to say, *Why? What the hell is wrong with you? Why are you wasting my time with this?*

"It's kind of degrading. . . ."

My dad's face grows dark and serious. "Listen to me, Freckles," he says, using a nickname I loathe. "There is no such thing as a degrading job. Except stripping." He pauses, deep in thought. "And prostitute. And hired goon."

Hired goon? "You need to quit watching *The Sopranos*, Papi."

He keeps talking like I haven't said anything. "When we came to Miami, we had nothing," he begins. Here we go. The Speech. How many times have I heard it? So many I can recite it, along with him, but I won't because I don't like to see him get mad. "We started from zero. And we worked hard. Everybody has to start somewhere. It's a great service you're doing to your uncle. You should be proud."

"I know," I say. When all else fails, say "I know" or "I see" or "You're right." It's a good policy, and it works for me. For the record, Dad was only seven years old when he came to Miami, and his parents had quite a bit of money. He acts like he went straight to work in a factory or something. Like he was some pauper begging on the streets of Calcutta. Weirdo.

"What's not to like about your job?" he asks, shrugging all the way up to his big ears and leaving his shoulders hitched up there for the duration of his monologue. "You have a nice desk, air-conditioning, you get to make phone calls. You're not out cutting sugarcane."

"I know." Sugarcane? Is he out of his *mind*? Dad is always mentioning cutting sugarcane, I have no idea why. No one we know has ever cut sugarcane. The people in our family are much more likely to cut the cheese.

Speaking of cheese. Grandma walks in, toting her Bible. She clutches it all the time lately. She never used to be terribly into the Bible, preferring the Cuban method of putting glasses of water behind doors and whatnot, but now, as she gets older I guess, she needs to comfort herself with the book. "'Beware of false prophets,'" she rambles in Spanish, "'which come to you in sheep's clothing, but inwardly they are ravening wolves.'"

"That's nice, Grandma," I say.

"Book of Matthew," says Grandma, waving her Bible at me. "Matthew 7:16." She opens the book and reads, "'A good tree cannot bring forth evil fruit, and neither can a corrupt tree bring forth good fruit.'"

I consider responding, but Dad gives me a look meant to silence me. I spy the day's mail in two neat stacks on the ornate Spanish-style dark wood coffee table, one for them, one for me. Yay! The new *InStyle* has come. I don't want to stand here with a towel on my head, arguing with my dad about why it sucks to be a laxative publicist. If a person doesn't *get* that already, like, from the get-go, I don't see how I will convince him. I just want to go to my room. Be alone with *InStyle*. Dad negotiates with people all day long, about rugs being taken from here to there, whatever, and he's basically not able to stop negotiating when he gets home. I find him exhausting and turn to leave.

"You can quit when you get married," he says, trying to bait me back in. I stop and smile. When I get *married*? What is this, the fifties? I look at his eyes and see that he says this nonsense without really meaning it, almost as if it is the duty of a father to say such things. He looks at me looking at him, and I can see that he knows I know he doesn't mean it. I wonder for a moment what he really thinks, but I don't have the patience or desire to ask.

"I know."

He points a finger at me, just so I know that he's, like, talking to me and not, I don't know, to the television. Ever helpful, my father. "Your problem is you want too much. You shouldn't need more than you find on the Miracle Mile. That street has everything a woman your age needs." Here he counts on his fingers. "Bridal shops, baby clothes, and cribs. That's what you should be worried about, or you should stop worrying." His eyes cringe, like he knows the modern world is going to slap him back one of these days. I don't have the heart to make that day today.

I say, "I know, Papi. Okay. Look. I have a headache. I'll be in my room."

I close the door behind me and flop onto the bed with the magazine. I prop up on my elbows and start to read. So many beautiful people, with such white teeth and pretty clothes. Sigh. And there, on page 97, is a feature story about Mr. Ricky Biscayne, his gorgeous Serbian model wife with the dark hair and wide-set green eyes, and their gorgeous mansion in Miami Beach. The article calls him "the quintessential family guy," noting that he is learning Serbian so that the children he plans to have someday will speak three languages. The article also says Ricky is a health fiend, drinking a broccoli-and-wheatgrass shake for breakfast every morning. His wife continues to model, and is to be featured in an upcoming issue of *Maxim*.

Life is *so* not fair.

I feel like crying again. Because I'm not Jasminka. Because I don't live in a mansion. Because no one would pay for a photo of me in a bikini. Because *People* magazine always calls Renée Zellweger the all-American Texan girl, even though her parents are immigrants just like mine, while continuing to portray "Hispanics" as spicy foreigners. Because I have to go on a Trust Cruise with my mother and sister tomorrow and I'm not even strong enough to refuse. My mom gets freebies like this cruise all the time, in exchange for a promise to talk about it on the show.

Just as I'm about to dive into a vat of self-pity, my phone rings. Yes, it's a Hello Kitty phone. I know. It doesn't help my cause. The caller ID reads Club G. Great. My glamorous sister has already gotten a phone number for the club she plans to open. She is a consummate optimist, another reason I hate her. Why can't she just wallow and complain and suffer silently like me? I don't feel like talking to her. She's just going to tell me how great life is. Correction: She's going to tell me how great *her* life is.

I leave her to the answering machine.

Hello. It's me, Milan. Leave me a message, and have a great day!

"Hey, M. You know, you don't have to say, 'It's me, Milan.' That's redundant." F-you! F-you! "Okay, so it's G. Just had lunch with Ricky Biscayne, and thought you might want to hear about it."

Excuse me? Geneva knows I'm the secretary of the unofficial Ricky Biscayne online fan club. She *knows* I've lusted after Ricky for years. You know what she is, my sister? She's like those people who toss food scraps to poor children. She is evil. I raise my middle finger to Hello Kitty, and realize how bad that looks, but still, it's not the cat per se. It's my evil sister.

Geneva takes what sounds like a long sip of water, followed by a vulgar gulp, and says, "I've convinced him to invest in my new club, and I think you'd be just the girl to do PR for it. What do you think? It'd be a three-, maybe four-month contract, with a good shot at lots more work down the road. He's looking for a new publicist, too, full-time, too, so it could be a two-birds one-stone kinda thing. Gimme a call if you're ready to get out of the constipation business with Uncle Messiah. *Ciaocito.*"

I lunge for the phone now. I am aware as I do it that I have the grace and ripple of a sea lion on rocks. The towel tumbles off my head and tangles over my face. I'm too late. Geneva has hung up, and Hello Kitty falls with a clatter to the white tile floor. Kitty's eye has popped out. I check to see if the phone still works. It does. And then, for the first time in I don't know how long, I voluntarily dial my evil sister's phone number.

*9*ill Sanchez stands in a tight, white vinyl cat suit behind the hot-pink podium, which is molded into the trademark hour-glass shape of her body, and watches as two slack-jawed lackeys lift the mink-trimmed red velvet sheet off the oversized poster for her new perfume.

A collective "ahh" rises from the crowd of loser journalists and entertainment industry executives, all of them trying to find a comfortable spot on the pillows and mattresses scattered across the floor of the trendy Miami club BED. It was not cheap booking this club for three hours for a private party on a Friday evening, but Jill Sanchez isn't cheap. In fact, she has worked very hard to associate her name and image with the very opposite of cheap. Still, she hates the idea of spending that kind of money for a bunch of news *reporters*. The ugly price of fame. The club overcharged, in her opinion, because they knew Jill and the press would be cleared out by ten, in plenty of time for them to get a solid crowd going for the night. But what can you do?

Jill smiles down at them like a parade-float queen as they smile up at the poster, and she basks in her own possibilities once more. She grew up always hearing about what a great businesswoman Madonna was, blah blah blah, Madonna, Madonna, Madonna. But Madonna has nothing on *her*, Jill Sanchez. No one wants to smell like *Madonna*, do they? Madonna looks like she smells like syphilis. Just like no one wants to smell like that scrawny barbed-wire sculpture called Celine Dion, either. Or, who is that other one who has her own perfume? Reba McEntire or something. Is that country bumpkin completely insane? No one wants to smell like a redheaded *elf*. But *everyone* wants to smell like her, Jill Sanchez, who, in her own estimation, is the sexiest, cleanest woman alive. Even when movie executives called her box-office poison two years ago, her perfume line continued to outsell all others in the land—to everyone's surprise except her own. Even

Beyoncé's perfume couldn't compete; and neither, in Jill's opinion, could her booty.

"Ladies and gentlemen," says Jill, giggling for effect, though she does not, in fact, see herself as the giggling type. She deliberately, cutely teeters for a moment on the superhigh, clear-soled platform sandals made especially for her and for tonight by the fine gentlemen at Prada, but catches herself before falling. Years of dancing coupled with the temperamental qualities of a hungry lioness have prepared her to rarely make a misstep, even here, in impossibly difficult and costly footwear, on the stage covered with two hundred thousand dollars' worth of Swarovski crystals. The crystals might have been overkill, but Jill has been wildly jealous of Britney Spears since she appeared in nothing but sparkling diamonds in the "Toxic" video, and this is Jill Sanchez's revenge on that Louisiana reject for having had the audacity to believe for one moment that she might outshine Jill Sanchez at her own game. One of these days, Jill will appear in public wearing nothing but a diamond thong and pasties.

"Gosh, it's big," she giggles about the poster, pretending to be as stunned as they are by it, even though she is the one who insisted on the gargantuan size. She has practiced this line, and the open-mouthed kissy lips in the style of Marilyn Monroe. She has meant for the breathy words to have a hint of sexuality to them, as if she were commenting on something other than a poster. The giggle is intended to offset the brazen sexuality, offering up saint and whore in equal doses. Giggling revolts her. But the revolting media seems to prefer her when she giggles revoltingly, so that's what she does when they are around. She rarely giggles otherwise.

"Okay, well, I introduce to you Flamenco Flame, the new fragrance by me, Jill Sanchez."

Again she giggles, lest it seem that she does, in fact, take great pride in branding herself like a cow. Even as she does so, Jill worries that the makeup and high-end studio lighting she paid to have perfectly in synch are somehow revealing her wrinkles and lines to a world that still doesn't know she has them. She will have to go in for Botox again soon, and perhaps some belly lipo. Belly lipo is one of the finest inventions of all time, in Jill Sanchez's opinion. A breast lift might also be in order, as all the dancing over the years has invited gravitational pulls she will not tolerate. Jill Sanchez believes she is superior to gravity and other science.

The poster is a life-size replica of the dewy peach-toned ad that will soon appear in fashion magazines and on the sides of buses worldwide. In the foreground is the pink hourglass bottle, in the shape of Jill's own heavily insured body, because in Jill's humble estimation there is simply no better shape to be found. It isn't vanity; it is honesty.

In the background stands Jill herself, nude as a wood nymph, though strategically positioned and airbrushed, so nothing that shouldn't be seen *could* be seen. She is curvy in ways the establishment used to think would not sell, until she began to outsell everyone else—smaller on top, bigger on the bottom. The vibe of the ad is misty, and hot, as if she stepped out of the shower and into your bedroom, aflame with Flamenco Flame, the new fragrance by her, Jill Sanchez.

The press begins to applaud. Jill acts all shucks and embarrassed.

"Stop it, you guys," she says sweetly, blinking the mink fur on her eyelashes. "Oh, come on, it's just perfume. Jeez!"

At that moment, the six hot girls who were hired because they were almost but not quite as hot as Jill Sanchez, start to circulate through the club, with silver Tiffany trays full of tiny fabulous bottles of Flamenco Flame, the new fragrance by Jill Sanchez. They spritz and spray, and those in attendance can't help but marvel at the perfect mixture of vanilla and lemongrass. Jill believes she is one of the cleanest women on earth, bathing several times a day, slathering her body in expensive creams that so far work in congress with Botox and exercise to convince the public that she, in truth thirty-seven years old, is a mere twenty-eight. Years ago, a profile or two had printed her true birthday, but year after year she got younger and no one seemed to question this, except *The New York Times*, which none of her fans read anyway. Literacy is on the decline in America, and no one knows this better than Jill, who keeps up on cultural trends the way a stockbroker attends to market fluctuations. Why worry about the print media when no one reads anyway?

"So, what do you think, you guys?" she asks, as modest and folksy as possible. She played a modest girl, a Mexican maid, in a movie once, and was almost nominated for an Academy Award. Or that's what she heard. She doesn't know for sure. She knows she deserves an Oscar *for something*, however.

The crowd bursts into applause and Jill Sanchez bursts into a grin.

"Oh, gosh. I'm so glad you liked it!" Hand to neck, beat. "I was so nervous!" In truth, Jill has not been nervous in seven years, since becoming one of the highest-paid actors in Hollywood. They say Cameron Diaz makes more these days, but that will change as soon as everyone figures out that La Diaz looks like a puff-faced munchkin on stilts and her success is due almost entirely to Ben Stiller's jism hair gel.

On cue, the lights go down, and the curtain on the small stage goes up. And there are Jill Sanchez's male backup dancers, including the two she slept with when she was bored on tour. She doesn't remember their names. And there is Jill's pin-on microphone, to aid the illusion that she is singing live. And there is the music, a hip-hop Latin-inspired jingle a young songwriter named Matthew Baker penned for the perfume, but for which she, Jill Sanchez, will get a 75 percent writing credit, because Jill Sanchez has one of the best entertainment lawyers in the universe and, as Ricky once told her, Matthew Baker, who she got through Ricky, is a bit of a sucker.

She begins to dance, and sing, pretending all the while to be surprised by her own sexy gyrations, a trick of the trade she gleaned from Britney Spears herself. Nothing appeals to America more than innocence paired with lust. Jill Sanchez takes great pride in the fact that she is much older than Spears, but just as relevant with high school girls—and boys. But even as she thinks this, she worries that the new crop of young singers might have something on her. There is a Lindsay something or other, and an Ashley, at least one, maybe more. She doesn't even know their names anymore, but if she did, she would never admit it.

After the performance, the crowd claps some more, and Jill Sanchez takes questions. Of course, most of them have to do with her engagement to Jack Ingroff, the handsome indie actor, screenwriter, and Rhodes scholar. She answers by holding up her left hand and squealing at the sight of her massive yellow diamond, as if she's only just now seen it for the first time, as if she were sitting in a group of girlfriends instead of in a room full of bloodsucking bastards.

"Omigosh! We're, like, *so* happy!" she says. "With him I'm just a girl who cooks, and he's just a guy who likes baseball and a beer."

"What do you cook, Jill?" asks a reporter. Somewhere in the back of the room, a male voice shouts, "*¡Si cocinas como caminas, ay mami!*" drawing a smattering of applause from the assembled Spanish-speaking men.

"Oh, my mother's *asopao de pollo*, it's this chicken dish with green peppers and garlic," she says, as if it has just occurred to her, when in fact she rehearsed this very answer with a media coach last night. "I just love my mom! She is such a great cook!"

Jill attempted this dish only once, and it came out half burned and half raw, with undertones of dishwashing liquid mixed in; Jack ate it because he's a nice guy and then he had diarrhea for days.

"Yum! Jack loves chicken. And I love to cook. I finally found a man who'll make an honest woman of me!" In truth, Jill Sanchez has three personal chefs and has not set foot in a grocery store in at least six years. She has come to think that refrigerators fill them-selves.

A hefty, homely, female entertainment reporter Jill recognizes from *The Miami Herald* approaches the stage, with a stern look on her face. With khaki pants that pull and strain across her sagging lower belly, she reminds Jill of a prison guard. The pockets on the sides gape open like holes in a carnival ball-toss game. Her name is Lilia, a name far prettier than the woman it belongs to, and she speaks with that lesbian lisp Jill despises. Even when Jill played a horny lesbian in a movie once, she didn't do that lisp. For Jill, it was too horrible to imagine that sound coming from Jill Sanchez's lips.

On top of that, Lilia takes herself and her work far more seriously than Jill believes she ought to, and never squanders a chance to skewer Jill in her "Lunch with Lilia" column, the only place on earth, Jill figures, that Lilia is allowed to feel beautiful and popular. Newspapers are for geeks and losers what the Internet is for sociopaths, meaning that they are the only place these losers can find to socialize.

"Rumor has it," Lilia grumbles, "that you've been seeing Ricky Biscayne again. Jill, what is your response to that?" "Seeing" comes out she-ing, from the lesbian lisp.

Jill giggles and looks surprised, cringing only internally at Lilia's odd placement of her name in the sentence. It's like the reporter was trying to sound the way reporters sounded in Bogart movies. All Lilia needed was a pencil stuck behind her big, meaty ear. "It's the first I've heard of it. Last time I checked, Ricky was married and I was engaged." Jill wiggles the yellow diamond for effect, and giggles. "I just love this ring! Don't you guys?"

"So the fact that one of your home employees saw you have sex with him in your pool house doesn't ring a bell?"

Jill squashes her blush impulse and giggles instead. "This is ridiculous, Lilia. Maybe you should go on a diet instead of making up stories. For your information, I don't even own a pool house."

Lilia blushes as her peers laugh at her. Though most reporters are ugly, few are as ugly as Lilia. Jill knows her outburst will likely make headlines, and that some enterprising reporter will investigate real estate records and discover that Jill does, in fact, have a pool house; but what the hell. Who would read it? Who on earth reads anything but headlines anymore? Who bothers to even read headlines, frankly, when the colorful photos are more than enough? All press is good press, even press that says she was having an affair with Ricky. Let that Eastern European dishrag Jasminka see it and weep. That's the thing so many of Jill's celebrity peers don't understand about the press.

The press are an instrument, made to be played, and in that craft Jill Sanchez is a virtuoso.

"I'm just joking, Lilia, you look great. But don't take that as a come-on. I know how you feel about me." More laughter, as Lilia stalks out of the room scribbling furiously on a notepad. Only the dishonest reporters use those things, Jill notes. The honest ones use digital recorders. She looks around the room and notices that no one has a digital recorder.

Jill giggles again, thanks everyone, offers them Champagne and gift bags, then excuses herself and leaves the club, saying she has a business meeting. Ricky Biscayne is back in town, and they have a date.

'm wearing a baggy Ricky Biscayne T-shirt and a pair of Old Navy capri jeans that I realize are not as trendy as I like to think. I got them three years ago. I know people have moved on from these, but they're comfortable and I am going to the book group. I should mention, too, that I'm wearing Easy Spirit shoes, flat sandals, because I like them. I like how they feel. I just passed a woman riding a bike in high-heeled pumps, which is typical for Miami. I don't always fit in here. Sometimes, I think I'd be better off in Denver, or San Francisco.

Because I couldn't eat much at dinner, with my mother smiling as if she hadn't spent an hour talking clits, and my grandmother crunching her food with her mouth open, I steer the Neon to the El Pollo Tropical drive-through and order yuca fries and a mango batido. Yum. I stuff it all in as I drive the ten minutes to Books & Books on Aragon. As I pass the bridal shops along the Miracle Mile, I try to block Dad's bad advice about marriage and babies. I mean, I'd like to get married and be a mom, but not as my *only* goal in life. I turn up the cassette in the stereo. I know. Cassette. You don't have to remind me. I would like to have a CD player, but it's an old Neon. What can I say? I'm playing, you guessed it, Ricky! Yay, Ricky! I know every word by heart, every harmony part, every kick of the *timbale*. These songs?

They're about *me*. He sings like a man who totally understands women. Ricky wrote these songs with me in mind. I know it. If I could meet a guy like that, I might have *use* for bridal shops. And you know what? If what Geneva said was true? I might be meeting Ricky himself, on this club project of hers. How cool is *that*?

All the spaces at the meters are taken, and I don't feel like going into the parking garage across the street. I pull into the alley behind the store and park illegally. I'm feeling risky tonight. All because Geneva told me I might meet Ricky, but I know I shouldn't put too much faith in anything my sister promises me; for all I know, it's going to turn out to be some kind of cruel joke she's played on me.

I trot to the store because I'm late and don't want to miss a single second of the best part of my week. I rush through the front gates, onto the patio. It's so cute, this place. There's a courtyard right as you walk in, with a refreshment stand and magazine stand, and all these little wrought-iron tables and chairs. My club girls are waiting for me here, outside. There are six of them, plus me. The store itself wraps around the outdoor space, giving it a Spanish touch that I adore. To me, this bookshop is the most peaceful, perfect place on earth, a place where I feel free to be entirely myself, to make jokes that my father might find off-color or inappropriate for a woman, to sit with my feet far apart, to dream about worlds greater than my own, and to place myself fearlessly in the shoes of the protagonist women who live in these pages. At Books & Books, I am no longer just Milan; here, I am Bridget Jones, Jemima Jones, Jojo Harvey, Emma Corrigan, Cannie Shapiro. Here, I am fabulous, grown-up, and allowed to be free. Here, I feel like I might one day wear fancy shoes.

Even if I don't own a single pair of fancy shoes, I can pretend. For the record, I will say that I would love to own expensive, sexy shoes, but I've never had a real excuse to get them, and also I know that once I give myself an excuse it is going to be very hard to stop with just one or two pairs; I am excessive in my consumption of food and television, and I believe I will be likewise in my consumption of beautiful shoes and clothes if and when I finally get around to it.

The six women from the book club, each with *Sex, Murder and a Double Latte,* by Kyra Davis, on her lap, smile and wave. The women are so happy, and perfectly happy, at least for these moments when we are all here, to live without men. Can I just say this, that I could *live* in this book club? Everyone already has a cappuccino and a pastry, or iced tea—in short, they are my kind of girls. Suddenly, I'm hungry again. I want my own goodies.

"Be right back," I say, setting my book on a chair.

"Take your time," says one of my friends.

I go inside, to the café, and inspect the pastry case. I order the mini chocolate Bundt cake *and* the frosted scone. You only live once. I also order a large, creamy iced mocha cappuccino. I thought about going on a diet, but I don't see the point now. I just ate yuca fries. Might as well go all the way. Pork out. Why not? I'm feeling good. I don't care.

As I turn back toward the patio with my goodies on a tray, I regret my purchases because there, standing in line with a tall, beautiful (black!) man, is my sister, Geneva, in yet another pair of slender, long jeans, another pair of breathtaking designer heels, and another fancy embroidered designer tank top that fits like it was made especially for her and her perky little boobs. The man is stupendously built and wears a bright yellow polo shirt with khaki shorts. He looks like a Ralph Lauren model and is possibly the most attractive man I've ever seen her with. I've long had a fantasy of stealing a man from her, to get even, but I seriously doubt this would be the one. He's way out of my league. He's almost even out of Geneva's league.

"Milan!" cries Geneva, obviously as surprised to see me as I am to see her. "What are you doing here?"

I want to hide the tray. Can't. I smile as if there is nothing to be ashamed of. Maybe she'll think I'm bringing back goodies for the group. "Book club," I say. "Kyra Davis." I am sure as I say the name of the author that my sister will have no idea what I'm talking about.

"Oh, right." Geneva smiles awkwardly and the man lifts his brows and stares at her as if waiting for something. My God. My sister has dated attractive men before, but nothing that looked like *this*. Geneva looks at him and laughs. "Oh," she says. "I'm sorry. Milan, this is my . . . friend. Ignacio. Ignacio, this is my sister, Milan."

Friend my *ass*. I wonder who she stole him from.

She smiles at the man, and he takes her hand. She doesn't pull it away. Geneva moves forward in line, dismissing me. "The reading's going to start in the other room in a minute. We should get going."

"Oh. Okay." Reading? Geneva? I back away. Lie: "Good to see you." How weird.

"Bye, sweetie," says Geneva, insincere.

I shoot Geneva a look of approval about the man, and Geneva, to my surprise, looks insecure for the tiniest of moments. Then her eyes light up, like my approval matters.

I return to my book group and take my seat. As soon as I join the group of book girls I feel the muscles of my back and neck release. It's like the air gets thicker and more comforting. My breathing slows, and I feel happy. We do the usual round of hellos and updates on work, men, mothers (why must we always talk about our mothers?), and money. Then, Julia, the group leader, takes the lead.

"Shall we?" she asks, holding up the book. Pink cover. So many of our books have pink covers. And long women's legs. And a gun. How many are there like this? But this book rocked. It was one of my favorites.

"We shall," I say. I bounce in my seat and feel like a kid at show and tell. Remember that feeling? Like you're about to say something really important to connect with your peers? That's what this book group is like for me. I like that I can make decisions here, that I do, that I step up, as it were, to make things happen. It's almost, almost, like I'm not a slacker after all.

"So, what did you like best about this book?" asks Julia.

"I love Sophie," says Debra, speaking of the lead character, Sophie Katz. "I love that she's biracial. I totally identify, as a black Jewish woman." For the record, Debra is constantly saying "as a black Jewish woman" for everything she says. Even things like, "I like food, as a black Jewish woman," or, "As a black Jewish woman, I use the can."

"Me too!" I say about the character. "I totally identify." They all look at me like I'm crazy. "What?" I ask. "I'm biracial."

They laugh. "You're Cuban," says Julia.

"My family in Cuba is black and white," I tell them. "You should see my sister. She looks light-skinned black. She's right there in the middle room if you don't believe me."

"You are the palest person I know," says Gina.

"Anyway," says Julia with a roll of her eyes. "Milan's African heritage aside, what did you guys like most about Sophie?"

"Her Starbucks addiction," I say. "I relate. Being an African woman and all."

"Oh, please," says Gina.

"I don't appreciate you making fun of me, Milan," Debra tells me.

"I'm not!" I tell her. "Oh, oh! And I think it's really cool how the author mixed chick lit with mystery." I feel my own caffeine and sugar high kicking in. "Like, didn't you guys just stay up all night to read it? I think I read it in one day."

"Yes!" they shout. I take over, as usual. When it comes to books and Ricky, no one can talk more than I can.

"The way she wrote about this guy who came up with all these sneaky ways of getting to her, making her look paranoid," I say. I take a bite of cake. "It was amazing, the plotting and everything."

"Absolutely," says Gina.

I take another bite of cake, and on it goes, me eating with abandon, talking with abandon, utterly happy and comfortable in the company of modern, literate women, finally completely free to be Milan the white (black) slacker Cuban girl who likes to read and doesn't like much else, except Ricky Biscayne and a good double latte. Now if I could only find a way to make a killer living off my intense, yet clearly limited, interests, instead of peddling poop-aids.

saturday, march 23

My daughters, who don't even look like they're related to me *or* to each other, sit in my new Jaguar as I pull into the parking lot at the cruise-ship docks. They say nothing. The tension is enough to kill a camel, or however the saying goes. I don't like to complain about my children, but these two are spoiled. Ungrateful, spoiled, and hateful toward each other. In Cuba they would never have been able to get away with being the way they are, so self-absorbed that they don't realize blood is thicker than water. I'm sick of it. If they knew how much we, their parents, have struggled to give them the lives they've had, they might realize how silly their petty issues with each other look to me. Don't they realize that in the end, all there is to count on is family? Don't they care? I don't know why I bother.

"We're here!" I say as cheerfully as I can.

"Yay," says Geneva, sarcastic as always. She is crumpled down in the passenger seat in the front, looking at some little thing she calls a BlackBerry. I hate all those metal things in her nose and eyebrows. She's been typing something on that little machine, and laughing. Lost in her own world, as usual. Geneva has never cared what I or anyone else thought of her. I admire it in her, as a woman, even though as her mother I wish she were different.

"Yeah, yay," says Milan.

"It's a beautiful day," I say. "Let's try to have a nice time."

I cut the engine, open my door, and stretch my arms over my head. It really is a beautiful day. Sunny, with a few clouds on the horizon to the east. All around us, people in touristy clothes park and hobble toward the ships with their suitcases in tow. The docks here are for nothing but cruise ships, and there must be six or seven of them docked at the moment, readying for various trips around the Caribbean. The cruise business is big business here, and I know this because I once did a show on undocumented sex workers on the ships.

My daughters emerge from the car. Geneva wears a sexy sarong and low-cut tank top, both black, with a teensy jeans jacket. She is beautiful in black, and every other color. She has her long hair curly today, held back in a scarf. She has a new tattoo, a ring of flowers around her right ankle. She looks very bohemian and artistic. Milan, on the other hand? *Ay Dios mío.* I don't know what to do with her. She is a pretty girl, nearly as pretty as her sister, but she doesn't seem to care. She seems to want to hide her beauty from the world. She wears a pair of stained sweatpants from college, with the words GO IBIS on the butt, and a large and baggy Ricky Biscayne T-shirt, the same one she wears all the time. I hate that shirt. I hate the entire outfit she wears. She looks terrible. And those sandals? They are the kind that hippie women wear, for women with hairy toes. Her hair looks greasy and shapeless. I've never seen her look quite so sloppy. I used to try to get her to take her clothes more seriously. I used to tell her that your clothes, the way you dress, is your greeting card to the world. I don't do that anymore because it never did any good. My husband, Eliseo, likes that she doesn't try to be pretty because he thinks that is a reflection of her devotion to him, somehow. He has issues about women, especially his own daughters. The prettier Geneva looks, the angrier he gets.

I myself wear a white linen Liz Claiborne shorts suit with beige pumps and gold jewelry. I've got my hat, too, a sun hat. I'm not supposed to get sun after the treatments I've had for my face. I take my suitcase from the trunk and the girls grab their bags. Geneva has a Vuitton. Milan has a backpack, like a sherpa. All she needs is a yak. I don't know how she fit any clothes in it at all. For all I know, she is planning to wear the same clothes again tomorrow.

"Ready?" I ask, trying to sound cheerful. Milan nods. Geneva pulls her sunglasses over her eyes and whistles in a way that communicates both boredom and arrogance. She pops her back, then her wrists, and

Milan gives her a nasty look. I wonder where exactly I went wrong with these two. Was it because I was so focused on the show I didn't love them enough? I don't know. Off we go.

The Rebuilding Trust Cruise ship is the fourth ship down, a smaller ship than the others but nonetheless sizable. There must be a lot of people who don't trust each other walking around in the world. The ship belongs to one of the big cruise lines but has been chartered by a local self-help author, who I can see standing at the base of the ramp, greeting everyone with a warm smile and an embrace. Her pen name is Constancy Truth, and I admire her very much. I've wanted to meet her for a long time. This is going to be so good for my girls. I can feel it.

As we walk past the second ship, a big white oceanliner, Milan gets a call on her cell phone, and we all stop walking so she can talk, because my sloppier daughter apparently cannot walk and talk at the same time. People swarm around us trying to get to their ships. Geneva sighs and looks at her watch. So far, this is not going as I'd hoped. I look at the ship next to us. It is enormous. I still don't understand how these huge metal vessels float in the water. This one, the one near us, is a Carnival ship, and it is loading now, too. She mouths "book club" to me, like this means something important.

"No," says Milan into the phone. "I've never heard of that book."

Geneva looks at me like I should do something about this, rolls her eyes when I don't. Milan and her books. She should be a librarian. I turn away and watch a group of unattractive people with guitar cases and other musical equipment making their way up the ramp to the ship. There is one woman among the group, and for some strange reason she reminds me a little bit of Milan. A pretty girl who makes herself plain. She flirts with a man who looks almost too hairy to be real.

"What's it called?" Milan shouts into the phone, plugging her free ear with a finger. She squints against the noise and commotion around us, trying to hear the bookworm on the other end. Those are her only friends, a bunch of ladies who read too much. Milan should be meeting men, and getting on with her life. "It's a kid's book? Teens? But you picked it for next time? What is it? *Loser?* Is that the title? Hello? Hello? Can you hear me?"

Milan pulls the phone away, looks at the screen, frowns, curses, and folds the phone closed.

"Crap," she says. "No signal."

As she fiddles with her phone, I see a bowlegged young man with red hair slink past the ramp once, then turn to walk past again. He wears rumpled shorts and a ratty T-shirt and looks familiar somehow. He is watching the woman in the group of musicians as she laughs with the hairy guy. I know I've seen this redheaded man somewhere before. He reminds me of a shorter Conan O'Brien. That's it! It's the musician from Ricky Biscayne's band from *The Tonight Show*. Milan, staring only at the screen of her phone, starts to walk around without paying attention to where she's going, trying to get a signal. Geneva huffs and turns to walk toward our ship without us.

"Catch you on board," she says.

I stay with Milan only because that is the way it is with my girls. Geneva can take care of herself. Milan wanders aimlessly through the crowd, dumpy, bumping into people and not even noticing, focused on what's in her own head and nothing else. I watch as she walks backward, and in her haste to find a signal she bumps into the red-headed man just as he is about to head up the ramp. She nearly knocks him over into the water, but he grabs on to the guard chain of the ramp to steady himself.

"God!" he cries. He looks down at the water with fear in his eyes. The woman with the musicians on the ramp sees him and starts to laugh. The man looks at her.

"What a loser!" she calls out to him.

He blushes, and turns to look at Milan. Still focused on her phone call, she looks at him with anger, like she thinks *he* bumped into *her*. He lets go of the chain, and straightens himself out, still dazed from Milan's bump. He smiles at her and I do believe he thinks my little Milan is *cute*. I know enough about men to recognize that face. I've never seen a man look at her like that, and it gives me chills. Yes! Please,

God, let her meet someone and move out of my house. I know you're supposed to love your children forever and always welcome them, but I always looked forward to the day my kids moved out. And Milan, as far as I'm concerned, is about six years over her limit.

But does Milan notice the man? Nope. She seems to have just gotten through to her friend because she holds her hand up to the young man and leans into her call. He shrugs, and waits for her to finish. Honestly, she owes him an apology. I think he's waiting for one. But all Milan does is give him a second look, like she's trying to place him, then, distracted, she turns away from him and shouts into the phone, "Loser!"

The young man's face falls and I realize he thinks she has insulted him. He looks up at the woman on the ramp, and his shoulders drop. He adjusts a baseball cap on his head like he's trying to hide something, and walks away. Milan comes back to me, her call over.

"You nearly knocked that young man into the water," I say.

"Oh, him? He ran into me."

"No, he didn't."

"Yes, he did."

"It was that guy from Ricky's band. Did you notice that?"

"What guy?"

"The musician."

"No, it wasn't, Mom."

"We're going to be late, Milan," I say. "Turn off your phone."

"Sorry," she says. "It was about our new book pick."

"Let me guess," I say. "Something called *Loser*?"

She nods. "How'd you know?"

"I heard you," I say. But what I want to say is that I think it might have been written about her.

I have a splinter in my butt. From the bleachers. Ow! I reach down with one hand, and there it is, right in the crease between my butt and my thigh. I've been popping up and down on these wooden bleachers, cheering my daughter, Sophia, on in her soccer game. She is not just playing, either, she is kicking *butt*. She takes after me, I think with a swell of pride. My kid is not only smart and pretty, she is a regular soccer prodigy.

So, anyway, here I am at the park, up one second, cheering and jumping around in my Target khaki shorts, canvas sneakers, and a long-sleeved yellow T-shirt, and the next, I'm sitting down and trying not to notice all the other parents staring at me.

"Gooooaaaalll," I bellow, like a reject from a Spanish-language sports show. Sophia looks up, embarrassed of me but proud of herself. She waves at me, then does a hand motion to get me to sit down. Parents must embarrass their children, I've decided. It's inevitable and a requirement. Ouch. I sit on the splinter. How do you remove such a thing? I'm going to have to ask Jim to remove it for me, later. I'm happy I have a Jim to remove my ass splinters. Life is good.

"Gooooall," I cry again. I pull at my short hair. I whoop and whistle. I'm making such a ruckus that my sunglasses clatter to the bleachers, then disappear beneath. I'm big, and I'm strong, and I am usually graceful, but not right now. I hardly notice. I squint against the harsh Homestead sun. "That's my girl!"

I feel the eyes of a few fathers turn toward me. It happens a lot. The wives growl at me. It's not my fault their men are hounds. It's not my fault I have to keep fit for my job and many of these women, apparently, *don't*. It's not that hard to be fit. You watch what you eat and you exercise. It's that simple. People try to make it so complicated with all the special diets and whatnot. It's all a distraction.

Sophia is getting entirely too pretty for her own good. The other day, I told her I was worried that she was becoming too beautiful, and she said something that surprised me. "You're beautiful, too, Mom. You look like Kate Hudson." It was the first compliment she's paid me in a couple of years. I'm hoping we've rounded some kind of corner, and that she's going to continue to be open with me throughout the rapids of adolescence. I hope she'll ask for my advice on dating, though I can't promise that I wouldn't say something stupid and overprotective, like, "Just wait, take your time, don't be like me, go to college first."

Don't be like me? Yeah, like I was with Ricardo Batista, aka Ricky Biscayne. I thought I was so in love back then, but in reality I didn't know squat about squat. I sit down and try to avoid thinking about Ricky. He's everywhere I go these days. Stores, TV, radio. I can't believe it. There was a time when I would have died for that boy, and now I don't know if he would even remember me.

The memory comes back like an unwelcome friend, but with exquisite detail.

English class. We are discussing *The Red Badge of Courage*, by Stephen Crane, and the teacher tells us the book was written in a matter of days. Several students, including me, say that isn't possible or that, if it is possible, no book written so quickly could ever possibly be any good.

"It's possible," says a young man in the back of the class. Ricardo Batista. Soccer star. Loner. Gorgeous. A kid who laughs for no reason, at jokes only he has heard. A young man I keep catching trying to make eye contact with me, but who I am too shy to let approach. In class, I feel like it is okay to look at him, because everyone else is also looking at him. He is beautiful, with a few pimples that don't detract from the rest. Those eyes. Wow.

The teacher, a young woman with long, curly hair, smiles. "You think, Ricardo? What makes you say that?"

"Well," he says. "I wrote a book of poems last week. Two hundred pages long."

Most of the kids in the class laugh, but the teacher doesn't. Neither do I. I like to write poetry, too, and can't believe someone else at this shallow school, where all it seems anyone worries about is clothes and popularity, shares my passion. Without poetry, I feel I will die of sadness and loneliness. My father's rage has been directed mostly at me lately. My mom has taken off for two weeks and no one knows where she is. She does this a lot, and always comes back. I avoid home as much as I can, try to excel in school, in band, in swimming, in everything, because even though I am only fourteen years old I recognize that education is my only way out of the life my parents have given me.

"What are your poems about?" asks the teacher.

This is the moment my heart sprouts wings for the first time, as Ricardo Batista, the boy every girl wants to want her, looks directly at me and points at me with his gray mechanical pencil. "Her," he says with the softest, sweetest smile.

"Me?" I point to myself. A few classmates laugh.

"You," he says. It is the first time he's spoken to me directly.

"Why me?"

"I've seen you," he says. "It ain't easy on you."

"Me?"

"Irene Gallagher," he says. "The most beautiful, tormented girl in this school. I call you my *mariposita rota*, my broken butterfly."

The teacher interrupts and asks us to continue talking after class, directing everyone's attention back to the book. I turn away from Ricardo, but I can feel the heat of his eyes burning across my body for the rest of the class.

"Goal!" cries Coach Rob, as Sophia scores again. Again! I almost missed it, thinking about the past. This is why I try not to think about it. I shake myself back to the present, but still feel the sticky fingers of ghost love drag across my skin. I stand and cheer.

All the girls on Sophia's soccer team start to shout and trill with laughter as Sophia runs across the field to celebrate her newest goal. Her teammates lift her onto their shoulders for an instant, before accidentally dropping her on the hard, wet grass. Thud.

"Sophia!" I cry, hand slapping over my mouth in horror. "You okay, kid?" I dash onto the field.

Sophia looks up with me with her crooked grin. Sometimes the child looks so much like her father it is actually painful for me to look at her.

Ricky was good at soccer in high school, back when we dated. He was a very smart boy who was good at lots of things, and from all indications his daughter is likewise gifted. I'm stretched to the limit paying for Sophia's music and dance lessons, and soccer. She's starting to ask for better clothes, the kind that you get in the teen section at the expensive department stores. I can't afford those clothes, and it pains me to have to say so. I've been stashing some money away in hopes of one day having saved enough to live on for six months, when the time finally comes for me to sue my employer for sexual discrimination. Sophia doesn't know about the savings, or the harassment. She just thinks her mom is stingy about money.

I feel guilty. I should tell her about her dad. Maybe arrange for them to meet. Maybe see if he will provide a little bit for her. My pride has stood in the way all these years, but it seems foolish now. I don't know. He was awful to me, I mean *really* awful. It would be like accepting his prejudice to go back now, wouldn't it? I don't know what to do about it. I never have.

"I told my moms about the baby," he tells me. We share an Orange Julius at the mall. We are kids.

"What did she say?" I ask. I hope Ricky's mother will adopt me, take me out of my home and raise me and the baby together.

"She wants us to get rid of it," says Ricky.

"What?" My heart stops, and the tears come. I don't cry much, having learned to keep it inside. But I can't stop it. I try and can't.

"She doesn't want us to have it."

"I'm Catholic," I say. "I'm keeping this baby."

"You can't," says Ricky. "She says we should put it up for adoption."

"What? No! I'm having it and raising it."

"You can't."

"I can and I will, and either you help me or you don't."

Ricky looks at the ceiling, at me. He looks angry. "Don't do this to me, Irene."

"Why doesn't your mom like me?" I've seen his mother a few

times at his house, and she is the kind of mother I always wanted. A stable, working woman who keeps her house clean.

Ricky shrugs. "I don't know."

"Yes you do."

He stands up, still angry. "My mom thinks you're white trash, Irene. Okay? You happy now?"

"What? How can she say that?"

"She doesn't want me to associate with you. She thinks you're bad news."

"What do you think?"

"Well, you have to understand why she'd think that. Your parents . . ."

"Ricky! I thought you loved me."

"We're too young. It's stupid. My mother is right. I think you should get rid of that baby. I gotta go."

I look up, surprised to find tears in my eyes. No. I won't reach out to him. I won't allow him to know this daughter of *mine*. He has no right to her, calling us names, looking down on us, demanding I give her away.

We don't need him.

Sophia shoos me back to the bleachers. I use the moment to crawl under them for my sunglasses. Then I sit and watch.

Sophia and the other girls consult with Rob, their young, good-looking coach, for a few moments, and then they are dismissed to their parents. Sophia runs to me on her long, tanned legs and buries herself in my embrace. She is almost old enough to be embarrassed by such behavior, but blissfully for me she still likes to cuddle—now and then.

"You're amazing, girl," I say, nuzzling her wild brown hair. "I am so proud of you, I can't even tell you."

"I've been practicing," says Sophia with a confident smile.

"I noticed." I gather my stuff from the bleachers and stand up. "You hungry, kid?"

"Could we get pizza?" Sophia loves pizza almost more than she loves soccer, and now that she is thirteen, she seems to be hungry all the time.

"Sure," I say. I try once again to sound like a mom who doesn't worry about things—money things. But I wonder if the checks I wrote this week have all cleared. If they have, there won't be anything left for pizza, or anything else. If they haven't, I might be able to juggle things until payday next week.

"Cool!" cries Sophia. Doesn't take much to make her happy.

Hand in hand, we walk across the field toward the parking lot. I see Coach Rob look over at us, and then here he comes, jogging our way. He's cute. No question. And I'm pretty sure he likes me. He always wants to talk to me. I have never flirted back with him because I think it would muck up Sophia's life if I got involved with her coach, especially if things went badly with him down the road.

"Uh, hey, Irene?" he calls.

"Oh, hey, Coach Rob. Great game! What a girl, huh?" I muss Sophia's hair.

"Sophia's the best," says the coach. He looks me up and down and blushes. His eyes turn guilty. "Um, can I have a word with you in private for a second?"

Sophia elbows me in the side. Wise beyond her years, my kid continues to walk toward our blue Isuzu Rodeo in the parking lot. "I'll meet you at the car, Mom," she says with a teasing smile. Sophia thinks Coach Rob has a crush on me. This is wishful thinking from a little girl without a dad.

Rob waits until Sophia is out of earshot to put a hand on my shoulder. Mmm. Feels good. I wish it didn't. I will away any feelings of interest I might have, and try to think of Jim the Christian cop. "I didn't want to say this is front of her, or anybody," he says, wincing. He lowers his voice. "But your check for the new uniforms didn't clear."

Ugh. No. My stomach lurches in fear, like I'm being chased. Money issues have that impact on me, fight or flee. My usual impulse is to flee. "That can't be," I lie.

"I'm sorry," he says. "I went ahead and gave Sophia her uniform, but I need you to get that sixty dollars to me as soon as you can."

"Sure," I say, humiliated to my bones. "No problem. It must have been a mistake from the bank."

Rob smiles, and his eyes dip to look at my mouth. "We all go through hard times," he says softly. "I'd really like Sophia to attend soccer camp this summer. We need her. I know it's steep. If you can't swing it, we have some parents who can help, I can try—"

"I *can* swing it," I lie. Three hundred dollars, though? Ugh.

"Okay. But I know they don't pay firefighters enough. It's wrong how they do that. You guys are out there risking your necks and all."

"See you next week." I turn away before I turn red in the face. Soccer camp? There is no way I'll be able to afford soccer camp for the whole summer. I hurry toward the Isuzu with tears burning my eyes. How did I get here? How? When did this happen to me? I had bigger dreams than this. How do I get out?

"You okay, Mom?" asks Sophia, leaning against the car, bouncing her soccer ball off her head and catching it with her hands. The kid is psychic sometimes. It is incredible how you can never really get away with lying to your kids.

"No," I say. I unlock the car. "But I'll manage. Get in the car."

We drive for a while without saying anything, and Sophia fiddles with the radio dial. I try not to cry, but I do anyway. If they'd just been tears of sadness, or just tears of rage, I might have been able to handle it. But they are both this time.

"What's wrong, Mom?"

"I'm sorry, Sophia. I should be honest with you. We're having some money trouble this week."

"Again?" She slouches lower in her seat, as if she doesn't want anyone to see her being poor in the car.

"Yes," I say.

"So no pizza?"

"Not tonight. I'm sorry. We can make something at home. Maybe Grandma already did."

"Yippee," says Sophia cynically. "Maybe she'll make mayonnaise sandwiches."

"I'm sorry."

"No, Mom, it's okay." Sophia sighs. "Really. I understand. It's been a tough week, with the windows and Grandma's teeth."

I'm amazed, *amazed*, by Sophia's resilience and maturity. Earlier in the week, someone threw rocks through four windows in our house. Then I find out too late that I accidentally let the home insurance lapse. So I had to pay for that. Then my mother's dental bridge fell out. The dentist said Medicare wouldn't pay for it anymore. So, yup. I paid for that, too. I also paid the mortgage and the bills. The starts of the months are the worst. There's just not enough money, it's that simple.

Sophia flips to a pop station, and immediately the English-language Ricky Biscayne hit comes out of the speakers. I reach out by instinct and turn it off.

"I'm up for promotion," I say. I know I probably won't get it, but it's worth mentioning.

"That's good, Mom. Would you work more, though?"

"Yeah." I'd have to spend as many as four days and nights away from home, at the station, a week. That's the main reason I let my mother live with us.

"Oh well," says Sophia. She looks sad. I've wanted to be a fire-fighter since she was a little girl, but it's a piss-poor career choice for a single mom. I know that now. But what am I supposed to do? I can't really get any other kind of job at this point that pays as well.

Ricky. To hell with Ricky. Ricky is rich now. He was fifteen when I last talked to him. That means he would be twenty-eight now. Maybe he's changed. Maybe he could help us. I don't want to need anyone, but *still*. God. I don't know.

"So, you got homework, or what?"

"Yeah, a little," answers Sophia. "Math."

"We *love* math."

"Yeah, *right*." Sophia is just starting to master the art of sarcasm. We both hate numbers. "I love eating. I'm starving."

I pull into the driveway of our house, cut the engine.

"Hey, Mom?" asks Sophia as we walk across the front yard. A thundercloud rumbles overhead.

"Yeah, puppy dog?"

"That guy singing on the TV the other night?"

My heart races but I try to act calm. "Yeah, what about him?"

"I think he looks like me." I feel her eyes on me, but I don't look back. Instead, I stick the key in the front door.

"You think?" I ask with a shrug.

"I do."

I try to laugh like I don't have a care in the world. "Sweetie," I say to her. "Go on inside." Sophia looks confused.

Sophia squints at me for a long moment before entering the house. It smells like hamburgers frying.

I say, "Looks like Grandma made dinner, Sophia. Isn't that great?"

"I'm not hungry," says Sophia, plopping onto the cheap Ikea sofa with a frown.

"But you just said you were starving!"

"Well, I lied," says Sophia, all sass and attitude.

"Why'd you do that?" I ask, absently.

Sophia stares hard at me until I finally return her gaze. "Because," she says. "Lying obviously runs in the family."

sunday, march 24

All I want to do is sleep, but the entire cabin rocks back and forth with such force I have to tense every muscle in my body so that I don't throw up. Geneva snoozes in the bed next to mine, like there's nothing wrong. Even with all the commotion and her sleeping, she manages to raise a wrist and crack it. In her sleep. How can she do that? She must be the devil. That's the only answer I can come up with. Only the devil could look *pretty* snoring, and snore through the rocking carousel that is our cruise ship cabin.

I get up and stagger toward the little bathroom, aware of the precarious drone of the ship's engines somewhere under the floor. I don't know where Mom is, but she's not here. Everything on cruise ships is nailed or welded to the floor and the walls. Now I know why. I look at the little round window and see water sloshing up across the glass. Nice. We're supposed to be five stories up from the surface of the ocean. Why is there water slopping around up here? Are we going to capsize? Is this normal? I am not the ship type, I think, as I trip and fall to the floor.

"Ow!" I scream.

Geneva stirs in her bed and peeks up at me with one half-open eye. She has no mascara smudge because, unlike me, she remembers to remove the stuff before bed. "You okay, Milan?" she asks. I can't tell if she's being sarcastic.

"I'm fine," I say. I get up and continue to balance my way to the bathroom. Cruises suck, okay? For the record and now and forever let this be known.

I make it to the little bathroom and close the door. It's almost as small as an airplane bathroom. I don't want to throw up. All I want is to pee. And go back to sleep. I look at my watch. It's six in the morning. I listen to the hot hiss of liquid squirting from me to the bowl and wonder how I ended up here.

I exit the bathroom and find Geneva sitting up on her bed checking her BlackBerry again. She's addicted to her e-mail. I can't believe it works out here. Where are we, anyway? Somewhere near Cuba, circling the island of the doomed like it doesn't exist. This is a lame cruise because it doesn't even stop anywhere. We're at sea the whole time, supposedly learning to trust each other. I wish Geneva were still asleep because I want to raid the bag of guava cream pastries I have hidden in my backpack, but I don't want to get that look from her.

The door to the cabin opens and our mother waltzes in like a sitcom mom, cheery and perky, her makeup and clothes perfect. Does she never look bad, my mother? When did she have time to iron a black linen pantsuit? She looks spiffy, with a yellow scarf tied just so around her neck.

"Good morning, girls!" she trills. She has two Starbucks paper cups of coffee, with lids. "Who wants a little caffeine?" she asks. "I've got Dramamine, too, for the tummy." She smiles like a schoolteacher. Geneva holds a hand out for her coffee and mumbles a thank-you. Is that a new tattoo on the inside of her wrist? I refuse the coffee, but Mom shoves the cup and the pills into my hand anyway.

"I'm sick," I say. I stagger to the bed and plop down.

"That's what Dramamine is for," says Mom. Yeah, thanks. I couldn't have figured that one out on my own.

I wonder how anyone can down pills with hot liquid, but I do my best. The boat shakes and pitches and it feels like the front end of it rises and slams back down to the sea, with a cold hard bang, like the water is solid cement or something.

"What was *that*?" asks Geneva.

"It's just a little storm," says my mother. I try to mentally calculate whether hurricane season has started yet. The boat veers to one side and my mom has to hold on to the little desk to keep herself from toppling over. She smiles nonetheless and smooths her hands down her sides the way she does when she's about to talk about a man. "I was just chatting with the captain, and he said it's nothing to worry about. It should pass in an hour or two, he said. He's very handsome. I'd like you girls to meet him." The ship shivers and dips as Geneva and I share a look that I take to mean we both wonder if Mom is sleeping with the ship's captain.

"Wake me up when we dock," says Geneva. She dives back under the covers and pulls them over her head.

"Oh, come on, girls!" Mom sips her coffee as she steadies herself against the wall. "Get dressed. There's a nice buffet, and after that is the nice Opening Our Hearts workshop."

"My heart is full of vomit at the moment," I say.

"Don't open it," calls Geneva. "It wouldn't be *nice*."

We laugh. Together. Me and Geneva. How about them apples? My mother doesn't laugh with us. Maybe Geneva and I will bond after all, at Mom's expense.

Mom's eyes narrow at me. "I've tried to be nice," she says. "But you two are pushing me to the limit. Now get up and get dressed and stop acting like a couple of spoiled brats. We're going to the darn breakfast."

Meow.

Constancy Truth looks like a cartoon giraffe that teaches aerobics somewhere in the 1980s. She has a long skinny neck, weird half-black, half-blond hair that flips up in defiance of gravity and good taste, and huge black eyes with fake lashes. She stands in the middle of a circle of people in a room that looks like any bland conference room in any hotel. She wears hot-pink short shorts and a sparkly silver top. The people are sorry. That's the only word I have for them. They look like they should be at an AA meeting or something, you know the type, sort of needy and desperate and wounded. People who will believe anything. Constancy is as jumpy as a toad. Wiry, too, and, I would suspect, on speed or something like it. She zips around the circle, shaking hands and looking a little too deeply into our eyes. Her feet are bare, though she does wear thick gray leg warmers. Where on earth did she find leg warmers? My mother finds her charmingly eccentric and original. I find her weird and terrifying. Geneva seems to agree with me, because she leans over to me and whispers, "Is she going to ask us to drink cyanide Kool-Aid, you think? Should we have brought black Nikes?" We laugh viciously and our mother watches with a look of concern.

"Okay, people!" shouts Miss Truth. She has an accent from one of the islands. Jamaica? St. Thomas? "Everyone join hands."

"Oh my God," I mumble. Geneva snickers. Mom grabs our hands and places them together.

"Please try to cooperate," she hisses.

"Say, 'I love myself!'" shouts the giraffe guru.

"I love myself!" shout the gullible masses.

"Shout, 'I love everyone in this room!'"

"I love everyone in this room!" they shout.

"Now. Everyone *quiet* your heart," says Constancy.

"Hearts," Geneva whispers to me. "We don't all share a heart. If we did, we wouldn't have trust issues."

Constancy continues, "I want you to close your eyes and feel the warmth and humanity of the persons beside you. Take a deep breath."

I inhale and I smell farts. Awful, wet, beany, sprouty farts. That's warmth and humanity, all right. Who was it? Not me. It's usually me, so I'm surprised. Oh my God. It really stinks. I open my eyes and look at Geneva. Her eyes are wide open.

"Eeew?" I whisper.

"I bet it's Mom," says Geneva.

We crack up. Constancy is still babbling something, God knows what, and my sister and I are trying not to choke. Suddenly, the boat lurches and half the people in the room tumble to the floor. Geneva and I stagger, remain upright, and just sort of look at each other.

"Not a problem!" Constancy is shrieking. "Do not let this be a problem! Trust that we'll get through this! Trust that the weather will improve! Trust that this was meant to be, to teach us all a great lesson!"

A couple of people have thrown up on the floor from motion sickness. It was just one person at first, a sad-eyed woman with frizzy permed hair, but another saw her throw up and that made *him* throw up, which made another woman throw up. Constancy practically screams, "Regroup! Regroup! Trust that we have the collective power to regroup and rejoice!"

Now the smell of farts is joined by the smell of barf. I'm going to die.

"We must sit on the floor like Indians," says Constancy. She is rushing around shoving people into a circle. "We must trust! Trust that by sitting we will not fall!" People moan and groan and the ship continues to rock violently. I am going to be sick.

"The smell," says someone with much bigger ovaries than mine. "Oh my God!" Good for her.

"Ignore the smell," says Constancy. She takes a hugely deep breath with a false smile on her face, raising her arms over her head dramatically. "Let us think of the smell as a gift from the universe, as a symbol of the very thing in our hearts that prevents us from trusting the people we mistrust. Trust in the smell to be sweet!"

"Isn't that denial?" Geneva asks me. Geneva looks at our mother. "Mom, Constancy's in denial."

Our mother places a hand over her mouth and nose as if this will somehow block the odor. "Let's make the best of this."

"Excuse me," I say, hand to mouth. I have the urge to throw up, so I run from the room out onto the deck. The cool air feels good on my skin. I lean over the railing and feel the spray of salt water on my skin. Geneva follows, and comes to stand beside me.

"Our mother is insane," she says. She rolls her head like a dancer and I hear the neck popping. Ugh.

"Ya *think?*"

"Trust in the *smell?* What *is* that? Why would Mom do this to us?" I breathe deeply. "I guess her boyfriend was busy this weekend."

Geneva looks at me. "You know about him?"

"Yeah," I say. "You?"

"Totally. I saw them at a café once. I ran out."

"He looks like Jack LaLanne, right?"

"Oh, God! Totally!"

We laugh wickedly. It's terrible. We *are* spoiled brats. But we have to relieve the stress somehow.

"Can you believe Mom's got a lover?" Geneva asks.

"More power to her, I say. Dad's been cheating on her for years."

"I guess, but it's weird anyway."

I feel a hand on my shoulder and turn to see our mother. I don't know how long she's been listening, but she has a strange, sad look on her face.

"Oh, hey, Mom," says Geneva, eyes wide with guilt.

"Don't tell him," she says. "Okay?"

thursday, march 28

Ricky Biscayne enters Jill Sanchez's white baroque Bal Harbour estate early Monday morning, in the back of a van from a local florist shop that makes daily deliveries there. The driver and Jill are tight, and she knows he'll keep it on the down-low. But even if he doesn't, no harm done, really, right?

Jill has dismissed her household help for the day, and she is alone at home except for the outside security guards. She waits for Ricky in her bedroom, wearing a short, white, transparent La Perla lace robe, a yellow-gold and diamond Rolex, her yellow-diamond engagement ring, Crème de le Mer moisturizing cream (which is meant for the face but which she uses everywhere), and nothing else, with a hundred white candles burning. Ricky steps into her bedroom, wearing ripped jeans that look like castoffs from Billy Ray Cyrus, a hockey jersey, and Diesel sneakers. His wedding band burns in his pocket.

No me jodas. This wasn't what we agreed to," he says, weakly, trying not to look at her magnificent body. He is here to talk business. He wants her advice on investing in this new nightclub, Club G, and on hiring a new publicist, now that Boolla Barbosa, his old one, will soon be going to prison for weapons smuggling and prescription-drug theft or some shit. Jill always knows how to hire the right kinds of people. He needs help. Business help.

But he can't think about that now. All he can think about is that body. How did she get her skin to look that soft and smooth? Jasminka is pretty, but pale and bony. Jill, though. *Her* body looks like it is sculpted out of hard coffee ice cream, or a hazelnut candle, and her breath smells of fresh, cool milk. "We said we'd be good this time. I just came to hear your tracks."

When she stands inches away from him and drops the robe, Ricky starts to shake and sweat. Her peppy, erect nipples are the most exquisite shade of reddish brown. They are small. Jasminka has droopy model breasts with those huge nipples he'd first seen as a little boy in the YWCA locker room with his mother, breasts like long British faces. He prefers Jill's tight little body to his wife's stretched, lean one. He *loves* Jill's body, he says, with mad passion, a longing he says keeps him awake at night. You can almost balance a glass of beer or a piece of sheet music on top of her ass.

Jill listens to Ricky's attempts to stop her. He loves his wife—he babbles about that, as he tends to do—but he says he never stopped loving *her*, Jill Sanchez. Jill can't be sure, but it seems like he is struggling not to cry. If she hadn't dumped him, he says, he would still be with her. He would never have married Jasminka. But he is married now and wants to do the right thing, to be honorable, to be a good man, the way his mama raised him. He doesn't want to be a *sinvergüenza* like his father, who is somewhere in Venezuela with a whole new family. Blah, blah, blah.

"Be with me now," she purrs. She draws one manicured foot up over the shin of the other leg. Jill's feet never look blistered or callused the way normal people's feet do. They looked like the feet of a wax figure. "It's never too late, is it?"

Jill kisses Ricky's cheek, then his neck. She eases her hand over his crotch, and squeezes. He resists for a total of six seconds before grabbing her and scattering bites across her sweet-smelling skin. Jill's personal perfumes all come from a small, private shop in France.

Ricky cups his hands over her breasts and ducks to take a nipple into his mouth. Jill groans dramatically, realizing as she does so that she might be overacting. "*Así, Papi,*" she says, Spanish for "Like that, Daddy." Ricky loves it when she calls him Daddy, and her Spanish inspires him to bite the nipple lightly. "*Así,*" she says. "*Muérdeme duro, Papi.*"

"You like it rough, eh?" he responds.

"The rougher the better, baby," she says. Ricky releases her breasts and grabs her hair and the back of her neck. He tugs her hair, and the pain makes her smile. "Harder," she challenges him. He pulls harder, arching her neck and back while pushing her down to her knees, maneuvering her head toward the zipper of his jeans.

"Suck it," he commands. *"Mámame el bicho."*

Jill unzips him and complies. Ricky's pants stop somewhere around midthigh. She is somewhat unimpressed with the semisoft state of his member, but moans and groans nonetheless, as if licking him out of mushiness excites her beyond words. She carries on with this, manually stimulating herself as she goes, until she decides she's had enough. Then, she stands up.

"Get on the bed," she says.

"Make me."

"Okay," says Jill. She turns her back to him, and bends over, using her hand to spread and display her carefully waxed wares clearly. She knows that in the peach light of the candles she will look smooth, succulent, and irresistible. Ricky watches and says, "Oh, shit, girl."

Jill slithers to all fours and crawls to the bed like a cat, rising and bending herself over the mattress. Feet on the floor, chest to the bed, she lifts her ass and arches her back, beckoning as she swivels her head to look at him. Her hair drapes across the peach comforter. Her crotch, like the rest of her, throbs for attention. "Come here," she says. "Spank me."

Ricky strips as he walks to her, littering the spotless, spacious room with his clothes. He has that violent look in his eyes, the one Jill loves. He's holding himself, stroking, as he comes to her. "Don't move," he instructs. Jill bites her lower lip, and waits. The spank comes quickly, not too hard, not too soft.

"I've been very bad," she tells him. "You can do better than that." He spanks her again, harder. Jill loves it. "I want you," she says. "I need you inside me."

Ricky obliges, and continues to slap her bottom as he goes *"¿Qué carajo quieres, eh?*" he asks. Jill closes her eyes and imagines what she must look like doing this. She's sure she looks beautiful. She releases the sorts of noises she has heard actresses make in porn movies, and it makes Ricky work harder. She knows just what to do to make him please her. Then, just as she thinks she has him in her control, Ricky surprises her by sticking a finger in her other opening. The pain is almost divine. She shrieks, and the sound is genuine. "You are so nasty," she says. "*Cochino.*"

Ricky removes himself from her and leans over to lick her there. Everywhere. In places people are not supposed to lick. The taboo nature of it makes Jill crazy. "*Cochino,*" she repeats, the Spanish word for "pig."

"I'm a pig, but you like it," he says. "*A ti te gusta que te doy candela por el culo.*"

Jill flips over and lifts her sculpted legs into the air. Ricky sticks his tongue into her exposed openings, then his finger, fingers. "I love you," she says.

"I love you, too."

"But I hate you," she reminds him.

He jams his whole hand into her and she cries out in agony and pleasure. He is rough by nature, but his confusion and agony make him rougher. Jill feels dizzy with excitement. With Jack, sex has become almost rote in the three months since they got engaged, after meeting on the set of a film they starred in together. Jack has this puritan thing where he can only get wild with women (or boys?) he hates, and he actually *likes* Jill. But with Ricky, the tension of unrequited love and mutual admiration, mixed with a subtext of genuine disrespect, keeps everything fresh, and he performs for her as if he were on an audition, doing things to all the openings of her body she can't imagine a husband doing to a wife.

When they finish, Ricky dresses quickly, with a dark shadow of shame across his face. "I can't keep doing this," he says. "I need you to respect what I want."

"I know what you want," says Jill. "And I think I just respected it."

"You know what I mean. I really am trying to change."

Jill lounges nude across her bed and grins like the Cheshire cat. "Divorce her," she says. "I'll leave Jack. We'll get married, me and you. Imagine the press!"

Ricky's face drops. He looks at her with longing and love, but changes his expression immediately. "No," he says. "I'm not falling for *that* again."

And with that, he storms out of the room. Jill puts the robe on again and pads across the pink and white travertine tiles of her hallway, following him to the kitchen, where he helps himself to a glass of ice water.

"I love my wife," he fumes, as she enters the room. "She's an incredible woman."

Jill yawns dramatically.

"You have no idea what she's been through in her life," he says, on the verge of crying. He feels sorry for Jasminka, Jill realizes; this is what cements him to her. But pity is no reason to remain in a marriage. Jill knows this for a fact.

"We've all had hard times," says Jill.

"Jasminka survived ethnic cleansing, Jill. Do you have any idea what that must have been like?"

Jill nods. She once played a woman who had survived something like that. She knows how it feels.

"I'm not coming here anymore." Ricky gulps down the water and refills his glass. He points a finger at nothing in particular. "This is the last time."

"Whatever you say," says Jill. She hops up onto the counter and hikes up the robe to expose more of her legs.

"Oh, God," he says, not wanting to look, but looking. "Why do you do this to me?"

"Because," says Jill, "I still love you."

Ricky actually trembles. "This is so unfair," he says, as the glass clatters to the counter. All is fair in love and war, thinks Jill, who believes herself to be at war with Jasminka.

"Come here," says Jill.

"No."

"*Come here.*"

Jill jumps to the floor, turns around so that her torso rests across the counter, and slides up her robe even farther, exposing her exquisite, caramel-candy ass. Ricky rattles the glass along the counter for a moment; then, as he's always done, he gives in to Jill's demands.

"It's too risky," she says as he enters her from behind, thrilled, as always, by danger and her own bad behavior. "The press and everything. After all, I'm America's sweetheart."

"Nah, girl, that's Julia Roberts," says Ricky. "You're America's rich Spanish bitch."

"Shut up," says Jill, biting Ricky's hand. It is supposed to be a playful nip, but it comes out a little too hard, a little too real. She tastes the iron of his blood on the polished white surfaces of her porcelain veneers.

Ricky recoils from the blow, then grabs her hard on the back of the neck. She loves rough sex. "Fuck you. Why do you hate me?" he asks.

"I don't know," she says, turning her head until she can lock eyes with him. "I just do."

He stares at her big, cold black pupils, growing more excited by the second, and thrusts harder.

monday, april 1

My forehead is numb from this morning's Botox injection. I also had it injected into my armpits, to help stop the sweating. As a mother of two grown women, I don't feel like I should be sweating in the armpits. It's not right.

I adjust my red beret over my blond bob, and swivel in the chair at the counter in the radio studio. I fix the headphones over the hat, then concentrate my attention on the three young men who sit across from me for my show. Dumb, dumber, and dumbest, I think. The men are today's panel, the topic of my show being "Cuban male prostitutes in Miami—why they do it, and who they do it with." It's a makeup recording session, a show I can store for days when I might call in sick.

"Welcome back to *The Violeta Show!*" I cry into the microphone, in Spanish. "We're talking today with men who have sold their bodies for money, and how the communists have driven them to do so in Cuba with alarming regularity, reducing real men to quivering communist whores. So," I say to the cutest of them, pointing at him with a red fingernail. "You're a handsome, intelligent man. No one would know to look at you that you sold your fertile young loins to women for money."

"Lots of money," jokes the ugliest one, who seems to be on drugs. I picked a winner this time. I cannot imagine for the life of me why any woman in her right mind would sleep with that man, much less pay to do so. There are so many willing men in bars. Not that I'd know. Well, actually, I would, but no one needs to know that about me, though I do suspect my daughters know about one of my lovers at least. I hope they don't tell Eliseo. There's no telling how he'd react.

I hold up a hand to silence the homely whoreboy who has spoken out of turn, and focus more intently on the cutest one, who, I should say, I would have done in a heartbeat. I have a much more active sex life than my husband or daughters know about, thanks to a few discreet gentlemen around Miami, including one in La Broward who likes to go with me to a sex video "newsstand" at least once a month. "Let me ask, what inspired you to go into this line of work? Did you have a difficult childhood, honey?"

"*Pues,*" he begins in his thick, street Cuban Spanish. "No. *Oye,* I had a normal childhood. I didn't grow up wanting to be *un jinetero.* It just happened."

"Yes, but *how* did it happen? Did the communists force you to do it for tourism? Tell me *exactly*—in vivid detail—how it happened. What was Castro's role in your degradation?"

"Well, you get naked and have sex with women and they pay you for it."

I suddenly regret having called him "intelligent." It is possible to be too generous to a guest. He appears to be about as smart as a paper cup.

"Yes," I say. "I think we all *get* that. What I *mean* is, how did you make the switch from being a normal working man to being a whore? Was it Castro? Did he have something to do with it? And if not Fidel Castro, was it *Raúl* Castro? Which Castro made you into a man-whore?"

"*Bueno*," he says, then launches into a story about how he once was a doorman at the Hotel Nacional in Havana, when a beautiful, older French woman tourist asked him to help her up to her room with her shopping bags. "And when I got there, she closed the door and started to remove her clothes. I did what any man would do, and when it was over she paid me. I didn't expect it."

The other panelists laugh knowingly and high-five each other. "But," continues the man. "I didn't mind the money, and soon enough the French lady told her friends, and I fucked a few and they helped me get out of Cuba, and here I am."

I look at the producer. I know he won't be pleased with the word "fucked." Oh well. It's a word, that's my opinion. All words have their place. He signals me to go to break by playing the show's break-theme song. "Fascinating," I say as a segue. "Okay, Miami. We'll be right back with more tales from the dark side of prostitution from these three charming young men corrupted by the Castro regime into a life of debauchery and debasement, and figure out what we can do to prevent our own sons from entering this terrifying and dangerous profession, right after this commercial break."

I look at the clock. It is five thirty and my daughters should be arriving at the studio any moment for our group shopping trip to get Milan something suitable for her job interview with Ricky Biscayne. I love my daughter, but she dresses like a retired schoolteacher. It's quite sad.

I remove the headphones and poke my head out of the studio, locking into the lobby area. Sure enough, my daughters are already

here. Milan wears another of her bag dresses, and sips a large iced coffee from a Starbucks; she's reading a book. Geneva looks elegant and
cruelly beautiful in her simple jeans, black top, and black sandals. It
looks like they're actually talking to each other. The cruise must have
worked.

I whistle to get their attention, and wave.

"Hi, Mom," say the girls in unison. They have that whipped-dog
look they get when my shows embarrass them. Like they never think
or talk about these subjects? Why do children expect their mothers to
be saints? It is too much pressure.

"Have you been listening to the show?" I ask. I want them to one
day appreciate that their mother is a maverick taboo breaker. The
girls nod, and it seems like Geneva tries not to laugh while Milan tries
not to cry. "Well, what do you think?"

Milan and Geneva exchange a look of bewilderment, and I get an
idea. Without waiting for the answer my kids obviously don't want to
give anyway, I say, "Why don't you girls come in here and help me ask
these boys some questions?"

"No, thanks, Mom," says Geneva, still staring at that computer
thingy.

"Oh, come on. It would be fun! It would be great to have a young
person's perspective on the whole thing. We could have the promiscuous single girl and the virgin."

That should get them. Yes! They look up, furious.

"I'm *not* promiscuous," says Geneva. Milan smiles at me in dis-
agreement.

"What?" Geneva looks at me for an apology. "I'm *not.*" Geneva
looks hurt, and turns to Milan. "You're not still a *virgin*, are you, Milan?" Milan stares at her book, blushing deeply. "Oh my *God*," says
Geneva. An evil grin creeps across her face. "You're lying to Mom and
Dad about that? Why?"

"I'm going back. Who's joining me?" I ask, hoping Milan is *not* a
virgin at twenty-four. Don't all rush in at once, girls.

"Uh, I *would* but, you know, I have to read this book before next week," says Milan. "Book club." She holds up the book. Something called *P.S. I Love You*. Her and her book club.

"And you?" I ask Geneva.

"I'll go," she says, flashing a competitive smile at her sister. "I'm not afraid to try new things."

My heart breaks for my Milan, who pretends to read her book but who, I know for a fact, took the comment very hard. As the door to the studio closes, I say a little prayer to the Virgin of La Caridad del Cobre that Milan will do such great work helping her sister publicize the club that Geneva will see what she has refused to see so far—that Milan is as smart as she is. Then maybe Milan will get some confidence and a better job, and see a little bit of the world. I want Milan to give Geneva a reason to be jealous of *her* for once. As a mother, I would like to see that.

My producer scurries in and sets Geneva up with headphones as I resume the host's position. I note the hungry way the gigolos stare at Geneva, and I don't like it. Thankfully, Geneva seems to have little interest in them.

"Hellllloooo Miami," I say. "Welcome back to the show. Today we're speaking with three of Miami's top male prostitutes about their profession, clients, and the difficulties—and dangers—of their work. For the last quarter of the hour I have a special guest, my own daughter, Geneva Gotay, the Harvard Business School graduate, to help me ask the questions I know all of you would like to ask if you were here with us. Geneva, welcome to the show."

"Thanks, Mom," says Geneva in sarcastic Spanish.

"So, aren't they handsome?"

"Yep," says Geneva, with a wicked grin that makes me nervous.

"Do you have any questions for them?"

Geneva nods and turns to the men. "So," she says. "Do you guys think my mom here is hot, or what?"

The men grin and whistle at me as if on cue.

"Oh yeah," says one. The ugly one. Of course.

"So you'd do her for free?" asks Geneva.

"Absolutely," says the cutest one. I don't blush easily. That's why I'm the queen of taboo radio. But this makes me blush for the first time in years.

Geneva smiles at me and says, "April Fool's, Mami."

I don't like to play favorites with my children. I don't. But this one, this girl? I'm telling you. But it was almost impossible not to admire Geneva and her *cojones*. In another time and place, I think I would have been just like her.

Talk about degrading. *This* is degrading. Climbing into the backseat of my mom's new Jaguar, a stiff ugly car that still smells like chemicals for car leather. Am I the only one who thinks the new Jags look like Ford Tauruses? Degrading because Geneva has taken the front seat, again. The passenger seat. Of course she has. Does anyone have more of a right to everything they want in life than her? Me, oh, you know, Milan doesn't want much, need much, just stuff 'er in the back. Let the two glamour girls sit in front. As kids, I always got the back. Geneva? Front. Always in the front. It shouldn't bother me this much. I realize that. I could just drive my own car, and follow them. But Mom wants us all to go shopping together, to pick out something for me for a job interview at Ricky Biscayne's house. Turns out he's looking for a new publicist, and Geneva recommended me. I'm still in shock. Mom wants us to shop, and have dinner together, and be like adult children who love hanging out together with their mom, a mom who spent the afternoon talking to Havana gigolos about work.

Have I mentioned I want a new life? I can't wait for this interview. My life is going to change. I feel it.

Mom folds herself into the driver's seat and starts the engine. It purrs smoothly. My Neon? It burps and backfires. Life is fair. Mom doesn't work for a living, but she gets nice things. I work, and get nothing.

"Where to, girls?" asks Mom. Why is she asking us both? It's *my* shopping spree, isn't it? Not Geneva's.

Geneva answers first, of course, because I am too busy fuming about the injustice of it all. "How about the Bal Harbour Shops?"

I want to scream. Only very tiny women with very tiny purses and very tiny dogs shop there. And tiny women with huge professional athletes for husbands.

"No, thank you," I say.

"No," says Mom. "Milan's right." Is this where she finally asks me, Milan, what I want? "It's too far," she says. *D'oh!* "Why would you want to do all that driving? How about Merrick Park? It's practically around the corner."

Geneva shrugs. "Fine with me," she says. "I was hoping to stop at my place to let Belle out for a potty break. But she can use the doggy door for the patio if she gets too desperate."

"It's settled then," says Mom. What? Settled? I didn't even get to have an opinion and it's "settled"? I want to pinch them both until they bleed. But all I can manage to do is utter a sarcastic, "Yay."

"Don't act so excited," says Geneva. She turns in her seat and looks at me, smug. "We don't *have* to do this, you know. We *could* send you on your interview looking like an Amish maiden."

I squint at her and hope she gets the point. I. Hate. You.

I tap our mother on the shoulder. "Oh, Mom, I meant to tell you I saw Geneva the other night, at the bookstore." I shoot Geneva a look to let her know I plan to tell Mom about Ig-na-cio the African Prince. Geneva panics. Her eyes get wide and she tries to speak to me telepathically. That's the only possible thing that facial expression can mean.

"What's wrong, Geneva?" I ask her.

"What were you doing at the bookstore, Geneva?" asks Mom.

"Buying *books*," says Geneva.

"With a guy," I say.

"A friend," says Geneva, flashing me the most threatening stare I have ever seen.

"Play nice," says Mom. She checks her lipstick and hair in the rearview mirror, the car still idling in the parking lot. Satisfied with her face, she snaps her lipstick closed, jams the stick shift into Reverse, and eases out of the spot. "We're going to spend a nice evening together, a mother and her two beautiful daughters, having a nice dinner and buying some nice new things for Milan so that she looks extra beautiful for her nice job interview. *¿Me entienden?*"

"Gee, Mom, think you might say 'nice' a few more times?" asks Geneva with a sarcastic snort, as Mom steers the shiny black Jaguar onto Red Road.

I could actually punch my sister and I wouldn't feel bad about it. That's what's scary. I can't stand her right now. And just when I thought maybe we were starting to get along. What's wrong with my clothes? Nothing. Just because I don't look like Geneva, or my mom. I'm fine the way I am.

"*Nice,*" says Mom to Geneva. "*You* could learn something about it from your sister."

I smile. Wickedly. But my moment of gloating doesn't last.

"And *you*," Mom tells me, catching my eyes in the rearview mirror, witchy. "*You* could learn a little about fashion from Geneva. I think we all have something we could learn from each other. That is the beauty of family. Now let's go shopping. No more cat fights."

Meow.

No more cat fights. *No more cat fights.* This is what I chant in my head as we walk across the parking garage toward the walkway to the mall. Mom and Geneva walk close together, each carrying her expensive handbag over her left shoulder.

"Is that a Tod's?" Mom asks Geneva, referring to her butter-yellow bag with the beige trim.

"It's a Carlos Falchi," says Geneva.

"Beautiful," says Mom.

I'm off to the side. Symbolic. This is my life. They are both tall and lean. Mom's in a black suit with that ridiculous red beret. Geneva in her jeans and perfect black top. I flap along nearby like someone's discount linen boat sail. My handbag is Cherokee, from Target. Very chic.

I try to stay a few steps behind them in the walkway itself. They ooh and ahh and point at the giant posters of Tiffany & Co. jewelry. Have to have it, says Geneva. So Asian. What's up with her and Asian things lately? I totally don't get it. She's wearing jade jewelry right now, that's what she told me, for good luck. Puh-lease. The most upsetting thing here is that Geneva looks so much like the model in the ad that Mom stops and puts Geneva in front of it. I can see the similarities, but Mom rubs it in.

"Milan, look at this."

"What."

"Geneva. The model. They're identical."

Geneva pulls away and surprises me by putting her arm through mine, as if we actually ever did something like that. "So," she says, rolling her eyes toward Mom. "What do you feel like getting?"

I shrug, even though I want to ask her why she's bothering to seek my opinion. I guess you could say I hold a little bit of a grudge.

We emerge from the outdoor hallway from the parking garage into the light of the outdoor mall. It really is very pleasant and pretty here. I have to admit it. I have only been here a couple of other times, both times with Mom. It is four stories tall, the mall wrapped in sort of a U shape around a lush green courtyard with fountains and palm trees. Each "hallway" balcony has dozens of large ceiling fans blowing the air around. We are on the second level, and I look over the balcony and see there are sculptures below, too. There's hardly anyone here, just a few ladies walking around with worried faces. Why is it that the more money people seem to have, the less fun they seem to have spending it? If I had that kind of money, I'd be happy about it. I see three women walking down in the courtyard area, near the purple and yellow flowers, and they all carry identical Louis Vuitton bags, the see-through-plastic kind everyone around here sports these days. The shopping uniform du jour appears to be tight pants, almost like riding pants, and high ponytails. Even women who appear to be in their fifties and sixties dress like this, chattering away on their cell phones in Spanish and, occasionally, Portuguese or English. The men have their hair slicked back like the evil men in Lifetime movies, most have puffy double chins, wear gaudy rings. I don't trust them. Their eyebrows are raised sardonically, like they don't approve of something, or like they want everyone to know they are rich. Miami men.

"Where to?" asks Mom, catching up to us at the railing. I look at her and see that she's sucking in her tummy. She does that in places like this. Age does nothing to cure vanity.

"I don't care," I say. I mean it. No matter what I get, it is bound to look bad on me.

"Neiman Marcus?" asks Mom.

"No," says Geneva. "Anthropologie. Milan's an Anthropologie girl."

So there they go, fighting about where to buy me clothes. It makes me think of the first time they tried to make me over, in junior high.

"Fine," says Mom, finally. "Anthropologie."

I follow them as they prance along, and I wonder what in the world can help me be somehow in the same room with Ricky's model wife. Nothing. But I guess it would be okay to look better than *this*. I am actually starting to get a little excited about it.

"Come on," says Mom. She grabs my hand and pulls me along with a grin. "Loosen up. This is going to be fun."

I'm trying to think "fun," but as soon as we walk into the store, I'm, like, uh, no. It's weird. First of all, it's not even like a clothing store. It's like a hardware and rug shop, with clothes thrown on tables with buckets and hoes. The shoes are displayed in suitcases on the floor. It is a store that tries too hard. And everything looks old and musty, only it is supposed to be new and trendy. Big poofy skirts, little embroidered sweaters. Poodle clothes. Geneva thinks I'm an "Anthropolgie girl"? Isn't that what she said? She's trying to insult me, is that it?

"*Pero*, browse, *ya*," says Mom.

"I don't know." I'm standing in the doorway like the biggest geek in high school at a dance.

"Come on." Mom rolls her eyes. "Just look *around*. It won't kill you to look."

I walk a little farther into the store and lift the price tag to a shirt. Ninety-eight dollars? For a shirt? Is this a joke? "I can't afford this," I say.

"You haven't paid rent in your entire life," Mom reminds me. "Where does your money go?"

"Savings."

"How much do you have saved up?"

None of her business. But it's close to twenty thousand dollars. I shrug. Mom shakes her head and says, "You have money. So spend a little."

Geneva dances over to us, grooving on the music that blares everywhere. "Come with me. Let's make this fast, and easy. I'm a shopping whiz. I should be a personal shopper."

I follow. She plucks things for me. I look at them and frown. She picks a few puffy knee-length skirts. There is no way in hell those things are going to look good on me.

"I'm not auditioning for *Grease*," I tell her. "I like them longer than that."

"You think I don't know that? You like to dress like a nun. No, I take that back. You dress like a *priest*. That's about to end."

"I look better in longer skirts. My legs."

"This isn't *Little House on the Prairie*, Milan. It's Ricky Biscayne."

"I have big ankles."

"Your ankles are *fine*," said Geneva. "*God*, why are you so insecure?"

Maybe because you used to call me a fat pig, I think. Maybe it's because every man I ever really liked left me for *you*. I shrug. She drags me to a dressing-room area with lots of doors, in a U shape around the room, with big velvet chairs for everyone to lounge about as I stuff myself into these clown clothes. How nice for them.

A salesgirl takes the clothes, opens a door, and ushers me in. I shut the door behind me and take a deep breath. I'm such a sucker. If I knew what to wear, I'd pick something for myself, but I don't know what works.

I take off the linen Dress Barn dress. It's sweaty on the back and in the part where my crotch was, in the car. I avoid looking at myself in the worn-out bra and granny panties with the rip at the waistband. To my horror, the door to the room opens at that moment, and Geneva stands there, staring.

"I thought so," she says, looking me up and down.

"What?" I slam the door.

"Next stop? Lingerie shop," calls Geneva. Bitch.

I lock the door. I put on the stupid clothes.

Only they're not stupid.

Wait a minute. I'm looking at myself in the mirror, and you know what? The fullish black knee-length skirt actually looks good. My ankles aren't bad. It's all very flattering. I turn around and around. Weird. How is that *me*? The shirt, too. I would never pick a shirt like this. It's sleeveless, for crying out loud, and puffy in the front, and low cut. I don't *do* sleeveless. Or poofy. Or low. But the shirt looks good. The bright colors and patterns balance the basic black of the skirt and my body seems to instantly come into better balance with itself. The puffiness gives the illusion of a bigger bustline.

The doorknob rattles.

"How's it going in there?" calls Geneva.

I open the door. Step out, blushing a little. I'm not half bad. I'm really not.

"Wow!" they cry. They are so happy. Why couldn't they be this happy when I read a book I loved? Or did anything other than look better?

"You've got the job," says Geneva. She looks as surprised as I've ever seen her. "I mean, you actually look like a celebrity publicist."

Yeah, I think. I *do*.

tuesday, april 2

I'm at my desk, windows open, and a cool breeze blows in off the trees. I love my office. It's actually the master bedroom of a two-bedroom apartment in a two-story deco building on Meridian, between Seventh and Eighth. It's a quiet part of SoBe, and I can hear birds. I used to live in this apartment, with its wooden floors and vintage appliances, on the quiet tree-lined street, before I saved enough from my party business to buy the condo in the Portofino Towers. I keep the apartment on Meridian as an office. I like the neighbors and the peacefulness of the location. I've got the place furnished with some sleek modern pieces and a collection of colorful deco ones. I have a Caribbean-painting collection on display. I love this place. Some nights, I still sleep here. It's small, homey, comfortable. This is where I started my career. I feel attached to it. In the front office, formerly the living room, my assistant is busy pricing drinkware and bathroom fixtures. In the back bedroom, my party planners work on another rap extravaganza. My second assistant is off today. I'm going to need a third assistant soon. I can't do everything myself, even though I'm a control freak and, honestly, I'd like to.

I sip Fiji bottled water—the only kind I'll drink anymore—and listen to the music. I've got CDs in a stack on the desk, and I'm listening to them all. They've been sent here by some of the top DJs in town—and in New York and L.A., actually—who got my letter requesting a demo based on the philosophy of Club G. There are some keepers here. And some losers. Also in a stack are the interior-design portfolios. I have to pick one of them, too. I've signed the lease on the building on Washington, and I am giddy. The way some women describe feeling about having a baby? This is how I feel about Club G. I am nesting, planning, getting ready. And you know what's helped enormously? Milan. Yeah. My sister. She hasn't had her interview with Ricky yet, but to get a leg up on it she sent out a press release on Ricky Biscayne's newest venture, Club G, and literally *hundreds* of media outlets picked it up. At that point, banks started calling me. Everything is falling into place, just like it is supposed to.

Belle sleeps in her bed under my potted palm, and kicks her feet as she dreams. As I listen to the reggaeton mix, I handwrite a list, on a yellow legal pad, of the services Club G will offer, how ours will differ from similar services at other clubs in town, and how I will implement the services. I write "Uniforms" on the yellow pad. *Custom-made harem and genie outfits, in lush reds, yellows, pinks, and purples.* I think about it for a while. The club will have male and female drink servers who not only work behind the bar but also circulate around the club. There should be three women for every male employee, for the simple fact that men and woman are equally conditioned to appreciate beautiful women, and men tend to be intimidated by attractive men.

The male servers should be shirtless, I decide, with golden armbands and short, intricately embroidered silver pants. The female servers should be of a uniform size, or should wear sizes two to eight, no bigger than that, both because it isn't attractive to have women larger than that wandering the club in revealing outfits, and because I don't want to have to spend more money on uniforms than I have to. If I order them in only three or four sizes, that solves the problem. I make a rough sketch of the ideal costume for a female server. Low-rise transparent harem pants, with jeweled thong underwear. Flat shoes that curl up at the toes. A bikini-type top, with a small, short, see-through jacket type thing over that. The servers should have long hair in high ponytails, and veils over their faces. This last part will be the most controversial, given the state of the Muslim world, and U.S. relations with the Middle East. But I plan to emphasize the Moroccan influence on Spain and the nations of the Spanish diaspora, most recently in the rhythms of reggaeton and Latin hip-hop, which draw heavily on Arabian popular music. Besides, few things are sexier than women with veils and beautiful eyes. They won't be the standard veils. They'll be see-through. The entire vibe of Club G will be sexy, haremlike, and deliciously immoral.

I search through my computer address book for the phone numbers of some local clothing designers I know. I call a few and describe the costumes, to see if they are something they'd like to try. They are all interested. They've all heard of the club because of Ricky's involvement. News travels fast in Miami. I ask each of the designers to come up with prototypes based on my descriptions. The winner gets the contract. And free publicity. They all agree to do it on spec.

I move on to the next item. Services. I want the usual assortment of services offered at upscale local clubs, including cleverly titled packages for purchase. Such as? I chew the end of my pen and think. I pull up Explorer and google Genghis Khan, scanning the information for key words. One sticks out. *Nokhor.* A Mongol word for "comrade," it sounds very much like "knock whore." I like it. Club G will offer a Nokhor package for women who want to go home with a guy they met at the club, but still remain safe. It will include, and I write this all down, condoms, edible body gel, various aphrodisiacs (from green M&Ms to vanilla and cloves), a disposable camera, and pepper spray and emergency numbers in case things don't go according to plan. How would they be packaged? I think about it. How about gilded plastic genie bottles with phallic-looking spouts? That's it! With red rope and tassels around them. Bingo.

"Brilliant," I whisper to myself, writing it all down. I have goose bumps. I get them when I'm on to something good. "This is going to be *so* good."

I hear a knock on the office door. I look up to see my fuck buddy Ignacio stick his head in. All my friends have fuck buddies. It just so happens that mine is really smart, with two psychology degrees, and I may be starting to fall in love with him. I made wrong assumptions about him when I first starting having sex with him, probably because he's really dark black and I'm an idiot. I assumed things like that he was just a fitness instructor. In truth, he's a famous ballet dancer from Cuba who defected a few years ago and brought his whole family here. My family would disown me if they knew I was dating a black man, even though we have plenty of features and history in our family to indicate that we are partially black ourselves. Welcome to hypocrisy, Cuban-style.

"Hi," I say. It's almost twelve thirty. I agreed to go to his one o'clock Zumba class today, but I lost track of time. That happens when I'm having a good time.

"Ready?" he asks. He smiles at me like he loves me. I melt. I stash the pen in the holder, grab my gym bag, and stand.

"Yup. Let's go, baby."

Station 42, in Pinecrest Bay, is a peach-colored Mediterranean-style building that looks like a really big house with a really big garage for the truck and the ambulance. It is a house, more than anything else, and the house where I spend forty-eight hours a week, nonstop, in the company of men. Of the twelve-man crew, I am the only female, which I guess means it's really an eleven-man crew. I walk in the front door and check in with the off-going lieutenant. He fills me in on what's happened in the last shift, which is basically nothing. I thank him with a "sir" at the end, and head to the living room.

Like any house, we have a living room, which we call the TV room. The television is usually tuned to news or ESPN, which is fine with me because I'm not what you'd call a TV watcher. A couple of the guys are here already, all of us wearing the dark blue pants and T-shirts that are our uniforms. We have a kitchen, where the men and I cook the meals we share together, and it looks out over the TV room. I greet the guys with a hello.

"Hey, Irene," one says. "What's shaking, beautiful?"

They smile. I smile back and act like it doesn't bother me. I know they're only trying to be nice.

"What's for breakfast?" I ask. "Which one of you ladies is cooking? Scrambled, not fried, for me, girls."

"I'll scramble ya," one jokes.

"I'm gonna set up camp," I say, heading to the bunk room. "Be back in a minute, ladies, and you better have my toast buttered."

I walk like a man, with no shake or jiggle, because I don't want their eyes on me. I also don't want to reveal to them any of the anger I feel. At first, I tried to avoid cooking altogether because I didn't want them to think I was some kind of girlie girl they could push around. I talked to my cop lover, Jim, about the way the guys treat me here, and he seemed to think that if they were talking sex with me there must be something I was doing to provoke it. That's what he said. I have decided it's time to stop returning Jim's calls. I don't need the stress of a born-again boyfriend who thinks I'm asking for it. If God, as he would say, wants me to have a boyfriend, he'll send me someone better than Jim. I have faith.

I enter the rear bunk room. We have two bunk rooms at this station, and two smaller private bedrooms for the captain and lieutenant. The bunk rooms are large and sparse, with white tile floors and lockers set up to section off the room into smaller compartments. Each compartment has a twin bed with a plain striped mattress—no box spring—and a little TV set, and, really, not much else. No posters, nothing that might offend or distract anyone. It's like a prison in design and function, mostly because our goal here is *not* to have a good time. Our goal here is to subsist, and to exist with the sole purpose of responding to a fire or other emergency. They don't design firehouses to be too comfortable.

I put my overnight duffel bag on the thin striped mattress and prepare to unpack it into my metal locker. I see that my locker is open a little, and inside is a new "gift." Not imaginative. Whoever does this has done it before. This time, it's a stack of porn mags, with a photo of my face taped over the women in the pictures. A scrawled note, I'm pretty sure in L'Roy's hand, says, "Youd look good like this." No apostrophe. No one ever accused L'Roy of being *educated*. At thirty-five, he's the world's oldest frat boy, minus, you know, the college part. He's a good old boy from Daytona Beach, who looked like Burt Reynolds in his younger years, a mistake of genetics that led him to believe he is invincible and entitled to treat women however he likes. And how does he like to treat us? Let's just say his favorite dining establishment is Hooters. He's been married and divorced four times. He asked me out once, and after I turned him down he began his campaign to win my affections, with gifts like this. I think of him as a Neanderthal. I honestly don't think he realizes what he's doing is wrong. He thinks it's going to make me like him.

I sigh and dump the mags into my bag. I'll store them in the bin in my garage at home, where I've stored all of these things. Who knows? Someday I might have a use for them. A legal use.

I return to the TV room and lean against the wall. Most of us are here, now, and the guys from the last shift are slowly leaving the building.

"Hey, man, where are my eggs?" I call, bravely and with the best "one of the guys" grin I can muster. "Ernest? Billy? Who's going to cook for me today?"

A young recruit named Kevin peeks up from the refrigerator. "I'll make your eggs, Mr. Irene," he says.

"Don't forget the toast, sister," I say.

As Kevin mans the breakfast, the rest of us line up for roll call in the office. I immediately notice there's a new guy. A *really* good-looking new guy. A really young, good-looking new guy. Most fire-fighter men are fit and attractive because of the job requirements of physical strength, but this guy has the face and the sparkling eyes to go with his excellent physique. Yowza. He's probably about twenty-seven. Most of the guys here are in their thirties, for whatever reason. The new guy is clean-shaven, with a distinct resemblance to The Rock. And The Rock is basically my ideal man. I have a major *thing* for The Rock. I mean, a *thing* thing. I like strong men. The new guy catches me looking at him, and I look away, embarrassed.

Captain Sullivan reads the roll. He calls my name last, for some reason.

"Gallagher!"

"Here, sir."

L'Roy makes kissy noises. His pals laugh. I ignore him. It's best to do that.

"Now," says Captain Sullivan, ignoring the boys, "I'd like to introduce you all to the newest member of our crew. This is Nestor Perez. He comes to us all the way from New York City."

The beautiful young man steps forward, smiles with a sweetness that catches me off guard. I have never seen a uniform fit a man quite that well, tight across the back and form-fitting enough in front to reveal a respectable, if not remarkable, package. "Make him feel welcome."

He dismisses us.

Perez, the new guy, falls into line at the rig check, and tries to seem as if he's always been here. Some of the guys shake hands with him. When Kevin passes around the coffee can to collect money for the day's groceries, however, Nestor Perez blushes and says he has forgotten to bring cash. It's just the advantage L'Roy and his insecure cronies are waiting for.

"What's a matter, Nest-boy? You don't eat?" L'Roy says. He seems to think it's his job to haze everyone. I do believe L'Roy would paddle us all if we let him.

"I eat," says Perez, wide-eyed at their hostility.

"Yeah, but do you eat *pussy?*" asks L'Roy. He grins at me. I shrug it off. "Some people around here like that, ain't that right, Irenie?"

"Yeah," I say. "L'Roy here loves to eat Kevin," I say. The men howl, but Nestor Perez looks very uncomfortable. It hits me that to normal people from the real world, this kind of locker-room humor might be pretty offensive. But hasn't he been in a firehouse before? He must be *real* new to this line of work.

Nestor Perez stares at L'Roy and his wide eyes narrow slowly. "I'm *sorry?*" he says, his forehead knotting with concern and disgust. Just like The Rock in that movie where he's a sheriff who takes on the whole town. I feel my womb tighten. He steps closer to L'Roy and says, "What did you just ask me?"

The guys chuckle, and I feel my breath catch in my throat. I open the door to the engine and check the oxygen tanks. Full.

"I asked you if you ate pussy," says L'Roy, coming to stand a little too close to Perez. This is so male, and so stupid, I almost can't even believe what I'm seeing. Perez straightens himself to his full height, a good two inches taller than L'Roy, somewhere above six feet. Yikes. He's pretty, so pretty. He puffs out his chest, turns his head fearlessly to one side, frowns, then speaks.

"I don't know you well enough to answer a question like that," says Perez. "And standing here next to you, I don't know if I like you enough to *ever* get to know you that well. But I *do* know there's a *lady* here, and what you said is completely out of line."

I blush at the mention of me. "I'm not a lady," I say.

Dennis checks the hoses and chuckles. "Irenie's one of the guys."

"What, you're a fag?" L'Roy asks Nestor Perez. I know L'Roy is just joking around, or at least I think he is, but it seems like Nestor doesn't share his sense of humor.

Nestor Perez shrugs. "I don't know you well enough to tell you that, *either*," he says suggestively, looking at every centimeter of L'Roy's face with deliberation and calm.

He's gay? No way! I can't believe it. Our first gay firefighter. And I thought *my* struggle was tough. This guy's in for it.

"But if I *were* a homosexual," says Perez, inching even closer to L'Roy, intentionally staring at L'Roy's lips and licking his own, "you wouldn't have a *problem* with it, would you?" It is the first time I've seen L'Roy dumbfounded. I don't think any of the men on the team are gay. "Teamwork is the essence of firefighting," says Perez. "I mean, that's what I read in my training manual. Teamwork, and respect. And I'd hate to think you discriminated against anyone, especially since it's your job to save all types of people."

"People have to *earn* my respect," stutters L'Roy.

"Let me tell you something," says Perez, easing even a little closer to L'Roy, and lowering his voice. He raises a brow confidently, licks his luscious lips again, and says, softly, "L'Roy. That's your name, right?" L'Roy says nothing. "Well, let me tell you something, *L'Roy*. Even if I *were* gay? I just think you'd like to know, you're not my type."

Perez smiles at me. I smile back. *Is* he gay?

At that moment, the tones begin to chime in the station, indicating a fire. The dispatcher calls out on the radio system in the office, for us and for several other stations. This means it is not only a serious fire but a *big* one. In that moment, each of us forgets our prejudices and differences, and we spring into action.

We hurry to the hooks on the wall and step into our bunker pants, our jackets, our big yellow boots. We move quickly and smoothly. Nestor follows the rest of us, and seems calm in spite of how green he seemed earlier. We slip on our oxygen tanks and place the helmets on our heads. And then we take our places on the trucks. I'm hanging on the side, near the cross hose. Nestor is directly opposite.

As the engine pulls onto the street, I can hear dispatch calling for reinforcements on the scanner in the cab. The siren engages, and we're off. The rush of adrenaline is like nothing else in the world. I don't want to admit it, but I'm excited—and in the end, that's what it's all about here, with these guys.

We might be different in background, gender, and other things, but deep down inside, each and every one of us is attracted to danger, and every person on this truck has a masochistic love of a good, hot fire.

My name is Jasminka, and I'm still starving.

"You need to eat more, Jasminka." The doctor, young black man with double chin, looks at me over top of his glasses, right into my eyes. "This is serious. If you don't start eating more, there's a very good chance you'll have a low-birth-weight baby, or, worst-case scenario, lose this pregnancy."

I sit up straighter, trying to reclaim some dignity. I hear paper of exam table crinkle beneath me. I must have some substance, to make it crinkle like that. I'm not completely invisible. "Okay," I say. "I eat more food, yes?"

"That depends on what you're eating." He sighs and sits on chair against wall, takes off glasses, rubs bridge of nose. I exhaust him. Why? I'm just a woman. "There are support groups for anorexia," he says. "I suggest you start going to one."

I shrug. "I am not anorexic."

He laughs. Are doctors supposed to do that? "Really. Hmm. Then bulimic? Listen, when a woman is five-foot-eleven and weighs a hundred fifteen pounds, and she's pregnant, there's a good chance she's got an eating disorder. There's no other reason to explain why you are dangerously underweight, unless you were ill, which you're not. It's a serious problem in your profession, and if you are serious about the health of your baby and your own health, you should take it seriously."

He's right. I know he's right. I just don't want to admit it. "Maybe," I say. "I eat more food. I eat, I eat."

He hands me some pamphlets on eating disorders and another on nutrition. He tells me to up my intake to at least 2000 calories a day. "While most women shouldn't gain more than 25 pounds during a pregnancy, you could easily gain 40 or more and be healthy," he says. "In fact, you could gain 40 pounds *without* being pregnant and still be healthy. Healthier than you are now."

I leave clinic and drive home in gold Cadillac Escalade Ricky bought for me. I'm pregnant. I'm pregnant! About ten weeks along. I'm going to have a baby. I can't believe it. I stop at McDonald's drive-through and order cheeseburger and french fries. I eat them as I drive, savoring every salty, greasy bite. I feel guilty when I'm done, like I have to find toilet to throw up in. I fight urge, and try to find something else to occupy me.

I head to the studio behind house, to see what Ricky is up to. I sit on tacky red and white Spanish-style sofa in little living-room area and listen to the sounds of a ballad coming out of the recording booth. It's a pretty song. Ricky's songs are all beautiful. I love his music. But the room? It makes me want to throw up again. The colors are bad. Red, white, yellow, and blue. Ricky's talented and attractive, but he does not know about decorating. I want to remodel entire house. It looks like it was decorated by drunk with squeeze bottle of ketchup. It is a very nice house, but falling apart. He told me he paid two million dollars in cash for the house. I wonder why he couldn't spend a little more to have it kept up better, or professionally decorated. He actually has pool table and jukebox in the living room. That isn't the kind of house I want to raise child in. This is—how do you say it? A bachelor's pad. It's like Ricky has not accepted that he is married man, or that I might have any right to change things here. Ricky still calls this Cleveland Road home "his" house, as if I were visitor. I'll have to talk to him about that.

I can see Matthew Baker through window of the mixing booth. There's something very comforting about his face. All of him, actually. He's very balanced. Spiritually. I like him. He also seems to be very talented, and devoted to Ricky. People can't help but be devoted to Ricky. He's got something needy about him that you want to rescue. Matthew looks up from turning knobs and buttons and smiles at me. He has humor in eyes, eyes that could melt woman's heart. He deserves good woman. Better than that eerie-looking Icelandic girl who stops by here sometimes when she is on shore from job on cruise ship. I don't like her. Eydis, that's her name. I don't know Matthew well enough to talk to him about it. But I'm good judge of character, and there is something compulsive about that girl.

Matthew opens door. "Hey, Jasminka, what's up?"

"Hello, Matthew," I say. "Where is my husband?"

"Right here, baby," says Ricky, peeking out from behind Matthew. He bounds over to me like happy dog. Kisses me. Kneels at my side and holds my hand. "What did the doctor say?" I tell him about the eating. He frowns. "What does that doctor know?" he asks. "You're healthy."

"He want that I am to eat more food."

"Then you have to eat more," he says. "I'll get my moms to come cook for you."

I wrap my arms around him and kiss his neck. I have nausea from the pregnancy, and the only thing in the world that seems to make it go away is smell of his neck. I love it. It reminds me of why I am this sick, because I have Ricky's baby inside of me, growing. He starts to rub my back, almost as if he knows it's sore. He can read my body sometimes, as if we were same person. It's amazing.

"More low please," I say.

"How's that?" He leans forward and kisses my collarbone, his hands working behind me. His arms wrap around the back of my neck.

"I love you," I say.

"I love you, too, baby," he says.

"Ah-hem," says Matthew.

Ricky kisses me on lips, squeezes me, and smiles at his production partner. "Sorry, dude," he says. "When you have a wife this beautiful, and she's carrying your baby, you know."

"You're—*what?*" Matthew looks at me and smiles. "Really? You're pregnant?"

I nod.

"That's fucking great!" he shouts. He runs over to shake Ricky's hand and give me pat on back. "Awesome. A little Ricky running around. Damn!"

One thing I've noticed about musicians is that they use foul language all the time, without realizing it. It's like their own little language. Ricky stands up and reaches for his Bambú rolling papers and harsh, raw tobacco from Thailand on coffee table. He's been smoking a lot lately. I have quit, and asked him to. He says he can't.

"Ricky, no smoke," I say. "The baby."

He puts the materials down and nods. "Right. Sorry. I forgot."

"Jaz, you have to hear this song we're doing," says Matthew.

"Crank it up," says Ricky to Matthew, who dashes to control booth and presses buttons until song comes on. He comes back, and he and

Ricky sit on the sofa with me. The song is lovely, a delicate flamenco-flavored piece, with lyrics about the pain of losing a woman to another man. Ricky and Matthew have wonderful musician's masculinity to them, the way they focus and lean forward, grinning at each other over things regular people do not hear or understand. I envy Ricky his brotherhood of friendship with Matthew. I wonder if I will ever meet woman I feel that safe with. With models, there's always competition that gets in way of true friendship.

I wish for a moment that God would send me a friend. A regular woman.

Almost as if on cue, the doorbell rings. I believe in signs. It is fancy doorbell, a doorbell like a melody, with a million notes that ring and keep ringing. I go in the main house. Cynthia starts to wipe her hands, as if she will answer the door. I am tired of feeling like this isn't my house. Like the hired help have more rights to it than I do.

"I answer it," I say. I walk to the house and go inside. Mishko limps in from the living room and wags her tail at me. Such good dog. My family. I love her. I scratch behind her ears. "Come with me, girl," I say in Serbian.

I walk down long hallway to the entry, smooth my hair back, more out of habit than anything, and open door. Standing on the front step is a plump young woman who looks so much like my mother I gasp. The universe works in such strange ways.

"I'm sorry," says woman. "Did I scare you?"

"No, no, not scare me," I say. She has shoulder-length blond hair, quite light, with highlights, cut in fashionable style. She has under-stated makeup in peaches and golds. And she wears a pretty, black ruffled skirt with red heels and red and purple sleeveless top. Over her shoulder is adorable Vuitton handbag, the clear one. I have one just like it.

"It's the clothes," says the woman, looking down at herself as if she wore something ugly. "They scared you."

"The clothes?"

"My sister made me get them." She tugs awkwardly at the hem of skirt. It reminds me of traditional Serbian skirt, sort of folksy in thick cotton, but modern, too. "I'm sorry. I'm Milan Gotay." The woman blushes and holds out her hand. Milan? Wasn't the song Ricky just played me about that city? Another sign. God has sent me a friend. I know it. "I'm here to interview with Mr. Biscayne for the publicist job."

Publicist job? Oh, right! Ricky has opening. His other guy is in jail. That's how it is with the people he usually picks. "Welcome," I say. I take her hand and shake. Her handshake, like her body, is solid but not soft. I find her stunning, and substantial, and am envious and drawn to her at the same time. I admire women with flat bellies and large rear ends. "I am Jasminka, I am wife of Ricky."

"I know who you are! You're so beautiful," gushes Milan, in a baby-like voice.

"I feel not so beautiful today. I am little bit sick." I want to tell her I'm pregnant, but Ricky and his manager want me to wait as long as I can. "Please come in."

The woman's face softens with awe as she enters house. At one time I might have thought it was luxurious home, but I've seen better homes since modeling, and I don't think Ricky takes very good care of house.

"You have a beautiful home," she says in that breathy, childlike voice. "Wow."

"I take you now to Ricky," I say. I pray he hires her. "Follow me."

The fire has engulfed half of a two-story stucco apartment complex in a poor part of Cutler Ridge, and I can feel the heat of it through my suit. It's like I don't even have the helmet or the oxygen tank over my face. I feel the heat as if someone were holding a torch directly to my skin.

I jump from the truck and grab an ax. It is one of the golden rules of firefighting that you always carry a tool, whether you think you will need it or not. I turn on my big red flashlight and prepare to meet this fire head-on. I'm not really aware of who each of the firefighters around me are anymore, as individuals. As a unit, we move toward the building. Captain Sullivan tells us that our station has been assigned search and rescue, meaning that there are still people in there. People who could be alive, or who could be dead. It is our job to get them out.

We rush to the burning building, altruistic, ready to give our lives. I never feel more alive than I do in these moments, tempting fate, saying to fire and other elements and forces that try to destroy me that they won't be able to win—not on my watch. I'm going to win this. Heat blasts me like a wind from hell, and I charge through a doorway and into smoke and near-total darkness. I breathe the oxygen, but the taste and smell of smoke is everywhere around me anyway. I hear crying and screams, and I follow the sounds through a smoke-filled hallway. I hear the creaking, unmistakable groan of wood in flames. I run, the weight of the tank and the uniform cramping my back.

I find a closed door at the end of the hallway. The cries come from the other side of it. I kick it open, and enter. Inside are three children, two of them standing shivering in the corner, and the other, a baby, lying limp on the floor. I grab the baby, and feel another firefighter at my back. I can't tell who it is. He rushes in and grabs both girls. "Let's go, book it," he says. I don't recognize the voice. We run back through the flames and smoke with the children, and back into the light just as a timber falls across the doorway, missing me and the limp baby in my arms by centimeters. I rush the child, a girl in a diaper, with pink barettes in her hair, to the nearest paramedics. They take her and begin to do their job of assessing life or death, and the horror of bringing her back to the living. The other firefighter, who I now believe is Nestor Perez, hands the two older children to the paramedics. They scream that their cousin is still inside, in her room, and their mother.

I run back to the building and try to find my way back down the hallway. There are two other firefighters here, and I recognize them as Dennis and L'Roy by the way they move and by their voices. They have the child. Dennis rushes past us with the boy, and shouts something about a man who refuses to leave the room. Nestor and I rush to the room with L'Roy and find a very drunk or drugged man who appears to be suicidal. He fights us when we try to get him out of the room. We gang up on him and lift him from the bed. Nestor hoists the man over his shoulder and hurries out of the room. L'Roy and I intend to follow, but as soon as we get to the doorway, it collapses and flames crash down from above, all around us. L'Roy is knocked to the floor by the crashing wood. I hear him cry out in pain. I look around the room for a way out, but there is none. Everything burns. The only way out will be through the window area, but it's blocked by debris and flames.

"Hang on, L'Roy," I call to him. "Can you move?"

"No! My fucking leg! Oh God it hurts!"

I act so fast I feel as if I watch myself from somewhere far, far away. I jump into the flames and begin to hack away at the wall around the window with my ax, praying I won't cause the building to cave in. I swing the ax like crazy, again and again, until a hole comes, and then, mercifully, a piece of the wall gives way and an opening big enough for the two of us appears. In all the swinging, my mask has come loose, and I feel the smoke choke me. I adjust the mask, but it won't go on right. I should leave now, but I can't let L'Roy stay here alone. I can't do it.

"Come on," I cry, rushing back to L'Roy. It is utterly counterintuitive to do this. I don't like this man. He doesn't respect me. I'm risking my life to save him, and I can't think of a good reason why other than the fact that he is a human being. I feel like I am on fire. I burn, every inch of me, and I almost can't stand the feel of it, needles on my skin, knives in my lungs. I am not going to let this man die here, I think. "Hold on to me!" L'Roy reaches up and wraps his hands around my neck, and I drag him toward the light. Through the flames, across the debris, and, God knows how, I get us out. I drag him as far as I can from the building and I drop to the grass with him and roll us to put the flames out. L'Roy screams in pain, but I don't care. He'll die if I don't get the flames off of us. And then we lie there, and the others come, and there is screaming and I'm dizzy. Someone picks me up off the ground like I weigh nothing. I look through his mask and see Nestor Perez, his eyes watering from smoke, or something else.

"Thank God," he says, his voice choked with emotion. "Thank God you're alive."

At that moment, a black Lincoln Town Car with dark windows eases past the guarded gate of Jill's ten-million-dollar Bal Bay Drive waterfront estate, onto the pink tile circular driveway, and stops at the rounded white turret that serves as the formal entry to the courtyard leading to the front door. For a woman who has made her fortune on songs like "I'm Still Ur Ghetto Girl" and her supposed "street cred," Jill is oddly enamored of formalities, the tackier and more garish the better.

Jack Ingroff, jet-lagged and with a painful hamstring pulled during a stupidly acrobatic bit of purchased sex with an absolutely gorgeous Japanese transvestite, opens the back door of the car. He does this even though the driver, a grossly underemployed physics professor from Azerbaijan, hurries as fast as his hefty frame will take him, from the driver's side around the back of the car, in a nervous effort to pamper Jack the way his fiancée demands she herself be pampered. But Jack, a socialist in theory if not in practice, and a man from modest means, doesn't play that way. He opens his own doors, pays his own bills, and, well, other than the whole paid-sex thing, considers himself a pretty damn good and normal guy.

"Dude, don't worry about it. Seriously, Yaver, don't," says Jack as he stands in his rumpled jeans and T-shirt, squinting in the bright South Florida sunshine. He notes the surprise on Yaver's face at the mention of the man's name, and figures it is because Jill has never bothered to learn the names of those who work for her. Or if she *has* learned Yaver's name, likely she has never bothered to use it. Jack, who was raised by a single mother who was a poet and college teacher in a small Massachusetts town, is continually surprised—and sometimes intrigued—by his future wife's natural callousness. As a sensitive writer type and a formerly scrawny asthmatic kid who now yearns to be seen in real life as the tough guy he once played (quite badly, in his opinion) in a blockbuster movie, Jack hopes some of Jill's cruelty will eventually rub off on him. If it does, he thinks, Hollywood and all the crap that goes along with it will be a hell of a lot easier to manage. If it does, he might even be able to stomach shopping in a regular store again, a grocery store. As it is, the mere sight of the checkout counter and all the gossipy rags that go along with it sends him into a panic. It is a good thing that Jill has personal shoppers to keep her house stocked with food and supplies, because otherwise Jack thinks he might never eat anywhere but restaurants. The thought of hiring someone to grocery shop for him makes him about as sick as the thought of waiting for a fat old Azerbaijani physicist to open his car door.

Yaver rushes around to the trunk and opens it, eager to open *something*. Jack notices the older man has a limp, and immediately realizes they both have limps at the moment. There is something sort of pathetic and almost noir about this, so Jack laughs. He has a bad habit of laughing at jokes he's told himself in his head, giving him the appearance in some circles of a crazy man. In other circles, he is considered simply a dick.

"I am sorry, sir," says Yaver, yanking one of Jack's two Louis Vuitton suitcases out of the trunk. "Did I do something to upset you?"

Jack places a comforting hand on Yaver's shoulder and shakes his head, smiling. "No, no, my man. Not at all. You've been great. I'll get the bags, though."

Yaver looks offended and confused by this last bit. "You are sure?" he asks.

"They're *my* fucking bags," says Jack, with a surprising burst of hostility aimed entirely at himself. He feels guilty and fraudulent for making upward of twelve million dollars a movie, when he is the first to recognize his own mediocrity. Jack is always looking for ways to blow his money, because the very feel of it in his bank accounts makes him loathe himself.

Yaver knows none of the reasons for Jack's outburst, and figures Jack is on drugs and possibly dangerous, neither of which is true but both of which are widely reported in supermarket tabloids. "I'm sorry, sir."

"No," says Jack, running a frustrated hand through his disheveled hair. "I didn't mean it like that. I meant I'm a schmuck for being in a position to have someone like you, a good guy like you, an educated man, carry my idiot fucking designer bags for me."

"Okay." Yaver maintains a distance from Jack.

Jack laughs again, with the wry half-grin that has caused millions of women the world over, even some in Azerbaijan, to fall in love with him. "I might look like a pansy-ass wimp, but I can still schlep my own crap. That's what I'm trying to say, Yaver."

Yaver bows slightly, making Jack feel horrendous. Yaver would like to look as "wimpy" as Jack and doesn't know what the beautiful young man has to complain about.

"Look, man," Jack says. "You don't have to do all that." Jack pantomimes Yaver's bowing and scraping. He lowers his voice and realizes that the five bottles of Sapporo he had on the flight haven't yet worn off completely. "You really don't. I know you're a physicist. You're ten times smarter than me or Jill. I recognize that and I'm sure you recognize that."

Yaver blushes intensely and stares at the ground.

"You do recognize that, don't you? Don't shit me. You recognize that you work for a couple of fucking morons, right?" Jack smiles. Yaver says nothing. "So," Jack continues. "We're cool, okay?"

Yaver nods without looking up. Jack sets the suitcases down and approaches the older man. Jack places a hand beneath Yaver's chin and lifts his face, their eyes finally connecting.

"You know I'm right about you," says Jack with the grin. He points at Yaver's chest. Yaver blinks a few times, and smiles.

"Yes," he says softly. "I believe so." Until now, only Yaver's wife has known the utter disdain with which he regards Jill Sanchez and her associates.

"Good man," says Jack, and smacks the man's chest. "Now if you'll excuse me, I have to hobble up the steps of this gaudy, idiotic cupcake of a mansion now."

"Yes, sir," says Yaver. He chokes back a laugh.

"It *is* gaudy, don't you think?"

Yaver examines the white Tuscan stucco of the mansion with the pink trim, the white marble columns, the cascading fountains with fat cherubs cavorting in the foamy blue spew. "I suppose it is, sir."

Jack shrugs, and lowers his voice and looks around like a conspirator. "I'm working on her, you know?"

Yaver nods solemnly and tries hard not to roll his eyes; he's seen other men work on Jill Sanchez, with the same luck as men who work on guiding Eastern Europe and Russia toward justice and honest government.

"I've got this plan," says Jack with dreamy eyes. "New Mexico. That's where I'd like to live. Somewhere close to the mountains, with big sunsets. Get us a little adobe casita, fill it up with art, raise some kids. Santa Fe. That's what I'm thinking. Like, a totally normal life, skiing, hiking. That's all I want, believe it or not."

Yaver smiles through his pity, and stops himself from bowing. "It's a good plan, sir," he lies.

"*Jack.* No more of this 'sir' shit, okay?"

"Okay."

"Okay, *Jack.*"

"Eh, okay, *Jack.*"

"We cool?"

"We are cool."

And with that, Jack turns toward Jill's house, leaves Yaver in the hot sun, and limps his way up the gaudy marble steps to the turret, dragging behind him the two stupidly self-conscious, hideously buttfucking ugly, and overpriced designer suitcases Jill bought for him.

Ricky's skeleton of a model wife opens the door to the recording studio in the backyard of Ricky Biscayne's house, and I step in. Have I mentioned I hate her? For being his, for being gorgeous, for having that exotic accent. I blink once, and there he is.

Ricky. In jeans and a simple white T-shirt, barefoot, with half a sandwich in one hand, chewing. So normal, and yet so godlike. Sigh. I start to shake. I don't mean hands, either. I mean I'm shaking, nervous, almost hyperventilating. I don't deserve to be here. Looking at him. Smelling the room, which smells like pickles and mustard and—what else?—cigarettes. Ricky doesn't smoke, does he? Maybe it's the other guy, who is turning around and staring at me with narrow eyes like he hates me. Oh my gosh. It's that little Conan O'Brien musician, the one my mom said was at the docks that day.

"You're the woman who almost drowned me," he says. "The one who called me a loser."

"I didn't push you," I tell him. "You pushed *me*." Ricky shoots him a strange look, and the redheaded guy continues to stare at me.

"Ricky, this is Milan," says the wife. "The publicist interview."

Ricky takes a few steps toward me and I almost hear violins. Oh, wait a minute. I *do* hear violins. They're listening to music, a Ricky song. Whoops! I'm standing in the recording studio of Ricky Biscayne's house, listening to a song no one else has ever heard before, and he's about to shake my hand. What would the girls of Las Ricky Chickies think of *this*? I can't wait to tell them. I should have brought my digital camera.

"Hi, Milan," he says. His voice is low and gravelly. "Geneva's told me a lot about you. Come in. Sit down. Can I get you water or something? Get comfy."

I decline the water. I feel too weird in these clothes to do anything normal like drink water. The model wife says she's going to the kitchen to eat. Good idea. She should eat for a year. The balding guitarist dude asks Ricky if it's okay if he adds some overdubs to the tracks, whatever that means. He's slightly chubby and has a hard-to-place accent. California? Because I'm a masochist about men and sex, I like the way he gives me the evil eye. Even though he is rude and almost pushed me into the water, I am telling you, if this guy wanted me, I'd do him. Maybe both Ricky and this guy, at the same time, like I've seen in photos on the Internet. Oh. My. God. That would be so awesome, a story to *not* tell my grandchildren.

Ricky introduces the guy in the cap to me as Matthew Baker, which makes me think of my grandma and how she's been spewing nonsense from the Book of Matthew lately. I think of sharing this detail, but think better of it. Rather, I shake Matthew Baker's hand. "Small world," he says, with attitude. He has pretty, expressive eyes.

I sit on the sofa and cross my legs. No need to show Ricky too much too soon, you know what I mean? No, I'm *not* joking. If he tells me I have to go down on him for the job, I will. I want to bite him, everywhere. I want to pinch him to see if he's real. He sits next to me and I smell grasslike cologne on him. I want to eat it. Him. The whole thing. Ravenous.

"Oh my God," I say. "I'm so nervous. I love you. I mean, I love your music. I'm seriously, I mean this, I am, like, your biggest, biggest, stupidest fan in the entire world. I'm, like, the secretary of Las Ricky Chickies? This Internet fan club for you? Have you heard of us?" I see the miniature Conan O'Brien roll his eyes at Ricky and I realize I've made a fool of myself. I backtrack. "I mean, I'm professional, too. I'm a good publicist. I really am. I just, oh my God. I don't know. I'm sorry." I look at my hands. "I'm acting like an idiot."

"You're cute," says Ricky, looking me up and down.

"But I'm not *actually* an idiot." I stop talking and it hits me that Ricky has just told me I'm cute. "I am?"

"Yeah, yeah," says Ricky. He's smiling and puts a hand on my knee. "Deep breath, Milan. Calm down." He looks at Matthew. "She's pretty, right?"

Matthew shrugs. "I don't think that's what you should be talking about," he says. What? *Matthew* doesn't think I'm cute? Not even after the full Geneva-inspired makeover, with highlights and a haircut and makeup lessons? I worked really hard to be cute today. Why doesn't he think I'm cute? I want them *both* to think I'm cute.

"Oh really." Ricky looks at him like these two argue a lot. "And what, exactly, do you think we should be talking about, Mr. Perfect?"

"Her résumé or something." Matthew gets up and shakes his head. "I'll be in the booth if you need me, Ricky. Milan, nice to meet you.

Glad you didn't kill me at the docks. Sorry you think I'm a loser. An apology would be nice. Don't let him do anything to you that you don't want him to do."

Ricky and I sit in silence until the door to the booth is shut.

"Don't mind him," says Ricky. "Jackass."

"Who is he?"

"My producer. He's just jealous. He's not very good with women, either. Especially cute ones like you. So. What were we talking about?"

"Uh, how you think I'm cute?" I feel like I'm watching a movie of someone else's life. This is ridiculous.

"Yeah." He scoots closer to me and lifts an eyebrow. "Like a girl next door or something." He's staring at my mouth. Like he wants to kiss me. That's weird. But not impossible. Or is it? Okay. Think, Milan. Why is he doing this? You just saw his wife. She is perfect. And you are not. You, Milan, are an average girl. But then again, this is the same guy who writes songs in praise of average girls. Maybe he actually means it?

"This is very strange," says Ricky, still close, still staring.

"What is?" Do I stink? I showered. I scrubbed. Shaved. I even bent over like a cat and shaved my *chocha*, just in case.

"I feel something about you I didn't expect to feel."

I stomp a foot just to make sure I'm not dreaming.

"Something?" I ask. "Like what kind of something?"

"Like a good energy with you." He stands up and offers me his hand. "Come here."

I take his hand and stand. This. Isn't. Happening. He pulls me down a little hallway, to a door. The hall is dark and the door is closed. He puts me in front of the door, facing it, and stands behind me, right up against my body.

"You have a beautiful body," he tells me.

I say nothing. There's a sign on the door that says OFFICE, which seems sort of redundant to me, but I am a subtle sort of girl.

"This here," says Ricky, "is your office."

"My office?" I squeak. "But you didn't ask me anything yet. I just got here."

He reaches past me and turns the knob. Pushes me into the darkened room. It's an office, with shelves and a desk, plants and a rug. It's a pretty nice office, with lots of space. The computer is really nice, a Mac with a huge screen. Framed posters of Ricky grace the walls. Ricky steps in behind me and closes the door.

"Milan," he says. I don't move. "Turn around. Look at me."

I do. He's gorgeous. I know, that's a lame description. But I don't know what else to say. I can't even breathe, much less speak. This is so wrong, a total lawsuit. If this were someone like Tío Jesús, it would be really, really wrong. But it's not. It's Ricky Biscayne. And I've made love to him thousands of times in my head. It's like he knows that, the way he's smiling at me. I feel like I know him already, like I've known him forever.

"Come here," he says.

"There?"

"Right here." I walk to him. He touches my face and says, "I don't do this. I don't usually have these strong feelings for women who work for me."

"You don't?"

"No." He looks into my eyes and I see that his are bloodshot. He must work a lot, sleep not enough. He needs me to help him. "But here's what you need to know about me. I'm very intuitive. I can feel things other people don't. I know when things are right or wrong, because I just feel it. It's almost like I'm psychic."

"Psychic?"

"Yeah. And I trust my instincts. I always do. That's how I've gotten here, where I am, that's how I've gotten to be Ricky Biscayne."

"What does this have to do with me?" I ask.

"I like you," he tells me. "I think we'll have a lot of fun working together. You like to have fun?"

What does this mean? I nod weakly. I expect he'll kiss me now, but he doesn't. He backs away with a grin, and turns on the lights, blinding me.

"Welcome to Ricky Biscayne Productions, Milan," he says. "This is your office."

What? No kiss? No sexual harassment? I don't believe it. After all that? Is this guy twisted? "You're hiring me?" I ask.

He opens the door to leave. "Yeah," he says.

"But you didn't ask me anything. You don't know anything about me."

He looks at me. "I know more than you think," he says. "And I trust your sister. You can start now. I have to get back to the studio. Let me know if you need anything, cutie."

He leaves. I stand there, humiliated for having thought he was going to seduce me. Totally, completely humiliated. I follow him down the hall. "Mr. Biscayne?" I ask. He stops in the little lounge area and we sit on the sofa again, side by side. "What do you want me to do? I mean, you want me to start, but with what, exactly?"

Ricky smiles at me again, and points to the window of the sound booth, where Matthew Baker sits at a large console, twirling buttons. "You like him?" asks Ricky.

"What?"

"Matthew. You like him?" Ricky looks at Matthew as if he dislikes him, for some reason.

"I, uh, I don't know him."

"My wife thinks women find him attractive. I think he's a troll. Whose side are you on?"

Side? I have to pick sides? Really? No way. That's not right. I want this job, though. And Ricky doesn't seem to use the regular kinds of employment tactics. "Uh, yours, I guess."

"You guess?"

"No. Yours. Absolutely."

"Matthew's a troll? Is that what you're saying?"

I nod, and hate myself for doing it. Why am I doing that? Why am I insulting some guy I don't even know? But, then again, he shrugged when Ricky asked him if I was cute, so it could be seen as revenge. Screw Matthew Baker anyway. He's rude.

"What kind of guy do you like?" he asks.

"Ones that look like you," I answer honestly. "I have pictures of you all over my room."

He turns toward me and grins. "You're shitting me."

"No, sir. I'm not."

"So maybe I should have kissed you in the office back there. I was worried you didn't want me to."

I'm speechless. Totally, completely. Words? What words? What are words? It's all I can do to actually just keep breathing and stay alive. He stands up and laughs.

"Hey, don't look so scared. You know I'm kidding, right?"

Huh? "Yeah," I say. But I don't know. I don't know anything. "Right."

"I'm just kidding!" he says, laughing loudly at my shocked expression. "You're cute. I meant that part. But, Milan, I'm a married man."

Dizzy. Breathe, Milan. I say, "I, uh, I met your wife. She's really nice."

"We're all nice. We're like a family here. And we joke around like a family. We flirt. Get used to it. Welcome to the craziest family since the Osbournes."

Ricky opens a bamboo box on the coffee table and pulls out a rough-looking little cigarette, sticks it in the corner of his mouth. No! He doesn't smoke! Does he? I never read anything about that. I have read in his interviews that Ricky Biscayne takes his health very seriously. I remember the article perfectly, how it says he has a broccoli shake with wheatgrass every morning. After I read it, I even tried blending broccoli with apple juice a couple of times, trying to be like him. It was puke-a-licious, and I lasted two days before going back to eggs and sausage.

I stare, with my mouth gaping.

"I have one now and then," says Ricky with a shrug, as if reading my mind. "But I'm trying to quit." He lights the match on the fly of his jeans, and I feel a tingle of excitement. He smiles and blows smoke in my face. So pretty. He's so pretty with his lips like that. I forget all about how much I hate cigarettes.

Ricky picks up off the coffee table a stack of photos of himself and starts sifting through them while he smokes. "What do you think of that one?" he asks. The photo is sexy, of Ricky in a wet shirt and tight jeans, leaning against a wall with a toothpick in his mouth. His abs ripple. Fuckin' A.

"I'd hang it up over my bed," I say. I realize this is a weird thing to say and clap a hand over my mouth. "Oh, God. I'm sorry."

"I like you." He winks at me. Did he actually just wink at me? Is he allowed to do that? Why am I sitting here like a little deer in the headlights of a big-ass Hummer?

"You do?" Duh. Stupid Milan.

He pushes a stray hair out of my face with his hand. "Let's see what you can do, cutie."

I gulp for breath, like the guppy I had that jumped out of the Tupperware bowl onto the kitchen floor that time when I was little and Mom told me I had to clean the fish tank. I saw it gasping, only I guess it wasn't for air. It was for water. But you know what I mean. "Okay."

He stares into my eyes. "Sometimes I think it's too bad I'm married," he says. He takes another drag of his cigarette, close enough for me to hear the embers crackling at the end, narrowing his eyes. "My manager's coming to town today to talk about strategy. We're partying at the Delano tonight. I want you to come with us."

"Me?"

Ricky takes one more long drag of his cigarette, pinching the end of it with the tips of his thumb and pointer finger, the rest of his fingers balled in a strong knot. He touches my chin with his hand and seems to size me up again. "You. I think Ron will like you. But, uh, you might want to wear all black. That's my suggestion. Actually, it's my only requirement. Oh, and your hot sister. Bring her, too."

"Sorry?" He's telling me what to wear? Hot sister? Hello? What? What is all this? Trying to seduce me, or pretending to, toying with me? None of this is allowed, is it? Why does it feel good? Why do I not mind at all?

"No offense, cutie. I have an image, and my people have to be part of that image. Most of the chicks who work here, I have a few on payroll, they wear jeans and heels and sexy tops. They look sexy. Lots of black, my favorite color. You look funky, and cute. But you don't look sexy." He licks his lips again. Comes close and actually brushes them very lightly against mine, not quite a kiss, but almost. I feel my loins catch a tight, painful bit of fire. Too. Good. To. Be. True. And he says, low, soft, and seductive, "I wonder what you'd look like sexy."

He backs up abruptly, shuffles through a few more photos, and stops on one of him in his underwear only, lounging next to a bright blue swimming pool. "How about this one?" he asks. "Good for publicity?"

I feel tears form in my eyes. I love this man. I actually do. "I can't believe I get to work with you. Thank you, Ricky."

He chuckles to himself, stabs the cigarette out on the back of one of the photos he apparently doesn't like as much, and stands up, suddenly seeming to lose interest in me.

"Must be your lucky day," he says as he walks away.

I guess so.

Ricky walks into the recording booth. He looks triumphant. Matthew looks at him and figures he got the psychotic job applicant to blow him. Matthew saw them kissing on the sofa just now. Disgusting. That's how he usually does his hiring, when the applicant is pretty and female. Fucks them, eats them, makes them blow him. He's a total fucking pig.

"She seems like a nice person," says Matthew. He feels sorry for the girl, even if she is rude, because Ricky is to rude what gold is to metal. She probably had no idea what she was getting into. Most of them are so starstruck they don't know how to say no. They want jobs, money, fame, and, yes, probably the majority of them want to fuck Ricky, too. Whatever. Matthew couldn't watch it—that's why he had to leave when Ricky got close to her on the couch like that. Knowing his wife was pregnant and everything, and he still did that? It was so weird. Ricky was a sociopath.

"You like her?" asks Ricky. "Little Milanesa?"

"I don't know her." Matthew tries to seem offended by the question, as a teaching tool. To show Ricky that you shouldn't screw around with women you don't know and just met, particularly when they are looking to you to hire them.

"You like her like that? Would you do her?"

"She's pretty," says Matthew. He shrugs. As a rule, he doesn't like to "do" women at all. He likes to make love to them, and only once he loves them, and to love a woman, you have to actually talk to her and get to know her. That's how Matthew sees it, but Ricky has never understood because Ricky is to insight what Abilene is to mountain peaks.

"Yeah, well, you can forget it," says Ricky, with an oddly triumphant look on his face.

Matthew feels a pit open in his stomach. "Why?"

"I asked her about you, man," says Ricky. "While she was going down on me."

"You're a sick fucker."

"You know me, I'm always looking out for you. Always trying to get you some."

"Yeah, thanks."

"And I have to be totally honest with you."

"Why do I hope you won't?" asks Matthew.

"Do you want to know what she said?"

"No." Matthew starts walking toward the door. He isn't in a mood for rejection. On a total losing streak, he'd called Eydis on the cruise ship last night, on her satellite phone, and begged her to come back to him. She'd laughed and said she would think about it.

"She said she thought you were a troll," says Ricky. "A loser."

"No, she didn't."

"Dude, I wouldn't say that if it wasn't true. I wouldn't do that to you."

"That wasn't a nice thing for her to say."

"I hired her," says Ricky. "She gives good head. I like that in a publicist."

Matthew is truly starting to hate Ricky Biscayne. He had figured, you know, that when he, Matthew, grew up, naturally his longtime friend and collaborator would, too. But Ricky appears to be going backward.

Matthew can't wait to get out of the studio and away from both of them.

There's this idea that firefighters are brave, right? And we are, when we have to be. But most of the time, our lives are pretty damn boring. This is one of the boring times. I've been instructed to show Nestor Perez, the handsome rookie from New York, how to clean the station windows, and so we stand in the hot white sun and sickening humidity, with buckets and rags, and a ladder, wiping. In downtime at a fire station, everyone does things that are actually traditionally women's work: cleaning, cooking, laundry. Ironic. I once read an interview with a commercial airplane pilot where he said he spent most of his job in a bored stupor and the rest of it in a terrified panic. Same here.

I needed to get out of the firehouse anyway. It's L'Roy. He has not once thanked me for saving his life. He acts like it never happened. No one saw it happen, and so he's started telling people that we got out of the fire at the same time. I told Jim, the cop I'm dating, about it, and his advice to me was to let L'Roy have his pride. This made me finally tell Jim the famous words: "This isn't working out."

"Like this," I say to Nestor Perez as I dip the sponge in the bucket.

"You sure?" he says with a wry grin. He's chewing gum. He's got a New York accent. "It's sponge in water, right? Not sponge on ground? Let me make sure I understand the basics of this window-washing thing."

"Very funny," I say.

"Thanks." He smiles and starts to wash a large window in great big broad strokes, his back muscles rippling through his shirt. Wow. So what that he's probably gay? He's still the best-looking, sweetest-smelling man I've been near. If he's gay? We'll talk boys. It will be heartbreaking at first, hearing about his conquests, but I'll get used to it, and then Sophia and I will have something in common—cute, gay best friends.

"Uh, so am I doing it right?" he asks, deadpan. "Not too hard? Too light? I mean, I want to make sure I understand this stuff."

I glance over at Nestor, and watch his biceps flex and contract as he rubs the grime off the glass. Yikes. "You're okay," I say.

"You're okay, too," he says. He flashes me the white grill again. Da-yum. What I might do to *that*. I try to think of something else. The first thing that occurs to me is Sophia, who has lately been hinting that she knows Ricky Biscayne is her father. She'll be out of school for the summer soon, with nowhere to go and nothing to do except punk around with her pal David, who will probably try to talk her into piercing something, or robbing someone. I want to trust David, to like him, but he is too wild and attractive for Sophia's good. I don't need Sophia falling for a gay boy, but then, look who's talking, right? I shudder to think that Sophia might be developing some sexual fantasies of her own. It is too awful to contemplate. She's my baby. She can't be growing up so soon. I just figured out how to be a mom, and now this, already? It's not right. I don't know how to handle Sophia anymore.

Captain Sullivan joins us outside with his beer belly, and observes our washing for a few moments before asking me to come with him to his office. My heart jumps and I feel a jolt of adrenaline. Why would he want to see me? I feel like I've been called to the principal's office. I set my bucket and squeegee down and remove the yellow rubber gloves with a snap.

"I'll take care of the rest," says Nestor. He smiles at me, blushes. Why is he blushing at me as if he's gay? He has perfectly white, perfectly straight teeth, with the tiniest of gaps between the top front two. Lovely.

Captain Sullivan leads me back into the station, to his office, and stands at the door until I've gone in. He shuts the door behind us.

"Have a seat," says Captain Sullivan. His belly slops over the front of his pants, and his skin has the gray cast of a man who eats too few vegetables. I sit on the rocky vinyl chair. "I know you've been studying for the lieutenant exam," he says.

I nod.

"You are aware L'Roy and some others want it, too?"

I nod again.

Sullivan looks at the papers on his desk and frowns, sighing. "I have to be honest with you, Gallagher. You're one of the most qualified candidates for the job. That's obvious. But as your captain I have to say I don't think you'd be the best match for the position at this time."

What? An invisible fist punches me in the gut. "What? Why not?"

He sighs and can't make eye contact, that coward. "The way this station is right now, with the particular personalities we have working here, I just had to make the decision I felt would be best for the whole team, not just one or two individuals."

"I don't understand."

Another sigh. He looks around the office, at everything but me. "What I'm saying is, I don't honestly think you should waste your time with the exam right now. You know, I just don't think some of these guys are going to take orders from you, Irene. Even though they should. That's not what I'm saying. I just don't think they're ready."

"Ready for what?"

"A female supervisor. It's nothing personal. It's all about the team." I say nothing, stare at him until he finally winces in my direction. The corners of my mouth harden. He says, "Now wait a minute. I'm not finished yet. I know a big part of the reason you want the promotion is because you're raising a kid by yourself. So I've decided to raise your salary to $41,850, even with the lieutenant position, so in a way it's like you got the promotion. At least from a money standpoint. I don't want you to think I don't appreciate how hard you work here."

"So you want to pay me like I got the promotion, without giving me any of the authority, sir?"

He sighs. "I know this isn't easy to hear, but in a field like ours you have to think of what's best for the function of the whole team, Irene. You know that as well as I do. And trust me, if you weren't such a team player, if you were more like those feminazis out there who sue over things like this, I wouldn't have been so up-front with you about all this. I'm sure you understand."

I thank Captain Sullivan with the usual "sir" at the end, and walk out the door of the fire house without responding to L'Roy's catcalls, and quietly resume my duties cleaning the windows of the station house.

"Hey," says Nestor Perez, tossing his rag into the bucket and trying to catch my eyes. "You okay?"

"Not really. But I'll be fine."

"Is there anything I can do to help?" he asks. I look from his rippling muscles to his earnest, square face, and think, *Yes, you can ravage me in the backseat of my car before I go home to my miserable mother and teenaged daughter.*

"Nope," I say. "Thanks, though." I start to whistle as I work, like a stinking dwarf. Like one of the guys.

Like I don't have a goddamned care in the world.

Swank. That's the word that comes to mind. I'm not a fan of the word. It's not a Milan word, see. But I have to use it because, frankly, there's no better way to describe the Delano Hotel, where I find myself at the moment. Swank. Say it like this: *schwank.* Lift a blue martini. Wink. Throw your head back and laugh like tinkling bells for the benefit of all those around who might not be having as fabulous a time as you are. Yes, dahling. That's it. You got it. You, too, now belong at the Delano. Smooches!

I've driven past this place a million times, and I've heard about it from Geneva and whoever. You know the place, even if you think you don't. Think massive white curtains, outside. Maybe they're a palest pink. Tall building, deco, matte, chalky white and rose, like after-dinner butter mints, only it's a hotel. The Delano is all about the huge white curtains, curtains two or three stories tall, perfectly clean and wrinkle free—God knows how—billowing slowly and gently, with fairy-tale calm. That's outside, in front. Inside, think minimalist, dark wood floors with huge fat white columns like giant pieces of sidewalk chalk, all of it so clean and fresh and white you want to take a minty deep breath that never ends and just sort of float away. Things are in odd proportions here, like a giant lampshade, white, hanging over a tiny sofa, also white. Interesting. I like it. I really, really like this place. It's *me* I don't like, *in* it. Until this morning, I was a poop publicist. That does a number on a girl's self-esteem. I don't feel like a poop peddler belongs here. Me, in the Delano, is clumsy, like a hungover birthday clown at a sushi bar.

This is my first time actually *here*. It's on the beach, in South Beach, and very pretentious, even though it claims to be "casual chic." I've just walked in with Ricky and his entourage. Can I use that word now? Entourage. I'm part of the *entourage*. Only I feel like, you know, the hungover-clown contingent of the entourage, while the rest of the entourage is people like Jasminka and her model friends, other people who look way better than me, and then Geneva, who I brought because Ricky wanted me to. Geneva "the hottie" fits in here, with her stinky little dog and her Fiji water. She even waves to the manager, after cracking her wrists, and then waves at some other people in the lobby because she knows everyone in town from her days as the party-planner girl. I watch her and try to affect the same posture. As part of the entourage, maybe I fit in better than I think. I don't know. But I do know I better stop saying the word "entourage" in my head because it's starting to give me a headache, and because I'm an idiot and I start to repeat things like that just for fun when I'm nervous, which would be now. Entourage, entourage, entourage. Speaking of the entourage, I wonder where that little redheaded man is. Isn't he part of Ricky's entourage?

We stroll along, the *group* and I, following Ricky and his manager, Ron DiMeola, who is married to Analicia, the Mexican *novela* star. A crew from the hotel escorts us. How cool is that? Normal people have to find their own way around. Ricky gets guides everywhere he goes. They offer him water in bottles, they bow and scrape. I would like to be bowed and scraped to. That would rock. I'm liking this job, even if I feel like a total impostor. I'll get used to it. No, really. I promise.

We go down halls that smell of wood and lacquer, past fabulous people eating fabulous food in fabulous cafés and swank restaurants. We walk out onto a ground-level patio spilling over with little pots of flowers that smell of citrus and soil. Sunset is coming, and with it the slowing of the pulses of sound in the air. I look at Geneva and she smiles at me. Without sarcasm. Like she's proud of me and a little bit excited about all of this.

"Nice, eh?" she says, as we keep walking behind Ricky.

"Thanks," I say, truly grateful for her help in getting me this gig. "I can't believe I'm here."

"Yeah," she says, scratching Belle's ears. "Maybe you should keep that thought to yourself."

Pop! So much for my little balloon of sisterly love.

We get to the beach, and it looks like a really elegant circus, with pastel green and white square tents set up here and there, and tents that are bars, and beautiful bodies in bikinis and, ew, Speedos. Hell-o? Shouldn't Speedos be illegal? I mean, for men? They are probably the worst invention ever for the male body. There's a guy in one right over there and he turns around and I see that, ew, ew, ew, it's actually a thong. Geneva gasps and grabs my arm.

"Nasty," she says.

We laugh. Ah, insecurity. Nothing makes you feel better about yourself than putting someone else down.

As we head toward our own little collection of pointed, pastel fairy-tale tents, I feel like I'm not as bad as I thought a minute ago. After all, Ricky hired me. He even tried to *kiss* me, but I'm not sharing that news with anyone. Maybe I'm just being overly judgmental because I still don't feel like I fit in here. And while, yes, I'd like to be taller, thinner, richer, with better clothes, and, yes, I'd like to be really tan, in something like a white curtain, something that drapes and flows and makes me look Grecian and statuesque, I'm okay. I'm not "chic," but at the moment I am starting to feel a bit schee*wank*. I want a blue martini.

Wearing a sexy white-mesh shirt and white linen shorts, Ricky comes over and puts his arm around me, ushers me and Geneva into a tent. Asks us what we want to drink. Geneva orders a cosmopolitan. I ask for the blue martini. Wow! It's like he read my mind or something. Off he goes. I can't believe the star is actually waiting on us. I feel like I should be doing that.

"He's cool," says Geneva.

I want so badly to tell her about our almost kiss, but I don't.

"You look good, Milan," she says, with a touch of surprise in her voice that I could do without. She clicks her fingernails, picking at them, and I put my hand over hers to stop her. I'm wearing the results of our late-afternoon emergency shopping spree: dark denim Moschino low-rise jeans and a sleeveless, puffy-front black Cavalli top, short-sleeved and cut in a peasant-blouse style. I like the clothes, but I worry that my crack shows all the time. Geneva thinks I have a pretty belly and that I should focus on that, but I'm always worrying about my behind. She has suggested I get my belly button pierced, but I would rather stick a toothpick in my eardrum.

Geneva wears her version of the same outfit, though her jeans have tiny back pockets. Geneva has forbidden me to wear any brand of jeans with tiny back pockets. The bigger the back pockets, the better, she says. We are both barefoot with our shoes stashed in our bags. Geneva knew we'd be on the beach and suggested flip-flops and big totes.

Ricky comes back with the drinks and gives me one of his looks. Like a seductive look. Then he goes to the next tent to do something else, with a quick look over his shoulder at me and a little wink.

"What was that?" asks Geneva.

"What?" I say.

"That wink."

"What wink?"

Geneva observes me over the rim of her cosmopolitan. "Just be careful," she says.

"What?"

"Don't do anything stupid." She touches my newly lightened and shortened hair, running her fingertips through its many layers. "I can't get over the hair. Why did you wait so long to get your hair done?"

"I don't know."

"Why don't you listen to me more?"

"Because I've hated you for stealing my men, Geneva. That's why."

She stares at the sand and shakes her head. "I'm sorry. I really am. I was immature and stupid. I'll never do it again."

"Okay."

"Will you pierce your belly button now?"

"I don't know," I say.

"You have to stop saying that all the time."

"Saying what?"

" 'I don't know.' You say it way too much."

"Sorry."

"Stop saying 'sorry,' too."

We watch the stars and models. "Just remember one thing," says Geneva, tilting her glass toward Ricky and his glamorous . . . entour-group.

"What?"

"They're human. And most of them are really insecure and really messed up."

"Why would you tell me that right now?"

"You look starstruck," says Geneva. "Don't get too swept up in it. He's not that great. He's just a guy who can't dress."

"Somebody's bitter."

"Just remember that and you'll be fine."

hree martinis and almost an hour later, and we're still sitting there, watching Ricky and his pals run around and drink. Belle is asleep, thank God. "Are we going to have a meeting, or what?" I ask. Geneva laughs at me. "What?" I ask. "Ricky said it was a business meeting. They've been drinking and prancing around for an hour."

Geneva shakes her head at me in shame. "You are too much," she says.

"What?"

"Partying *is* business in Miami Beach, sweetie, didn't you know that? They're all watching each other. Survival of the fittest."

I watch. Lots of drinking, eating, and making out. Jasminka's back, in her bathing suit and sarong. Every time Ricky leans over to kiss her, I feel, like, pain in my body. He's mine. Doesn't she know that? I growl, and realize too late that I've done it out loud. Shouldn't drink on the job, I s'pose.

"Forget it," says Geneva, with an ankle rotation and a pop.

"What?"

"You can't have sex with him."

"Who?"

Her look tells me she knows I know who she means, and, furthermore, she finds me idiotic. "Even if he *offers*. Say no. You have to say no. Got that?"

"What?"

"Never mind."

Jasminka and her model friends traipse off to swim in the ocean, their flat bottoms barely jiggling as they skip and cavort. They remind me of a herd of very small deer. Finally, Ricky, Ron, and Analicia join us in our little tent. Ron closes the curtains. I take a notebook out of my tote bag. Geneva says hello to everyone and Ricky introduces her as his new business partner in "a hot new club." He introduces me as his "new right-hand girl," whatever that means.

Ron is drunk, and fat, and old, with a body like Jack Nicholson's. With his suit jacket and no shirt, his long hair slicked back over the bald top of his head, he looks overdressed, sweaty, and greasy, like a Hollywood movie stereotype of an Italian mobster. Why does he make himself look like that? You'd think if a guy was Italian-American he might actually try *not* to look like that stereotype. And why did Analicia, a *novela* star and pop singer adored by everyone in Latin America and many other parts of the world, choose him to marry, of all the men on earth? She was already rich, wasn't she? She was also adorable; with her pale skin and freckles she was almost like a much more beautiful and slender version of me. I don't understand what a perfect and successful woman like Analicia sees in a sleazy slob like Ron DiMeola, a man who, if I understand correctly, was fired out of his high-powered record-company job last year. But that's none of my business. He has to be at least twenty-five years older than she is, too. If I looked like Analicia, I'd find a guy like Ricky. *En punto.*

"Shall we get started, gentlemen?" I ask, trying my best to sound confident and like I belong here. Geneva rolls her eyes and laughs at me. Thanks for the support, *man stealer.*

"Yeah, just as soon as I get some vitamins." Ron takes a silver tin out of his pocket. Ricky watches as he opens it to reveal a tiny mountain of white powder, and smiles. Analicia stares off into space and pretends not to watch as Ron sticks one end of a little silver tube into the tin, and the other into his big fat hairy nostril. Uh, okay. I didn't expect to be caught in the middle of a bad episode of *Miami Vice.* I really didn't. All that's missing is Don Johnson and a peach-colored men's blazer.

I guess my jaw drops as Ron takes a snort like a pig in truffles. He looks up at me with that "you lookin' at me?" face. "You want some, Milan?" he asks, in a tone that lets me know *he* knows I'm a drug virgin. The tone also implies that if I rat him out, I will die soon after. I look at Analicia, but the starlet still stares off, twirling a piece of her curly brown hair with her fingers.

"No, thanks," I say.

"Geneva?"

"No."

I'm remembering that a couple of years ago Analicia did a bunch of Spanish public-service announcements about how bad drugs are for kids. How could she lie like that? I'm starting to feel less like a hungover clown and more like a kid who has awakened to see if Santa Claus came, only to find her mom and dad in a three-way with a reindeer under the tree.

Ron offers the cocaine to Ricky. Ricky looks at me and Geneva, then shakes his head. "No, thanks, man."

Ron laughs. "Suit yourself." He turns to me. He doesn't have meat in his mouth, but he looks like he should, a big raw bloody piece. "Now, so, Milan, like, if Ricky had just done coke, which the little prick isn't doing because he wants to make a good fucking impression, *this* is one of those things I obviously don't want you to tell reporters about."

Ron, Analicia, and Ricky laugh. The martinis have gone to my head and I feel like I should laugh, too, but I'm not sure why. I smile like a jackass, trying to fit in. Geneva watches it all without changing her disapproving expression.

"Of course," I say.

"Look, kid. Now and then you get a smart-ass who asks about this kind of thing," explains Ron. "And what do you tell them?"

"I tell them nothing?" Is that the right answer? I have no idea.

"Wrong," says Ron. Okay. Now I have an idea. "You tell them they're fucking crazy. You tell them Ricky is as healthy as Jane Fonda." He shoots Ricky a disgusted look, and slaps his own pudgy knee. "Who the fuck did you hire for a publicist, Ricky, Betty fucking Crocker?"

"Milan's had a long day," says Geneva, coming to my defense. "And this," she points to Ron, the drugs, "isn't exactly professional behavior."

Analicia, wearing a miniskirt and a bustier, climbs onto her husband's lap, smoking a cigarette. No way! She *smokes*, too? "Who's Jane Fonda, baby?" Analicia asks Ron in her thick Spanish accent, tracing his lips with her fingertip as if he were not as repulsive as a zoo gorilla eating its own mucousy yellow turd.

"Nothing, forget it," says Ron to Analicia. The feel of her body on his lap must have calmed him down, because he stops talking and just grins. Then, in front of everyone, he grabs one of her breasts and squeezes it. "These are so fucking great," he says of the breasts to Ricky. "They're new. She got 'em lifted up and filled out. They're like beach fucking balls. What do you think?"

"Yeah, man," says Ricky as Analicia giggles. Ricky shoots me an apologetic look. I feel sorry for him. I don't think he's liking this, either.

"Here," says Ron. He takes Ricky's hand and places it on his wife's breast. Geneva and I both gasp as Ricky squeezes it and Analicia throws her head back and laughs. What is wrong with these people?

"Very nice," Ricky tells Ron in a flat tone, once again wincing at me. He's embarrassed, poor thing.

"You think that's good, look at this." Ron uses his hands to spread Analicia's legs. She isn't wearing underwear. Okay. What the hell? I turn away. "Prettiest shaved kitty in the world."

"Oh my God," whispers Geneva, hitting my leg with her own.

"Brazilian wax," corrects Analicia. "No one shaves anymore, baby. Razor bumps."

Geneva and I lock eyes. We've entered the fun house. Fallen down the rabbit hole. Whatever. This is another universe. And Geneva, who I would expect to be able to handle something like this? I don't think she knows what to do, either. I peek back just in time to see Ron lick one of his fat, grubby fingers and stuff it into his wife. *Ugh!* Analicia groans with pleasure and kisses his neck.

Ricky turns away and smokes his cigarette. Another cigarette? *Man.*

"I think we'll step out until this is finished," says Geneva, grabbing my hand.

"No, hold on," says Ricky. He turns his attention to his manager. "Ron, I think you're making the ladies uncomfortable. We should chill a bit."

"Fine," says Ron. His eyes appear suddenly alive with energy, and with Analicia nibbling his neck he removes his finger from her and she sucks it clean.

"Jesus," whispers Geneva. She looks at me with wide eyes. "What did I get you into?"

"Me? You just cashed the guy's check, Geneva. Us. We're in this."

"Us," Geneva corrects herself. Analicia has the blank eyes of a drug addict. "What did I get *us* into?"

"Milan," says Ron. "Let's talk fucking business. Let's figure out how you," he points at me as if he hasn't just said my name, "and me are gonna make him," he points at Ricky, "the next hottest-shit boy next door in American popular music. A squeaky-clean all-American guy, with Latin hips." I feel like crying. I don't know why, exactly, because I'm a little drunk and freaked, but I just want to curl up and cry. "What's the matter?" asks Ron. "You nervous?"

I look at Geneva, and she's clueless. We're both clueless. It makes me like her. My sister. God, I'm glad she's here. I like her again. You bond in moments of natural disaster.

Ron looks at Ricky with disapproval. "You should have checked with me before hiring her," he says. Uh-oh. Is he going to fire me? That would be sad. I would be fired without ever having gotten to have sex with my employer.

"It's not her fault," says Geneva. "You guys are acting like assholes. What do you expect?"

Ron shrugs and seems to ignore Geneva. "But now that she's here, and now that she knows certain things about us that we don't want nobody to know, we have to fix the problem."

His New York accent, piss-poor syntax, and mobster appearance make me think I'm about to be offed, as in killed. Geneva looks like she thinks the same thing. What the fuck? What did she do to me? Why couldn't I just be the secretary of the online fan club? Why did I want this job again?

Jasminka sticks her head into the tent. "Hi there," she says to Ricky. "How's everything?"

"Good," says Ricky. He forgets to mention the porn show.

I see Analicia's eyes narrow competitively at the sight of the beautiful Jasminka. She's jealous? How weird. Me too!

"We're going up to the suite," says Jasminka. She sees me and smiles warmly. "Hi, Milan! I'm glad you're to be working for Ricky! We need someone like you around."

I smile back, weak. Jasminka waves and ducks back out of the tent, clueless about what just happened here.

"How much is he paying you?" Ron asks me. I tell him. It's a good salary, almost a third more than I made working for my uncle.

"Triple it," he says to Ricky.

"Wow," says Geneva. Six figures? I am now making more than my *sister?*

Ron continues, "And get her a new fucking car. I saw the piece of shit she drove here. What was it?" He looks at Ricky.

"A Dodge Neon?"

Ron shakes his head as Analicia laughs. "Unacceptable. Tell him what kind of car you'd like."

I blink. "I'm sorry?"

Ron nods impatiently, like he's hearing something for the hundredth time. "Go on."

I stutter, and Geneva jumps in for me. "Mercedes," says Geneva. "My sister would like a white Mercedes."

Hello? I mean, it's true. But still. Why is she doing this? Shouldn't I just quit? This is weird. But maybe this is how it is in the big time. Geneva knows. I don't.

"Done," says Ron.

I stare at him, speechless. What the fuck?

"What, you want some clothes, too? Chicks always want fucking clothes. Ricky?"

"Yeah?"

"Triple the salary, get her the car, and get your wife to take her shopping. That make you happy, Milan?"

I don't move. Don't speak. I am drunk and weirded out. I want to go home. Ricky gives me another apologetic look, and now I want to do Ricky like I've never wanted anything in my life. Why? Why is he looking at me like that?

"Milan," he says. "Can I talk to you outside for a second?"

I look at Geneva for permission. Don't ask me why. Habit. She smiles and shrugs. I follow Ricky out of the bungalow, into the night air.

"I have to apologize for Ron," he says with a look of agony on his face. "He's going through some weird times right now. I can't get into it, but . . ." He pauses and chews his lower lip. I see how tortured Ricky is, and feel bad for him. Maybe this isn't really how Ron behaves all the time. Maybe this is rare. Maybe it will all be okay. "I am really, really embarrassed about this," says Ricky. "The record company made me hire him for the English stuff, and I've been planning to get rid of him for a while, but I haven't found anyone else yet. I'm really sorry. Okay?"

He touches my face.

"Do you still want the job?"

"I think so," I say. He is so earnest, so normal right now. Like a real person, not like a star. I want to hold him. For him to hold me.

"I'll have a talk with him," says Ricky, sniffling and wiping the end of his nose with the back of his hand. He stares with fierce eyes back at the tent. "He works for me, not the other way around."

"Okay, Ricky."

"No, I mean it. He's always doing shit like this. His ass is so fired."

"Okay."

"I swear, Milan, it won't happen again. Do you believe me?"

He steps close, and pulls me in. And kisses me.

Kisses me.

On the mouth. With a bite, small and sweet, to my lower lip. Holy fuck. I can't breathe. Where am I? Where are my legs? I can't feel my legs.

He pulls away and I grin up at him. I think I'm going to fall to the floor, or the sand, or whatever is under me, I can't remember right now.

"Sorry," he says softly, his eyes closed, then open and looking into my soul. "You just have the sweetest little mouth. I had to. I've wanted to do that since I met you. I don't like these people. Know that. Do you believe me?"

I don't know what to believe. But I still love Ricky Biscayne more than any other singer in the world. Nobody is perfect. I have stored up years of adoring him inside my heart. And he is such a soulful singer and songwriter, I don't think it's possible for him to be as crude and disgusting as the man in the tent. I smile at him. I love his music. That, more than this nightmare with Ron, speaks of his soul. I know him from his music. I love him. "I believe you."

"My wife and I, it's not what it seems like, we have issues. I have a separate room for her here tonight, and I want you in mine, with me. I know it's forward. I am impulsive. I told you that. I feel something for you."

"Me?"

He looks sweetly embarrassed. "I'm sorry. I'm just a man, and I feel something for you, Milan, something I've never felt before. . . ."

Geneva comes barreling out of the tent like someone tripping alone in a bad comedy sketch. "Hi," she says, blinking sarcastically.

"Hi," I say. Did she see? No. There's no way. Geneva takes me by the arm and pulls me away from Ricky.

"What are you doing?" I ask.

"They're having sex," says Geneva with a fake-ass smile.

"Who?"

"That fat pig and Analicia."

"What?"

"Like seals. Milan, you don't have to take this job. I can find other investors."

"No, it's okay. Ricky apologized. He said he's gonna fire Ron."

"You sure? You can handle this?"

"Yes," I say, the full knowledge that I've just kissed Ricky Biscayne coming down on me like a flock of doves. "It's just Ron. It's not Ricky. Ricky's fine. His label forced him to hire that guy."

"I'm sorry I got you into this," says Geneva. "We should go home now."

"Uh," I say. I want to stay, go up with Ricky. But I can't tell Geneva, and she's pulling me away. I don't know what to do. I look over my shoulder at Ricky, and this time it's me with the apology in my eyes. I see him receding, gorgeous, understanding, gentle, with love in his heart for a plain, interesting woman like me. He's not happy in his marriage. He told me so. And now Geneva is pulling me away? This isn't happening. Can't be. To me? Really? No. There's no way.

"Come on," says Geneva, rotating her neck in little pops. "I'll take you home."

"I have my car."

"You're drunk."

As Geneva pulls me through the pretty, swanky lobby, her fury speeding us along, I see Matthew Baker sitting alone on a chair. He's reading a travel book on Milan, of all places. Weird. He's kind of cute. He looks worried about something. He looks up and sees me, watches me with strange, sad eyes, and waves as I pass by.

"This loser of a troll will see you Monday, publicity girl," he says, like a coworker. Like I have a normal job, with normal people, which I totally do not. "Have a good weekend."

The Second
Trimester

sunday, may 5

Sweaty from the three-mile bike ride across Homestead, Sophia chains her pink Huffy to the base of a sickly baby palm tree in the parking lot of the Wal-Mart supercenter and walks across the enormous, crowded lot to the store. She has not counted on so many people being here. Maybe Sunday isn't the best day in the world to go shoplifting. But it is the day her mom is at work, and she's out of school, and that means it is her one big chance.

Sophia wears the same Faded Glory jeans and T-shirt from this very store, clothes she wore to school just yesterday with shame, clothes that would have been fine a year ago but that seem pathetic now that she is in middle school and clothes *matter*. She hopes she doesn't see anyone from school who might realize she is repeating an outfit two days in a row. Her mom hasn't exactly been good at getting the laundry done lately, and her grandma is next to useless. Sophia figures she'd better start doing her own laundry, but the thought of pretending to care about these pathetic loser clothes makes her angry. Why can't she have at least *one* nice pair of jeans? Why does her mom have to be so stingy about everything? Other parents work normal jobs like Sophia's mother, but they all seem to have more money than Sophia's family, for some reason.

Sophia enters the store and says hello to the comatose man in the blue Wal-Mart vest by the shopping carts, who is supposed to be there to say hello when you walk in but who in reality looks like he wants to kill himself. The store is crowded with families and the usual collection of crazy people, some without shoes or teeth. This is where Irene does the family's grocery shopping, once a week, armed with coupons, and Sophia is as familiar with the layout of the store as she is with her school or her home. Sophia is the only girl her age alone here. Her heart pounds with anticipation as she walks the aisles, trying to look like she might be searching for her parent. And, in a way, she is.

She gets to the music section and immediately sees Ricky Biscayne's crossover album, *Nothing for Free*, displayed along the top row in the pop music area, with the singer smiling in his tight shirt and jeans. He looks *exactly* like her! Anyone with half a brain could see that. Mom might try to pretend, but Sophia isn't stupid. She knows the deal. This guy is her father. Her mother knows it, and so does Sophia.

She picks up one of the CDs and turns it over, finding Ricky without a shirt, covered with tattoos, a fedora perched over one eye like an old-time gangster. He looks tough and smart. If *he* drove her home from soccer, none of the neighborhood girls would ever pick on her again. They'd take one look and be, like, oops, we were wrong about you, Sophia, you *are* cool, even in those Wal-Mart jeans. Of course, if Ricky Biscayne was her dad, then she probably wouldn't have Wal-Mart jeans and she probably wouldn't have any problems at all. Sophia has tried to talk to her mom about it, but it has always been the same thing: Your dad is a man we are better off not knowing; maybe when you are grown-up you can meet him but it won't do us any good right now.

Her pulse quickens as she imagines how it will be once he founds out he *has* a Sophia. He will take her out of Homestead and give her a big room in a house with a pool. She'll have cute clothes just like Raven and all those pretty girls on the Disney Channel, and shoes! Lots of shoes. Right now she only has two pairs, one for school and one for soccer, and they are both sneakers. She is at an age where she wants to at least *try* more girlie shoes, but her mom, this superbutch firefighter who hates men, doesn't have anything girlie of her own, and would probably never get anything girlie for Sophia, either. Kids at school tease Sophia that her mom is a dyke, but she doesn't think it is true. Or at least she didn't *used* to think it was true. The way Sophia's mom ignores that adorable coach Rob, when he obviously *wants* her, makes Sophia think her classmates might be right. That would *so* suck. Then she'd not only be fatherless and poor, but she'd have a mom everyone made fun of, and no hope of ever getting a skirt or lipstick. Flash! That would *so* suck.

Sophia has to find a way to meet Ricky. Once he sees her, he'll know they are related and he'll rush to save her from this life. She'll get her very own room with a view of the water, with a bunk bed, but not like a little bunk bed—a *big* bunk bed, like a queen-size one—and she could choose each night whether she wanted to sleep on the top or on the bottom. She could get up in the middle of the night and switch beds if she wanted to. She'd have one of those fake-fur white rugs shaped like a polar bear, and she'd dig her toes in to keep them warm because they'd have the air-conditioning on all the time, not just during the hottest three hours of the day like they do now. The screens in Ricky's house would be perfect, not like the ones at home, which have holes from where the cats hung on them, trying to get into the house, holes that mosquitoes used later to get in and bite her as she slept because her mom was too cheap to use the air conditioner at night or get the screens fixed. Sophia hates her mom sometimes.

Sophia will feel terrible just leaving her mom like that to move in with her dad, after all these years, but maybe she won't have to. Maybe she could make Irene and Ricky fall in love again, and then she and her mother would move to a mansion. If her mom wasn't a *lesbian*, that is. They'd loved each other once, hadn't they? That's how she, Sophia, got here. They could love each other again. They probably still secretly love each other but don't know how to admit it, and now here is Sophia to help them past their shyness with each other. They'll get married and she'll wear a beautiful sparkly dress and hand

Ricky the ring and he'll put it on her mother's hand. God, she'd love to see her mother in a dress, just once! With makeup and her hair done. Or if Ricky was already married, maybe he'd give Sophia and her mom a lot of money and they'd get a better house, and then Sophia could have holidays and weekends with her dad the way other kids with divorced parents did. Just the sound of the words "my dad" makes Sophia feel excited. She's never had one, and now here he is, one of the most famous men in the world! She is one lucky girl.

Sophia clutches the CD and looks for others in the Bs. There is only this one. She finds a female employee sorting Christian books and taps her shoulder.

"Excuse me," says Sophia. "Do you have any other albums by this singer?" She holds the CD up, thinking, *By my dad*, but not saying it, her belly filled with bubbles at the thought that she is related to such a special, important man, and also at the thought of what she's about to do.

"Ricky Biscayne?" the worker asks with a Spanish accent, her face lighting up as she spies the CD. "Oh, yes, we have lots of records from him. I love him. Don't you just love him? He's such a good man. I seen him on Cristina and he said he was a real family man."

She leads Sophia to a section with a MÚSICA LATINA sign over it and points out a section with at least four other Ricky Biscayne albums. "We don't have them all, but there are some."

Sophia thanks the worker, and spends the next ten minutes poring over the album covers. Ricky Biscayne sings in English and in Spanish. No wonder Sophia has always felt a love of Spanish, even though no one in her family—or no one in the family she has so far known about—speaks it very well. You have to speak a little bit to get by in this area, but Sophia's grandma isn't exactly fond of Latin people.

Sophia waits until no one is looking, and then she rips the plastic wrappers off two of the Ricky Biscayne albums, including the part that she knows will set off the metal detectors. She hides the wrappers in the bins, under some CDs. She stuffs the CDs under her large T-shirt, and tries to look casual. She finds the worker again.

"I lost my dad," she says. "Could you page him for me?"

"Sure," says the worker. She leads Sophia to the front of the store and tells her to wait right there while she makes an announcement. "What's your daddy's name?"

"Rick," she says, thinking, Ricky Biscayne.

Then, as the announcement rings throughout the store, Sophia makes a run for the parking lot, the CDs burning with promise under her shirt.

*9*ack lounges on Jill's expansive white-fur bedspread, reading Howard Zinn's *The Southern Mystique* (*Radical 60s*), feeling very socialistically nostalgic in honor of National Worker's Day in Cuba. He's been visiting Jill in Miami for a full month now, and he is getting tired of the place. People say Miami is an international city. They say it is the capital of Latin America. But to Jack Ingroff, it is a provincial southern backwater with a Spanish accent, run by a bunch of Cuban Nazis who try to get sympathy from the public and the press by pretending to be Latino in the way Mexican farm workers are Latino. What a joke.

He hasn't bathed in two days, and takes strange, sticky comfort in the grease of his butt crack and the raunchy aroma of the stretched-out collar of his Boston Red Sox T-shirt. His boys swing free in the breeze under his gray drawstring sweats. His feet steam in their mismatched athletic socks. He feels like a guy, and feeling like a guy feels good. All that is missing, in his opinion, is a big honkin' grease box of pizza and a six-pack of Sam Adams. Then it would be a perfect evening.

In the next room, technically a closet, but Jack thinks of it as a room because it is bigger than most of the apartments he lived in when he was at Emerson College, Jill primps and preens, getting ready for their dinner date. The stereo system in the closet (the irony of such obscene excess is not lost on Jack) blasts her own voice, an early remix of the single "Born Again," which the label has picked to be her first single when the album comes out in a couple of months.

Jack knows that if he, say, heard the song casually, like if some stupid fucker was blasting it out the open window of his Honda street racer or something, he might find it appealing. But right now he thinks his fiancée sounds like one of the Little Rascals on helium. No one should sound like that when they sing. Jack prefers old-time blues, Bessie Smith or even Billie Holiday. Something with grit and soul and meaning. Jack longs for the days when singers didn't have to be beautiful.

Basically, tonight, Jack wants to stay in, to finish his book, but Jill is ovulating, and he knows what that means. It means Jill needs even more attention than she usually does, and no amount of attention he can provide will be enough. She needs the attention of the masses. When he first met her, on the set of a movie they did together that bombed, she seemed so sweet and charming, so sort of innocent, always laughing at his jokes; he realizes now that this was only because she was so into her character—a sweet, charming, innocent woman— that she believed it was herself for a while. Now, sadly, she's back to her real, miserable, shallow self.

"Jack!" she cries. "Get in the shower! We'll be late."

"Take the day off, Jill," he says. "It's National Worker's Day in Cuba."

Her voice drips with annoyance. "What?"

He calls out to make sure she hears him, "Yeah, a day celebrating the spirit of solidarity among those noble people who work for a living. Oh, wait. We wouldn't know anything about that. Sorry. Forgot."

"Get up."

"Okay, okay," he says, distractedly, continuing to read as he heaves his feet off the edge of the bed. "You should read this book, Jill. It's amazing. It will change your life. It will change the way you think about the South forever."

Jill appears in the doorway, scowling at his laziness as she stuffs herself into a vintage white corset top with ribbons and shreds hanging in all the right places, and painted-on low-rise white Jill Sanchez jeans with rhinestones. Her hair is pulled back in a long, high ponytail, and gigantic diamond hoops flash on her earlobes. He looks up, pleased at the sight of her calculated curves—but frightened by the curdled expression on her face. For a beautiful woman, she has a rare gift for meanness.

"What?" he asks. "Why are you looking at me like that?"

"We have ten minutes, Jack. What have you been doing?"

"Reading."

She rolls her eyes. "Unless it's a script, there's no time," she says.

"What's that supposed to mean?" Lately, she's been on his case for not having as many movies as she does, and just last night they fought about who, of the two of them, was the more naturally talented actor. He doesn't have as many movies because he is starting to get picky about what he does, unlike her.

She ignores the question. "I've laid out your outfit in the bathroom. Please hurry. If you're not ready in five, I'll have to leave without you."

"Why are we in such a hurry? It's *dinner*. We don't have lives like real people. You don't have to be there at any certain time, Jill. Why can't you go to a restaurant like a normal person?"

"Because I'm *not* a normal person." She says this as if it makes her superior somehow. He laughs out loud.

"No, you're not," he says as he scratches his dangling boys. "You are most definitely not a normal person."

"Please hurry."

"Why? We can go when we want."

"No, we can't. I had it leaked that we'd be there at seven, and we should be there at seven."

Leaked? Jill is in the habit of having publicist pals like that disgusting Lizzie Grubman fill reporters and photographers in on her whereabouts, ensuring, in her mind, the nonstop splash of publicity that guarantees a long and healthy career in the entertainment industry. Hasn't she heard of overkill? People are getting sick of them. Hell, *he* is sick of them, and he *is* them. Know what else he hates? The way Jill started to call South Beach "SoBe," like somebody who doesn't know how to pronounce "sorbet." It is pretentious and trendy, just like her. Jack is a man of classic interests. But Jack is losing Jack. His friends don't come by anymore when Jill is around, and they try to talk him out of the relationship.

Jack pushes off the bed and stalks to the large marble shower in the master bathroom, sneaking past the chosen outfit on his way; it is laid out just like it might have been in a boutique, matching down to the freaking socks and shoes. Jill certainly has an eye for design, he gives her that, even if it tends toward the gaudy, or, as he likes to call her furs and stilettos, the *Gotti*. Slacks, shirt, and tie, slick and shiny, no doubt clothes made by another one of those stupid fucking designers who all want Jill to be their walking billboard. It is *so* not him. He laughs at the clothes, and then laughs at himself in the mirror. He doesn't want to go to Rumi, the pretentious restaurant where Jill has made reservations and where they will undoubtedly spend the most self-conscious and awkward evening of his life with flashbulbs popping every thirty nanoseconds. It calls itself a supper club. What crap. And he doesn't want to wear these stupid clothes, either. He picks them up and looks at the tag. Prada? What the hell kind of fag wears this crap? His friends don't recognize him anymore, now that she has him wearing velour jogging suits and crap like that, like some kind of designer dog she likes to match her all the time.

He tosses the clothes back onto the counter as if they are empty hamburger wrappers. He wants to read and scratch his balls and belch, and if they are going to eat out, he would have been happier at some hole-in-the-wall joint on Calle Ocho, where he can watch some old guys fight over dominos. Rumi? Fuck Rumi. If he is lucky, he'll end up seeing somebody like Robert Downey Jr. get his *ass* kicked by somebody like Pauly Shore.

Basically, Jack wants to get out of this relationship with Jill, but he doesn't know how. Well, part of him does. Another part of him thinks that maybe her gloss and shine can help ease the rough edges of being a regular guy with some sexual quirks he'd like to get rid of. A while back, he figured that being married to something as sexy as Jill Sanchez might cure him of the need to seek out wild sex with weird partners, but he has since realized that, like most things about Jill Sanchez, the sexy image is just that. An image. The real Jill Sanchez is always too busy to have time for sex, and when she finally gets around to it, it seems she is much too concerned about how she looks to the invisible camera that is always filming her in her head than with pleasing him in any way. The most pleasing thing to Jill is Jill herself, and she figures that pleasing herself will automatically make everyone else happy. It does not make Jack happy anymore.

"This is so fucked," he says to his reflection as he tosses the Howard Zinn to the floor next to the toilet and strips out of his beloved weekend Joe clothes. He picks up the underwear she's laid out for him. Versace? With a thong ass? Is this some kind of a joke? Is Ashton Kutcher going to jump out of the linen closet and yell, "Punk'd"? He points at his reflection with a furious smile as he readies to hop into the shower to get his ass clean enough to be threaded through with ridiculous underpants. "You know how fucked this is, right?"

saturday, may 11

Saturday. Matthew dreads Saturdays, mostly because they, more than Sundays, even, remind him of exactly how alone he is in his universe. In the name of keeping the existential grief of Saturdays at bay, he's taken up cooking, and is, at the moment, attempting to coax a large Calphalon wok out of a cardboard box. He has this dream that, if he weren't a musician anyway, he would have been a TV chef. There are lots of guys on the Food Network who aren't necessarily handsome but who the ladies seem to find sexy because of their way with food. Look at that Bobby Flay dude. He isn't anything to look at, really, just a redheaded guy like Matthew, but he's married to a model because women dig food. They say the way to a man's heart is through his stomach, but it's true of women more than men. This is Matthew's newest idea for making women want him. He'll cook his way into someone's bed.

The wok finally loses its hold on the inside of the box, and Matthew holds it up like a newborn baby. "Beautiful," he says, and runs his fingers along the pan's smooth, round lines. He likes smooth, round lines. Lately, he's taken a particular liking to the smooth, round lines of Ricky's new publicist, the one who called him a loser at the docks and then called him a disgusting little troll. Well, maybe she didn't say "disgusting." Or "little." But she most certainly said "troll," which *implied* disgusting and little.

Why Matthew always has to fall for the most impossible of women is beyond him. But it's tricky not to fall for Milan Gotay, with her flirty blond hair and her amazing backside. Ricky makes fun of the size of Milan's ass, and Matthew is like, What the fuck are you talking about, dude? She's *spectacular*. Ricky says he's "had" Milan, and that she was "okay," but Matthew doesn't believe it. Doesn't believe it. Even though he saw them on the couch that time, pretty close. Ricky's such a jerk. Even after claiming to have "done" Milan, Ricky talked about how he wants to have sex with Milan's sister. Ricky thinks Milan's sister, Geneva, is more attractive than Milan herself. Most men would probably agree, but that's because most men are drawn to the obvious. Not Matthew. He is drawn to the subtle beauty of unassuming women, and his taste in women has nothing to do with fashion magazines. Women like Geneva are like simple melodies, like nursery rhymes. You can transcribe their essence in a nanosecond. But women like Milan are layered, contrapuntal, with twists of melody you have to listen to very closely to detect. He senses that Milan has a wild streak. A longing inside of her. Ricky is a dumb-ass. How could any normal man not be affected by a rump like Milan's? Evolution has programmed men to appreciate a woman's swellings. Matthew is start-ing to wonder if Ricky is actually part of the same species as other people. As Matthew sets the wok down in the sink to wash it, he wonders if Ricky isn't secretly gay. Not that it would matter. Plenty of Latin-pop singers are gay. Most of them, it seems. But still.

Troll?

"Fuck," says Matthew. He runs the water until it's scalding.

As he sets the clean wok on the plastic drainboard, Matthew hears a knock at his front door. Only door. It's a small apartment. Surprised, he dries his hands on a paper towel, tosses it in the wastebasket under the kitchen sink, and strides across the living room on his short legs. He peers through the lookout hole in the door.

"Fucking shit," he says. He runs his hands across his thinning hair, and searches the room for a baseball cap. TV remote, *Details* magazine, dirty socks, a week's worth of *Heralds*. No caps. No. Please tell him he isn't washing all of them, at the laundry down the street. Please tell him that isn't what he is doing. He considers tying a shirt around his head, but realizes that the dignified thing to do is deal with his balding head honestly. He opens the door, and there she is.

"Eydis," he says.

She has on jeans and a cheap-looking sparkly shirt, sneakers, and the sad, childish face she wears when she is about to ask him to take her back. She carries an orange duffel bag and her fingernails have chipped purple polish on them. She's a complete, lovely mess.

"Can I come in?" she asks as she chews the tip of one of her fingers.

"Uh, sure," says Matthew. He stands to the side, and resists the urge to kiss her. Nothing has changed. No matter how desperately he wants things to change in his feelings for her, they never do. As she walks to the sofa, he watches her beautiful bottom.

"What are you doing here?" he asks. He looks at his watch. He has dinner plans with a Cuban rapper named Goyo, from Los Angeles, later, to talk over a couple of tracks for his new album.

She plops down on the sofa and looks around. "It's a mess," she says.

"Yes, and it's my mess. That's why it's my house. What are you doing here?"

Eydis shrugs and her eyes begin to fill with tears. He hates when she cries. He has to be tough with her this time. He has to say no this time. Maybe he could have sex with her and then he could say no. No. It doesn't work that way. He has to get her out of here.

"He left me," she whines.

"Who?"

"Shasi. The drummer."

"The hairy Israeli."

Eydis smiles a little, still crying. "Yeah," she says, dreamy. "He's very hairy."

"Why?"

"His genetics."

"No, I mean why did he *leave* you."

"Actually, I caught him sexing with the massage therapist on the ship."

Matthew sits on the floor near the sofa but not near enough for Eydis to reach him. He loves her accent when she says "sexing." Quite adorable, actually. He also thinks of how cool it would be to fuck a massage therapist. They probably know all kinds of tricks. Then he wonders how massage therapists deal with men as hairy as the Israeli. Shave them first? Extra oil?

"That's sad, Eydis, but it still doesn't explain why you're here."

She looks at him. "I love you," she says.

"Funny how you always love me when you're feeling rejected."

She's about to speak, but is cut short by the ringing of Matthew's telephone. She jumps to answer it, which Matthew finds alarming and frightening—and sexy.

"Hello?" she calls in her throaty alto. She screws up her face like she's tasted something bad. "May I ask who's calling? Milan?" She looks at him with jealous rage in her eyes. What is her fucking problem? Milan? Milan is calling him? Eydis continues to talk. "Hello, Milan. This is Matthew's girlfriend, Eydis. Oh? You work with him. Okay. Hold on."

Matthew bolts for the phone. Eydis hands it to him with one brow raised in accusation. Matthew snatches the phone from her. As it turns out, Ricky has asked Milan to call Matthew about some tracks that are missing from the studio.

"Tell Ricky I took them home to work on them here over the weekend," says Matthew.

"Okay," says Milan.

"Wait a minute," says Matthew. "Why is Ricky making you call me on a Saturday?" Ricky is a dickhead dictator.

"I'm not sure."

Matthew has a sudden, overwhelming urge to kick the ass of everyone in his life. Eydis, for being a conniving, jealous, heartless bitch. Ricky, for being a lazy dictator. And Milan, for having a voice as beautiful as her face, and for calling him a troll. A *troll*?

"Just tell Ricky to calm down and stop bothering people on the weekend," says Matthew. Milan laughs.

"Okay. Have a good weekend. Sorry to interrupt."

"No, you're not interrupting."

"See you on Monday."

"Okay."

Matthew hangs up, marches directly to the door of his apartment, and opens it. "Out," he says to Eydis. She stares up at him with her clear blue eyes, in shock.

"Sorry?"

"Out."

"But where will I go?"

"I don't know," he says. "But I hear hell is nice this time of year."

"You're not serious." Eydis stands up and lifts her bag.

"Very serious."

"You never turn me away."

"I do now."

"Can we talk?" She tries to touch his face but he swats her hand away.

"No."

Eydis begins to bawl. Don't give in, Matthew tells himself. Don't. "Don't you love me?" she asks. "You said you'd always love me no matter what I did. I made a stupid mistake."

Matthew pushes her out the door. "That was before Shasi," he says. "Have a good life."

Matthew closes the door and locks it. He is not a goddamned troll. And he is not a pussy.

M ilan stands just outside the doorway to La Carreta, with the phone to her ear. She looks pretty, fashiony, and worried, three things I don't think I've seen her look all at once before. "Okay, Ricky," she says in a way that tells me she wants everyone around us to know she is on the phone with Ricky Biscayne. How lame. "I know. I called Matthew earlier, I told you, he's got the tracks. Please calm down."

My sister is working too hard for Ricky. It's Saturday, and she's not supposed to be working. She's supposed to be having the weekly family dinner with me and Mom and Dad and our grandparents. The penance, as I like to call it. I've left Belle at home. I have also decided to rock the familial boat this evening by announcing my love for the black ballet dancer Ignacio, *el negrito más lindo del mundo*. That should be interesting. My parents are terrible racists.

I walk up to Milan. She looks me up and down. What, she's judging me now? Who does she think she is? Please. I'm wearing a BCBG silk mini kimono-style dress and East Indian head scarf, with a liver-shaped Dior detective handbag, in red, and matching sandals. I'm trying to get the whole exotic vibe in every part of my life, to match the essence of the club. People stare. But what else is new? Milan looks good. I mean really good. It's weird. She wears a new shirt, in bright green. She actually shopped for it herself. Not everyone's color. But with her newly blond hair, she looks good. It's unnerving. I'm used to being the only pretty one. I'm not sure I like it.

Milan hangs up. "You look . . . interesting," she tells me.

"Trouble in Ricky land?"

Milan looks tormented. "He's so devoted to his art," she says. "He's, I don't know."

"Obsessive? Tyrannical?"

"Yes." Is it my imagination, or does she look lovelorn? She puts her hands over mine and says, "Please stop with the fingernails, G, I'm not in the mood." I didn't even realize I was picking them.

"You have to set limits with him," I say.

"It's just, I keep listening to his album, and he's so amazing. He has these insights into things, Geneva. His music is so awesome. It's that soul of his. God. I love him."

"Let's go inside." And please stop fawning over that sleazy man. Why can't she tell he's sleazy? We enter La Carreta, one of the top Cuban family restaurants in Miami, and join the motley collection of Gotays at a large round table. I swear to God, at the sight of me their faces droop in disappointment.

"Are you trying to look like a geisha, or a slave?" asks Mom.

"Good to see you, too." I ignore the jab. We girls circle the table, leaning down to hug each person and deliver one quick kiss to each of their cheeks. We take our seats. I quickly unfolded my napkin and put it in my lap. Seeing me do so, Milan follows. That's how she is. She's capable of intelligent choices, but flaky.

"Ricky Biscayne already gave your sister a raise," says Mom. Is she trying to make me jealous? All my life, or at least the part of my life in which Milan has been around, my mom has seemed to want to constantly make Milan feel like she's as good as I am. Which, I should say, only communicates to both of us that Mom prefers me and feels sorry for Milan, but whatever.

"I'm aware of the raise." I am also aware of why. Something to do with coke and sex and a sleazy manager. "I was there."

Milan blushes. "Let's talk about something else."

"She bought clothes and perfume," Mom tells me. Brag, brag, brag.

Dad studies the menu with a frown. "There was nothing wrong with her job before," he says to the menu. "And she's starting to dress like . . ."

"I hear the shrimp is good tonight," says Mom, over the top of Dad's head. Protective of Milan, sweet little defenseless "virginal" Milan. Why can't they see Milan for what she is?

He lowers the menu and points a finger at Milan. "Your uncle, my brother, gave you a very good job, Milan. And now who is Tío going to hire, eh?" He turns his attention to me, still pointing. "And you. You shame the family with your adventures with boys. Why do you need to flaunt your dating? The two of you girls, I don't understand it. You have perfectly good lives, and you want more, more, more, better, better, better." He points a finger toward the ceiling. He's always pointing somewhere. "In Cuba, you would never have been this spoiled."

The waitress comes and takes our orders without a notepad, having all but memorized our choices, which rarely vary. *Masas de puerco* for Dad. Chicken soup for Mom. Shrimp for Abuelita. Chicken soup and Cuban steak for Abuelito. *Vaca frita* for Milan. I get my usual: Cuban steak with french fries, and a creamy, sweet mamey shake.

"I think I'll have the club open by fall," I blurt after the waitress goes. They all murmur their congratulations. Don't be so enthusiastic, I think. They don't understand me, or what I do.

Most miserable-looking of all is Grandpa. And he isn't the only one. All the old men in the restaurant look depressed as hell. I feel bad for them, but in a way, they have created their own misery. They could have spent the last forty years making the best of things, or at the very least learning English, but they haven't. They complained their way through four decades, the ultimate procrastinators. I have no patience for procrastinators.

Dad takes over the conversation, to talk about his own business. I guess it was too threatening for him to consider that I might be doing as well as he is. Or better. He talks for a half hour, and then the food comes. After that, Dad starts to talk about all his friends who have daughters who are getting married, and how proud the parents are of them. Blech.

Time to rock their world.

"I don't think I'll ever get married," I say. "I like being single. I mean, why tie yourself down to a domineering creep if you don't have to?" Yes, Dad, I'm talking about *you*.

Milan's eyes wander to the front door, and she gasps. We all turn to see what she's looking at. I see two men, a black one and a balding redheaded one, standing in the entry waiting for a table.

"What's wrong?" I ask Milan.

"Nothing, it's just that *guy*." She lowers her head as if she doesn't want to be seen.

"Which one?"

"The redheaded one," she says. "I work with him. His name is Matthew."

"That's the one you knocked into the water at the docks," our mother says to Milan.

"Quit exaggerating! He ran into me and no one fell into the water, Mom. God!"

Taking her cue, our grandmother begins to babble. "Whoso shall receive one such little child in my name receiveth me," she says. "But whoso shall offend one of these little ones which believe in me, it were better for him that a millstone were hanged about his neck, and that he were drowned in the depth of the sea."

"Cheery," I say.

"What is he doing here?" asks Milan. "I see him everywhere. It's very weird."

"He's freakin' *hot*," I say of the black one. "Wow." I recognize him as a famous Cuban rapper named Goyo, and tell the table. None of them seem to have heard of him, but that is the way it is in my universe. They know nothing of the things that I value.

Milan makes eye contact with Matthew, and they wave awkwardly to each other before the two men are ushered to a table in a far corner of the back room. Grandma falls silent, and we all resume eating. Milan's cheeks are flushed red, and I wonder if she's falling for Ricky and every other man at that office. What have I done to her? I should have never thrown her into this world, made over her clothes and hair. It's all over now.

As everyone eats, my mother asks, "So, Geneva. Who are you being *single* with these days? Anyone special?" The look in her eyes tells me she knows I'm seeing someone new. Did Milan tell her about Ignacio? I shoot Milan a look, and she shakes her head as if to say, *I didn't say a thing.*

I hold a piece of meat in the air near my mouth. "Yes, actually," I say.

Milan asks, as if she did not already know, "Who is he? Do we know him?"

"He's a Cuban ballet dancer," I say.

"Ballet!" screeches our grandfather. "*¡Qué cosa!*"

"From Cuba?" asks Dad.

"Yeah. Fresh off the boat. And he's black." I grin and sip my shake.

Mom gasps. Dad slams his fork down on his plate. Abuelo stares miserably at the wall, mumbling something to himself, and Grandma is the first to speak, crossing herself.

"Well, there you go. I told you all she was no good."

She did? I thought my grandma liked me.

"He's a really nice guy," says Milan. "I met him."

Mom stares in shock at Milan. "You met him? You never told me you met him. You said you *saw* him, but not that you met him."

"You told her about Ignacio?" I cry. "*Kennedita!*"

"No," says Milan. "I mean, yes." Mom finds something interesting on her shirt, and Milan tries to look pathetic. I don't know these women. I don't.

My grandfather speaks. "No granddaughter of mine is going to marry a black man!"

"Who said I'm getting married?" I say. "We're just having sex."

Everyone gasps. Grandpa looks like he is choking.

Dad hisses, "Do not speak that way at this table."

I say, "Can someone in this family please tell me what the problem with black people is? Look at us. Am I the only one who notices that Dad's side of the family looks black? Grandpa, your own dad was black because your grandma got it on with her hired help. Everyone knows that."

"Don't say that," says Mom.

"Why? Because it's the truth?"

"It's not true," says Mom.

"Trust me. If you people went to any other city in this country, you'd see that everywhere else in the United States people like us look black. Except you, Milan. I don't know where you came from."

"Postman?" jokes Milan. Dad reddens in the face. "Cable guy?"

"You girls can't do this to your family," says Dad. He tosses his napkin onto the table to let everyone know exactly how he feels. Suddenly, it seems like everyone is talking at once, angry about a man they've never met, angry about the first man in my life who actually makes me happy.

monday, may 13

The feeling of hip bones spreading apart to make room for growing womb is at once horrible and amazing. It's like when ship gets waterlogged and starts to crack apart. I ache. Everywhere. In breasts most of all. I gained twenty-five pounds already, and can still wear my favorite old Yanuk jeans, but only with zipper down. I wear big shirt over it and no one knows the difference.

I'm sitting in sunny breakfast nook of large gourmet kitchen in my house, which really still feels like Ricky's house. I asked if I could start to redecorate, and he has limited me to baby's room only. Unfair. When you're married, you're supposed to share everything fifty-fifty, but Ricky doesn't seem to understand that part. Or he doesn't want to. He is very possessive of house the way it is.

I sip iced ginger tea Ricky's mother, Alma, has prepared for me, out of favorite blown-glass, blue-bottomed drinking glass. I think it's Kate

Spade, but who cares? I am sick of designers, names, trends. I hate modeling and all the stupid people involved with it. I should never have fallen into that hole, but it's how it happened and it's done and I have to move on now. Without modeling, I wouldn't have met Ricky. And life is about something else now. This baby. My body growing. Colors. They are so much brighter when pregnant. Smells, which for me have always been very rich, are so much richer. Pregnancy takes knob on your "life panel" and cranks it up. I am superhuman, or at least that is how I feel, in a very nesting, nurturing sense.

Alma pads around kitchen, worrying over me, preparing things she thinks I need and storing them in plastic containers. She is kind woman, but prickly. The cool, rich color of blown glass matches the bay out window, and soothes me. At three months pregnant now, I feel horrible nausea beginning to subside in afternoons, but not in mornings. This morning, I felt little sick, but also very hungry. Mishko lies on cold travertine tiles at my feet, panting a little and waiting for something delicious to fall to into her universe. I want to be like Mishko, taking what comes, not wanting or asking for too much, content to rest and simply be.

Alma stands at stove preparing banana pancakes. Lately, I can't get enough with blueberry syrup. I don't know what magical ingredient they contain, but I need it. As I stare out window, I see Milan teeter past on a pair of high heels and tight jeans. I still admire the way curvy Milan's clothes fit her, but I don't like way she looks at my husband. She worships him, and I think she wants him the way a woman wants a man. It makes me sad. So many of young women who come to work for Ricky have that look in their eyes. I believe he is faithful to me, but I know Ricky is weak and that biggest need in life is to be loved by women. I seen him look at her body. You might think because I have been model I would be secure about my looks in comparison to a woman like Milan, but I'm not. There is kind of beauty that goes on magazine pages, which I think is admired most by other women and gay men, and then there is animal attraction that men feel for bodies like Milan's, bodies that feel good to touch, to move

against. I am jealous. And I think best way to make sure Milan does
nothing to Ricky is to become friends with her so that at least she
feels some loyalty toward me and at most I can know her well enough
to read her.

Maybe once baby is born I'll have hips and body like that, too. I
don't know. Ricky has started to complain about weight I've gained.
I'm size eight now, and he told me he wants to build me a home gym
so that I can get back down to "normal" size after all this. But he
doesn't realize I have no intention of doing that. I am going to stay
this size, or bigger. Before I left my home country, I was big girl, probably equal to American size ten. I like how my feet feel upon ground
now. I feel solid. I'm not going back.

I sigh with thought of Ricky. Why such heaviness? We have not
made love in two weeks. He says he doesn't feel like it. I feel like it all
the time.

I turn away from Milan and back to Alma. With her sophisticated
silver bob, peach skin, and dark eyes, Ricky's mother is truly striking,
and steady. Even her clothes seem steady, never wrinkled in any way.
Today, Alma wears tidy, pale yellow pantsuit with beige sandals. She is
always nicely put together, like many middle-aged women I've seen in
Miami, a city where women worry about beauty until they die. I love
Alma for steadiness. Alma has worked all her adult life as paralegal for
same firm and isn't the kind of woman who takes a lot of chances. She
likes things predictable, which might explain why she doesn't seem to
approve of her own son, my husband.

"Drink," says Alma with her thick Spanish accent, pouring a bit
more tea into my glass before returning to flip pancakes. She grew up
in Mazatlán. "It will help you feel better." Alma leaves pancakes to
brown and turns attention to box of pastel soaps I brought out for her
to sample. I make them in one of guest rooms, a room I've converted
into soap factory with all my potions and chemicals. She picks up
sage-colored bar, in the shape of leaf, and sniffs.

"Exquisite," she says. She does the same with half-dozen other
soaps, all delicately scented and beautifully molded. I put all of the

love I feel for my child into my craft. I enjoy it. "I can't believe you did all this here in your house," says Alma. "You are very talented, *mija*."

"No," I say. "Is just hobby."

"You get good packaging, you could sell these on the Home Shopping Network. They're as good as anything out there."

I smile and sip tea. Alma is very kind—to me. More so to me than to Ricky. I am feeling better. Of all Alma's remedies for morning sickness, this cold tea works best. Sea-Bands are waste of money. Meditation does not help. Ginger is a good thing, though. A very good thing.

"Feeling better?" she asks. I nod. "Good enough to catch the movie?" She scoops pancakes out of pan, puts them on thick blue dinner plate, and sets plate in front of me. We've made plans to see romantic comedy together, and I feel well enough to go. I tell her I still want to go and she smiles. I think she likes having someone to do things with. I don't think Alma has many friends. I drench pancakes in blue syrup and dig in.

"Is delicious, Alma. Thank you."

Alma looks at me with sadness in eyes and answers in slow voice. "You're too good for my son," she says. I suspect this is compliment.

The back door opens with squeak of hinges. Ricky doesn't keep house up as he should. I need to call someone to fix door and other things. Milan peeks her head in to say she is just checking to make sure everything is all right. Alma's nostrils flare and her eyes narrow. I can smell Milan's perfume on breeze that blows in. Something yellow and sunny.

"Did Ricky tell you to check on her?" she asks Milan.

"Uh, well, sort of," says Milan.

Alma shakes her head as if this greatly annoys her, and Milan apologizes.

"We're fine, thanks," I say. I try to seem friendly. It isn't Milan's fault Ricky doesn't trust me. "How's it going back there?"

"I'm just about to take my lunch break," says Milan. "But it's good." A huge smile takes over her face. "I am so, so happy to be here.

You have no idea how much fun this job is for me. I call people, and they listen to me. In my old job it wasn't like that. People love Ricky."

"They do," I agree. "I know."

Milan beams and bounces a little on her toes. "I just landed a pro-file in *Details*."

"Good for you, honey," says Alma. "Ricky's lucky to have you."

"Come with us to movies," I blurt. It's probably inappropriate, but this occurs to me too late.

"Really?" Milan looks around as if someone might have overheard. "I don't know. I have some work."

"Do it later," says Alma. "Ricky wants you to spy on his wife, so we'll do even better. Come with us. Let's have some fun."

"Really? You think that'd be okay?" Milan comes into kitchen and closes door.

"Absolutely," I say.

Alma nods, says, "Girls' afternoon out."

I feel good. Eating, in kitchen full of solid women, my belly filled with fresh life. I feel as if small roots are sprouting on bottoms of my feet, attaching me, at last, to the earth. I look around the room, and my eyes stop at knife block.

For the first time in the longest time I can remember, I am com-pletely free of the urge to cut myself.

What am I doing? Going to a movie with Ricky's mom and his wife? After kissing him? And after feeling every single day like I want to take him away from this woman? This is crazy. Before he left on this latest trip to New York, Ricky hinted that he wants us to get closer when he gets back. I've resisted him so far, because it seems stupid to do anything else, but I don't know how much longer I can. I really don't.

Mrs. Batista drives us in her Toyota Camry, which rattles and thumps like it needs a tune-up. I'm ready to hop in the back, as usual, when Jasminka tells me to take the front seat. Huh?

"Really?" I ask.

"Yes, I need space to stretch. And you are guest."

Imagine.

As Alma eases out of the driveway, I see Matthew unchaining his bike to go to lunch. He's all sweaty-looking. "Ay, poor Matthew," says Alma.

"Why poor Matthew?" asks Jasminka.

"Ricky doesn't appreciate him," says Alma.

"I think he does," says Jasminka. She sounds annoyed. Like maybe Alma insults Ricky all the time.

"He's a good man, Matthew. He'll make a woman quite a husband someday," says Alma.

"I hear he has a girlfriend," I say, thinking back to the phone call and that weird girl who answered.

"No, he does not," says Jasminka, surprised.

I say, "No, he *does*. I called him on Saturday and this woman said she was his girlfriend. She had a weird accent." I realize too late that I am speaking to two women who have accents. Oops.

"Oh no," says Jasminka.

"What?" asks Alma.

Jasminka sighs. "He's back together with her. I thought he was done with her."

"He's sort of cute," I offer. I mean it, but I also think that to seem interested in someone else will help to erase the scent of Ricky on my lips.

"There's something about him, no?" asks Alma, with a smile at me. "He has passion and compassion. Passion without compassion is useless."

"I can't believe he took her back," says Jasminka.

Alma nods. "Ricky lacks compassion."

What is *that* about? Why would the mother of one of the most successful recording artists in the world say something like that? How weird.

Jasminka leans forward and puts a hand on Alma's shoulder. "Alma, with respect I ask you: Why you are so hard on Ricky?"

Alma shrugs. "With men, you can never be too careful." Hello? This is too weird. "Ay, Jasminka. I know you love my Ricky, and I am blessed for that. A saint like you to fall in love with my son and bear him a child."

Jasminka says, "Ricky's amazing. Why you don't see that?"

Yeah, I think. Why don't you see that? I see it. I shouldn't, but I do.

"He's a good man," says Ricky's mom. "But he's a man."

"I don't know what you are supposed to mean," says Jasminka.

"Ricky has his weaknesses. I worry about him, and about you. That's all."

"No, Mom, there's nothing to worry about." Mom? She's calling this woman Mom and they're talking about how much "Mom" hates her own son. Weird. Creepy.

"I hope not," says Alma. "Ever since he was little, Ricky has liked danger. There was the time he tried to jump over a canal and almost drowned in it."

She pauses, as if this might have some meaningful bearing on Ricky's life now.

"He was little boy, Mom. Little boys do things like this." Jasminka retreats to the backseat again.

"He used to tie up lizards and hit them against the wall. Did you know this?"

"You told me."

"I used to cry." Alma sniffles as if she might start anew. "The lizards all bloody and dead in the yard. I thought he'd be a serial killer. I used to look at him and say to myself, My God, where did this boy come from? Who is this child? How is this person from my body? He was so different from me."

Now? Now I'm feeling like a total intruder. They're talking like I'm not even here, and really I shouldn't be. It's not good.

"I think Ricky would like it very much if you were proud of him, Ma."

"I am! I love my son." She is fully crying now. Hello? Get me out of here. I kissed Ricky. I'm horrible. I'm a horrible person. "I'm so proud of him. I love him. I just worry about him. He makes bad decisions, Jasminka. You don't see this in him yet. But I am telling you." She looks at me, finally. "I'm glad he hired you. Make sure he's surrounded by good people, because if he's left to pick them on his own, he won't make good choices. He makes a lot of mistakes."

Yeah, I think. Like me.

Jasminka steps to his defense again. "He has good people. I'm proud of Ricky, and happy for him."

Alma Batista eases the car to a stop at a red light and turns to look directly at Jasminka. "You're such a sweet, loving girl," she says, as if this were the saddest thing in the world.

Chester, the black tomcat adopted by rookie firefighter Nestor Perez when less-than-kind neighbors moved out of the apartment complex and left the creature stranded, meows. Actually, Nestor supposes, Chester *thinks* he is meowing. In truth, Chester makes a noise somewhere between furious banshee and infant with sprained ankle: *Wrrroooowwww!*

"What is it, buddy?" Nestor kneels on the floor of his small kitchen and scratches the base of Chester's mangled ears. Years of fighting for proprietary rights in the middle of Kendall have made Chester tough, but a recent neuter operation has made him whiny.

Wrrroooowww!

Chester rubs against the soft gray cotton of Nestor's pajamas, and purrs. The veterinarian told Nestor that purring was a good sign, a sign that the cat had not always been feral. Someone, somewhere in Chester's history, had once loved him. Nestor Perez takes comfort in the fact that Chester has found love again, and hopes that one day he can say the same of himself.

"Here you go, bud," says Nestor, popping the top on a can of cat health food, the kind in an orange can that you can only buy from a veterinarian. The stuff is expensive, but, as the only love in Nestor's life at the moment, Chester is worth it.

As Chester gobbles from his blue dish with the fish decorations, Nestor opens the refrigerator to forage for breakfast. He hates days off. There is too much to think about, things in the past that he doesn't want to think about. He takes a carton of orange juice and a bag of scones from the refrigerator and shuts the door. Then, he stands looking at the photographs taped there. The chubby woman with the cornrow braids has a smile that threatens to take over her face. She holds a little girl of two who looks exactly like her in miniature; the girl holds a tiny Dominican flag on a little wooden stick, a relic from their day at the Dominican Parade. Together, mother and daughter sit at the top of the big slide in the playground in Central Park in New York, the summer sun dappling the ground in a million shades of peace. Nestor had snapped the photo one month before his wife and daughter died in a fire in their Washington Heights apartment building while he was away at night school studying to be a civil rights attorney. Lisa, his wife, had owned an art gallery on 125th Street, dedicated to Afro-Dominican diaspora works. Their daughter, Fabiola, had just started preschool and made her first best friend.

For months after the fire, Nestor slipped into the deepest depression of his life, turning to alcohol with a vengeance that dissipated only after his parents and siblings, and Lisa's family, had an intervention in his childhood home in the Bronx and insisted he get help. He'd gotten help, and though his heart continued to exist in tatters and smears somewhere inside his lower stomach, he made the decision to become a fireman instead of a lawyer, so that at the very least he might one day save another man like himself from his own fate.

He'd trained in New York, but that city was full of ghosts now. The museums and independent movie houses were unbearable because it was Lisa who had introduced him to these places. The sounds of children laughing or even crying anywhere in the city drove him to thoughts of suicide. Where was his little Fabiola? What had happened to that person, such a spirited being, so full of life, more alive than anything he'd known? Though the warm scent of her hair had long since faded from the pillow on which Fabiola used to sleep at his mother's house now and then, Nestor continued to sleep with it clutched to his chest, his nose desperate for some small trace of her. Where the hell was she? How could the most important person in your life just *disappear*? Was she afraid on the other side? Did she need her father? Was he selfish for living, with her needing him somewhere in heaven? Sometimes for entire weeks Nestor Perez intentionally stopped checking for cars before crossing the street, praying that God would take him to his family so that he might nuzzle Fabiola's hair once again, and feel Lisa's breath against his skin.

Finally, Nestor's mother suggested he leave town for a while and try to make a life for himself somewhere else. He had an aunt and some cousins in Miami, so that's where he decided to go. It couldn't be worse than New York.

But now that he has his first job in firefighting, now that he's made a home for himself in a clean, anonymous one-bedroom apartment, and now that he's found the lost soul of Chester to comfort, Nestor finds the monumental sorrow in his body turning to rage. His hands tremble as he sits at the small dining table and pours himself some orange juice. He feels unhinged by the tremendous injustice of the world, by the natural disasters that take innocent people by the hundreds of thousands, but also by the many close-minded, small-thinking people who make life miserable for those who are left behind.

Chester, the world's fastest-eating cat, is already finished, and has found a comfy chunk of sunlight on the living room carpet in which to bathe himself, licking with his eyes half-closed in utter content-ment. Nestor envies the cat his peace and pleasure. He's forgotten how to laugh. How to relax. Nestor bites into a grocery-store raisin scone and promises himself he will try to begin again to enjoy simple things: food, sunlight, a warm shower. But it will not be easy. His life here seems almost as painful as his life in New York. Ghosts know no state boundaries. Ghosts live in your very cells.

"What are we going to do today, Chester?" he asks. The cat re-sponds only by slightly flattening his ears. The licking is all-consuming. That's okay, thinks Nestor. He knows what he will do to-day. He'll do what he does most of the time when he doesn't work. He'll ride his hybrid street bike until he can't ride any farther, and then he'll turn around and force his exhausted body to pedal home again. He's programmed his iPod with happy music, merengue mostly, in hopes that the combination of music therapy and endorphins will rocket him out of his private hell. It usually works for a few hours, but then the guilt returns. The heavy truth of his loss.

Nestor's mother, a nurse-practitioner in a mental health hospital, believes the only solution is for him to find love again, a woman who might rescue what is left of him. Nestor does not fall in love easily; but he is starting to feel something small and soft hatching in his soul for Irene Gallagher, the beautiful, fierce-eyed firefighter.

His new coworkers are bigots. They pick on the weak, the lonely, the tragic. Women. Nestor has always thought of firefighting men as gentlemen, or at the very least as gallant. But now he knows better. And in the past, Nestor might have assumed that someone like Irene, with her blond hair and blue eyes, could never have had a harder life than his dark-skinned mother had, for the mere fact of Irene's white-ness. But now, since the fire, Nestor finds that he doesn't differentiate between races anymore. The fire that took his wife and child had not discriminated—it had taken white people, black people, Puerto Ri-cans, Italians, anyone who had been sleeping in the night in their beds. And Nestor has seen the grief of the survivors of all those lives taken, and that grief looks the same. Life and those who stagger through it, looking for meaning, are colorless to Nestor Perez now.

If nothing else, his suffering has made him particularly able to sense sorrow in his fellow human beings, and in the person of Irene Gallagher he senses solitude and tragedy almost as deep as his own. He doesn't know her story, not entirely, but he will. He won't push her. He'll wait.

Unable to believe completely in the randomness of life after the two most precious people in the world were stolen from him, Nestor has become convinced that there's a higher order to things. He now believes he's been sent to this place and this time to save not a victim of a fire but a victim of the fire *department*. His goal now is to become Irene's friend, and persuade her to fight the idiots in charge. He knows enough about the law, having been only one semester removed from his degree, to know that she might have a discrimination case. He also knows that she is an uncommonly attractive woman, and that he has always been drawn to women of strength and humor.

Convinced for the past six years that he could never love again, Nestor Perez has begun to doubt that conviction, thanks to a cat named Chester.

tuesday, may 14

I'm going home in a damn good mood, with the intention of drinking a protein shake, stretching my sore legs and back, and going to sleep early. Just as I was leaving the firehouse today I ran into Nestor Perez in the parking lot, on my way off shift as he was coming on. When I first saw him he was bent over, getting his overnight bag out of the backseat of his car. Lord God. *That* was a lovely sight, about the loveliest sight I have seen in years.

He actually brought me a present, if you can believe that. A small box of Godiva chocolates, and a card that said, "Let no one hold you down," about the lieutenant position. He included his phone number in it and said that if I ever felt unsafe or afraid at work and he wasn't on duty, all I had to do was call him and he'd be there in a matter of minutes to help out. "Think of me as your big brother," he wrote. His script was neat, deliberate. I realized when I saw his handwriting that Nestor was a calm, organized man. He *had* to be gay. A brother? Think of me as your brother? That didn't sound good. Oh well.

I walk into the house and find my mom sprawled on the sofa, asleep with a bag of Doritos on her chest. Sad. I hear loud music coming from Sophia's bedroom. I recognize the singing voice, and feel my blood run cold. Ricky Biscayne? Oh no no no. *Hell* no.

Okay. So it's normal to find teenagers listening to loud music. It's almost a cliché. But it is not normal to find girls like Sophia listening to the racy lyrics of one Mr. Ricky Biscayne on the little stereo boom box I originally bought for myself but which my kid has stolen. I used to use if for my Norah Jones and Paula Cole CDs, but it's Sophia's now. Single mothers own very little of their own.

I set my bag down in the hallway and open my daughter's bedroom door.

"Hello? Knock?" cries Sophia, offended, her hand over the mouthpiece of the phone. Right. I should knock. But I'm too angry to knock.

"Who are you talking to?" I demand.

The girl sprawls on her belly on the twin bed, with the sleeves for what look like two or three Ricky Biscayne CDs open and spread out around her. She wears her soccer shorts and a large T-shirt, with yellowed sports socks. I need to buy her more socks. How could I keep forgetting that? She's needed socks for months now. I'm so tired.

Sophia holds her hand up to silence me. She has the phone to her ear with a shoulder, and she's scribbling something on one of her school notebooks. Next to the notebook is a gossip magazine with a photo spread on Ricky Biscayne and his Miami Beach mansion and beautiful model wife. I read the headline upside down: AND BABY MAKES TRES. I feel sick.

"Okay, thanks," Sophia says into the phone. "So I take the seventy to the one and transfer there? Do I have to pay twice? Okay. I appreciate it."

She looks up at me with an expression of betrayal of her face.

"You can't just walk in here, Mom. I need my privacy."

I walk to the stereo and turn it off. "Who were you talking to?" I feel my blood slow down, even as my heart speeds up. The body preparing for a fight. I hate this. She better not have been talking to Ricky. There's no way Sophia could have gotten in touch with Ricky, is there?

"No one." She sounds bratty. I hate myself for even thinking the

word "bratty," which my mother used against me when I was only de-
fending myself.

Sophia sounds "girlie." Let me change it to that. I'd hoped my
daughter would never be the kind of kid who sounded like that, a
"back-talker" as my mother called it. I was a hell of a back-talker in
my day, and though I know this very defensive quality might serve
Sophia well later in life, I don't want to butt heads with her. It is too
painful to lose my baby girl this way, to see her transform into a surly,
and, yes, bratty teenager.

"I was *listening* to that," says Sophia, pointing to the stereo. "Put it
back on." Sophia sits up, pouty. "Now!"

How do you talk to a daughter like this? Grounding her doesn't
work, because Sophia just ignores the punishment. I'm never around
to enforce it. And Alice? Useless. I rub my temples with my fingertips.
"Not right now, Sophia. I have a headache."

"You *always* have a headache." Her voice is accusatory.

I flop down on the floor next to my daughter's bed and stare up at
the ceiling. It has a water-leak stain. I've been meaning to fix it, but
forgot. Sophia has pasted glow-in-the dark stars there to cover it up. I
had no idea. I hate that I don't know things about her, obvious things
like this. "I know. I know I always have a headache. I know you can't
stand me. I know you need your privacy. Now tell me who you were
talking to."

Sophia gets up and turns the music on again, lowering the volume.

"So, like, I like the third song the most," she says. She presses the
buttons until the song comes on. She surprises me by singing along, in
Spanish, reading the words off the CD jacket. I don't understand a
whole lot of Spanish, but enough to know that the song is a lie, something about love and devotion, love until the end of time.

"Turn it off," I say. "Now."

Sophia glares at me. She looks like a grown-up, like she could beat
me down. Scary. "Make me."

I turn my head and look at her. Take it all in. She's tall and defiant,

with eyes like her father's. You don't raise them to be like their fathers, but it happens anyway. I sit up and stack the CDs neatly in the
center of the bed.

"Where did you get these?"

"A *truth* fairy left them under my pillow."

"Very funny. How did you pay for them?"

Sophia shrugs and grimaces, sarcastic. "I didn't know Ricky's kids
had to pay for his music. Did you?"

My headache gets worse. "Sophia."

Sophia mimics me. *"Mother."*

"Who were you talking to?"

"Not to Ricky Biscayne, if that's what you're worried about. But I
will. You'll see."

What can I do? Get another job that pays as well as the one I have
now? No. But I can't keep working these hours, leaving this girl on her
own. She needs me now more than ever. She might look grown, but
she's not. If I don't do something, and quickly, at this rate Sophia is
bound to end up like all the other fatherless girls around here, pregnant and on drugs, rebellious. Something has to give.

"Where did you get the CDs, Soph?"

"If you must know, I stole them from Wal-Mart."

"Well, put on your shoes." I stand up, stretch, crack my back.

Sophia looks insulted. "Why?"

"We're going back to pay for them."

Sophia stares angrily at her me, her eyes slowly filling with tears.
"I hate you. You knew. You knew all along, and you never told me.
Why not?"

I feel the pit of unease solidify in my gut like a cold chunk of granite. "Come on, get your shoes on."

"No. I don't want to get my shoes on."

Sophia grabs the CDs and runs from the room. The young woman
she will soon be has disappeared for the moment, and the child she
has been returns. "I hate you!" she screams.

I follow her to the kitchen and corner her by the small wooden table. "You can't just take things from stores, Sophia," I say. "You know better than stealing, honey."

Sophia dries her eyes with the back of one long, lanky arm, and stares at me. Hard and cold, like a cat. "So do *you*," she says. "You're nothing but a hypocrite."

I shake my head to let Sophia know I don't understand what she means. But I do. I know. She's right. I know it. I know, and it hurts like hell.

"You stole my *father* from me," the girl shrieks, pounding her chest with one hand. "And I think it's time you paid me back."

"Why do you think he's your father, Sophia?" It's a last ditch effort, but I have to do something.

"I don't just think, I *know*," says Sophia. She hits her chest with a fist. "Here. I know it here, Mom. I know."

We share a long look, and then I feel tears begin to form in my eyes. I sit at the table, and am pleasantly surprised when Sophia does the same. Alice, for her part, continues to sleep through it all. I wonder if my mom's doing drugs again. Probably.

I start to cry a bit and wish I could stop it. "I just didn't want him to hurt you the way he hurt me," I confess, at last.

"Just because you hated your dad doesn't mean I have to hate mine," blasts Sophia, unaware of how deeply wounded I was by the hands of my father. No one but Alice knows, and she probably doesn't remember all the times my dad beat me nearly unconscious in drunken rage.

"That's not it, Sophia," I say. It probably is, though. I have a smart kid. "Ricky left me when I was pregnant, because his mom said I was white trash. Okay? That's the truth."

"That's stupid," says Sophia.

"I know."

"No, that you'd say that. Mexicans can't be racist against white people."

I laugh. Yeah, right. "People are complicated, Sophia. His mom comes from money in Mexico."

"That's stupid."

"No one in his family called me back after I had you. It was like they thought we were untouchables. Like in India. That's how they treated us."

Sophia's eyes narrow. "Maybe Ricky hurt you because he hates you just like I do."

Ouch. Jesus God, but ouch. I feel like someone has struck my body with a belt buckle, the way my dad used to, and I gasp. How can my kid be so horrible? Sophia smiles at the face on the CD cover. "But he'd never hurt *me*. I know that for a fact."

friday, may 24

*J*ill Sanchez smiles as the flashbulbs pop, and does her best to seem like she is giggling and ducking her way past mildly annoying paparazzi and reporters in the back of a shiny white Lincoln Town Car. She pretends to be shocked that they have the nerve to invade her privacy, even though she is actually castigating her fiancé, Jack, who sits at her side, aping the photographers.

"Quit pouting and smile," she says through clenched, smiling teeth. It isn't her fault that they have to run damage control on more stories about Jack's strip-club habit. It is his fault. And this evening, damage control involves an outrageously flirty petticoat minidress by Dsquared, bodicey and tight up top, yet roomy enough in the lower half to invite speculation that she might be pregnant, even though she, of course, isn't. There is no better trick for keeping your picture and story in the magazines than pretending to want to be pregnant, and teasing the cameras. Dowdy, it is not, however. It is very short, and her legs are creamed and glittered to perfection, the golden thighs peeking ever so expertly out of the soft, beige suede knee-high stiletto go-go boots. Jill Sanchez wants the look to say "one sexy mama, maybe," and it does.

"Rumi sucked, and this Tantra shit will suck, too," says Jack of today's outing. He wears another one of the outfits she's picked for him, intended, she says, to give him a "Ward Cleaver meets Kurt Cobain" vibe. Just the kind of dad you want, he thinks; goes to the office in the morning, shoots his fucking brains out in the evening. He wears a button-down shirt, open, and dark jeans that he actually kind of digs. With sandals that he fucking hates. He is happy to note to himself that he has a business trip coming up in his favorite city of Los Angeles, and he will soon be out of this nightmare and back in his own neck of the woods.

Jill has chosen Tantra for their "date" because of the sexual connotations, because she wants to convey an image of love and joy in her relationship, as a form of damage control. The restaurant and nightclub in South Beach is known for its unblushingly sexual menu, filled with racy quotes like "a woman should never be seen eating and drinking unless it's lobster, caviar, and Champagne," and dishes guaranteed to enhance, increase, and otherwise really rev up the libido.

Only happy, horny lovers go to Tantra, in the estimation of Jill Sanchez. They come to Tantra to share the Tantra combo: Pacific oysters, shrimp, calamari salad, sweet-soy-grilled eel, lobster wontons, crab claws, tuna sushi, and wasabi sorbet. It is a place not for the prudish or shy but for hip young lovers who are unashamed of their passionate romps, even if they are on the way to the stodgy old altar.

In reality—a realm Jill Sanchez chooses to inhabit as infrequently as possible—she and Jack have been arguing violently enough the last day or two to have left a scratch from her fingernails on his upper arm. Of course, he hadn't scratched or hit back. He wasn't that kind of guy. He'd just stood there laughing at her with one of his stupid books in his hand. She does not like to think about how physical her relationships sometimes get, because that would be to admit a sort of defeat. Jill Sanchez isn't finished battling this particular demon yet, and so will not be bothered to think about it until it is slain.

Jill doesn't look at Jack again, but she suspects he is still making sarcastic faces at the paparazzi outside of Tantra, even though she's explained it to him a million times: Sarcasm comes across as ugly in photos. And angry. She doesn't want the tabloids speculating about their bad relationship. She wants them noting how happily in love everyone seems. She needs to counter those awful stories they've been running about Jack screwing boy-girls in Tokyo, and that can't very well happen with Jack mocking the reporters, can it? He should nuzzle her neck, or kiss her as if the media weren't there. He should do something to show how desperately and madly in love with her he is, just as she smiles and smiles until her face hurts to prove to the world that she is, in fact, the happiest, luckiest, most beautiful, and richest woman in the world, a woman you'd want to dress like, smell like, and sleep with.

It annoys Jill Sanchez that Jack Ingroff does not take acting as seriously as she does.

Jill Sanchez is pleased that she is able to act at all times, even when she is only acting like herself the way she would like people to think she is.

"Smile," she repeats. "Don't make ugly faces."

Jill Sanchez is not ugly, and she doesn't think her men should be, either. There was only one exception to that rule, and it was D-Kitty, a mealy mouthed rapper with enough money to summer on Cape Cod year round, making his own sunshine and heat with electricity. There were photos of him out last week, playing tennis at his Cape house in the cold, warmed by giant lights and personal-heater holders. Jill continues to admire his style and panache, even though she is not sure exactly what the latter word means. She dated him just long enough to witness some dudes in his crew shooting another rapper, and then she was out, giggling her way through the interviews in which she didn't sob, and sometimes doing both to pump up the sense of her innocence and helplessness in the whole ordeal. The public seems to have forgotten all about how the gun was found stashed beneath her very own seat in the Escalade limo, or about how she'd worn a bandanna around her head like a gang member during that phase of her life. She likes to take chances, but an ugly mouth and a violent crew are not chances worth taking more than once, if you intend to rule the world, which Jill Sanchez does.

Pop! More flashes light up the darkening air of South Beach as Jack and Jill step out of the Town Car and onto the crowded sidewalk. Jill wears sunglasses for the ruse of not wanting to be recognized, but since the shades are her "own" design for her clothing line—indeed with her brand name, JSan, emblazoned in gold leaf across the sides of the frames—it is hard to mistake her for anyone else. She holds her new handbag, a square, butter-soft yellow Celine tote she hopes conveys just the right mix of "diaper bag" and "sexy sack" to create the image she wants. One thing is certain—as soon as the photos are out, everyone in the world will want a bag like this. Lucky Celine.

"This blows," says Jack, as Jill's bodyguards and the poor driver, Yaver, push tourists and other assorted wannabe stars out of the way.

"Jill Sanchez!" people cry. Gasping. Jill Sanchez loves the fact that she has this impact on people. Everyone needs a hero. Better her than some other people she could think of.

They point and stare. They thrust their pens and baseball caps or T-shirts at her in hopes of getting an autograph. A few people ask for Jack's signature, including one very geeky man who only wants Jack's, but most of them want hers, proof that she is right in their ongoing argument about which of them is the more naturally talented celebrity. Jack does not sing. He does not dance. He does not have the creative fire in his belly that Jill does, and Jill is happy to see that all of this is not lost on the public. Jill signs a few and then gives the guards her secret sign, two quick nods, and they cleave a path to the door for her.

"What are you doing here?" someone calls out.

Jill turns before entering the restaurant to get a better look. It is a reporter she recognizes from *People* magazine, so she decides to answer.

Giggling, she waves as if she's just seen an old friend, shielding her eyes as if she cannot quite make out who asked the question, and calls out, "Sometimes you just get a craving for some really good sushi! But no raw fish for a while." She places her hand over her belly, as if she were pregnant and famished, and she giggles.

And with that, she ducks inside as if she is surprised by all the commotion and photographers.

As they settle in at their table, Jill pulls the fawning, overjoyed owner aside and asks that he station four busboys at her table to hold up large white napkins for the duration of their dinner, to obstruct her and Jack from the view of the rest of the people in the restaurant. The owner obliges. Jill is shocked when one of the busboys says hello and asks her how she is doing; he comments that he didn't like Jill's last movie as much as her earlier ones, suggesting she get back to "films of substance."

What? It is not his place to do that. She does not answer. Rather, she quickly asks the owner to replace this particular busboy for invading her privacy. Once his replacement is in place, Jill Sanchez has her bodyguards arrange the men and the napkins just so, giving one or two choice photographers out on the sidewalk a good, if "secret," view of her, while keeping the others guessing.

"Perfect," she says.

"Oh, please," mutters Jack. "You are so full of shit."

"A true star has to work at it," she says, digging once more into his most sensitive spot. "Or it disappears."

"A true star is someone like Don Cheadle or Gael García Bernal," says Jack, babbling again about someone or something irrelevant, "who actually makes a difference in people's lives." Jack is so boring. Jill has a sudden urge to be as far away from Jack Ingroff as possible. He is weird, and he is cramping her style. With that in mind, she takes a deliberate, delicious sip of Champagne, smiles for the cameras in the street and kisses him passionately on the lips. The happier they seem now, the more press their breakup will generate later.

She misses Ricky terribly.

Jill Sanchez needs a real man around. A fearless man.

A man like Ricky Biscayne.

monday, june 3

It is Monday, and school is out for the summer. Sophia is officially out of middle school. In the fall, when she goes back, she will be in high school. And she isn't about to go to Homestead High. She deserves better than that. She is sick of the schools around here, and if her mom isn't going to do anything about it, she'll have to fix the problem herself.

This is why Sophia is walking from her house to the city-bus stop with her best friend, a wispy, attractive fifteen-year-old boy named David. Nearly six feet tall already, with his tattoos, swishy walk, and fresh crew cut, David lives in a cheap apartment with his stock-car-racing mom and likes to joke that he is "the original gay redneck." He is really good-looking, funny, thoughtful, a hell of a budding comedian. Sophia feels closer to him than to any of her female friends. They share a massive crush on the same kinds of guys, too, with the bonus that there will never be any sense of competition between them. If a guy likes Sophia, he probably won't like David, and vice versa. At the present time, both teens have a thing for the singer Mario. He's skinny, and cute, and both Sophia and David want to protect him. Truth be told, Sophia has a crush on David, too, but she can't tell him. There is no point.

"Weeere *off* to see the wi-zard," sings David, skipping sarcastically along the sidewalk next to Sophia. "What do you think your mom is going to do when she finds out?"

"I don't care," says Sophia. Her mother, hard at work being Little Miss Firefighter, does not know she is going anywhere, and if all goes according to plan, she will not find out. If everything goes as planned, Sophia will meet her dad, and still be home in time for dinner with her mom and grandma.

They wait for the bus in the bright early-morning sunshine. Sophia tries to look brave and tough in her well-worn jeans and

T-shirt. She wears her backpack over both shoulders, even though David swears she looks like a loser and begs her at the very least to drape it casually over *one* shoulder. In it, she has family photos, her birth certificate, and everything she has so far collected about the man she is sure is her father—magazine clippings, CDs, and even a DVD of a sold-out concert he once gave at Madison Square Garden. Sophia can't risk having it all stolen by wearing the pack the cool, insouciant way. She feels anything but insouciant.

Waiting at the bus stop with them are two men who look homeless and drunk. When the bus finally comes, the drunks don't get on. Sophia realizes they were using the bus stop as a place to sit down and nothing more. Some people have it worse than she does, she thinks.

"Hi," she says to the bus driver. No answer. Grumpy bus driver. If Sophia had to drive a bus, she'd be grumpy, too.

"Have a nice day," says David to the driver, sarcastically, hoping to get the driver to realize the rudeness of his ways. To Sophia he then says, "Honestly, I don't know what's *wrong* with people."

They take seats in the back, and David starts to sing "Redneck Woman," which, coming from him, makes it sound like *he* is the woman. He draws some disapproving looks from people on the bus, and Sophia tries to quiet him. "Do you want to end up getting beat up?" she asks. "Calm down."

Sophia has never taken the bus. Her mother doesn't allow her to. She tries to look like she knows what she's doing. The trip is long, mostly because of all the waiting at different bus stops, but otherwise it is exactly like the lady from the transit authority had described to her on the phone.

By the time they finally get to Miami Beach, it's late afternoon, and they are starving. Sophia's shoulders are droopy, cramped, and her arms are sunburned. "Do you have any money?" she asks David.

"Are you on crack?" he replies. "I used all my money on this hellish bus nightmare. I'm as broke as the cars in my granny's yard."

"I didn't think it would take this long. I'm hungry."

"Me too. Let's just pretend we're supermodels and enjoy starvation," says David. He takes a deep, dramatic breath with his arms over his head. "Let's live our starvation, shall we? Feel it. Really feel it."

From the final bus stop to Ricky's house, it's about five blocks. Sophia used the Internet to create a map to Ricky Biscayne's house, but what the map hasn't told her is that there is a gate and a guard preventing them from entering his neighborhood at all. She and David spot the guard from two blocks away, and duck away into a patch of palmettos to come up with a solution. They watch several cars come through and then see a woman walking two dogs march past the guard without even looking up. No one tries to stop her.

"Just do that," says David.

"What?"

"Walk like you have purpose and meaning," he says.

"Really?"

"Girl, just look like you belong here. If they ask, you're Ricky's niece and I'm your boyfriend. That's all you have to do. I'll handle the rest."

"No one is going to believe you're my boyfriend," says Sophia.

"What?" He looks hurt. "I can do straight." He stands tall and puffs out his chest. "Me Tarzan, you Jane."

"You look like an angry hairdresser," says Sophia.

"You little bitch," says David with a wicked smile. "Let's go. I promise I won't act gay."

Sophia lifts her head, straightens her backpack, and starts to walk and whistle to herself, as casually as she can. David trots along beside her, doing his best "straight guy." She doesn't look at the guard house at all, just follows the sidewalk through the little opening in the wall. She tries not to show her amazement at the size of the houses beyond the wall. They are palaces.

"Hey, you two!" The woman's voice is harsh. Sophia turns and smiles with a wave.

"Hi!" says Sophia. She quickly reads the woman's name tag. Myrna. What an ugly name.

"Where do you think you're going?"

"Uh, Myrna?" says David, in full actor mode. "Don't you remember us?"

The guard's face quickly turns from menacing to insecure, and Sophia mentally congratulates David. Sophia touches her chest and smiles kindly. "It's me, Sophia? Ricky's niece? I come here for tutoring?"

The guard squints. "I don't remember you. Nobody gets tutoring in the summer."

"For singing they do."

"I'm Sophia's boyfriend? We're both going to be contestants on *American Idol*? Ricky's helping us?"

Sophia sneaks a look at the guard house and notices a large light-green bottle that she recognizes as Arizona iced green tea. "Last time we were here, we talked about iced tea? You forgot? I had a green tea, you told me you liked it, too?" She tries not to show how thirsty she is.

"So many antioxidants," says David. Sophia glares at him because he sounds *way* gay.

Still confused, Myrna shakes her head slowly.

"We can call her uncle if you want," says David with a shrug intended to be threatening. "But I'll tell you right now, he was pissed the last time we did it, because he gave you guys instructions to let us in whenever we came, and he's working on a new record and doesn't really want to be bothered unless it's something urgent. But, if you want, we can go call him right now? I can call him on my cell phone." David takes his cell phone from his pants pocket and starts to pretend to dial a number. "He hates when we interrupt him, though, doesn't he, baby?" David asks Sophia.

"Big time," says Sophia with a nod.

"If we get in trouble, it's your fault, Myrna."

Myrna smiles and shakes her head. "That's okay. I remember you now."

Yes! Sophia believes David will become an actor yet.

"Cool. Good to see you again. Have a good day!" Sophia turns and walks past the palaces, toward her father's house. David grabs her hand and squeezes it. They continue to hold hands, to aid in the illusion, even though David skips.

I could get used to this, Sophia thinks of the beautiful neighborhood with the luxury cars and acres of lawns. Even holdings hands with a boy she loves. Yes, she thinks, I could.

'm lying on my yellow bed in my yellow room, after having just had a conversation with Ricky Biscayne by phone, in which I told him I would be honored to be his secret lover, and I'm wondering what mess I've just gotten myself into. I'm sipping an iced mocha my mother made for me (thoughtful, actually), and wiping the crumbs of a pineapple *pastelito* binge from the front of my shirt. He told me things I've never heard from a man before, like "destiny threw us together," and I know I shouldn't believe them, but I do. We are soul mates, I've known this in the center of my spirit for years. I am just amazed that he feels it, too. I have resigned my post as the secretary of Las Ricky Chickies, citing a conflict of interest. I got a few nasty e-mails from members of the group, accusing me of being arrogant. It's hard for me not to log on to the group site all the time, as I used to, out of habit.

I try to read a few pages from this week's book club pick, Jane Porter's *The Frog Prince*, but I can't focus. I'm behind in book club. I show up and don't know what anyone's talking about, and they know it. I'm not myself, they say. They don't trust me in my fancy clothes, either. They think I've stepped out of their league with my new job, or something. It's not the same anymore. I don't know what's happening to me. In a very short time, my life has taken a surreal turn. My dad isn't even talking to me because he thinks I've betrayed him by accepting the perks of my job—the car and the clothes and all that. He thinks I'm dressing like a prostitute, which is sort of true—but so? I'm *happy*. Can't anyone in this house appreciate that? My mom seems happy for me, but worried. Everyone in my family worries when things are going well for others. Like there's something wrong. Like it can't possibly last. Like there's a catch. So, naturally, I am certain there *is* a catch, and I think it has to do with the fact that destiny has lined me up to be Ricky's new woman. I don't know how people will react to that. I don't even know what to do about it. I just know that I love him. I think I'd make a very good wife of a rich and famous man. I could definitely get used to that.

Okay, time to get up and get ready for work. Is it still work if it doesn't feel like work? Is it still work if it feels like the world's longest date? I don't know.

I walk to the bathroom in my robe and slippers, strip, shower, shave, exit, wrap my head in a towel, put the robe back on and go back to my room. I open the closet door and search for something to wear. It didn't used to be such a monumental decision. I used to wear a lame dress, and that was it. I kind of liked life better in those days, only because it wasn't so much work. This whole business of trying to look good for Ricky is wearing me out. It's silly. I don't know how other women have the stamina for this every day. All the work it takes to be a pretty girl. I thought I'd like it, but I really don't. I really find it kind of annoying. I really just want to wear sweats and read magazines all day, but that's not an option anymore.

It's late afternoon. I know. Most people would be at work by now. But I have a good reason. I'm hosting a listening party for the press in Ricky's studio tonight. Well, not all of the press. Just the ones who matter. *The New York Times, Billboard,* and *People.* Oh, and a guy from the Associated Press. Everyone is under the impression that they are getting an exclusive sneak peak at the genius Ricky at work on his new Spanish-language album, and I have also told each and every critic I invited that I value their opinion above all others and therefore really want them to give it a listen and tell me what they think. Reporters respond to nothing so much as to flattery. But I guess that's true of all people, including me. I mean, why else am I standing here considering the seductive properties of various articles of clothing? For work?

I pick a pair of black DKNY crop pants and a tangerine Dolce &

Gabbana tank top and a light, black cotton shawl. I'm starting to sound like Geneva with all the brand-name nonsense. These are all courtesy of Ron DiMeola and his drug addiction. These are the clothes I got on Ricky's dime. I feel guilty and weird about it. Dirty. I like feeling dirty, but I don't *like* that I like it. I justify this whole growing mess by telling myself that my new job comes with a responsibility to uphold Ricky's trendy image with the members of the press.

I slip into the clothes, then take down my newest purchase—a pair of matching tangerine sandals from the Jimmy Choo shop at Merrick Park. I really don't care about shoes, but I feel like I should because I used to watch *Sex and the City,* and there's that whole scene when Sarah Jessica Parker thinks her married friend should get her shoes as a present for being single, and there's like this reverence she has for a pair of Jimmy Choos. Eh. As far as I can tell? They're just overpriced shoes. There's nothing really all that different about them. I'm sure there are people in the world who think otherwise. But as I slip them on, I'm, like, whatever. I would actually rather wear sneakers. Is that so wrong? Is it? I mean, six hundred bucks for a pair of shoes? With people going hungry in the world? How *stupid* is that? Pretty stupid. I thought I'd like shoes more than this. Our society brainwashes women to think shoes are special.

Now the truly annoying part. I head back to the bathroom for hair and makeup. Hair and makeup, so you know, are the most colossal of all the colossal wastes of time in girl-landia. I have to look at notes from the stylist about how to make my hair look right. I still can't do it without cheating. And the whole makeup thing? It's fun now and then. But every day? It's exhausting. It's a little disgusting, too, smearing all this dye on your face. I don't get it. I mean, I get that people respond better to me when I have it on. Men open doors for me. Ricky, uh, kisses me. Stuff like that. Little stuff.

Okay, big stuff.

I use the hair dryer until my hair is almost dry, then use the straightening iron to make it smooth and sleek, all the better to emphasize the highlights. I use a little white makeup sponge to coat my face with NARS liquid foundation. While I can't tell the difference between expensive and inexpensive shoes, I can really tell the difference between makeup. NARS is the best thing I've ever put on my face. I use Benefit cheek and lip glimmer next, in a creamy peach color. I leave my lips pretty neutral, and emphasize my eyes with NARS eyeshadow in shades of charcoal and lavender, and a couple coats of black mascara, Maybelline's Great Lash, which Geneva and every other woman I know swears is still the best on the market, even if you *can* buy it in a pharmacy. When I'm finished, I set my face with a light dusting of Clinique blended face powder. Perfect.

Mom and Dad are at work. I don't know what Mom's show is going to be about today. I don't remember. Or I choose *not* to remember. She told me. And if I think hard it will come to me. Uhm . . . oh. Eew. Right. The dangers of smegma.

I seek out my grandparents to say good-bye. They still talk to me. They talk to me to tell me to tell Geneva to get rid of the *negrito* before she destroys our family reputation. What family reputation? Please. Anyway, I find them both on the back porch, playing cards together and talking about the big party they are helping to organize for all the exiles in town from the city of Trinidad, Cuba. They have done this party for years. The sight of them is so sweet, and somehow so sad, that I rush over and give them both big hugs. "I'm going to be at work until late tonight," I tell them. "Don't wait up for me."

"Why would we wait up for you?" asks my grandmother. "That's what your mother is for."

Gee, thanks. Okay.

I leave the house and get into my Mercedes. Did I say my Mercedes? It's not right. It feels very sick to have this car, like I am being bribed to keep my mouth shut. Oh, wait. I am. That's right. Okay. Anyway, it's not like it's really mine, because Ron only leased it, in the company name, for me to use. Still. A white Mercedes, all my own? To use, I mean. It is too weird.

I get in the car, press Play on the stereo. A demo of Ricky's CD, the one the critics are be coming by tonight to listen to, spins into action. Note to self: CD players *so* kick ass over cassette players. Second note to self: Mercedes *so* kicks ass over Neon.

I ease out of the driveway. The song makes me want to sing to the stars. I love it. I love that Ricky writes and sings lyrics like this. He's amazingly talented. I am more in love with the music than the body, now that I am around the body so much it doesn't seem that unusual. And this? It's the best album Ricky has ever recorded, full of the sappy ballads I adore, but also the upbeat dance numbers that the rest of the world has come to associate with World Cup soccer anthems.

I turn the volume down, and as I drive through Coral Gables I dial the office on my cell. See how that sounds? Dial the office on my cell. So chic. Not at all swank. Very cool.

I reach Ricky's assistant, a girl named Penelope, and ask her to patch me in with the caterers for tonight's listening party. Patch me in. Chic, right? Anyway, I want to make sure everyone is on the same page, ready to go, etc. I almost believe I'm qualified for all this. I watch myself and think I'm doing a damn good job of fooling everyone. It doesn't get better than this.

I turn onto the Dixie Highway, and confirm that the caterers will be coming by an hour before the first guest arrives, with appetizers and Champagne. As I turn north on the highway, really more of a boulevard in this part of the city, I call Ricky's assistant again and ask her to confirm with all four critics that they will in fact be attending. Then I hang up, crank the music, and drive.

When the Dixie Highway merges with 95 North, I floor the Mercedes, just to feel the incredible pickup. The Neon always sort of lagged behind at this particular spot on the commute, saggy and wimpy while every other car passed it. Even though I seriously doubt Ricky Biscayne wants to be my lover, I know that he has said he does, and that's enough to make me drive fast to get to him. No one passes me anymore.

---

park the Mercedes at Ricky's house, late afternoon, and I'm just in time to see Matthew Baker returning from somewhere on his little red bicycle, wearing his baseball cap and Green Day concert T-shirt. There is something very manly and natural about him. Something very un-Miami.

I wave. He seems to smirk before waving back, and doesn't hold eye contact. What's up with that? He's so unfriendly to me. I wonder if he knows about Ricky. Probably. Disapproves, and I would, too. I am starting to think I did a bad thing, kissing my employer. My married employer. My famous, married employer. Not a good decision. And now that I actually like Jasminka enough to not be able to hate her, it's even worse.

I step out of the Mercedes, push the key fob to lock it. Matthew hurries ahead of me.

"Late lunch?" I call, hoping he'll stop. He does. Stuffs his hands in his pockets and looks at me like I've just tried to insult him.

"Yes, actually," he says.

"Was it good?" I catch up to him and try to act like a normal, chatty coworker. I still can't figure out what the Matthew connection is in my life, why I keep seeing his name, and him, everywhere I go, and why he hates me so much. It's masochistic on my part, but when someone dislikes me it is a challenge I can't refuse, to try to get them to change their minds.

Matthew pats his belly and smirks again. "Do I look like the kind of guy who ever has anything other than a good lunch, Milan?"

"Well, okay," I say. I don't know how to answer. "Is Ricky around?"

"I haven't seen him all day." Matthew opens the gate to the backyard and holds it for me. I wait for him. But he sort of strides past me and doesn't wait in turn. He's in a hurry. Or he hates me. I don't know which. I mutter, "Nice talking to you, too," but not loud enough for him to hear.

I stand in the yard and try to gather my thoughts. I listen to the waves lapping against the retaining wall of the yard. I hear someone zipping past on a Jet Ski. What am I doing again? Right. The listening party. But Ricky's not here. I decide to go in the main house and ask Jasminka if Ricky has mentioned the party to her. If he remembers. It would be a shame to throw a party if the host didn't show, now wouldn't it? I ring the back doorbell, and almost immediately Jasminka answers, like she's been watching me. Creepy.

"Milan, you don't have to knock, you can come in anytime," says the model. She looks round and pretty. I want terribly to hate her so that it might be easy to steal her husband, but I don't. She's too nice to hate. She even hugs me, and I can hear her breathing, shallow and somehow very pregnant. I'm a bad person. So selfish.

We go into the kitchen and I ask her about Ricky. She tells me she hasn't seen him all day, either. She shrugs. "He's been spending a lot of time out," she says. She seems sad about it.

"Lots of work?"

"Not really. He's spending time with buddies mostly."

"Okay, well, if you see or hear from him, could you tell him to be sure to show up at the listening party at seven? It's really important."

"Sure." Jasminka holds a box of soap out for me to smell. "I just came up with this," she says. "I call it Celebrity. It's supposed to smell like pine trees and mint."

I sniff. Man! That's awesome. It's got a menthol quality that makes my eyes water. It wakes me right up. "You made that?"

"Yes. It's hobby."

"That's pretty great."

"Keep it," says Jasminka. "I have to go get ready for manicurists. They're coming here to house." Jasminka looks around like she doesn't want anyone to hear what she is about to say. "I don't know if you know this, but Ricky won't let me leave house anymore. He says it's not safe." She rolls her eyes. "So from now on, everyone has to come to me. The stylist, the manicurist."

"Wow," I say. What? Did she just say Ricky won't *let* her? What does that mean? I didn't realize grown-ups could be forbidden to, like, leave their own house. "Sounds . . . nice?"

Jasminka studies my face for a moment, and I feel like the ickiest, most dishonest person in the world. "Not to me," she says. "It's not nice. I don't think so."

Whew. So it's true. They do have problems. Ricky's been telling me the truth. He's going to leave, once the baby is born.

Less guilt for me.

I retreat to my office and make some calls. Television media, mostly, on the West Coast, where it's still fairly early. I make notes to myself on a new pitch I've come up with, aimed at getting Ricky coverage in travel magazines. As I'm writing, I hear a man's fat thighs rubbing together in suit pants, then I see the corresponding big, bulky grease spot in my peripheral vision. I look up. It's Ron DiMeola, waddling in without knocking, like everyone else in my life.

"Ron!" Blink, blink. Fake smile. "How are you?" Isn't he hot in that suit and shiny tie? It's a million degrees. He looks very out of place. He looks at me with a steady eye and smiles with only one side of his face. "You look good, Milan," he says. "Much better than the last time."

I try to erase the image of this man exposing his stoned wife to complete strangers, but I can't. I thought Ricky was going to fire him, but he's still creeping and oozing around. What the hell is he doing here?

"So, you might be asking yourself why I'm here," says Ron.

"No, not really." Huh? "You're always welcome here."

Ron continues as though I haven't spoken. "Why is he here? you say. I'm here because I personally wanted to congratulate you on doing a good job with Ricky."

Huh? "Er, thanks."

"I've been keeping up with the work you do. I seen the piece where you got Ricky to talk about organic gardening. The one about his charity work." He laughs out loud. "Shit. It's great."

"Thanks."

"You know, when I first met you, I didn't think you had it in you

to lie, I have to be honest. But now? I thought *I* was the big liar."
He's chuckling, with his chin tucked into his neck. "But you? Now
you are a world-class liar." Liar? Ron DiMeola just called me a liar?
There *is* a God.

"What do you mean?"

"Ricky? Health nut?"

"He's pretty healthy."

"How do you sleep at night?" he asks with a wicked smile. "That's
all I wanted to know, Milan. How you live with yourself."

It's a good question, actually. "I don't know what you mean, Ron.
Ricky's a pretty good guy."

A slow, soggy grin spreads across Ron's face, and he laughs again.

A t roll call, I notice with a jolt of happiness that Nestor Perez
is on. In the two months since he started the job, we've become friends in the way people become friends with those
they work with. We eat meals together. We talk about TV shows and
sports teams, or politics. We actually agree on politics, so that's good.
He spots me on the bench press, I spot him. I talk to him about my
family. He never talks about his family. I don't know if he has one. He
doesn't talk about a personal life at all, except to tell me he likes bike
riding and he has a cat. This tells me he's gay. I'm sure of it. All of the
guys in the station are sure of it, and they talk about it behind Nestor's
back all the time; none of them mention it to his face, but they do
avoid spending too much time with him, like being gay was a disease
they might catch or something. I'm stupid, too, because I've begun to
wear mascara and blush to work, because of him, but I realize how in
vain my vanity is; he's gay. Mascara won't change that.

Captain Sullivan announces it's a slow moment and gives us window duty again. We head out with the buckets and sponges, and exchange pleasantries. We work in silence for a while. I catch Nestor
staring at me.

"Everything okay?" I ask. He tosses his rag into the bucket on the grass down below.

"Irene. Can I ask you something?"

"Sure," I say as I scrub a bird crap stain with conviction. How do birds manage to crap sideways onto windows? Is the wind in South Florida that strong?

"Why do you let them push you around like they do? L'Roy and all them."

I laugh it off. "Push me around? Them? Please."

"I know you act like it doesn't bother you, but it must," he tells me.

"There are bigger fish to fry."

"You should fight back," he says. "What they're doing to you is illegal."

I shrug. "I guess I'm not that worried about it."

"Well, you should be," he says.

At that moment, L'Roy and his cronies come outside to do some work. Nestor retreats down the ladder to retrieve his rag once more. "Let's talk about this later," he says.

"Okay," I say.

"I'm off early today," he suggests.

"Me too."

"Dinner?"

Dinner? Really? My heart flutters as I think for a moment that he might be asking me out on a date. Unlikely. Gay men don't date, you know, women. Even if the women wear mascara to work.

"Sure," I say. "Dinner would be nice."

hold front door to house open for two women from nail salon. The heat of midday summer sun steams through oppressive humidity of Miami Beach. It makes me want to sleep. I'm tired. More tired than I've ever been.

"Thank you," says first manicurist, Shelly, as she and partner, Diana, bring in boxes of equipment. Their real names are something else, something Vietnamese, and I have hard time understanding their accents.

I'm about to close front door when I see young girl sashaying up the driveway, next to young man. The girl is tall, and pretty. I squint to see if she might be young model I met somewhere. But no. The girl with plain jeans and simple, sweat-soaked red T-shirt has nothing of model quality to her. She is confident and strong as athlete and seems unaware of her beauty. The young man is also attractive, but obviously gay, touching girl's arm and giggling like girl himself.

The girl looks at piece of paper in her hand, checks address on the wall surrounding house, and then seems to take a deep breath and comes fast up the brick drive with boy behind her. I hold door open and watch girl until she gets close enough to hear me.

"Hello there? Can I help you?" I call.

Girl looks up, and when she smiles, I feel dizzy, afraid. She looks exactly like Ricky. I feel flesh on my arms rise.

"Hi," calls girl. Her voice is richer and deeper than you might expect from child. She marches right up to front door, and stands with hands on either side of her body. Her posture reminds me of Ricky. The goose bumps crawl across my arms and back. "I'm looking for Mr. Ricky Biscayne, please." The boy catches up and waves with silly smile.

"He's not here at moment," I say. It's true. Ricky is not here, never here anymore. I don't know where he's been going. He's supposed to be back soon for some kind of listening party, that's what Milan says, but I don't know if he'll make it.

"We'll wait," says boy.

"Can I help you with something?" I ask. They smell like sunlight and sweat.

"You're his wife, Jasminka, the model," says girl. "You're Croatian."

"Serbian."

"Serbian," says boy, mock-slapping the girl.

"Right. Sorry," says girl, mock-slapping him back.

"And you are?" I ask.

The girl smiles harder, like it must hurt her cheeks, and holds out right hand. "I'm sorry. How rude of me. I'm Sophia, Ricky's daughter. And this is my friend David."

"The original gay redneck," says David, with curtsy.

I grab door to keep from falling. Dizzy. "What did you said?"

"I know it's a shock," says the boy. "But some of us *are* gay."

"No, not that," I say. "About Ricky."

"He and my mom were high school sweethearts," says girl. "Don't feel bad. No one knows. I just only found out, too."

My face is hot with blood, and I begin to blink, not knowing what else to do. This can't be true. He would have told me. But she does look like him. She truly does. What is going on here?

"Don't worry," says girl. "Ricky doesn't know about me either. My mom never told him." She rolls her eyes. "I hate my mom sometimes. She's a real piece of work. I can see why he dumped her, actually."

Boy speaks. "Can we come in? It's really hot out here."

I stand in doorway. Confused, hurt. Sick to stomach. "I don't know," I say. "How can I be sure you are who you say?"

"Hello?" says boy, turning girl's face toward me. "*Look* at her."

Girl removes backpack and digs in it, pulling out one of Ricky's CDs. She holds it up to her face and imitates pose, a scowling, serious face. "See?" The girl removes another CD from bag and does that pose, a happy, joking face, as well. She has no idea this might hurt me. She's innocent and hopeful, and whole thing crushes me.

"I don't know what to say," I tell them.

"How about 'would you like a glass of water?'" says boy. "We just spent the whole day on buses and trains. We live down in Homestead."

"Homestead?"

"It's down south," says girl.

"In the 'hood," explains boy, with laugh.

I stare at them. "How did you get past security?"

"We lied," says boy. "Can we come in now?"

"Uh, yes. Come in," I say. I stand to side to let them in. "I was just to have manicure."

I bring them in. I watch as they look at house. They are open-mouthed at sight of house.

"Su-*weet*," says boy as he runs fingers across everything in entry. Then he sees living room and crosses arms, scowls. "But that pool-table-in-the-living-room look is very, very last year, homegirl. It is so last year, it's last *decade*."

"So this is where my dad lives," says girl. She looks proud and uncomfortable. "Cool!"

David purses lips. "I thought it'd be better. It's a nice house, but, what is that thing? A jukebox? No. No, no, no. I mean, no offense, Miss Serbia, but you people need a designer makeover." He snap, snap, snaps like guest from Jerry Springer's show.

"I disagree," I say. "Ricky likes it."

"Ricky be a fool, then," says David. Then, he hugs girl. "I'm sorry, sweetie. I know he's your dad. Where *are* my manners? Straight men have no sense of style. Tragic, really."

I take them to master bedroom, where manicurists usually set up in alcove with massage table. Shelly and Diana wait for me, a foot spa steaming. The enormous room is decorated in royal blues and golds, with some kind of fake coat of arms on everything.

"Uh," says David. "This is like a bad college president's suite."

I like boy. Girl I'm not sure of.

"This is where he sleeps?" asks girl, in awe.

"We sleep here," I say. Usually, though, it's just me. I don't know anymore where Ricky is sleeping.

"Wow."

"Hello," Shelly says to girl. "Are you having a manicure today, too?"

Before I can answer no, Sophia chimes in.

"Sure," she says. She pads softly across room and sits lightly on side of bed.

"Ooh, ooh!" cries boy, waving his hands. "Me too!"

He runs and dives onto bed. They tumble on bed like they own it. Girl smiles at me, and says, innocent, "I've never had a manicure. But, you know, under the circumstances, I guess I better get used to it."

I don't know what to say.

Ricky finally shows up for the listening party, with barely twenty minutes to spare. He comes straight to my office, and shuts the door behind him, a little sweaty and a little out of breath. He's wearing carpenter jeans and a Red Ringer T-shirt and looks like he's gotten a bit of sun today. He looks healthy and happy and entirely . . . edible. My heart almost gives up and quits right there under my sternum.

"Hi," I say. I blush because of the conversation we had earlier, on the phone, where I promised to give him . . . all of me. I don't know what to do with my hands, my body, all of me is in the wrong place, doing the wrong thing. At least my clothes are good, I think. I'm wearing a pair of black DKNY crop pants and a tangerine Dolce & Gabbana tank top. Can I just say I am sick of working so hard on the clothes? It's like it takes half my mental energy just to do this. But I suppose it's a job hazard.

"I've missed you," he says. "I couldn't wait to get back here and see you."

Before I know what's happening, he has locked the door and closed the shades. He's on top of me in my chair, kissing me. I can't believe this is my life. I feel like I'm floating above myself, watching it all, like those people who are near death, only I am near to life. I can feel my spirit sprouting wings, about to take flight.

Ricky pulls me by the hands and we tumble to the floor in a mess of kisses.

"The critics will be here any minute," I say. "And Jasminka. She's home."

"Fuck that," he says. "It's you I want." He pulls back from me and looks deeply into my eyes. "Do you know what it is to be trapped, Milan? To be trapped and unhappy, and then to have the woman you've dreamed about, the woman you've written songs about, just show up on your doorstep? Do you know what kind of pain that causes?"

I shake my head. "No. I'm sorry, Ricky." I kiss him again, softly, almost maternally, trying to soothe him. I want to take all his pain away. "What would make it better?"

"Let me go down on you," he says.

This strikes me as not a very big request, given the enormous nature of his grief. But, you know, he asked. "Are you serious?" I instinctively close my legs tighter, self-conscious. I have never known a man to actually like doing that, much less ask to. Usually you have to push them there, or beg, or, like Whoopi Goldberg once said, you have to use a Life Saver candy to train them.

"Of course I'm serious. I love giving women pleasure."

"Women?"

He rolls his eyes. "You. I want to give *you* pleasure, Milan. You deserve it."

"I don't think we have time," I say. We really don't. I take *forever*.

"I'll be quick," he says.

Now there's a line every woman wants to hear, I think to myself. Why is this so funny and sad at the same time? He is unbuttoning my pants, and I'm wriggling out of them for him. I can't believe this. I'm weird-looking, so big in the back, but he doesn't seem to care. I should not be doing this.

"You are so beautiful," he says. He stares at my body like I'm a fine painting, like I'm hanging in the Louvre.

"I can't believe this is happening," I say.

"Believe it," he says. "You were made for me."

Ricky removes my pants, and my underwear, and he does what he's asked me to let him do, me in my office chair and him kneeling on the floor. I can't believe Ricky Biscayne wants to give me pleasure this way. It is the most erotic, emotional moment of my life. He's pretty good at it, too, and I'm so wound up I explode in a matter of seconds. He smiles up at me from *down there* and keeps going, even though I'm

so sensitive now I want him to stop. He doesn't. And, to my great surprise, I climax again, instantly. I didn't know I could do that. I knew
they talked about it on that Berman sisters show, and my mom's vile
show, but I didn't know I was able. Ricky has magical powers over my
body. I begin to babble. I tell him I've never felt like this, that I think
this is love, that he is my soul mate, how the lyrics to his songs have
made me value myself and love my life, that I am the most blessed
woman on the earth.

"I'm glad you liked it."

"I loved it." And I love *you*, I think.

"Now," says Ricky, undoing his own pants. "My turn. Let's knock
da boots, girl."

Knock boots? Is that the sort of dated slang you use on your long-
lost soul mate? Sometimes Ricky speaks so plainly it's hard to imagine
he's the same man who writes such spiritual, poetic songs. Still, I'd
love to make love to him. But we truthfully don't have time. We only
have a minute or two until the critics get here.

Ricky rolls me onto my belly and pulls me up onto all fours. I hear
him unwrap a condom and crane my neck around just in time to see
him roll it on. Then he sticks himself inside me before I even have a
chance to realize what's going on. Thwack, thwack, thwack. Mechanical. It's okay, but not the loving moment I was hoping for, you know?
It's sort of annoying, actually. My desk phone starts ringing, and then
I hear Matthew on speakerphone, announcing the arrival of the reporter from *The New York Times*.

"Please hurry," I whisper to Ricky.

"I'm almost there, baby," he says. Knock, knock, knock. Boots,
boots, boots. Yawn? This shouldn't be yawny, should it? I grin and bear
it, so to speak. It's not awful, but it's not what I'd hoped for. Before I
know it, he's collapsed on my back, crushing me as he convulses and
moans. "Jill," he says.

I push him off. "Excuse me?" I scramble to find my pants and underwear.

"Mil," he says. "It's my new nickname for you. You like it?"

I must be hearing things. "It's cute," I say.

He kisses me once, then bounds up and starts to fasten his pants. "Thanks, baby. Let's go to the party," he says. He winks. "That was fun. I knew it would be."

N estor picks Irene up at her house in his silver Mitsubishi Galant. He rushed home between work and here to change clothes, spritz his body's various nooks and crannies with Calvin Klein cologne, and swish deodorant across his armpits. Her green stucco house and several of the others are well kept, but he sees the telltale signs of ghetto-ness all around—men sitting around outside with nothing to do but drink, girls in clothes too revealing for their age, teenagers smoking and staring down unfamiliar cars, like his own, with their hands in their coat pockets like they carry weapons. He doesn't want to stick around here too long.

Irene comes out of the house before Nestor has a chance to get out of his car, as if she has been watching for him. She wears basic jeans and a long-sleeved T-shirt, which makes Nestor instantly feel overdressed in his black dress pants and baby-blue silk guayabera. He has thought of this as a date, but suddenly realizes she hasn't. She probably doesn't date coworkers. She has no reason to trust them, anyway, with the way they carry on with her. Maybe he's not her type. Humiliation burns his gut.

"Hey," she calls, with a wave. Nestor sees the front window curtain pull back and senses he is being watched from inside. He gets out to open Irene's door, but she insists on doing it herself. Of course. Not a date. Not a date.

"That's okay," she says as she pulls it open. "I've got it." Even though she hasn't dressed up, Irene *has* done something with her hair, and put on makeup. He thinks that's a good sign. Nestor thinks she is one of the most alluring women he's known; she reminds him of Kate Hudson, with her wide-set eyes and milky skin, but with a confident walk and a graceful, powerful body he can't stop thinking about. She looks worried, and tells him that her daughter hasn't come home yet. He feels a sudden panic, but mentally calms himself. Ever since the fire that took his wife and child, he has had to rein in his emotions around everyday happenings, to stop himself from thinking the worst. He suggests with some effort that the girl might be with friends. Nestor gets the sense that Irene is a person who, even though she tries to come across as easygoing and jovial, rarely stops worrying long enough to really, truly relax.

Nestor makes sure she's buckled in, then pulls out of the driveway. Where to go now? He asks, "Do you want to stay in Homestead?" He didn't mean for his voice to sound fearful. She shoots him a curious look.

"Uh . . . we can go somewhere else," she tells him. "What kind of food do you like?"

"Most," he says.

"Italian?"

"Sounds good."

"There's an Olive Garden in Pembroke Pines," she says. He gets the feeling she is looking at his dress-up clothes in confusion and her own form of embarrassment.

"That sounds perfect," says Nestor, though he really prefers independent shops and restaurants to big chains. This is the awkward dance of getting to know people and their tastes. He hasn't done this for a long time.

As he drives, they talk about work. Mostly, he asks her how long she's been putting up with harassment from L'Roy and the others. She tries to laugh it off, but eventually admits it has been going on since she began at the station five years ago. Then she tells him, like it's nothing, that Captain Sullivan suggested she not try for a promotion, out of concern for her male colleagues and their egos.

"Why would you take that from him?" he asks.

"I have a kid to support, Nestor. It's not that simple." Nestor thinks of his mother and the way she consistently protested whenever she was being treated unfairly, whether it was on the subway or at work, and how that drove him to want to work for justice in the world when he grew up.

"Have you ever thought that it might help your daughter more to see you fight back?" he asks.

"Nah," says Irene. "I just don't tell her how bad things are."

Nestor drives in thoughtful silence, takes a deep breath, and says, "Kids are amazing. They know more than we think they do."

"What's that supposed to mean?"

"I just wouldn't be surprised if your daughter was more in tune to your feelings than you think. You can't protect kids from everything."

"Sophia's cool," says Irene. She's smiling, but there's a hint of sadness around her eyes.

"I don't mean to say I know anything about your daughter," he says.

"Good. I have this policy that men without kids shouldn't lecture women who have them." Irene folds her arms across her chest and looks at him in a way that seems to dare him to come back with something better than that. She's so accustomed to being tough, he wonders if she'll ever be serious with him about her feelings.

"I used to be a dad," he says softly.

"What? Used to?"

"My daughter is dead," he says. It is the only way to say it, and as he speaks the simple words he can hardly believe them himself.

"Oh my God. I'm sorry."

Nestor pulls his car into the Olive Garden lot and parks. "Her name was Fabiola," he says as he opens his car door. "Shall we?"

They walk from the car to the restaurant in silence, and Irene doesn't speak until they reach the table and their water has been poured.

"How did she die?" she asks.

"House fire," he says. He lifts his glass in a sad-eyed toast. "Here's to our profession."

Irene doesn't lift her glass. "Were you a firefighter when it happened?"

Nestor shakes his head. "*Because* it happened."

"Did you have a partner?"

"Dead too."

"God. I'm so sorry."

"Don't be. Not your fault."

"What did you do before?"

Nestor tells her he'd been on the path to becoming a civil rights attorney. "That's why it bothers me to see you in the situation you're in at work, doing nothing about it. You have the law on your side, Irene, if you have evidence."

She laughs. "I've got truckloads." To his surprise, she tells him that she has documented everything that has been done to her for years, with the hope of one day fighting back.

"You could fight them, too, for discriminating against *you*," she says.

"For what?" he asks.

"You know, for being gay."

Nestor feels confused for a moment and then remembers the first day of work. For the first time in a long while, he laughs spontaneously.

"What's so funny?" she asks. He likes the way her cheeks flush pink and peach when she gets upset or defensive. She is beautiful, and powerful. And has no idea.

"I'm not *gay*, Irene," he says.

She looks surprised, then confused. "I'm sorry," she says. "It's just . . ."

"I know. I give L'Roy that impression because I want to screw with him, excuse my French." He looks at her with a grin. "Is that why you said 'partner' just now? You thought I was gay?"

Irene nods and smiles, and Nestor feels relieved for the misunderstanding. It's made the mood light again. He doesn't want to think about the past right now. He wants to come to life again.

"I was married. To a woman. A great woman. I like women, Irene. A lot."

Now, Irene laughs, and blushes. "That's great," she says, then seems embarrassed for having said it.

"That's great? Why?"

"I mean—I guess I've had a little crush on you."

"Oh, really?" Nestor smiles suggestively and scoots closer to Irene in the large corner booth.

"But let me ask you something," she tells him.

"Sure."

"Are you, like, really religious?"

Nestor shakes his head. "I have a relationship with God, but it's very personal and I don't like organized religion much."

She smiles at him as if this brings her a sense of relief. "I like your take on it."

He takes this moment to attempt to kiss her. Nothing big, just a sweet, little, innocent kiss. It is crass, yes. But he's out of practice. *Way* out of practice. They aren't children. So why does he feel so inexpert? She looks at him and asks what he is doing, with that half-smile women get when they know *exactly* what a man is doing, but feel obligated to ask anyway. He moves in, slowly, his heart beating too fast for its own good, and then . . .

Her phone rings. With the *Star Trek* theme.

"Oh, God, sorry," she says, backing away and looking for her purse. She fishes through it for her phone, takes it out, looks at the number on the screen, and asks him to excuse her. "It's my mom," she says. "Hold on one sec."

Nestor sits back and eats bread sticks, still smiling from the misunderstanding. That explains it. Gay? Please. Irene is really quite sensual, even just the way she holds the phone, a very physical woman. But as she speaks, his happiness at being out for the first time on something that feels like a date is marred by the shifting emotions on Irene's face.

She scribbles what looks like an address on the napkin, curses a few times. She hangs up the phone and immediately starts to gather her purse and keys.

"I'm sorry, Nestor," she says. "I have to go. It's my daughter. I need to get to my car as fast as I can."

To Nestor, the noise of the restaurant suddenly has a backward effect, like a turntable forced the wrong way. "Is it an emergency?"

"She's at her *dad's* house," says Irene, as if this might be a dangerous thing. "And her *dad* wants someone to come pick her up immediately. He's such an asshole, I can't even believe it. And her! She's in trouble. I can tell you that right now."

"What's wrong with her being at her dad's?"

Irene looks up at the ceiling for a moment as she takes a deep breath, then she speaks clearly, but softly. "Her dad is a famous man. She just found out. He's an asshole famous man, but famous. And she went to his house in Miami Beach without asking me or him and now he's denying she's his, which is not true." She sighs and rolls her eyes. "It's complicated."

"I can take you," says Nestor, not wanting to be alone in the backward silence again. Plus, he wants to know now who this famous man is who fathered Irene's child. Lovely Irene gets more interesting by the minute. "I mean, it'd be faster if we didn't have to go all the way back to your house, right?"

"Fine," says Irene. "But it's all the way in Miami Beach."

"I know, you just said that," says Nestor, happy as he says it that he'll get to spend that much more time with Irene, figuring out why she has this sort of reaction to her child's father.

He also doesn't mind that he will have the long drive back with an angry woman and a sullen child in his car again. He doesn't mind women's mercurial moods. In fact, there are times he's promised God he'll stop caring about PMS, as long as he gets his heart back someday.

This, Nestor thinks, might be the day.

Nestor is a good guy to drive me all the way up to Miami Beach, but as we pull into the driveway of Ricky's single-story house on Cleveland Road, I wish I were alone. Actually, as I look at the overgrown lawn and the scrappy palm trees around the large, plain, rectangular white house, which is not as nice as I might have expected it to be, I wish I were alone and *not here*. I don't want to be here. I do not want to get out of this car and face Ricardo Batista, or Ricky Biscayne, or whoever he thinks he is.

"You okay?" asks Nestor.

"Uh-huh." I cringe.

"You want me to go get her? I'm happy to do it."

"No." I open my door. I can hear the sound of a boat motoring along on the bay behind the house. I hear crickets and night birds. It's peaceful here, yet I have the same adrenaline pumping as when I go into a fire.

Nestor gets out, too, and stands with me. Ricky opens the door as we walk up to the porch, like he's been waiting. My breath catches in my throat at the sight of him, and Nestor places a comforting hand on my back, between my shoulder blades, as if he knows how I'm feeling. Ricky stands in the doorway to the house in a pair of green basketball shorts and a plain white T-shirt, with no shoes. I can barely make out his face because he is in silhouette from the light behind him. I can see straight through the house from the front door, through the entry and living room and out to the back. The light shines off the hardwood floors inside. The entire back wall appears to be made of glass, and I can see the turquoise shimmer of a swimming pool lit up, and beyond it, the bay. It looks like he has a boat dock.

"I'm right here," says Nestor, low. "I'm with you, Irene."

"Ricky," I say. I smile in spite of myself. He steps forward a little bit and smiles back. I can see his face better now, and he is the same as before, but older around the eyes. He's still as pretty as he was back in high school. For a moment, it feels like no time has passed at all. His eyes lock with mine, and for the smallest of seconds I can see that he remembers it all, too. Ricky's eyes harden as he sizes Nestor up. I see a woman I recognize as the model he is married to peek out from behind the door, and she calls my daughter's name. I feel a blast of cool air escape from the house into the thick, humid night air.

"Irene Gallagher," says Ricky, as if my name were the punch line to a bad joke. "Pretty amazing how my life turned out, eh?" He gestures to the house, as if I should somehow be proud of him.

I think of him as a fire I've been sent to put out, as the enemy. "Where's Sophia?" After all of this, after us sharing a child, this is all he can think to say to me? The pain, all of it, washes over me. He was a broken, selfish boy then, and he's a broken, selfish boy now. The only difference I can see is that now he has a pool house and an expensive wife.

Sophia and her friend David appear behind Ricky and he steps out of the way to let them leave.

"Sophia! Lookie! It's your mom and a really hot guy!" squeals David. He elbows her playfully, trying, I think, to lighten the mood with humor, as is his specialty. "I didn't know your mom knew hot guys! Did you?" David looks at me. "I mean, no offense, Miss Gallagher, but I thought I was the only one who knew hot guys."

"Mom!" cries Sophia when she sees me. She's angry. "Tell Ricky he's my *dad*. You *know* he's my dad. He acts like he doesn't know what I'm *talking* about. He's telling me he doesn't have any kids, and that's not *possible* if I'm his kid. *Tell* him."

David steps down onto the driveway with a goofy grin. "You have to admit, Irene, Sophia does look an awful lot like him." He turns to face them, hand to chin. "The crazy eyes, the wacky hair, the long grasshopper legs."

I look at my daughter next to her father and they are nearly identical. I am suddenly aware of a wave of nausea. Have all of these years been a mistake? Did I do the wrong thing, keeping these two apart? Then Ricky crosses his arms over his chest and avoids eye contact with me, with anyone. Sophia crosses her arms exactly as her father has done, without realizing it.

"The closed-off body language," continues David as he holds his chin like *The Thinker*. "The whole package, really."

"David, be quiet," I say.

"Yes, ma'am." His face mocks me.

"I mean it," I say to David. "Shut. Up."

David pretends to lock his mouth with an invisible key and dusts his hands together before prancing off to the car.

"Come on," I say to Sophia. "Let's go home. We'll talk about this later." I am not going to dignify Ricky's presence on earth by admitting that he is the father of this incredible, talented girl. He doesn't deserve her. She is mine.

"Later?" cries Sophia. She charges down the steps toward me. She stands in front of me and shoves me. "Why are you doing this to me? Why are you hiding this from me?" Her eyes spill over with tears, and her mouth contorts in anguish. I grab her hands to stop her from hitting me.

"Sophia, let's just go," I say.

She rips her hands free of mine and pushes me again, then turns to face her father with fury. "Both of you are disgusting!" she screams. "You *know* I'm your daughter! You *know* it! I can feel it, but you don't want to take responsibility for it, and my mom for some stupid reason doesn't want to make you take it, either." She spins on her heel and glares at me. "I hate you!" she yells.

"Sophia!"

"I hate you!" she repeats. "I hate you!"

"Maybe you're wrong about all of this," I suggest, not knowing what else to say. Sophia storms past me toward Nestor's car.

"And maybe you won't have a daughter to count on," she wails. "Maybe your lies are going to push me away just like you pushed Ricky away. Maybe you're going to end up all alone in the world just like your mom because no one loves you!"

I look to Ricky, but he has already turned his back to go inside. The front door closes, without so much as a word from him.

"I'm sorry," says Nestor. "Kids say things they don't mean. Just remember it's not you."

Blinded by tears, I walk toward the car. "Sometimes they mean it," I say, realizing that I was only a little older than Sophia when I got pregnant with her. I was as stubborn as she is, and I thought I hated my parents, too. And in my pain, I ran to the arms of the first boy who loved me. I realize in that moment that if I don't start dealing with the pain in my child, I am going to lose her forever. I feel Nestor's arms wrap around me in a gentle, supportive embrace, and I thank God he's not gay—and that David *is*.

sunday, june 23

I stand in the half-dark of the belly of the abandoned hotel on First and Washington, with my interior designer, Sara Behar-Asis, at my side. We're here to assess, to visualize the future. I take off my sunglasses and glance at Sara's outfit. You don't want to judge other women by their clothing choices, but you do, every second of every day, especially in Miami. We even judge each other by what our dogs wear. Today, mine wears a bikini and sunglasses. I scratch Belle's chin, and look around.

Sara is medium height with blond hair and blue eyes. She's wearing an elegant white linen pantsuit, with a pink silk top and beige strappy sandals and a matching handbag. I don't know the brand but guess it to be Ann Taylor or something similar. Basic, elegant, functional. Makes me feel a little too casual, actually. I wear jeans, ripped at the knees, with a simple white tank top—no bra—and beaded slides. My hair is back in another high ponytail, with a scarf around my head.

"So," says Sara. "What do you think?"

Carpenters and other workmen hammer away, knocking down walls and erecting others. "Looks good so far," I tell her. It does. So good I get chills. I'm actually doing this. Can't believe it. I roll my head and shoulders.

"Ouch," says Sara, wincing. Maybe Milan has a point about me cracking joints too much.

"Sorry," I say. "Bad habit."

I picked Sara for this job because she came up with the best computer model, the one that most closely reflects my vision for Club G.

Sara gets the whole harem vibe, and she ran with it in directions that never occurred to me. Like "scent branding," with an original incense that will burn in gilded holders throughout the club, and small bedouin tents scattered here and there, filled with pillows, able to be closed for privacy. Sara also had this idea to have a traveling circus in the club, a troupe of acrobats that performs for the crowd in the same way strolling mariachis perform for people in Mexican restaurants. Very Chinese, she said. Brilliant!

"I am so, so excited," says Sara. "I love that we've gotten started."

"How much longer do you think it should take now?"

"It depends. But I think we could safely plan for a late summer opening. Maybe August or September."

August sounds just right.

wednesday, june 26

Ricky, in Yves Saint Laurent aviator sunglasses, a shiny vintage white Adidas sweatsuit, and bare feet, chews his breakfast toast on a lounge chair on the patio in the backyard, and looks at the small news article about the teenage girl from Homestead who claims he is her father. She'd been here only a few days ago. How could there already be a news story about it unless these people were out for his money? It was a campaign, probably orchestrated by one of his competitors. It had to be. At least that's what he tries to tell himself, even though he knows the truth. That she is his daughter. Anyone who looks at the two of them can figure that out, but he doesn't need this shit right now. *This* is the problem. If she had come to him two years ago, or five years from now, it would have been different. But right now, Ricky Biscayne is becoming the all-American Latin heartthrob. He doesn't need a scandal. He doesn't need people to talk about what an irresponsible boy he used to be. He does not, most of all, need to have his name associated with Irene Gallagher, a girl he'd loved once but who had been, and would forever be, a poor, pitiful scrap of white trash. He would even have been willing to talk to them about it one-on-one, maybe make some quiet arrangements, but now that they've gone to the press? Forget it. It's war now, baby.

He turns to Jasminka, who's staring out at the bay like she always does. She's on the patio tiles in the shade of a palm tree, wearing a pair of silk pajamas. She hasn't bothered to get dressed because she says she wants to sleep all day. She's eating a bagel with loads of cream cheese on it. She never used to eat things like that. Look how fat she is. *Caraculo.* Even her face looks fat. Everything about her. Does she think it's okay to let herself go? You marry a model, you don't expect *this* shit. Jill would never let herself go like that during a pregnancy, he knows that for damn sure. Jill would exercise her way through, like a real woman. Something is wrong with Jasminka, depression or something. He's sick of it. He's sick of everything and everyone. He just wants to get away, with Jill, to a quiet place where they can be at peace and understand each other. She is right, about him. Ricky needs to be surrounded by the right kind of people, Jill's kind of people. Jill understands him. She'd know what to do now. Not Jasminka. Look at her, blubbery as hell and eating more. She is always eating. She claims the doctor wants her like this. It's disgusting. This whole thing with the Homestead people was her fault, too. She didn't have to let them in the house, but she did. Why did she do that? It was stupid, and crazy. She didn't have good instincts, that was her problem. She didn't know right from wrong.

"Never," he says, tossing the article in her face. "*Never* let anyone into this house again without asking me first, you understand? This is your fucking fault. All of this."

Jasminka chews her lower lip, a bad habit that tells him she fears him. She'd suck at poker. She looks at the photo of the girl in the paper. "Girl is your child, yes?"

It takes everything Ricky has not to slap her. Why is she baiting him about this? Maybe the child *is* his. He doesn't fucking *know*. Probably. But he isn't going to tell her. Or anyone. And he sure as hell isn't going to be taken for a ride by some cracker bitch he dated in high school just because he's famous now. You can't trust people, you really can't.

"No, she's not *foquin mine*," he says. He suspects it is a lie as he says it, but when you get used to lying, you learn that you have to be consistent. You have to lie to everyone. Even your wife. Even yourself. You have to believe it, and even though Ricky—some part of him, anyway—remembers Irene telling him she was pregnant, telling him she wanted the baby, telling him she would have it with or without him, and him telling her that Alma had demanded he stay away from her, he doesn't want to remember it now. Now, he wants the life he has built. His empire. He doesn't like the past. He doesn't want to remember that time at all, because it was then that the man he'd come to trust as a substitute father had molested him. He doesn't want to fucking think about that shit, or any of this. He wants his life back, calm. The way it is. He wants nothing to do with his past. They got this far without him, those people. Why are they trying to ruin him now?

"I sorry," Jasminka says, getting up inelegantly, supporting her back with her hand. She turns away from him and walks around the pool toward the house. Ricky shoves a piece of bread in his mouth and follows her. You don't just walk away from Ricky Biscayne. Nobody does that. He needs another hit of coke. The one from earlier has worn off already, and that is the other fucked-up thing. Ron is scamming him with all this bad, weak coke. He knows that motherfucker is stealing from him somehow, but he doesn't realize until this very second that it is through the coke. What is Ron doing, cutting it with flour? Something. He needs some real fucking coke, not this lame-ass shit that Ron is giving him. Coke, man. That's the only thing that might make him calm down right now. He needs medicine, something. He feels sick and alone.

"Get back here, woman," he shouts.

"She looks like you, Ricky. What you want me to do? I try to be nice." Is she fucking crying? What the fuck? This is so messed *up*.

"Don't walk away from me, you fat bitch," he says.

"You've been sniffing," she says. "We can talk when you come down. Right now I want to rest."

He grabs the neck of her pajama top to stop her. "You'll rest when I say it's time to rest," he says. "And from now on, you'll eat when I tell you to eat, *mamabicho*. And start speaking normal. English with *the* and *a* and all that shit you're too lazy to remember."

Jasminka looks him in the eye, and he sees, again, that she fears him. "Let me go," she says weakly. "Please. I'm going to be sick."

Sick? From what? Ricky remembers that Jasminka is carrying his child. Another child. Great, just what he needs. "Do you know how old you look to the public once, you know, when you have *children*?" he asks. She casts her eyes down. "I'm not old enough to have children," he says. "I shouldn't even be *married*. You know that? I wish I never married you. *¡Vete pa' el carajo!* Do you know how much better everything would be if I never *met* you? Look at you. You're getting *huge*. You look terrible. I married a model. What the fuck happened to you?"

Jasminka starts to cry, and he lets her go.

"You're pitiful," he says. "*Más fea que un culo*. You're not even worth getting angry at. Cry, cry, cry. That's all you fucking know how to do, complain and cry, and eat. You're stupid. I don't know how you lucked out and survived the dynamite back home."

"I love you," she says, her face tortured. "Why you are doing this to me?"

"Look at your stomach," he says. "It's disgusting. Who wants a woman all fat like that? No one. Stupid assholes, that's who. I'm a fucking *star*, Jasminka. I can have any woman I want. You shouldn't let yourself go, knowing that, you know that? How can you be so stupid?"

"I'm pregnant, Ricky." She sobs and her face looks like a monster. She is so ugly right now. He hates her.

Ricky points to her belly. "I don't *want* that baby. I don't *want* kids."

Jasminka sobs. "You said you did. What is wrong with you?"

Now it is Ricky who turns away from her, bouncing on the balls of his feet. He remembers there's coke in his pocket—yes—and takes it out, snorts out of her view. Then he bounces some more, hyped and ready for a rumble. He can't wait to be rid of her right now. He needs more coke. He snorts it all, and immediately begins to soar, above everyone. She is baggage, weighing him down. And Ricky is capable of flying. That's what Jasminka doesn't understand. He's *superman*. He doesn't have power, he *is* power. There is nothing that can stop Ricky now that he is a star, and that includes women and children. No one will get in his way.

"Get out of my face, bitch," he tells her, and Jasminka runs into the house.

Ricky sprints across the short yard to the end of the wooden dock, shouting as loud as he can to the sky over the bay, "I'm a fucking superstar! You hear me?" He picks up a rock and throws it toward the mid-morning sun. "I'm a fucking star!" The rock, obeying the laws of the universe that Ricky believes himself to be immune from, drops back to earth and lands on Ricky's head.

"Fuck!" he screams. "*¡Canto de cabrón!*" He feels his scalp for blood. "I've been fucking shot! I'm shot!"

"Ricky?"

He looks up to see Matthew Baker stumbling out of the studio with a confused look on his face. He rushes to Ricky's side, the humble slave. "You okay, man? What's going on?"

"That stupid bitch," Ricky roars.

"Okay, calm down, man." Matthew tries to hold Ricky, to keep him still, but Ricky isn't having it. What is he, gay now? What *is* this? "Walk it off," says Matthew. Walk? What the fuck is he talking about? "Calm down for a second. Let's talk about this."

"I'm a star," says Ricky. "That's what she needs to realize."

"Who?" Matthew looks confused. He always looks confused. *He* isn't a star. He is too weak and soft, like Jasminka and that Homestead girl and her sneaky, lying, white-trash bitch of a mother.

"Every bitch in my life," he says. "All of 'em."

Milan appears in the doorway to the studio and offices, with that look of shock on her face. Why does every fucking thing *shock* that bitch? He has been trying to keep her quiet by giving her what she wants most, which is the thought that he, Ricky, wants her. You control people better when they think they're in control. "That includes you, Milan!" shouts Ricky.

"Me? What?" Milan looks at Matthew.

"*Tú sabes*," says Ricky. "What? You don't remember?"

"He's having, like, a breakdown," says Matthew to Milan.

"Can I do something to help?"

"Go back inside," says Matthew. "You don't need to see this. Forget you saw this."

"Uh, okay."

What, was she raised on a farm? She's weak, too. The whole bunch of them. All of them, weak. No one has the kind of strength Ricky has. Jill is the only person worthy of him in the entire fucking universe. She has power and strength. What does Jasminka have? A flat ass and a bunch of stupid soaps she messes with in one of the spare rooms that she's turned into some fucking laboratory. She's like Frankenstein, he thinks, too tall for a woman and with those big, weird eyes like a space alien.

"Fuck you, Jasminka!" he cries toward the house. "You won't bring me down, *tú no me jodas*, bitch! You hear that? Not you, not any bitch!"

She has this idea that she's going to bring me down with the kid and the baby, he thinks as he searches the dark shrubs and trees with his eyes, looking for the shooter. Ricky lunges away from Matthew, dashes down the dock and past the pool to the shrubs at the side of the house. He starts sticking his hands and feet into the bushes. "Go ahead, *pendejo*! Shoot me again! You can't kill me! I'm invincible!"

"Ricky?" Matthew steps toward him like a snake catcher toward a cobra, motioning for Milan to go back inside the office. What, Matthew thinks he's he-man now? "You want to come inside for a little while, man, chill out?"

"Come here," says Ricky to Matthew. He sits in the cool grass. It feels like tiny hands across his skin. "Let me tell you something, *bellaco*."

"Sure," says Matthew, stupid corn-fed motherfucker. Look at those glasses. What does he wear that shit for? Doesn't he know it makes him look like a loser? He has a double chin. "What is it?" Matthew sits in the grass with Ricky. "You should lay off the coke for a while, Ricky," he says, softly. "Get your voice back, do some thinking."

"My wife, I don't trust her," says Ricky in a low, raspy whisper.

"Why? Jasminka's okay."

"I want you to do me a favor, *mamón*. When I'm not here, I want you to keep an eye on her."

"What do you mean?"

"I'll double your salary. Just don't let her *chocha* out of your sight. She's trying to ruin me. She's getting out of shape, man."

"Uh, okay, Ricky. Whatever you say, dude."

Matthew doesn't look like he believes Ricky. But then, maybe Matthew is in on it too. He acts like he doesn't want money for the songs, but Matthew does. He wants to be the star, doesn't he. That's what this shit is about. Jasminka's always talking about how sexy Matthew is, how nice he is, how talented. Maybe it's his baby, eh? But here's the news: Matthew isn't the star. Ricky *Biscayne* is the motherfucking star.

And stars can't trust nobody.

tuesday, july 2

'm at a lawyer's office and it's nothing like they show it in the movies. For one thing, it isn't as nice as you'd expect; I mean, it's nice in that it's downtown, in a high-rise, and it's spacious. But every inch of space is covered with papers and trash. He's a slob. You don't want a slob for a lawyer, do you? You want your lawyer neat and organized. Nestor found him for me. His name is Sy Berman, and he's supposedly one of the best labor lawyers around. So why is he wearing sweats and a baseball cap? Why is he eating fried chicken out of a Styrofoam container on his desk?

"Come in," says Sy Berman through a mouthful of food. "Sit."

Nestor is with me. Sy Berman shakes my hand first. I like that. Most of the time, if you have a man with you, other men go to the man first.

"Good to meet you, Irene," says Sy Berman. "Call me Sy. Sit. Can I get you anything? A soda? Something?"

"No, thanks," I say.

Nestor and Sy shake hands, and Nestor sits next to me and also declines to take a drink.

"Fucking construction," says Sy. He points a piece of chicken out the window. "Condos. Everywhere you look they're putting up a goddamn condo down here. I used to have a view of the water. Not anymore. Condos blocked me." Sy burps into his fist, and takes a long drink from a large paper cup.

I feel overdressed. I went to the Dadeland Mall last night and got clothes for this. I thought I should dress up. I took Sophia along, and bought her some clothes, too. It cost more than we could afford, but sometimes you have to splurge. We actually took an *InStyle* magazine and used it for reference, and laughed together about how clueless we were about fashion. I told her about the lawsuit, and she looked proud of me. "You'll win," she said. "And then we'll get all the clothes we want."

I'm wearing something called "dress jeans," in a dark, thick kind of denim, with a black short-sleeved top from Express, and black pointy-toed shoes. Very basic. Nestor keeps staring at me. I like it, but I wish I didn't. Ever since the night at the Olive Garden we haven't discussed my crush on him. I don't even know if he's interested, and I can't bring it up. This is probably the worst possible time to get involved with a man I work with. Right? I mean, I'm about to sue for sexual harassment, and I think I'm in love with Nestor. Stupid. To use a work-related cliché, playing with fire.

"Let me ask you," says Sy. He looks distractedly at a copy of *The*

Herald on his desk, the sports pages. "You two, you romantically involved?"

What, the guy's a psychic? I look at Nestor, and he at me. I shrug. He shakes his head. "No," he says.

No?

"You sure?" asks Sy. "I need to know, because that could be something they'll try to use against you, and I know I just met you, but I'm not an idiot." He stirs the air in front of him with a chicken leg. "You two have chemistry."

"Pardon?" I say. How rude.

"Yeah, you look at him, he looks at you. I see it."

"With all due respect," says Nestor. "Why are you asking about that?"

Sy wipes his mouth with a paper napkin, crumples it, and tosses it to the floor. He sits forward and makes eye contact, steady eye contact, with both of us. He's very intelligent-looking. "I approach cases from the opposing point of view," he says. "I have your information here. I know you've got a good case. I also know you are two of the better-looking people I've ever seen, and that they'll use it against you in some way, Irene, especially if there's sex here."

"There's no sex," I say.

"Or affection," he presses.

Nestor looks at me, then at Sy. "I like her, Mr. Berman," he says. "I don't know how she feels about me, but I'll be honest. I like Irene a lot."

"In that way?"

Nestor nods. "I think so, yes. In that way."

Sy smiles and shrugs. "Not a problem. The problems occur when you're not willing to be totally honest with me, when there's something I should know about that I don't."

Sy looks at me. And waits. Like I should say something. "What?" I ask.

"You like him?"

I shift in my seat. "Yeah," I say. "Pretty much." Nestor grins at me in surprise.

"All right," says Sy. "That's out of the way. Just take my advice and do what you can to avoid letting the guys at the station know. You can have all the hanky-panky you want off duty, but don't get too close at work until this is all behind us. You got that?"

I nod, offended. "But there's no hanky-panky," I repeat. "We just hang out." Why do I feel like I'm in high school? In fact, we hung out last night, watching fireworks with Sophia, who, it turns out, told the *Herald* about her dad and who still couldn't be consoled, it seemed, about the chilly reception her father gave her. But I'm working on it with her, being honest with her and trying to come up with something to help her through this.

Says the lawyer, "Whatever. My point is, you don't want to give them any reason to fire you, none at all."

I know. Honestly, though? I don't care anymore. I almost wish they would fire me, so I could collect unemployment and spend more time with Sophia.

Sy takes a cardboard box out from under his desk, all droopy and stained. He lifts it and dumps it next to his lunch. "Here's what we've got," he says. It's all the evidence I've been collecting, which Nestor had me send over here a few days ago. Sy smiles like a kid. "There's some really good fucking stuff in here," he says. "And if you can get your captain telling you on tape that he doesn't want you to apply for the lieutenant position . . ."

"I can do that," I say.

"Then I'd say you have a rock-solid case."

I stare at the dirty pictures with my mug taped over the faces, the grubby men's fingerprints obviously visible on the surface of the photos. Sex toys. Obscene notes.

"These men—and I use that word liberally here—have been arrogant and sloppy," says Sy. "They weren't worried you'd fight back, Irene. Either that, or they're retarded."

"Probably both," says Nestor.

Sy sighs. "I want you to know what you're up against, Irene. I'm happy to take the case. But these 'men' will try to vilify you in any way they can. They'll insult you, degrade you, drag you through the mud. They might even threaten you." His eyes lock with mine. "Are you ready for that?"

I smile. Ready? Is he joking? I say, "You just described my typical workday."

The lawyer laughs, but Nestor doesn't.

"They'll probably try to link this with the article Sophia landed in the *Herald,*" says Nestor. I feel a pit open in my gut.

"You're right," says Sy. "I was coming to that. They'll say you are out to get money any way you can." He pauses and picks his teeth with a pinky. "So, you still want to go ahead with this thing?"

I nod, and say, "I don't honestly see what I have to lose."

"Let's kick their asses then," says Sy Berman. I'm starting to like him, chicken and all.

Ten minutes later I sit in the passenger seat of Nestor's Mitsubishi and let him drive me home. I sink into my seat, relax my body, completely and totally let him *drive*. Against all my finely honed self-protective instincts, I let someone else worry about life for a moment, while I merely breathe. I've never done this, by the way. I close my eyes and think of kissing Nestor. We have not yet kissed. It's like we're both afraid to. Or something.

"Irene?" he asks. "Tell me what happened with Ricky. Why do you hate him so much?"

I would normally have closed up immediately. But I can't follow instinct anymore about my life. It hasn't worked. Right now, I just want to follow Nestor. For some reason, I feel like I've known him longer than I have. I feel safe with him. So I tell him. About the abuse in my childhood home, the homelessness, the pain, the poetry. Ricky and his poetry. His pain. How we made a connection based almost entirely on pain, and about how, in the throes of adolescence, in the empti-ness of a home where I never felt love, Ricky felt like home. Weird thing is, I now realize I fell in love with his mother almost as much as I fell in love with him.

"Meaning what?" asks Nestor.

"Meaning that I loved the idea that this sober, together woman might like me and take care of me."

"Survival instinct," says Nestor. "Seeking surrogates. Totally nor-mal."

"I guess."

"You have a lot of it." He looks at her. "That instinct. You're a *survivor*."

I relax a little more, and tell him the rest. About Sophia. The pregnancy, a surprise. The sex, which had never been good, or slow, or wonderful, the way it's supposed to be. It had been my first, and my last. And the heartbreak as Alma talked Ricky out of loving me. As he rejected me and disappeared from my life at the most horrific mo-ment. The beatings from my father. The name-calling. Having to leave school. The "special" school for pregnant girls. The jobs, one lousy one after another. The awful apartments. Doing the best I could. Running. Feeling like I've been running, and not just running, but running for my *life*, for years.

"It never stops, you know?" I say. "The running. The adrenaline."

"Are you tired yet?" he asks. We stop at a red light.

"Exhausted." I feel tears. But not sad tears. Another kind of tears altogether.

"You want some company in the race?" He leans across the seat, toward me. Brushes his hand along my cheek. "You're an amazing per-son," he says. And then Nestor kisses me. Finally. Warm, soft, with closed lips, a kiss more tender than has ever been given to me by a man for any reason. A healing kiss. The tears spill over the edges of my eyes, and I smile.

"Thank you," I say. The light turns green, and Nestor wipes the tears away with his thumbs before he returns to the task of driving.

"Amazing woman," he repeats. He drives safely, always using the turn signal, always checking the blind spot. I feel so, so *safe* here. I look out at the passing palm trees and shiny cars of Miami. Why are the colors so much brighter up here than they are in my part of the world down South? Why don't I live in a colorful place? I like it here. Surrounded by colors, with a man I trust driving. What is this feeling?

"You okay?" asks Nestor. He peeks over at me, then focuses on the road again.

"I'm fine." Really fine.

"Tell me what you need, Irene," he says. "Food? Coffee? You want to go home? You want to go for a walk? What can I do? Whatever you want. Tell me."

I look up at him. How is this happening? He couldn't be more spectacular-looking if he tried. He's Dominican. I got that much out of him. His parents are from the Dominican Republic. But he is so different from Ricky and his mom. Nestor doesn't have prejudices. He loves people. Truly loves them. He is gentle. Refined. You look at a guy like him and you think maybe he's a wrestler or a bully or something, just because of his muscles and the cut of his jaw, but he isn't. He's like a really sweet pit bull. Only better-looking, of course. What I *want* to say is that I want to be in his bed, under the covers, with him holding me. I want to know what that's like, to be a grown-up who isn't always joking her way through difficulties, to know what it's like to share the most intimate of spaces and thoughts with someone gentle, and safe. And *gorgeous*.

But instead I say, "Coffee would be good."

He puts a hand on the back of my neck and rubs gently. "Coffee it is."

It feels so good. So much better than when Jim touched me. Nestor's fingers have electricity in them, and I can feel it, and my body responds to his touch in ways I don't anticipate. I want him to hold me. I want him inside me. Moving. Softly, and then maybe not so softly.

"Actually?" I say. "I don't want to be in public right now."

"Okay. You want me to take you home?" He looks at me with an innocence and kindness that leaves me ashamed of wanting him so carnally. I don't know how to ask this man to take me to bed. How do you do that? I look at Nestor, the wide bundle of biceps that pulls on his shirtsleeves, the flat stomach, the masculinity of his neck and hands, and I feel my body ignite. What I really want is to go to his house. How do you say that? You don't. I can't.

"Yeah," I say. "Just take me home."

"Whatever you want," says Nestor. He seems disappointed. Doesn't he? Or is it my imagination? "Just tell me."

"Actually, I can't tell you what I want," I say.

"Why not?"

"I don't know."

"Don't you trust me?" he asks.

Trust. That's the word was searching for. I trust him completely. That isn't the problem.

"I don't trust *myself*," I say. "With you. Alone with you. With you in that suit. You look good in that suit. You. Okay? That's what I want. You." My cheeks catch fire, and I can feel pressure behind my eyeballs. I'm embarrassed. Afraid. On fire, with no way to put it out.

He smiles at me and lifts one brow. "Oh, boy," he says. "I like how that sounds."

"Oh boy," I repeat. And I smile.

He clears his throat and takes my hand in his. His hand is warm. So warm. He says, "Well, how about this? We go to my place, and see what happens."

Flames in every single cell. I look out the window and smile to the sky. "Okay," I say. "Deal."

The lust I feel dissipates as soon as I enter his apartment, replaced by fear. Nestor still has photos of his dead wife and child everywhere. I can't bear to touch him while their eyes watch us, and I actually do feel that they are looking at us. He senses what I feel by watching me.

"I'm sorry," he says. "I should have taken the photos down."

"No," I say. I take a seat on his sofa. "You'll take them down when you're ready."

He sits next to me and holds my hand. This is the extent of our physical contact for the next two hours, as we make even deeper contact. We talk. We talk about our lives, and reveal the pains that bind us.

wednesday, july 3

I am feeling very fruity and flirty. I don't know if that's good or bad. Black skirt, tangerine top. Lime-green shoes. I'm getting adventurous. And I feel like I'm developing a sense of style, though I'm not bold enough to ask other people because they might tell me some other version of reality, like, say, that I look like sherbet vomit. That would be bad.

Lips wrapped around the green Starbucks straw from an iced latte, I waltz down the hall and open the door to my office, half expecting to find those little helpful birds from Disney movies in here, weaving useful things with their beaks for me. Instead, I find . . . Ron. Eew. Nothing like a Disney bird. Everything like Gollum from those Hobbit movies. Gollum in a bad suit. Which might be redundant, because Gollum, even if he were in a good suit, would look bad. Gollum, by his very Gollumness, would make bad a good suit. Leaky and oozy.

"Milan," he says with that weird smirk of his. I still think of him stuffing his hands in Analicia. So. Disgusting.

I peel my eyes from the Gollum and see that he is not alone. El Ricky is here, in shorts and a tank top and looking mighty fine and edible, and with him, Jasminka and her dog. They look unnervingly alike at the moment, the woman and the dog. Sort of sad, sort of hot, sort of tired. I want to pet them both, but that's probably a bad idea.

"Is this where you yell surprise, and I remember it's my birthday?" I ask. Weak attempt at humor. In truth, I feel invaded. Violated. Creeped out. I approach my desk gingerly. "Is it okay if I, like, sit down?" I'm amazed at my boldness with these people. The fruity flirty thing is making me brave.

"Sorry to surprise you," says Ron. Then, almost as if it is a joke, he cracks his knuckles. *Okay.* This is where the hired goons my dad always talks about pop out of the supply closet and pelt me with paper clips. Is that it?

"What's going on?" I ask. Might as well be forthright.

"Have a seat, Milan," says Ricky, with a charming smile. That seductive little smile. Is he crazy? In front of his wife he's doing this? He says, "It's not as bad as it looks." I set down my handbag and briefcase and sit at the desk.

"Ricky needs your help," says Jasminka, droopy and wilted. After that scene in the yard where he insulted her, I don't understand what she's doing here. She, like her dog, is loyal to a fault.

"Actually, we all do," says Ricky.

Uh-oh. I study their faces. Feel my blood run cold. This is bad. Something tells me. Ron leans forward and clears his throat. I hear a sound like fabric ripping. I think he just split his pants, but this is a guess. I'm not willing to lift his suit jacket to confirm. He says, "First, let me say I love the press you got Ricky on the album. *Rolling Stone,* Milan?"

"Yeah."

"How the fuck do you do it?"

"Flattery," I say. "Lies." They all laugh like I'm joking. I'm not.

"That's a good one," says Ron, his face suddenly changing to serious. The serious Gollum. "Here's the deal. Ricky's facing an issue right now. A big issue." Jasminka bites her lower lip. Mishko whines to see her owner uncomfortable, and nudges her hand.

"The girl?" I ask. What, they think I don't know all of this?

Ron nods, and Ricky looks hurt and confused. "We got reporters calling from all over," says Ron. "And each of us is denying it, in our own way. But I wanted to have this meeting here today to make sure we're all denying it in the same way."

"Damage control," I say. "I was planning to do the same thing."

"Exactly. Good."

Jasminka speaks now. "It's not really damage control, Milan, be-cause there's no damage. Ricky swears that girl isn't his, that these people saw an opportunity to make money and ruin our lives, and they grabbed it."

"What's the story with her, anyway?" I ask.

Ricky and Jasminka look at each other, then she speaks again. "Milan. First, I have to say something. The other day, what you saw here, with Ricky?"

The breakdown? The cocaine? The crazy man? I shrug like I don't know what she's talking about. In truth, I've tried to block it out of my mind. I've decided that brilliant men do this kind of thing. I've never known a brilliant artist up close, so I assume they are all sort of like that. They're like that in the movies, anyway, so why not in real life?

"He had a breakdown from the stress," says Jasminka. "That's all it was."

"Nothing else," says Ron. It comes out as a warning of some kind. Hmm.

"Even if someone tries to say there's something else going on," be-gins Ricky. Jasminka and Ron shoot him a look. "That's not what it is. I don't take stress well. I'm very sensitive."

"Which is why we need you to put this thing to sleep as quickly as possible," says Ron. "Ricky needs to be on top of his game right now. We can't have him breaking down over some shit lies."

"Okay," I say. It must really suck to have the world watching your every move. To worry that if, say, your PMS is a little stronger than usual, the tabloids are going to claim you're insane. I call it "Mariah-ing," this tendency of the press to label crazy anyone with a little cre-ative genius and physical beauty. The press don't like attractive creative people. That's the problem. They're jealous. "I'll defend you, Ricky. That's my job."

"Seriously fucked up," says Ricky. "This whole thing."

"I know," I say, adding silently, *baby*. I want to call him baby and nibble on his ears. I love him. I hate that I love him so much. He's probably not going to be good for me, but I love him anyway.

Ricky goes on to tell me the story of Irene Gallagher. That he went to high school with her "back in the days," but that he was never close with her and hasn't spoken to her since their junior year. His guess is that the whole family is trying to get money and attention from him just because he's turning into a big star.

"That's disgusting," I say. And exciting, from a professional standpoint. I feel like a racehorse in the pen, excited and fruity and ready to take on the scumbags of the world, especially when they're attacking my Ricky. Mine. He's mine. I turn to him, girded for battle. "What do you want me to do about it?"

Ricky runs his fingers through his hair and looks at my desk with a faraway gaze. This must be what he looks like when he's writing music, like Mozart in that *Amadeus* movie, like he's searching for a sign from God. He looks tortured and it breaks my heart. "That's why I hired you," he says, lowering his eyes until they lock with mine. There's a secret in them, our secret. I wish in this moment that Jasminka would disappear. I want to take him from her. I want to fire Ron and be Ricky's wife and manager. We'd be unstoppable. He says, "To fix this kind of problem for me. We thought you would know what to do."

"I know," I say. "Do you know if they've gone public with this anywhere but the *Herald*?"

"Not yet," says Ricky. "I was hoping it would just go away, get buried after the *Herald* thing, but Ron flew down from New York last night because everyone's up in his face with this up there. It looks like everybody's going to."

"We can handle it," I say.

Ricky bites his lower lip and stares at the floor again. "I don't know, Milan."

"Just the press alone could ruin us," says Ron.

Ricky looks at me with love and longing. "I'm leaving it in your hands."

I want *him* in my hands. *Now.*

Ron clears his throat again. "Did you get that, Milan? He knows the mom. But he's not the kid's father. I need you to find any dirt you can on this Gallagher woman and discredit the fuck out of her."

I nod. Damn straight I will. "Whatever it takes."

Ron smiles high voltage, and gets up, coming over to place a goopy Gollumy hand on my shoulder.

"Good girl," he says. He smells like wet laundry that got left to mold in the machine overnight. He asks Jasminka if she's ready to leave. "I'm taking her to her ob-gyn appointment," says Ron. Huh? That's so weird I don't even want to ask.

I guess Ricky's preparing Jasminka for his leaving her. Yay!

Ricky looks at me and, as if sensing my question, says, "I have to go to the studio all afternoon, and I don't think Jaz should be alone right now."

How sweet.

Jasminka and her dog follow Ron out of the room, with good-byes all around. Then, it's just me and Ricky, looking at each other. He shuts the door. Closes the shades. I feel my body catch fire. "Thanks, kid," he says, coming up behind me and wrapping his arms around my neck. He leans over and plants a kiss on the top of my head. I can smell his grassy cologne. He smells so good. I want him. Now. "I knew I could count on you."

I swivel the chair to face him, and he stands before me. My face is, oh, right about there. You know where. I look up at him, and before I know what my hands are doing, they're on either side of his pelvis, just sort of running up and down, lightly.

"I'd do anything for you," I say.

He steps closer. I try not to think of Jasminka. She's a good woman. But she doesn't satisfy Ricky. They're not a good match. I know this. I lift his shirt, and see the line of dark hair on his hard belly. I twist the hairs around a finger, delicately. I can't believe I'm doing this.

"Anything?" asks Ricky.

"Anything," I say.

I lean in and kiss his belly. His skin is cool on my lips. I must be burning up. I feel his hands in my hair, and then he's directing me, moving my head. I kiss lower, through his shorts. And then I feel his hardness against my mouth. Oh, God. He presses into me, and next thing I know he's pulling his shorts down.

There it is, Ricky's confident, slightly purple and brown thing. I am sitting in my office, eye to eye with the very erect thing of Ricky Biscayne. I've had this fantasy so many times, but it never looked or smelled this good. I touch him first with my hands, stroke him, give that bobbing member a place to rest. He groans a little.

"You know I'm crazy about you," he says. "I can't stop thinking about you."

I smile up at him, and our eyes lock. He smiles back. It's a dream come true. I can't believe I'm here. I look straight ahead again, and move in, brushing my lips against him. Gently. These things are so vulnerable, I think, just out in the open like that. I feel sorry for men. But not that sorry. I kiss him. Up and down the thing, little dry kisses, with my hands on either side, and then, the top. And I lick him like a Popsicle. He tastes good. I remember everything I've read about fellatio over years and years of women's magazine articles, and tuck my teeth under my lips. I take him in. And I feel a spring open between my legs. I'm swelling everywhere, deliciously so. Up and down I go, him in and out. I do want him. Inside me. I want him so bad I feel like crying.

"That's good," he says. "That is so good, baby."

I look up at him. Ricky has closed his eyes, and he's smiling a little. He reminds me of a statue. I'd do anything for him. I feel the little words bubbling up from my soul, and I can't stop them. I take him out of my mouth for a moment and say, "I love you."

Ricky doesn't open his eyes. "Thank you, baby," he says. He reaches a hand down and holds his thing, and pushes it back toward my face. "Don't stop, Milan. Keep going."

"Ricky," I say, taking him in again. Mouth full, I mumble, "I'll do anything you want me to." I'm hoping he'll say he wants to make love to me.

Instead, he says, "In that case, I want to come all over your face."
Strange words for a sensitive and brilliant bard.

Very strange.

*J*ill rushes down the stone driveway to the mailbox in her short
shorts and tank top, barefoot yet coiffed enough to look good
in the random photo taken from the trees around her estate,
to get her copy of *People* magazine, runs back into the house, and settles down on the squishy white sofa in the living room to flip
through, looking for pictures of herself. Sure enough, the photos of
her and Jack at Tantra are there, with two headlines right up to:
MADLY IN LOVE, and FETCHING MORE THAN WATER. The accompanying
captions say that she and Jack are passionately in lust with each
other, unable to keep their hands off each other, and make note of
Jill's demands for privacy. Perfect. They've fallen for it again, the
dumb-asses.

Jill marvels at how well she and Jack photograph. She is the better
actor and celebrity, but he is almost as gifted as she is in the photo-
genic department. What a chin. What dimples. What good hair he
has, without even trying, a little curly and very shiny. They would
have produced gorgeous children. It is almost sad that she will have to
dump him soon. But she'll survive. Jack, on the other hand, will not.

Jill closes the magazine, then starts to flip through it again, this
time from the beginning, doing reconnaissance on what all her competitors are up to. There's Beyoncé, with her rapper boyfriend, eating
Popeye's chicken again, licking her fingers like the country girl she always claims to be. Shame, shame. The girl has zero discipline. Doesn't
she know country girls all end up fat and at the Cracker Barrel? And
there's mama Britney, pulling her thong out of her crack. Delightful.
That girl was not long for the scene, destined for a trailer park. Jill
considers getting pregnant for a moment, but rejects it. Why ruin her
body with *that*? Jessica, fighting and fornicating. Jill admires Jessica

Simpson for her ability to turn her marriage and separation into a viable commodity, and kicks herself for not having thought of it first. What better way to make America love you than by being the bombshell hottie housewife everyone loves to watch and wants to screw? She laughs her way past the Paris Hilton and Nicole Richie stories, but stares for a long while at the photos of pasty white actresses like Cate Blanchett and Hilary Swank. They puzzle her. If there is one kind of person in the world Jill Sanchez is intimidated by, it is gaunt, independent actress types, who don't seem to care about how they look but who look beautiful anyway. These are the actresses Jack is always talking about with reverence. They belong to a calm, elegant world Jill does not have membership to, a world where, if Jill were to walk in the door of some private party, they might all look up with amused expressions and laugh. They are destined to have long careers, like Susan Sarandon, because they play strong women and are taken seriously. Jill sometimes thinks that if she could do it all over again, she would go that route. But she doesn't have it all to do over again, and now she has an image and an empire to uphold.

She flips another page and finds Ricky Biscayne staring back at her. It is a most unflattering photo, with him screaming violently at someone, probably a photographer. He looks like a scrawny rat. Ricky hates the press and does not hide his feelings about them. The headline screams BISCAYNE BAY-B?

What?

A photo of a gangly, attractive young woman, maybe about thirteen, in soccer shorts and with a laughing smile, is superimposed over the screaming Ricky. Jill gasps and bolts upright. She knows better than to believe what she reads in these rags, but the truth is, they get most of the things about her life right most of the time, even when she doesn't want them to, and there is a possibility that this news is actually true.

The article says that a girl named Sophia Gallagher from Homestead, Florida, is contacting the South Florida media claiming to be

Ricky's long-lost daughter. There is another photo, of a woman in a firefighter's outfit, saying that the woman was Ricky's high school sweetheart. Jill remembers having heard Ricky mention her name. They dated for a year or so, long ago. The article says Ricky denies being the girl's father and claims he knew the girl's mother only as an acquaintance back in school.

Jill holds the magazine up to the light and examines the little girl. She looks a lot like Ricky—same dark curly hair, same honey-colored eyes. Jill feels adrenaline begin to rush through her veins. It isn't ideal. She doesn't like it. She plans to marry Ricky, and abandoning a child is not good, press-wise. But there is nothing Jill loves more than a challenge, a publicity puzzle to be pieced together, bit by clever bit, until the exact picture she wants to create exists in living color.

She reaches for the phone and dials Ricky's cell.

"Hey, Sugarface," he says, answering with her pet name.

"So," she says. "Is that kid yours?"

There is a long silence, then Ricky sighs. He is good at lying to most people, but with her, he loses the ability to be in control. She knows she has that effect on him. Jill feels the corners of her mouth curl up in a smile.

"No," he says. "She's not mine."

"You're cute when you lie," she purrs.

"I'm not lying," he says. His voice cracks.

"You're a terrible actor," she says.

"So are you, according to the critics."

Touché. Jill balls her fist and grins. "Come over," she says. "Say that to my face."

"I'm not coming over," he says. "I'm changing my ways."

Jill laughs.

"No, I am. I really am this time. I love my wife. I have to do it right this time."

"This time?"

"I want to be a good man."

"You are. You're the best I've ever had."

"Jill, don't. Please don't."

"I'm naked," she hisses. "Be here in an hour."

Ricky pauses, then says, "Okay."

monday, july 8

Dirty, dirty, dirty. That's how I feel. I'm having breakfast with my mom and dad in the spotless white kitchen with the red counters, the kitchen I cleaned this morning because it is expected of me. I'm supposed to be getting ready to go to work, and all I can think about is how badly I behaved with Ricky. It is *so* wrong. Isn't it? On so many levels. But I loved it. And I can't stop thinking about it. But I'm losing interest in everything that used to make me myself, including my book club, which I'm always too busy these days to attend. The girls in it have even stopped calling me to see if I'm coming. And Las Ricky Chickies? They won't even speak to me, like I'm some kind of traitor. I'm unrecognizable to my old friends, just as I'm unrecognizable to myself. I look at my *pan tostado* and ask the bread, *What have I become?*

"What's wrong?" asks Mom. She stares at me like a bird of prey and sips her strong cup of Bustelo espresso Cuban coffee—coffee I made for everyone in the thousand-dollar espresso machine, thank you. (Dad has no problem spending money on the "important" things.)

"Wrong?" I ask.

"Something's wrong."

My dad, for his part, ignores us both. He is disgusted with the women in his life. All of us. Or at least me and Geneva, one in love with a *prieto* and the other in love with her married *mexicano* boss. All he ever wanted was for us to marry successful white Cuban men. He has given up, and has started talking about how he wishes he'd had sons.

"Nothing's wrong."

"You're in love with your boss," she says.

I look at my watch. "Gotta go, Mom, Dad. Love you guys." I scoot away from the table and stand up. I take my dad's used plate to the sink for him. Mom is still staring at me. I think I'm blushing. I hurry out of the room, then out of the house, into my new car.

I listen to Ricky's music as I drive to work, and I feel heartbroken. I don't want to be la *otra*. I don't like it. But being Ricky's *otra* is better than being a normal guy's *mujer*. That's how I see it. It's a tradeoff. Why do I feel so conflicted about it. Guilt? Yeah. That's pretty much what it is. I like Jasminka. But even as I think this, I realize that Ricky's wife isn't my responsibility. She's his responsibility. Or her own. The signs are there. If I were her, I'd know he just wasn't that into me, as the book says.

As I drive from 395 across the MacArthur Causeway toward Watson Park, I see a familiar figure on the shoulder, hunched over a set of handlebars, with a black soft guitar case over his shoulder. Matthew Baker? What is he doing, trying to kill himself? It's boiling hot out there, and he's glistening with sweat. The causeway is high at this point, right over the bay. This is not the safest place to ride a bike. Precipitous drop to your death by water on one side, squishing death by speeding automobile on the other. Is he out of his mind?

I slow the Mercedes alongside his bike and press the button to lower the passenger-side window.

"Hey," I call. But he's got headphones stuck in his ears. He doesn't notice me, even though the cars behind me have noticed and begun honking like crazy. Finally, he looks over. His face registers surprise, and then the bike starts to wobble like he's going to crash into the road. Oh, great, I think. I'm going to end up killing the guy.

He stops. Takes off the headphones.

"Oh, hey, Milan," he says. Sweat drips into his mouth.

"What are you doing out here?"

He laughs like I'm not very smart, listens to the Ricky Biscayne

song on my CD changer, and laughs again. Why did I stop again?
Matthew is so mean to me. "I'm riding my bike," he says.

"I can see that. Do you want a ride?"

He shakes his head. "No, thanks. I need the exercise."

Is he implying that I could use exercise, too? He always does that.
"Suit yourself," I say.

"Besides, I get some of my best ideas while I'm riding," he says. He
makes a face. "You're listening to Ricky?"

"Yes."

"Don't you get enough of him at work?"

"Ricky's a genius."

He frowns.

"Okay . . ." I say. "See you at the office."

"Okay, see you."

As I drive away, I see Matthew blow me a kiss in the rearview mirror. He's so *weird*.

I get to work, and hide myself in my office. I seem to be the only
one here. That's good, because I don't want to waste any time
having sex with my boss. Okay, that's a lie. But still. I have a lot
of work to do.

By one o'clock, I've landed seventeen articles on the false father-
hood accusations against Ricky Biscayne, devoted family man. I'm
driven to prove my love to him. Don't ask me why. And yes, I realize
that my motives are unprofessional. But I truly believe in Ricky Biscayne. I feel like a soldier, rescuing my love from the jaws of the enemy. But the effort of talking about Ricky, looking at his photos,
listening to his music, just makes me horny and greedy. I don't want to
share him with anyone anymore.

As I'm chatting with a reporter from *Entertainment Weekly* and doing Kegels to get my muscles in top shape for my boss, Matthew Baker
walks in all red-faced, with a notepad. I stop the flexing and hope he

didn't notice. He's changed his clothes but still looks flushed from his ride. What does he want? He wears a Bob Marley T-shirt and long, baggy black cotton shorts, and his legs are hairy and muscular in a way that reminds me of photos of river rafting in men's magazines. I miss the days when I used to dress like Matthew Baker. He and I both have a natural style that fits better somewhere like Colorado than Miami. Life was so much easier when I didn't have to worry about how I looked every day. Even flushed, Matthew looks easygoing and comfortable, approachable and cute, like the not-so-handsome guy next door who is so nice that girls like him anyway. I bet his girlfriend is pretty. And wholesome. A lot nicer and cleaner than I am.

"I'm going to order out for lunch," he says. "Do you want anything?"

Matthew hands me a stack of stained, dog-eared take-out menus. I've been so busy I haven't thought about food, and I'm hungry. Very hungry. Everything looks good. If I were alone, I'd order a lot of food. But around a guy? Not much. I pretend like I'm not that interested in lunch.

"I had a late breakfast," I lie. I had an early breakfast, with my mother's nonstop inquisitions making it impossible to eat the toast and eggs I made for everyone.

"Oh, come on," he says. "The Thai place is really good. Do you like Thai food?"

I love Thai food. I love men who love Thai food. I am boy-crazy and it humiliates me. "I like all food," I tell him, truthfully. I order a salad. Very girlie to order a salad.

"You have to get more than that," says Matthew.

"Why?"

"I like a girl who eats," Matthew says with an embarrassed smile. "I mean, I think women should eat as much as men. No, wait. I mean I think it's really cool when a woman isn't afraid to eat."

I try to figure him out. Is he being sarcastic? Is he going to start laughing again? Why did he blow me a kiss before? What is this guy's deal? I look at the menu again, suspicious.

I ask, "Does your girlfriend like to eat?" Oops. The word "girl-friend" came out sarcastically. I didn't mean for it to. It just did.

"Who?" Matthew looks genuinely surprised.

"Your girlfriend." I cough into my hand. I regret having brought it up. Very unprofessional.

Matthew laughs. "Oh, *her*. Well, you know. Blow-up dolls don't eat much, Milan."

I look confused. "What?"

"Never mind. You can tell me the truth," he says. "You just don't want to eat lunch with a loser and a troll. It's okay. I understand." He smirks again.

Troll? "What troll? What are you talking about?"

Matthew blushes and moves closer to me. He looks around, like he's paranoid, and goes back to shut the door behind him. "Look," he says. "I have to be honest with you, Milan."

"About what?" Oh, God. Does he know about the blow job? Is he going to ask for one, too? Is that it? I'm the office slut now?

"About me. I'm, I'm weird. Granted. I know that. I get that part. But I have to tell you something."

"Go ahead."

"I've had feelings for you ever since you started here, and they make it really freakin' hard for me to get my work done."

"What kind of feelings?" Like he hates me?

"Man—woman feelings. Even trolls have them."

"But your girlfriend. Does every man around here cheat?"

"What girlfriend?" he shouts. "I don't *have* a girlfriend, Milan. I just told you that!"

"You did?"

"Yes! Well, actually I said I had a blow-up doll for a girlfriend, which was a lie." He smirks again. "I don't even have a blow-up doll. They find me unattractive."

"Well, when I called you some woman said she was your girlfriend."

"She lied. She's my ex. She's a psycho."

"That's what they all say," I joke. He doesn't laugh. He looks angry.

"She's crazy. She's inconsequential. The real problem here?" He takes a seat on the edge of my desk and starts to play with my stapler, opening and closing it. "You think I'm a disgusting little troll. That's the problem. You think I'm a loser. You thought that from the very first time you tried to drown me at the cruise docks."

"Why are you always talking about trolls, Matthew? It's very weird. Do you have a troll fetish? And why do you keep saying I called you a loser? And I didn't try to drown you! You bumped into *me*."

"You called me a loser as you tried to kill me."

"I didn't even *talk* to you! I was saying the name of a book we read in book club."

"Oh," he says, like he doesn't believe me. "And it just happened to be called *Loser*."

"Yes, it did. It's a good book. You should read it."

"I think I should write it," he says. "It could be an autobiography."

"Maybe that's your problem," I tell him. "You're projecting all your self-esteem issues onto me."

Matthew balks. "Did you *not* call me a troll when you started?"

"What?"

"Ricky said you thought I was a troll."

"Ricky? What? No. I never," I stop. I remember my first conversation with Ricky, when he almost insisted that I say Matthew was . . . a troll. "Oh, that. He kind of pressured me into it. I didn't think he'd tell you."

"So you do. You think I'm a troll. And a loser."

"I never called you a loser, Matthew. Quit saying that."

"Fine. That's fine." He gets up to leave, huffy.

"No, Matthew, I don't think you're a troll. I didn't mean it. I wanted a job. This job, I mean. I was a huge Ricky fan, and I did what he wanted."

"Wait a minute," cries Matthew. "*Ricky* made you say I looked like a troll?"

"Sort of. No, not exactly. I don't know. Yes. He did."

"What?"

I try not to laugh. But I do. It's funny. In a tragic kind of way. "Sorry," I say. "You're not a troll. I never called you a loser. I never called you a troll."

His eyes warm to me a little. He tries not to smile. "There's really a book called *Loser?*"

"Yes. By a guy named Jerry Spinelli. Look it up."

He frowns again. "I hate Ricky."

I shrug. "I love him," I say. I don't know why, but it feels like the right time to bring my love to light. Matthew laughs bitterly.

"You 'love' him?"

"I love him. Yes." I shrug with the truth of it all. And, I add to myself, I think he loves me.

"Has he made you blow him yet?"

My jaw drops open. *Made* me? *Yet?* "Yet?" I ask. "What does that mean?"

Matthew blows air out of his mouth and shakes his head. "He did. Oh well. Predictable."

"What? What's predictable?"

"Nothing."

"What? Tell me!" My heart feels like it belongs in a nervous mouse. How is the magic between me and Ricky predictable? Ricky loves me. He has said so. Or at least I think he has. On second thought, maybe not. Maybe he hasn't.

"Milan. Ricky gets blow jobs from every woman who works for him. It's common knowledge. Dude likes BJs."

"What?"

"It's an obsession for him. I don't know. Just be warned. If you haven't already done it, he's going to expect it."

"What?" I am crushed, and from the sorry look Matthew gives me, it must show on my face.

"Oh no," says Matthew. "Not you, too. Let me guess. He told you his wife wasn't passionate enough. He told you he felt something special for you the moment he saw you. He told you your souls match. That he wrote his songs for you."

I say nothing. All I can do is blink back the tears and try to keep my mouth closed.

Matthew sighs and says, "I've known Ricky for ten years. Trust me. He talks a good game, but when it comes right down to it? He's all about the BJ."

We stare at each other for a moment without speaking.

"I didn't do it," I lie.

"But he wanted it."

"Yeah."

Matthew laughs. "Let's change the subject. I'm losing my appetite."

"Okay."

"Okay, so I don't have a girlfriend. You didn't blow Ricky. You don't think I'm a troll. I'd say we're in good shape. You want lunch?"

I want to cry. That's what I want. I'm not the only one? I'm not Ricky's only one? He doesn't love me? He's not going to leave his wife for me? "I guess," I say.

"Don't pout."

"I'm not pouting."

"You're pouting. You love Ricky and you thought you had a chance with him."

"That's not true."

He looks like he feels very sorry for me. "I've seen this same story so many times it isn't even funny, Milan."

"I didn't say it was funny."

He looks at me with sympathy. "Ricky's hot," he says. "I'm a guy, but, to be honest, I'd probably blow him if he asked. Women want his body. No harm in that, girl. You're normal."

"It's not Ricky's body I want," I say, tears forming again in my eyes. "It's his soul."

"I think he sold that to the devil a long time ago."

I'm confused. "I love his soul. His music. His lyrics. His voice. His brain. That's the part of Ricky that makes him so special."

He cocks his head to the side. "You mean that?"

"Yes," I say, wiping the tears away. "Without all that, he'd just be a model. There are lots of good-looking guys in the world. There aren't lots of singers and songwriters like Ricky."

"You mean that?"

"If Ricky got burned in a fire and he was all scarred, I'd still love him because of what's inside."

"Yeah?"

"Yeah."

"Even if he looked like a troll?"

"Even if he looked like a troll."

"Or a loser?"

"Yeah."

"What if he looked like me?"

"Are you fishing for compliments?" I like Matthew. He's nice. He's not weird after all. He's just nice.

"No," he says. Matthew stares into my eyes as if he has something really important to say. He opens his mouth like he's going to say something, and stops.

"What?" I ask.

He smiles sadly and shakes his head. "Nothing. It's just nice, it's nice of you to say that. About Ricky." He shakes himself a little and tries to seem upbeat. "Now, about lunch. Let's order."

The ringing phone jolts me from my sleep. Who is calling me this late? What time is it? Midnight? It better be good. With deltoids aching from lifting weights with Tommy and Nestor at the station yesterday, I grope for the cordless on the nightstand in the dark.

"Hello?"

It's a reporter, that one from *The Miami Herald*. The one who did the original story on Sophia. "I'm sorry to bother you at home, but I've only just now gotten through public records, and I wanted to make sure you were the same Irene Gallagher that's filing a discrimination suit against the Pinecrest Bay Fire Department?"

"Yeah," I say, groggy. "That's me."

"And you're the same one who's got the kid who claims Ricky Biscayne is her dad?"

"Yes, but that's not me. She did that on her own."

"Nothing else, ma'am. I was just fact-checking. Sorry to bother you. Good night."

I say good night and hang up the phone. I have a very bad feeling about all this. Very.

monday, july 15

Sophia is so bored that she has started naming the leaves on the houseplant on the kitchen table. She started with Disney characters and moved on to DreamWorks. Even though her mom got her piles of teen-girl books with plaid covers at the library, and made lists of things for her to do to keep busy, and even though she has one or two friends left who don't think she is some kind of psycho for stalking Ricky Biscayne (that's what everyone else in the neighborhood thinks, by the way), she can't stay busy enough to keep from getting bored when she's not at soccer camp. David got a job at a grocery store, to earn extra money that he's stashing away for college, so he's hardly around anymore. She's lonely, Sophia. That's the problem.

She grabs the soccer ball from the back of her closet. She needs fresh air. Something. She needs to get away from this place. Now. She doesn't want to be here cleaning the cat box and listening to Grandma laugh at the game-show contestants when they mess up. Like Grandma could do any better? Please.

Sophia leaves the house and walks two blocks to the empty field where they've just started construction on a bunch of new homes. The earth has been cleared and leveled. She drops the ball and starts to kick it around, practicing her drills. She doesn't dare go to the park anymore. All the kids who hang out there think she's a lunatic. She hates them.

It's lonely being Sophia. But right now, compared to the things people are starting to say about her, Sophia finally agrees with the line her mom always says when she asked her why she never dates men: It's better to be alone than to be in bad company.

I wake up to bitter brown scent of coffee brewing, and it does not make me ill. Amazing, I have appetite. An appetite, I mean. I've been forcing myself to eat since I got pregnant, but now I crave soft give of bread on my teeth. And there is something I want to eat very much: waffles, with butter and syrup.

With Ricky still asleep, I kiss his warm, soft, man-smelling cheeks and step out of bed. I go downstairs. Cynthia, our cook, is already up, tidying and preparing sofrito for the day's meals. Since finding out I was pregnant, I've avoided Cynthia's kitchen in mornings, as scent— the scent—of simmering onions and green peppers nauseated me deeply. But this morning is different.

"A good smell, yes?" I say.

"Someone's feeling better," she says.

I ask Cynthia to make me a Belgian waffle, then turn my attention to *The Miami Herald* on the breakfast table. I read usual assortment of depressing international news. Things do not change much in the world, and I don't think they ever will.

I turn to the Arts and Entertainment section, to read about latest movies, wondering when, if ever, I will be "allowed" to see a movie in theater again. Before Ricky, I used to love going to movies with friends. But now Ricky says he doesn't want me hanging out with beautiful women who might draw attention to me. So, he's demanded that I stop hanging out with models. Models are only friends I have—

the only—other than Milan and Alma. After Ricky, I realize, I don't have many friends left. I never leave the house.

I flip to front of the section, looking for movie news, but I see something else. Ricky news. My breath catches in my throat. Since Sophia came to the house claiming to be his child, press have gone crazy with the story, running something nearly every day for a month now. I feel sorry for the girl, actually. And I still suspect Ricky is lying. How could he not be her father? She looks exactly like him, and he went to school with her mother. And even though he told reporters that he hardly knew Irene Gallagher, the girl had snapshots of the two together in prom outfits. Ricky claims that she had just wanted to have her photo taken with him, but Sophia says that is a lie. I will have to ask Ricky's mother. She probably knows truth. *The* truth.

This new article is about Irene Gallagher, the mother and Ricky's alleged high school girlfriend. That's what article calls her. I have not learned this word yet, "alleged." I ask Cynthia what it means. I am try-ing very hard to improve English—my English, I mean.

"It means 'supposed,' " says Cynthia. "When they write that in a news story it's like saying the person who said it is lying."

"Really?" I thought the American media were supposed to be so fair, but it doesn't seem fair to have way of using English that says someone is lying without coming right out and saying so.

The article says that Irene Gallagher is not only trying to extort money from the delightful Ricky Biscayne, devoted husband and fam-ily man, but that she is also trying to claim that her employer, the Pinecrest Bay Fire Department, discriminated against her because she is a woman. "Sources say Gallagher, who lives in a less-than-modest home in Homestead, will stop at nothing to get the money she thinks she needs. A banking source confirmed that an Irene Gallagher of Homestead had been recently placed on Check Systems, a database flagging those who too often write bad checks."

The article quotes Ricky's new publicist, Milan Gotay, as saying that Ricky is "beside himself with grief at these accusations. Nothing could be further from the truth. In high school, Ricky was a serious student and athlete, focused on his dreams of one day having a career in the arts. He hardly even knew Irene Gallagher."

I look at accompanying photo of Irene Gallagher and try to understand what it is I see in the woman's eyes. I have known many liars in my short life. And in this woman's eyes, I do not see a liar.

Lilia twists her chin hair and sits at her drab desk in the middle of the bustling *Herald* newsroom. She is excited. The more excited she gets, the faster she twirls the hair. It grows out of a mole. The hair, not the excitement.

The excitement burbles out of her gut. Or is it the chili cheese fries? She can't be sure. But what she does know is that this is the first time she has been truly excited about doing a story at the paper in the past five years. It is also the first time the editors have pulled her off the "Lunch with Lilia" column; they are short staffed and need someone with the inside celebrity scoop to help out with a breaking story about a possible illegitimate child belonging to Miami's own crossover Latin singing sensation, Ricky Biscayne. Lilia, for the record, is not aware that her very thoughts, like her writing, come tumbling out in predictable clichés. Clichés, like excitement, inspire Lilia to twirl the hair.

The phone rings, and the security guard downstairs tells her that Milan Gotay is here to see her. Right on time, thinks Lilia. She likes a punctual publicist. In Miami, that is sometimes hard to come by. "Tell her I'll be right there," says Lilia. She hangs the telephone headset on the stick-on plastic hook she has affixed to her computer terminal, tosses the paper plate from the cafeteria's chili fries into the wastebasket, logs off her computer—you never know which of these other reporters might try to break into your databases and address book when you are away—and barrels down the escalator like a bull.

Milan Gotay stands in the entry vestibule in tight designer jeans, a black top, and black strappy sandals, with a bag Lilia recognizes as Louis Vuitton, with a clear plastic Starbucks cold-drink cup in one hand. The Miami hot-girl uniform. She smiles when she sees Lilia, and Lilia feels as if she were meeting an old friend. She doesn't like that feeling. Usually, Lilia likes to feel hateful and envious of the people she interviews, because it makes it all that much easier to eviscerate them in print. It will be difficult, Lilia thinks, to disembowel the adorable, sweet-faced Milan.

"How are you?" asks Milan. "I am really happy to finally meet you. I've been a big fan of your work for years."

They all say that, thinks Lilia, as she shakes Milan's hand. She likes the feel of Milan's skin, and for a brief moment she imagines what this young, sweet thing might be like in bed.

"I especially liked the piece you did back in 2000 on Kid Rock," says Milan. "You wrote that he smelled like a white-bread sandwich in a trailer park. I'll never forget that line. So original."

Lilia studies Milan's face for a moment. Every publicist likes to compliment her, but few, if any, can remember a single column she's ever written. "You really read that?"

"I read everything you do." Lilia can't be sure, but it seems that Milan is flirting with her.

Lilia smiles, and signs Milan into the guest book at the security desk. "Let's talk upstairs," she says, imagining as she says it that she is at her Kendall condo and not here in the lobby of her workplace.

"Okay," says Milan.

Lilia leads Milan to the newsroom cafeteria. "Get anything you like. There's a secluded balcony we can go talk on."

Milan gets some bottled water and a cookie, and even though her belly has begun to churn and grumble with the last batch, Lilia gets another order of chili cheese fries and a jumbo root beer.

They settle at a table on the deck outside. Lilia is proud of the deck, which overlooks the water and has a stunning view of the downtown skyline. How many newspapers could say that? She'd interviewed at a few others around the country but had decided to stay here because of the views and the women.

"It's gorgeous," says Milan. So are you, thinks Lilia.

"So," says Lilia. "Tell me about this kid in Homestead. What's the real deal here, Milan? Is she Ricky's kid?"

Milan shakes her head and furrows her brow. "Absolutely not. Ricky doesn't have any children. Lilia, you know lots of celebrities. I mean, you're practically a celebrity yourself. And you know how people are."

"I'm not a celebrity," Lilia objects.

"What do you mean? You're famous! Everyone knows you. 'Lunch with Lilia.' It's every star's dream to be in your column."

It is true. Lilia is famous. Usually it bothers her that celebrities and their handlers don't acknowledge her power and prestige. But this cute little number is different.

"Anyway," says Milan. "This is just another case of a nobody trying to make themselves a somebody—and a few bucks—by associating their name with a somebody. You know how it goes."

Lilia nods. "But the girl looks like Ricky in the photos I've seen. Don't you think?"

"Exactly. Think about it. If you were broke and unstable, and you were having problems at work that looked like you were going to get fired or something, and your kid looked like Ricky, and you'd gone to school with him once, it would be a perfect plan."

Lilia listens as Milan describes Irene Gallagher in Homestead as a typical lowlife in search of money, and as the publicist lists the names of other celebrities who have been slapped with false paternity suits, she begins to believe her. Lilia also begins to really *want* her. Such sweetness. Such a tiny bow tie of a mouth. Such cute freckles and pretty eyebrows.

"You're not like any other publicist I've ever met," says Lilia.

"I'm not?"

"No, I mean, I'd actually like to hang out with you sometime."

Milan smiles, and coughs into her hand. "Uh. Hmm. That would be . . . fun."

"How about this weekend?" Lilia surprises herself with her forwardness. She has been on a losing streak with the ladies lately and thinks it can't hurt to be direct. After all, she can tell Milan wants her.

"Uh, sure. I guess."

Lilia writes her home number on a piece of paper. "Call me. I know this amazing Brazilian restaurant. It's new, lots of celebrities.

"Do you like going out to cool places? You seem like the type." Milan coughs into her hand again. Is she sick?

"You need a lozenge?" Lilia whacks Milan on the back with one beefy hand. "There. That help?"

Milan winces and coughs again.

"I have some lozenges back at my desk." Lilia likes the thought of walking through the office with Milan in tow, because people will talk. Journalists tend to gossip, and they all know Lilia is a lesbian. They've seen how cute her girlfriends are.

"No, no, I'm fine." Milan stares out at the water with a pained expression. Lilia thinks it is cute that Milan is so nervous around her.

"Yeah, I know all the hot spots."

"Wow," says Milan. "That's great. In my opinion, the real story, the one you guys might want to pay attention to, is about a place that I think you'd really love."

"What's that?" asks Lilia, adjusting herself in her seat to give Milan the best view of her arms. Lilia has a set of dumbbells at home and she pumps iron every night. She has very imposing arms.

"Ricky's invested in a new club here in town, called Club G, which is going to be the hottest thing in Miami since Mansion."

"Mansion's okay," says Lilia. She wiggles her brows at Milan. "But have you ever been to Lady Luck?"

Milan chokes on her water and smiles at Lilia at the mention of the newest lesbian nightclub in town; Lady Luck has taken the place of Godyva. Some people call the club "Lady Lick," which Lilia finds amusing and exciting at the same time. Lilia can tell from her reaction that Milan has heard of the club; hell, thinks Lilia, she's probably even been there. As Lilia suspects, Milan is a closet lesbian. She can sniff them out a mile away.

"I'd rather not talk about that right now," says Milan.

"What would you like to talk about?" Lilia leans closer and does her best at flirting, rolling her shoulders back and baring her teeth like a wild animal. "You? Me? Us?"

Milan's nostrils flare and she blinks quickly, as if she has dirt in her eyes. "Ricky's new club. You *have* to write about it. I promise you, it's a much bigger story than this whole thing with the kid."

"Only if you go with me to Lady Lick," says Lilia, emphasizing her creative alteration of the club name by lingering on the *L*s, tongue to teeth.

"Uh, hmm. Well. Er, uh. Hmm."

Lilia beams and licks the tip of her pencil without taking her eyes off Milan. "So. Tell me about Little Ricky's new nightclub."

thursday, july 18

Jill Sanchez adjusts her bright white sweatband, pumps on the StairMaster, stares at her reflection in the mirror of her home gym, and listens to the day's news as Rigor, her personal trainer, reads it to her in a strong Austrian accent. She doesn't have time to read to herself, and reading on the stair-climber makes her sick to her stomach.

"Ya," he says. "It says here that Ricky Biscayne is investing in a hot new Miami Beach club called Club G."

"What else does it say?" Jill admires the sinew of her thighs as she pumps away, both the way it looks in the mirror and the way it feels as she steps down hard. She feels a flutter of adrenaline as she imagines the moment she and Ricky go public with their rejuvenated romance.

"It says the club is very cool," says Rigor. He sounds to her like a mix of Curly from the Three Stooges and Arnold Schwarzenegger.

"Rigor, read the actual article please. I don't want your synopsis."

Rigor frowns and obeys. The story, by that horrible "Lunch with Lilia" woman, tells of a trendy new club financed by Ricky Biscayne.

"The sexy new club already has waiting lists for the VIP section with celebrities like Shalim and the Olsens." Jill's nose wrinkles. Lilia still has no clue who is cool in the celeb world. "Biscayne's club will have a Moroccan-style style. Biscayne's stylish new club promises to put Biscayne on the map as the single most powerful mainstream entertainer in Miami, dethroning the voluptuous vixen Jill Sanchez once and for all."

"Read that part again," says Jill, her eyes narrowing with competitive energy. Rigor reads it again.

"What a little bitch," hisses Jill.

"Who, me?" asks Rigor. "What did I do?"

"No, not you, stupid," says Jill. "Lilia. She hates me."

Rigor sighs and says with the limpest of voices, "How could anyone hate you, Jill?"

"Shut up and bring me the phone. That club is mine."

I've never spent much time in Allapattah. Okay, well, none. I've spent no time here. As one of the poorest, blackest neighborhoods in Miami, near the Civic Center and the Jackson Memorial, it wasn't exactly on the top of the list when I was growing up for places my family was dying to go. In fact, we pretty much avoided it altogether. Because it borders Wynwood and my parents didn't really want us girls hanging out with Puerto Ricans (I'm telling you, my parents might as well join the Klan and get it over with), I am almost totally unfamiliar with this part of Miami.

As Ignacio drives me to his mother's Allapattah house on NW Thirty-fourth Street, near Twenty-second Avenue, the house where he lived with his mom from the time he came to the States, before he got the apartment on Collins that he lives in now, I look out at the run-down buildings, crumbling sidewalks, sickly vegetation, and mostly dark faces. African faces. My heart races with fear. Why? It's stupid. I realize how stupid it is, but it happens anyway. Brainwashing. I try to consciously release all of my prejudices, all of the nonsense and fear that has been drilled into my psyche since I was a little girl. I remind myself that 70 percent of the neighborhood are Cubans, black Cubans, and that, in a sense, I'm among my people. Ignacio's people. This is the Cuban Miami no one outside this city knows about, because it doesn't fit America's limited popular view of who Latinos are and how we look. I'm going to go out on a limb here and say Cubans in general do not fit that stereotype, in any way.

"That's the library," he says as we pass a low gray building. I'm surprised there's a library in Allapattah, which is wrong of me. After all, we're going to a dinner celebration in honor of Ignacio's niece, who will be leaving for Stanford in the fall and who graduated at the top of her class just last month.

We pass a newish-looking house and he says, "That used to be an empty lot where my little cousins used to play baseball with their friends." He recognizes someone on a porch, and waves. He rolls down the window to yell out, "How's the family?" in Spanish. I hear music from passing cars. Cuban music, loud rap in Spanish, and *timba*. I also smell Cuban food in the air, that distinctive aroma of grease, pork, and white rice. I hear children playing and laughing and calling out in Spanish.

The house itself is small, and bright blue. It looks like illegal additions have been tacked on, wooden rooms that slope and slant, a slab of metal here, a mesh of sheets in a window there. Honestly? It looks like something from the third world, but something lovingly cared for. The front yard has a chicken coop and potted tomatoes.

Ignacio parks at the curb and comes to open the door for me. Three children spill out of the front door and tumble toward us, laughing. I turn toward them and they stop in their tracks and stare. Surprised. They're well dressed and clean, healthy and attractive. I think Ignacio's entire family must be attractive. Ignacio introduces them as his nephews and niece, and I wave hello. They are suddenly shy, and the littlest one runs back into the house, shouting in Spanish that Ignacio has brought a white girl home. Ignacio looks at me with an apology in his eyes, and I smile to let him know it's okay. I do not tell him that "white girl" is much nicer than what my family would say about him if I brought him home.

Ignacio holds my hand as we walk up the steps to the front porch. I remove my sunglasses and see the silhouette of a woman behind the screen door. The door opens, and an elegant-looking woman steps forward, wearing a tasteful beige linen pantsuit with an elegant gold necklace and matching earrings—just the sort of outfit my own mother might wear. Her hair is cut short in a way that flatters her pretty, angular face. Her dark brown eyes take me in, wary. Ignacio introduces her in Spanish as his mother. He introduces me as his girlfriend. As I shake hands with her, I wonder how old she is. She looks much too young to be his mother.

"Come in," she says, in Spanish, adding a slightly unconvincing, "Welcome."

The aroma of garlic and green peppers overtakes me as I step into the little living room. The floors are wooden, and the room is cool. The walls are painted a peach color and decorated with dime-store framed religious paintings. A group of kids, maybe six or seven of them, sits around a small television, playing video games and cheering the way kids do. Several adults sit watching a baseball game on a bigscreen television, and I can feel them size me up, even though they are too polite to simply stare. I see the classic Cuban altar on a table in the corner, with La Caridad del Cobre and a number of Santeria Catholic saints. Almost everything else appears to be covered with a doily, and there are many framed photos of family members.

A man who looks like an older, pudgier version of Ignacio pushes himself out of a brown armchair and ambles over to me as if he has a backache. He wears a green polo shirt and khaki shorts, and extremely white sneakers with long white tube socks. Unlike the woman, he does not smile at me. He looks concerned as Ignacio introduces me to him.

"Geneva, this is my father."

I hold my hand out to shake, and Ignacio's father simply stares at it. After a moment, he reluctantly takes it, and shakes briefly.

"He's a good boy," says the man. "I don't want anyone to hurt him."

Ignacio's mother rolls her eyes at me to put me at ease, and as her husband shuffles back to the chair, she leans in and says in my ear, "Don't mind him. He's very protective of his children."

Ignacio introduces me to the rest of the group. Most are relatives. Ignacio's sister Magdalena, a narrow woman with a stylish puff of Afro and long wooden earrings, comes into the room wiping her hands on a dishtowel. She seems suspicious of me and doesn't return my smile. She looks me up and down with a sniff. My jeans and beaded flip-flops suddenly feel too informal, and I am very self-conscious of not having worn a bra. All the women here are dressed much more conservatively, and much more formally. Even Ignacio wears khakis and an orange silk shirt, with woven sandals. He's dressed well. Why did I wear jeans? I cross my arms over my chest and will myself to be invisible.

Ignacio's mother disappears and returns a few moments later with some drinks on a tray. "Who wants a *doncellita?*" she asks. She hands me one of the drinks without waiting for me to answer. *Doncellita* is a traditional Cuban drink that I love, made with cocoa liquor and heavy cream. They are served in thick, tall glasses, with cherries on top, and straws. It's like a chocolate shake that gets you drunk before you know what's hit you, really. For the children, Ignacio's mother has plain chocolate milk, with whipped cream and a cherry on top.

"Come, sit," says Ignacio. We go to the dining room, which has a view of the kitchen through a narrow door. We sit at the table and sip our drinks. It has to be one of the most delicious *doncellitas* I've ever had, and I compliment Ignacio's mother. She nods at me without smiling, then goes back into the kitchen and joins her daughter and a woman Ignacio tells me is his aunt.

"Can I help with anything?" I ask. They say no, it's almost ready. Then, his mother opens the oven and brings out three platters of appetizers and sets them on the large dining-room table, which appears to have been "let out" for the event and takes up almost the entire room.

She calls to the people in the other rooms to come get something to hold them over until dinner. She sets out little paper plates and napkins, then returns to the kitchen. The appetizers consist of familiar foods, Cuban. There are croquettes, what looks like ham, yuca, and malanga, a root vegetable. There are also olives, about six different kinds, and something I don't recognize, which Ignacio tells me is a kind of plantain tamale. He explains that his family is originally from Oriente, and that they have some foods that are more like food you might find in Haiti. I taste one of the tamales and am surprised by the chili heat of it, and the mix of flavors. It's delicious.

Ignacio leans close and pops a croquette into my mouth. I have an urge to kiss him, but tamp it down. I already look underdressed and out of place; the last thing I need is to look easy on top of that. People circulate all around us, and there's the drone of a dozen conversations happening all at once. They tell jokes, some of which I get, and others that seem very inside. He asks me what I think so far. I tell him I like his family. They feel a lot like my family, only less crazy.

As the women cook, they call out through the door to ask me the usual questions—where I'm from, what I do for a living. It's awkward, but becomes less so as there is less *doncellita* in my glass. Soon enough, I'm feeling pretty relaxed. And, as I often do when I'm relaxed in unfamiliar territory, I just sort of sit back and watch. I'm disappointed again and again by my primary response, which is to think something like, Wow, they're people just like us. But I think it. I'm not proud of myself. In fact, I hate myself. I wonder if that feeling will ever go away, or if my parents and society have ruined me forever for issues of race.

Ignacio's mother calls everyone to dinner. The grown-ups, having had their drinks, too, are somewhat chummier toward me than they were. I am even loosened up enough to help clear the appetizers and set the table. Ignacio stands off to one side, watching me with a silly grin on his face. He is so sexy I feel like I want to jump him, right here, right now, in the middle of his mother's dinner table. I wonder if I have had too much to drink. What did she put in those *doncellitas*?

The small kitchen, dated yet tidy and well organized, has miraculously produced an abundance of food. I wonder why people like me, who rarely cook, need such big, flashy kitchens, with our stupid granite countertops and our stainless steel appliances. If anyone should have a difficult kitchen, it's me. I don't use it. If anyone should have an easy kitchen, it's Ignacio's mother.

I join the other women in loading the mismatched earthenware platters onto a buffet in the dining room. There are stuffed green peppers, and yellow rice with chicken. There's roast pork, and white rice with black beans. There's *fufú*, a plantain mash with garlic. There are also fried plantains, the dark, sweet kind. There's boiled yuca with olive oil, lime juice, and garlic. There is also soup, an *ajiaco*, or stew kind of thing.

"You ladies have been busy," I say. Ignacio's mother looks at me as if to say, *It's nothing, really,* and the other women don't look at me at all, just sort of raise their eyebrows to each other. Everyone lines up, plate in hand, and starts to pile it on. I get in line. Ignacio stands behind me, nuzzling my neck.

"I'm so glad you're here," he says.

I turn to face him, and kiss him lightly on the lips. I don't care if his dad is watching and hates me. I love this man, and I'm tipsy. "Me too," I say.

I hear a familiar trilling sound across the room. My cell! I hand my plate to Ignacio and run to pick it up. I know it seems rude, but with Club G on the verge of opening, I can't afford to miss a call. I burrow through my bag like a squirrel on the trail of a nut, and extract the phone.

"Hello, this is Geneva Gotay," I say.

"Geneva, this is Jill Sanchez."

Huh? I say nothing. The woman on the other end repeats herself.

I say, "Jill Sanchez? Like the movies and singer Jill Sanchez?"

"You forgot fashion designer and dancer," she says.

I say nothing.

"I want to talk to you about investing in your nightclub."

"Uh, okay." I step into the living room for a little bit of privacy.

The person claiming to be Jill Sanchez says, "Whatever Ricky Biscayne put in, I want to double that. What do you say?"

I want to say yes, thank you, but I can't speak. Is this for real?

"Hello?" asks Jill Sanchez. "Okay. Quadruple it. You there?"

"Yes, I'm here. That would be great. I mean . . ."

Suddenly, Jill Sanchez interrupts me, speaking louder and faster than most of the people I know. She tells me, "I have another call coming in. Hold on. I'll be right back."

I hear a click, but the call fails to go over. Next, I hear Jill Sanchez's voice purring smooth as syrup in my ear. "I miss you like crazy, Ricky. My thong is wet just thinking about you doing me *por detrás*."

I clear my throat. "Uh, Jill? It's still me. Geneva." And, I think to myself, you could not pay me enough money to *ever* make me do Jill Sanchez *por detrás*. There is silence.

"Ricky must have hung up," I say.

"Yeah," says Jill, giggling. "Well, it wasn't important."

Jill goes on to tell me that she wants to invest in my club. I can't believe it. She wants to invest a whole heck of a lot in my club, in fact. I arrange to have a meeting with her, try not to sound too excited, but when I hang up, I let out a whoop and hop up and down a little. Ignacio finds me in the living room and asks me what I'm happy about. I tell him, and he shares the news with the family, dragging me into the dining room and ringing his spoon against the side of his glass.

"Attention, everyone!" he calls in Spanish. One by one, the family members quiet down. "I want to announce that my lovely girlfriend, Geneva, has just, at this very moment, in our very humble home, scored a substantial business deal with none other than the Puerto Rican superstar Jill Sanchez."

People murmur. Then Ignacio's father begins to clap, and slowly, one by one, the other family members join him. They smile at me with a sort of respect they didn't have before, and when I sit down to my meal, I, the woman no one wanted to talk to before, am suddenly of great interest.

No American, no matter how recently arrived, is immune to the lure of celebrity.

friday, july 19

M ilan, *hija*, you are breaking my heart with this lesbianism of yours."Mom is, like, staring at me over the top of her big bumblebee sunglasses. She looks like a face double for Elizabeth Taylor, before Elizabeth Taylor puffed up.

"What?" I ask. Behind us, a waiter drops a tray and breaks about a million glasses. Ouch? My ears? We've just finished a "delightful" mother-daughter lunch at a very pretentious Miami Beach diner called Big Pink, recommended by Mr. Ricky Biscayne himself. I was hoping to tell Mom about me and Ricky, in delicate terms, of course, so that she might actually give me advice. Her shows are goopy and gross sometimes, but overall my mother is pretty good at giving women advice, which is why she's still on the air. But as it turned out, I didn't have the guts. I was too embarrassed, and she acted so proud of me and the job I'm doing that I didn't want to burst the bubble and let her know the truth about me—that I'm a homewrecking *puta*.

The noise settles down, and she's still staring at me like that, bug-eyed. Like she didn't even hear the crashing. She's got nerves of steel, or else maybe she can't move her face at all.

"Mom?" I ask. "Why are you looking at me like that?"

"Because," she says, as if I am the dumbest bird in the tree. "I can't believe you just told me you're going to a lesbian club."

Okay, let's backtrack. Before the crashing plates? I had told Mom I was doing Geneva a favor by going to a club with that *Herald* reporter, Lilia, to schmooze her into a huge feature on Club G. I did *not* mention that it would more than likely be a lesbian bar.

"I didn't say anything like that," I protest.

"You think your mother was born yesterday?" Mom taps her head, as if her temple has something to do with being born yesterday.

"No, actually, I think you were born almost sixty years ago."

Mom looks offended and scoots closer. "Shh," she says. "Don't advertise that information, thank you." She narrows her eyes at me. "I know you're going to a gay dyke bar because I know Lilia's parents, and they tell me she is a gay dyke."

I cringe at her repeated use of the term "dyke." It sounds so wrong coming from her lips I can't even tell you, but anyway. It's not like I'm not used to it. Mom saying off-color sexual things, that is. In fact, she just told me—with some glee, I might add—that she's heading to the station to do a show on elongated vulvas as the result of excessive promiscuity. I want to ask her what "excessive" promiscuity is, and I wonder if I qualify for the "simple" promiscuity moniker. But I leave it alone.

"Mom, I don't know where we're going. She asked me to hang out, and I said yes. I didn't think she was asking me on a date. Jesus, Mom."

"*Pero Dios mío*, Milan! What has gotten into you! That reporter is as butch as a bulldog's balls!"

I cringe again. My mother.

"You're not going to mention any of this to your father," says Mom.

"Well, duh," I say. Like I'd consider such a thing.

Mom folds her arms and cocks her head. Purses her lips like she knows something no one else knows. "Is this why you never date men? Because you're a lesbian?"

"I'm not a lesbian, Mom!"

She shrugs like she doesn't believe me. "You can tell me if you are. It's okay. It would break my heart, but I'd get over it because I love you and I'm your mother and all I want is for you to be happy, even if you can only be happy as a lesbian."

"I'm not!"

"Plenty of women are curious . . . I mean, once I even, well, that was a long time ago. . . ." Her eyes grow unfocused as she remembers something I really, truly do not want to hear about.

"Mom! I'm not gay!"

She plants her elbows on the table with the philosophical look she gets, the one that I hate. "You know what I think? I think we evolved to live in harems, and that women are by nature bisexual."

"What?" I stare at her in shock, realizing my mother has munched clam. This is very upsetting. "You *do?*"

She shakes herself and smiles. "But that's not what we're talking about. We're not talking about me. We're talking about how you feel about Lilia. How you are a lesbian."

"I'm *not* a lesbian!" My mom is bisexual? *Eeew.*

"Then why are you going to a lesbian club, Milan? Don't lie to your mother."

"It's like bribery. I don't know. I wanted Geneva to get a good story about her new club."

"Bribery?" Her face twists in disgust. "Who are you? What happened to my daughter?"

"It'll be fine, Mom. It'll be interesting."

"No, it won't. What's wrong with you?"

"Nothing. It's for Geneva."

Mom looks confused. "*Geneva's* a lesbian?" Now she looks enlightened. "That explains a lot."

"No, Mom. No one's straighter than Geneva. I'm doing it to get coverage in the *Herald* for her new club."

"Geneva can take care of herself. You're *not* going to go to that club."

"But what if the reporter gets angry and takes revenge on us?"

Mom shakes her head as she places her platinum AmEx card on the bill tray. "*Mira,* Milan. I know that she-man's mother and father. Lilia is the one who should be worried that it gets out she's trying to screw her sources. Did you know that they measure the clitoris of lesbians, and it is usually much bigger than the clitoris of straight women?"

"Mom!" I am going to puke. No, really. I am. "Stop it. Please. Let's talk about something else."

Mom smiles. She loves to make me sick. "*¿Qué?* That's not what she's doing? Hitting on you? That's what she's doing. You know that."

"I just don't want to think about it."

"*Sí, cómo no.* Me neither. But listen to me. If she bothers you, I'll talk about it on my show. And then I'll call her parents. She's not going to bother you." Mom looks at her watch. "Is there anything else you wanted to tell me, Milan? I feel like there's *something* you're not telling me."

I think of my intimate relations with Ricky, and shake my head with a smile. "Nope," I say. "Let's get out of here."

The scent of my body, body steeped in liquid of lifemaking and the scent of sleep, comforts me so much I can't bear to leave protection—the protection—of these soft white sheets. I am warm here, and the air of the bedroom is cold from the air-conditioning. I am alone. I don't know where Ricky is. I just know that this baby is taking all of my energy today, and that I can't get up. But I have to. I don't want to. I want to close my eyes and sleep forever. On my side, of course. I miss sleeping on belly. You can't do that when you're pregnant.

My back aches, and I think that it would be nice to have husband to rub it. But my husband seems much more interested in hanging out with his "boys," meaning the group of guys he's known since he was in high school. "Guys" is generous word; they are not mature enough to be considered guys. They are boys, without any of positive associations you might have with that word. They are a bunch of derelicts. And Ricky? Maybe it's hormones, but I suspect he is the King of Derelicts. Success has done nothing to change his party habits or his companions. I'm entering sixth month of pregnancy. You'd think he might be around more. But Ricky doesn't seem interested in this baby, or me, or anything but his friends, parties, and—I have to finally come to terms with this—cocaine. I don't know how he gets work done, actually. It's very strange.

I push myself up to sitting position and look around the room, stretch my arms over my head. I wear large white cotton nightgown, sleeveless Laura Ashley. I see pile of Ricky's dirty clothes on the floor. That shirt with the thin colorful stripes smelled like someone else yesterday. Lately, he's smelled of another woman. He denies it, but I have a good nose. I know perfume, and soap, and lotion. For better or worse, I know the smell of woman. I know that the scent Ricky carries even on his skin—and on his breath, oddly—is not mine, and not his. It is also unmistakably female, and feline, with undertones of blood. Like someone, something, in heat. I know, more or less, what Ricky is trying to hide, but I don't have energy or resources to deal with it right now. If ever there were a perfect time for a man to decide to start cheating on his wife, it is in the sixth month of pregnancy, when woman has no employment of her own and no family members to help her.

Ricky just called, half laughing, half apologetic, saying he spent night at his friend Hughie's house, after partying with friends from "back in the days." He promised to be home soon, and asked me to tell Matthew to get started without him. "Call him yourself," I said. I hate that Ricky always seems to make other people take care of the irresponsible things in his life. Ricky hung up on me, meaning that either I go down now and tell Matthew he is going to be late, or no one will.

I force myself out of bed and wrap my body in a thick white robe. I feel off-balance because of bulge of baby. I've gained fifty pounds, and I do love eating. I wear woman's size ten now. I go to my closet, and stuff myself into my favorite pair of Robert Rodriguez jeans, fly down for comfort, with an Elie Tahari peasant blouse that obscures my belly from sight. I realize I still weigh less than many nonpregnant women, but Ricky keeps telling me I'm fat. I don't like that, or his cheating, or anything about him now. He has no interest in me sexually. The pregnancy has not reduced my sex drive. I thought it would. You see pregnant women on street—the street—and you never think of them as horny. But that is exactly how I feel right now. Hornier than I've ever felt. I wonder what the purpose is, from an evolutionary standpoint. Why don't men understand that a woman never feels sexier than in the last two trimesters of pregnancy? I am embarrassed about this, but I've never masturbated more in my life than I do now; there must be scientific reason for it. Maybe the body wants to make strong the muscles of lower abdomen to prepare for pushing? Something.

I push myself to go downstairs, and walk in flat rubber gardening clogs across the backyard to the studio. I keep these shoes on back porch. I'm feeling very powerful and grounded. I will not remain with Ricky for much longer. How can I? I cannot. I will leave him once baby is here and I have the energy to fight back. I'm not a dead girl anymore. I'm woman. A woman. I have never felt more like a woman, uncut, unalone, carrying in my body a soul.

I enter the offices to find Matthew waiting in lounge area with his headphones on, eyes closed as he concentrates hard on the music. He strums an acoustic guitar, flamenco-style. It sounds haunting and beautiful. I watch him for a moment and think how incredibly sexy he looks. People are never sexier than when they are creating, be it life, music, literature, or, I like to think, soap. Again, it might be just hormones, but Matthew has an artistic intensity to him that radiates out like bright white heat from star. I fantasize for a moment of seducing him, but it's a ridiculous idea, that he would want pregnant wife of Ricky's. I tap him gently on the arm, and he jumps. The music stops.

"Oh, hey, Jasminka!" He takes off the headphones and smiles. Matthew is always on time and always seems to be in good mood. His cheeks are so pink I want to pinch them like a child's. There is a small crease in the space between his eyebrows, from his concentration. It will fade. He is so alive and pink. He must eat a lot of leafy green vegetables to have breath as clean as he does.

"Ricky called just a minute ago," I say. "He said he is late and for you to start without him."

Matthew glances at his watch, shakes head in disappointment. "Dude has my cell number," he says. "I don't know why he doesn't just call me, you know?"

I sigh and join him on hideous red sofa. I can actually feel the heat of his body against skin of my arm, even though we are a foot apart at least. He smells of heat and shampoo. "Is something you can do without Ricky?"

Matthew laughs to himself and looks as if someone just suggested he get a sex-change operation. "Uh, yeah," he says. "Yeah," he says softly, and, it seems, to himself. "I think so. In fact, I could do Ricky's entire album without him."

"What you are saying?" I ask.

Matthew stands up and paces the room for a moment.

"Can I ask you something?" he replies. I look at him with wide eyes to indicate that I'm listening. "How much do you know about your husband?"

I shrug, wondering if he knows about the affair. Maybe he knows who she is. I don't think I want to know. "I don't know," I say. "As much as wife—a wife—knows of her husband."

He speaks as if to himself only. "I shouldn't do this." He looks at me, pained. "Yes, I should."

"Matthew," I say. "If it is about Ricky and the other woman . . ."

He looks confused. "No," he says. His confusion melts to compassion; he feels sorry for me. He knows about the woman, but has not told me. He is surprised I know. "That's not it."

"Oh."

Matthew holds his hand out to me, smiles gently, and says, "Come with me. I want to show you something."

I follow him to the sound studio. He offers me the black leather swivel chair, flips the On switches on computers and other assorted electronic equipment, then stands at my side and begins to punch buttons. Soon, Ricky's current big hit, "You're the Girl for Me," begins to play. I smile in spite of myself because Ricky told me he sang this song just for me. The song plays, but the vocals do not start in the usual spot.

"Okay," says Matthew. He pauses song where it is, and rewinds it little bit. "I'm going into the recording studio." He points to the room on other side of the big glass window. "And when I get in there, I want you to punch this button, and then this one. Okay? Can you do that?"

I nod. Matthew goes into the recording booth. He points, and I do as he's instructed. The song begins again, without the vocals. Matthew opens his mouth and starts to sing. I feel the flesh rise on my arms. I watch his mouth move, but hear *Ricky's* voice. When Matthew stops singing, Ricky's voice stops on recording. After a few moments of this, Matthew returns to the mixing booth.

"I don't understand," I say.

Matthew frowns. "Neither does anyone else," he says. "That's the beauty of it."

"But Ricky is a great singer," I say. "Everyone believes so."

"He's a really *good* singer," says Matthew. "But he's inconsistent. His, uh, *recreational* pursuits sometimes get in the way these days."

"The drugs."

Matthew shrugs. "Drugs?" he says sarcastically. "What drugs? Ricky's a health nut. I read it in *Newsweek*."

"It is not true, this article," I say.

Matthew smiles and I realize I've missed his sarcasm. "I know, Jasminka," he says gently. "I've known for a long time."

"He is an addict," I say.

Matthew nods. "Yeah. It's sad. He knows it and I know it. I guess I'm glad you know it, too."

"I know for a long time, Matthew."

"I think Milan's the only one who doesn't get it," says Matthew.

"She does not know?"

Matthew makes a face as if I've asked him if he was Mozart. "Uh,

no. Milan's only the nicest, most sheltered woman on the *planet*." Do
I see love in his eyes? I do. Matthew likes Milan. I don't know why, but
I feel a tinge of jealousy.

I look at equipment and studio. All of it smells of electricity and
rubber. "How much singing you do on Ricky songs, Matthew?"

He shrugs. "I don't know. I've been here from the start, fixing
things for him."

"*Fixing* things? What does this mean?"

He looks at me as if I have failed to understand the simplest of
concepts. His eyes narrow as if he awaits a blow, and he says, softly, "It
means that I sing most of Ricky's parts on his songs, Jasminka."

I feel my heart squeeze hard in my chest. "Not possible." For all his
faults, I've always been able to point to Ricky's talent and art as valid
reasons for loving him. If they aren't real, then what do I have? What
do I have? It's almost too horrible to imagine.

"Thanks to the wonders of modern technology, anything is possible," says Matthew. "Anybody can be a singing star. With the right
people behind the scenes."

"Why you should let him do that?"

He shrugs. "It seemed like a good deal at first. We were friends. I
was the gringo who loved salsa, and he was the good-looking guy who
loved attention. Back in college, nobody could make me laugh like
Ricky, man. I loved him, like a friend, you know. I got to sing salsa,
which I love, and I got to hear my songs on the radio, without having
to get a face-lift."

He laughs as if this last part was funny, but I don't understand the
humor.

"But Ricky is millionaire," I say. "And you . . ."

"I'm a short, broke bastard, I know." As he smiles, I feel something
like holiness from him. He is not the things he says. He is gift. I feel
things like this, and I feel it now, for him.

"Why, Matthew?"

"I'm short because I don't like to wear heels," he jokes. He looks at me but I don't laugh. I can't. "Look," says Matthew. He leans against the control console. "I don't really care about money. I never have. I care about *music*. Ricky was basically a way for me to get my music out. I dug that, actually." He shrugs self-consciously and apologizes, then says, "For me, it's always been about the music, the creativity. For Ricky, it's always been about the fame, and the stage. It was like we were made for each other, at least for a while."

"So he is liar," I say. "A liar."

"I guess we all are," says Matthew. "But some things have happened in my life lately that made me think it's better to be honest with people. I'm starting with you."

"So you should be star?"

Matthew shakes his head. "Nah. I don't *want* to be a star. I'm no good onstage. I don't, like, dance around and hump the air. I'm overweight. I have red hair, and not much of that, either."

"But you sing songs and write them?"

"We used to do about the same amount of singing. But lately, for this English album, I did most of the singing. But Ricky sang a lot of it, too. We had to cut a lot of it. He doesn't know."

"But with not your voice, it does not sound like Ricky Biscayne?"

"Here." Matthew punches some more buttons. I see jagged lines move across a large computer screen, like lines of a hospital heart monitor. The song begins to play with just one lone voice singing. Ricky's voice. It sounds good, but nowhere near as great as it did when Matthew sang along. Actually, it sounds a little thin, anemic—the way I used to be—up high.

"He's not real good at harmonies and the upper-register stuff. And with this new crossover stuff, he doesn't do real well on the gospel kind of pentatonic riffs. So I help him out. I got schooled on gospel in the church." He grins. "My folks were missionaries."

I lift my eyebrows to acknowledge this last surprising statement. But I can't talk. There's too much heaviness in heart for that. We sit in silence. I feel loss, an emotion that has become familiar to me as breathing. Loss. It begins to make its slow new trek through my body, numbing me to what I have heard.

Matthew lifts his chin with confidence I've never seen from him before. He is, in fact, "heartthrob" material, if he wants to be. He just doesn't know how good-looking he is. Doesn't he realize that women find even ugliest of men beautiful if they are artists? And he is not ugly.

He says, "The weird thing is, though, the more the world believed it was all Ricky, the more *he* started to believe it, you know? To the point now that he acts like he doesn't really need me. And that's starting to piss me off. I have to be honest with you."

I get up. It's too much. I have tears, heat, pain. What else has Ricky been lying about? "I am sorry," I say. "I have to go see someone."

"Don't confront Ricky about this," warns Matthew. "Especially if he's high. It won't be pretty."

"I do not see Ricky." I push off sofa, big and exhausted. "I do not *care* about pretty. I hate pretty."

"If Ricky comes back, what should I tell him?" asks Matthew. "Nothing."

"He asked me to watch you, remember? Like I'm the guard of the fucking harem. Why do you let him treat you like that? It's insane."

Rage pushes through my skin like fine, new hairs. I feel like an animal pursued. "Tell him I escaped."

n tears, I steer Escalade SUV to Ricky's mother's house on Southwest Fourth Street in Fort Lauderdale. It's pouring rain. There's lightning. Thunder like someone scooting a heavy piece of furniture across an upstairs floor.

I pull into driveway of the small, yellow stucco house and park just behind Alma's Toyota Camry. As I look at the house, I feel a melancholy sort of respect rise in my throat. I want to yell. But I can't. I have such sadness, such large sadness. What is it, exactly? Something about suffering of women. Something about anonymity of pride. Something of the hormones brewing in my bloodstream as I create a brand-new life. And something of the shared universal sorrow of motherhood, into whose collective conscience I recently tapped. Children come from you, but they are not you. They are of you, but you do not control them. And sometimes, they outlive you in extreme. Sometimes you have to leave them alone in world to find their way.

I get out of car and hurry through rain to the front door. I feel the cool drops of rain on my scalp, cheeks, arms. I want to stay in rain, cleansed. I knock, then ring the bell. Several moments later, Alma opens door, wiping her hands on a worn but clean dishtowel. Even though she isn't expecting company, Alma is neatly put together in her red velour sweatsuit and gold earrings. Her bob seems freshly brushed, and her face still bears traces of makeup. I doubt she ever looks a mess.

"Jasminka!" she says, surprised. "What are you doing here? Are you okay? Get in out of the rain. You'll get sick out there." She pulls me into house, shuts the door, and takes my hands. Concern lines her face. "What's wrong?" she asks, looking into my eyes.

"I do not know," I say. Alma leads me to small, tidy living room and sits me on the sofa. Unlike Ricky's house, Alma's home is modern in design and decor. She doesn't have a lot of money, but what she does have she spends wisely, on pieces from Crate and Barrel and that kind of store. Ricky's house, for all the people who work on it all the time and all the money he spends hiring them, seems to be falling apart for sheer size. Alma's house feels like home, cozy and warm, inviting. I never want to leave.

"What did he do?" she asks. I tell her about faked recordings. Alma does not seem surprised. "And?" she says. "This is *news* to you?" Alma looks as if she pities me yet finds me humorous.

"You knew this?" I ask.

Alma laughs. "Of course I knew. He's my son. You think a mother doesn't know her own child's limitations? You think I don't hear those songs on the radio and realize they don't sound like the child who called for me in the middle of the night to get him water? A mother knows her son's voice."

I frown.

"What?" says Alma, standing. "You think that's cruel?"

"Yes."

"I'll be right back. I have something on the stove."

When, Alma comes back, she brings two glasses of ice water with neat wedges of lime in them. "Here," she says. "Drink. You need water. You look pale."

I take water and say, "Alma, I am not here because of songs."

"I'm listening."

"I come because of the girl in Homestead."

Alma nods and sips water. She knows exactly who I am talking about. "Sophia Gallagher. What about her?"

"Is she Ricky's daughter?"

Alma chuckles again, and again gives me look of mixed pity and amusement. "Of course."

"Of *course*?" I can't find air. I'm dizzy. Alma knew and didn't tell me?

Alma sighs. "Ricky loved Irene. All this nonsense he tells the papers now is as fake as his songs, *mija*."

I feel like someone is tightening belt around my rib cage. My forehead scrunches into knots. I try hard not to cry. Alma's eyes soften. She touches my hand with hers.

"I'm sorry," she says. "You're such a sweet, naïve girl."

"About this girl, you are sure?"

Alma nods, stands, and leaves room again. I break into sobs. When Alma comes back, she holds a large photo box. She sets the box on sofa, removes the porcelain knickknacks from coffee table, and puts box there. She lifts the lid, sets it carefully on dark wood floor.

Inside box—*the* box—are relics of Ricky's childhood, the sorts of things my parents once collected for me, things that were blown to pieces with my past. At the sight of them, memories of my lost childhood return to me.

Alma sifts through items, removing some to set them on the table. I watch. I'm surprised by her facial expressions. Sorrow, joy, all as she remembers her little boy. Alma holds up a sheet of lined paper with capital letters scrawled across it in thick pencil lines.

"He was a wonderful child," she says. "So sweet, so bright. Brighter than you could imagine. Did you know Ricky spoke his first sentence before he was one year old?"

I didn't.

"He did. No one believed me. But he was a brilliant child. He taught himself to read at age three. Quirky. Difficult. And brilliant."

Alma continues to dig through contents of the box, pausing on the plaster mold of child-Ricky's hand. She digs until she finds what she is looking for—a manila envelope, the kind you see in offices, with a string and a circle of cardboard for a fastener. Alma unwinds the string and dumps contents of envelope onto the sofa between us. It's a pile of letters in envelopes, some in Ricky's handwriting, others in an unfamiliar script that I recognize as very American and girlish.

"Love letters," says Alma. She opens one and reads it. The letter is from Irene Gallagher, to Ricky, gushing and enamored. It speaks of her love for him, and of how excited she is that he loves her, too. The letter is childish, sweet, and almost embarrassingly naked.

"This is from the woman in Homestead?" I reach for letter. Alma places it gently in my hand with a nod.

Alma removes another letter. "This one is from Ricky to her, but he was too lazy to send it."

The letter is beautifully written. I had no idea Ricky possessed that sort of talent. He speaks poetically of Irene's beauty and begs her to let him take her virginity. Alma's voice breaks with emotion as she reads it. She finishes reading, removes her glasses, and rubs her eyes and bridge of her nose.

"Actually, it wasn't laziness," Alma says. "I can tell you why Ricky never sent this. He's a perfectionist. He didn't think it was good enough."

I feel shock of new pain. "Yes," I say. "I know this about him."

"Ricky has always been this way, even as a very small child. He wasn't like the other kids, who'd fall and cry for their mothers to pick them up. If Ricky fell, he got angry at himself. It wasn't anything I did. I didn't raise him to be that way. He just was. It used to make me cry that he was so closed off from me, that he didn't want his mommy to help him feel better."

"He is this way now with me. He never thinks he is good enough."

"Well, with music he might not be," says Alma. "Ricky's real talent always lay with writing. He was a beautiful writer. But he thought writing was boring. He wanted to be on the stage, loved by women, women he could see."

Alma sifts through letters to a stack of photographs held together with a rubber band. She unwraps the band and looks at them. She hands them to me when she finishes. The photos show very young Ricky with his arm around a pretty, young blonde, both of them with tennis rackets over their shoulders.

"Part of it was my fault," says Alma.

"Your fault?"

"I didn't like her family," says Alma. "They were poor, and white. I didn't trust them. That girl was homeless when Ricky got her pregnant."

"Not her fault? She was with child then?" The weight of what Alma has just told me crushes me. Ricky abandoned homeless, pregnant girl?

"I know. But the parents were drug addicts and bikers. They were bad people. I didn't want him around that kind of people. I told him to avoid her," says Alma. I look hard at her face. Alma has small tears in her eyes. "He told me she had an abortion and that they'd broken up."

"My God, Alma."

"It was a hard time for Ricky. He stopped talking to me. He stopped writing. That was the worst part. He has a gift for it, Jasminka."

"Probably this was more hard for the girl, Alma."

She stiffens her lips and sets her jaw, hard. "Has Ricky told you about Alan?"

I shake my head.

"Around the time Irene got pregnant, we had a neighbor named

Alan who used to come over and help out with things around the house; and he was our friend. He was a writer. Ricky admired him. He told me he wanted to help fill in for Ricky's father, take Ricky fishing, do things like that, and I let him." Alma's lower lip begins to tremble. "And the son of a bitch molested Ricky on his boat."

"What?" I'm stunned.

"He doesn't like to talk about it. I don't know exactly what happened because Ricky never told me. He said the guy forced him to do oral sex on him, and the other way around. So I know that much. So all that was happening at once. It wasn't easy for either of them."

"God."

I look at pictures in my lap. The photos show happy teenage couple, silly at the mall, silly at the beach, and in a shiny prom dress and tuxedo.

"May I?" I ask, reaching for the letters.

Alma nods. "I feel terrible about it, Jasminka. I want to meet them, but I don't know how to reach out now, after all this time. After what I said about her."

I spend the next hour poring over letters sent to Ricky by Irene Gallagher. In the beginning, the letters are sweet and full of hope and excitement. The sixteen-year-old Irene writes that she looks forward to finally giving in to Ricky's requests to let him be the one to "deflower" her. They set a date for it, the prom. After the dance, the tone of the letters changes. Irene wonders if her father knows, because he has started to drink more and abuse her for being what he calls "a common whore." And then, a month later, big news. Irene writes that she has taken pregnancy test and it is positive. She wants Ricky to talk to her about it. The next letter pleads with Ricky to respond to her. She writes that she has been calling and he has been avoiding her. A few letters like this were written. Then there are the last ones. Irene writes she can't believe Ricky wants her to abort the baby, which she calls the "unexpected but nonetheless joyous product of our union." Apparently, Ricky never answered, because there are only two other letters after that. One saying she is going to have baby without him, and that she is giving him one last chance to change his mind and "act like a man about this." Then the final letter, saying he has lost his right to this child, because, and she swears this, she will never tell the child who father is, because a father who denies child doesn't deserve to know that child. "And when your son or daughter goes on to achieve great things in life, do not, I repeat do not, come knocking on our door asking for a handout. We won't know who you are. Mark my words."

I fold the final letter and place it softly on the top of pile.

"That's what happened," says Alma.

"Why he is so cruel to abandon the girl like this?"

Her eyes grow distant. "I don't know. But it might have to do with the fact that it's exactly what his father did to him."

'm at a lesbian bar, waiting for, just, you know, probably the *ugliest* lesbian of all time. Dad says he doesn't know me? I mean, I don't even know me. Waitin' for a butt-ugly gay girl, wearing what I think is a flattering open-backed Y-Yigal dress, in pink, only I keep thinking my butt cleavage is showing too much or something. And this music! What is up with the nineties revival? "Rhythm Is a Dancer"? Please. What's happened to my life? I thought my career was supposed to be getting better, but at this moment, I can honestly say I'd rather be a laxative publicist, in a pair of good old sweats.

I pull the chiffon scarf down over my hair and push the dark glasses up higher on my nose, feeling very Madonna-in-park. I don't want anyone to see me standing outside Lady Luck waiting for Lilia. Most of all, I hope Lilia won't recognize me and she'll mosey on. That would be cool, if she just came and left. I could go home.

No such luck.

Lilia comes charging across the street in a strapless black dress, clomping in chunky sandals, with the grace of a narrow-gauge steam engine. She looks like a barrel-chested bulldog in a tube top, and I half expect her tongue to loll out of her mouth.

"Milan!" She pulls me into a big powerful hug, her arms over mine to pin me down. She's ugly, and she's got a future in men's wrestling. "Glad you could make it."

Ick, ick. Get it off me.

We enter the club, and Lilia pays my cover. I don't want her to. She insists. "Take off the glasses and the scarf," barks Lilia. She sounds like a comedian making fun of Janet Reno. "Let's go dance."

"Lilia," I shout over the din of dance music. She grins and tries to impress me with a countrified two-step. She has a future in wrestling, and on *Hee Haw*, should they ever revive it. "I'm leaving."

"What? Why?"

"I shouldn't have come here. I mean, I meant to tell you when you got here that I don't want to come here. I'm not gay. I didn't realize this was what you had in mind."

Lilia smiles as if I were the cutest little thing in the world, which, you know, I am. But still. You don't want a countrified wrestler girl thinking that. "I get ya," she says. What is she chewing? Cud? "Still stuck in the old closet."

"No, it's not like that. I only came here because I appreciate the help you gave to me with Ricky, and . . ."

"Help? Journalists don't 'help.' We write the truth, and that's it. I'm offended you think I helped you. Don't say that again."

"Sorry. I want to leave now."

"Okay, okay."

Lilia walks out of the club with me. Just as we step out, Matthew Baker rides past on his bicycle, in plaid Bermuda shorts and a Hawaiian shirt, whistling an eerie melody. He sees me and does a double take.

"Milan?" He almost falls over and his bike wobbles to a stop. Why is this man always falling over around me? Lilia growls at the sight of a man coming near me, and tries to put a protective arm around me. I grab it and throw it toward the ground. Looks like I'm gonna have to break out with my mad wrestling skills, too.

"Hey," says Lilia.

"I'm not gay." Turning to Matthew, I say, "Hi there! I'm just here with Lilia from the *Herald*, doing a little work on the whole Homestead Ricky thing."

Matthew takes in the scene, including two lipstick lesbians who have started to make out near the front door. He grins the way most men would at such a sight.

"Wow, Milan. You are the most complicated person I've ever met," he says.

"No!" I cry. "I'm not. I'm really not. I promise."

"Okay, well, don't let me keep you," he tells me, preparing to take off again.

"No!" I wail. I lunge away from Lilia, who claws at me. "Please. Keep me." I look into Matthew's eyes. "Please." Under my breath I add, "I don't know how the hell I ended up here, and I don't want to be here. Take me away?"

Lilia comes over and stands territorially near me. "Hey, who is this creep? Is he bugging you?"

"This is Matthew, one of my coworkers." Matthew and Lilia nod an awkward hello. I scramble to think of something, and blurt, "And, uhm, my boyfriend."

Matthew's brows shoot up in surprise, and stay up in what I think is pleasure. "Yeah," he says, almost too quickly. "I'm her boyfriend." I laugh too quickly, and feel my tummy flutter as he grabs my hand. Matthew addresses me directly, with a smile in his bright, humor-filled, and, I think, pretty, little eyes. "I was wondering where you went. When you told me to come pick you up at Lady Luck, I had no idea it was this kind of place."

"Me neither," I say. He's cool for playing along. What a good guy.

"Hey, wait a minute," says Lilia. "I thought this was pleasure. Not work."

"I guess we misunderstood each other."

"Milan's straight," says Matthew. He looks at me. "Right?"

"Very," I say. I lean my head in what I hope looks like a playful gesture on Matthew's shoulder. Truthfully, I've fantasized about a threesome with another girl, or even some girl-on-girl action if I was really drunk, but the girl in my dreams never looked anything like Lilia; the girl in my fantasies looked more like Shakira. "So I guess I better get going."

"Her dad's real sick, and he asked me to get her home."

"On a bike?" asks Lilia.

"We better hurry," says Matthew. "Where's your car?"

I point to the lot across the street. "He always meets me and I give him a ride home. Bike goes in the trunk and all."

Lilia growls.

"Keep in touch," I say as Matthew and I walk his bike across the street. "It's been fun. Thanks again."

We load Matthew's bike into the back of my Mercedes, as Lilia continues to watch us suspiciously. "Get in," I whisper. "I'll explain it in a minute."

We get into the car, and I pull out. "She's still watching us," I say.

"Well, let's give her something to see," says Matthew as we stop at the corner stop sign. He leans over and kisses me on the lips. I feel my heart flip in my chest. I can't explain what makes this kiss different from, say, Ricky's. But it's different. Not unpleasant, anyway.

"Wow," he says. "You're a great kisser."

"No, I'm not," I say, embarrassed. I so do *not* want Matthew Baker to think he has a chance with me. I'm heartbroken, but my broken heart belongs to Ricky. Then again, what better way to get over a broken heart than to replace one man with another? Except, like, they probably shouldn't work together. That would be bad.

"Yes, you really are. You have great lips. Nice breath."

I blush, and drive Matthew home, under his direction, and park in front of the two-story apartment complex.

"Thanks for doing that," I say. "You saved me. I appreciate it. You didn't have to take it that far, but I really appreciate it."

"No problem," he says. "Would you like to come up?" Uh-oh.

"Have you heard that I'm the office slut or something?"

He looks offended. "No, nothing like that. I just thought you might want to watch a movie or something, hang out, like friends."

"Oh," I say. "I was just kidding about the slut thing."

"Good," he says. He looks like he knows something about me, though. He knows what I've done with Ricky. "I've got some DVDs from Netflix if you want to join me. *Ocean's Twelve, Meet the Fockers, Hitch.* I don't get a lot of company."

I think about it. Eh. I have nothing else to do. Why not?

I turn off the ignition.

Matthew's apartment is basic, a contemporary little box with white tile floors, plastic window shades, slider closets, a bean bag, an old futon sofa, but also cables and cords everywhere, attached to all sorts of keyboards, amplifiers, computers, and speakers. He has more speakers than a stereo shop. In fact, his apartment *looks* like a stereo shop.

"I'm a mad scientist," he says by way of explanation. "I'm making my own monster."

He helps me step over some cords by holding my hand. I catch one heel of my fabulous pink Via Spiga sandals on a cord and fall anyway. This is a hazard of wearing stupid heels. Fortunately, my skirt does not go over my head. Matthew apologizes and helps me up.

"I was gonna offer you a beer, but I see you've been drinking heavily," he jokes.

"A beer would be nice, actually," I say.

Matthew puts me on the sofa, then jumps over wires toward the kitchen. I watch his body move. He has a strange sort of grace to him. Not like Ricky's grace, which is obvious and sensual. But an understated sort of certainty about his place in the world, a spiritual grace. He is exactly where he wants to be. He's not bad-looking, actually. He comes back with two bottles of beer, opened. "Here you go." He grins. Cute. So cute. "Cheers," he says. Tilts his bottle toward mine.

"Cheers," I parrot. What now? What do I say now? "Uhm, nice

place you have here." Ugh. Not that! Anything but that! Stupid Milan. I hate myself sometimes.

Matthew laughs. "You're funny. A funny girl."

"Why funny?"

"Hmm. Well, this place is many things. But nice isn't one of them."

We look at each other, smile stupidly, then each of us looks away in embarrassment.

"This is weird," I say.

"Yeah," he says.

"We work together."

"Kind of."

"And Ricky," I say. Oops. Did I say that?

"What about Ricky?" he asks.

I think about this. Should I tell him? No. There is no godly reason why Matthew needs to know I've been with Ricky.

"Nothing," I say.

He takes a long drink, wipes his mouth on his arm, and says, "So, have you blown him yet?"

I choke on my beer, and spew like one of those people in a bad comedy skit. Beer everywhere, including on Matthew's face. He smiles anyway. I say nothing, just look away, humiliated.

"I know about it," he says as he wipes his face on his shirt.

"You do?"

"Ricky tells me everything. I'm like Ricky's own personal Ann Landers, only he never takes my advice."

"Oh, God," I say. I want to leave. Would that be rude? Wait a minute. Talk about rude! How *dare* he.

"How dare you," I say.

"Pardon?"

"That's a very personal thing."

"Sorry. You're right. Movie?" He grabs a copy of *Napoleon Dynamite* off the floor, from under the wires.

"Nice filing system," I say.

"Thanks. Works for me."

He gets up and puts the DVD in across the small room, and comes back. As the previews roll, he grabs the remote and mutes the volume. "So, Milan," he says. "Just curious. Why'd you do it?"

"Do what?"

"Ricky."

"Movie's starting," I say. I look at the television, but I feel Matthew's eyes on me. "What." I look back and he's grinning.

"Why'd you do it? What is it about him?"

"I fell in love with Ricky years ago."

"Yeah, but why?"

I shrug. "His music."

Matthew's face lights up a little. "Yeah?"

"Yeah. Movie's on."

He unmutes the television and scoots closer to me. "Massage?" he asks. He sets his beer on the floor.

"That's a weird thing to offer right now," I say.

"I'm generous. I give good hand. I might be a troll, but I give good hand. Fingers. You know." He cracks his knuckles and smiles at me.

"I never said you were a troll," I protest. I stare at the television even though I am actually carefully watching Matthew out of the corner of my eye. He's odd.

"I'll take that as, 'Yes, Matthew, I'd like a massage, thank you.'" He slides over to me, and turns my body so that we are still sitting side by side, but my back is to him. Then, he begins to rub. And he is right. He gives good hand. *Great* hand.

"Oh, God. That feels good," I say.

"Good," he says. "You have pretty shoulder bones."

"Shoulder bones?"

"These." He presses on the bones in the round part of my shoulders.

"That's a weird thing to notice."

"I notice things about women most men overlook."

"Oh."

"I forgot to ask you, have you seen this movie?"

"Yes," I say.

"Me too."

"Why'd you rent it?"

"I don't know. I hadn't seen it before I rented it. Then I saw it. But it's still here. Let's do something else." He jumps up, turns off the DVD player. "The whole movie thing was just my ploy to get you up here."

"Why?" I ask. "So you could grill me about our boss?"

"Kind of." He grins like a maniac. "Music?" He points at me, and opens his mouth to do a little shuffle-step. Why do people open their mouths when they wait for answers? To hear better?

"Uh, sure."

"What kind of music do you like? Please don't say Ricky Biscayne."

I shrug. "I actually love Ricky Biscayne."

"I was afraid you'd say that. You already told me that. How about something else. David Bisbal. Close?"

"Sure."

Matthew turns on the CD. He comes back to my side. "That's better. So," he resumes the massage, "which is your favorite Ricky song?"

"'Not Complicated,' the one about the plain girl," I say.

Matthew laughs and takes a break to guzzle his beer. "Yeah? What do you like about it?" His hands move lower on my back, to the space between my shoulder blades, and it feels like he's using his thumbs now, to knead the flesh between my blades and spine. *God.* It feels amazingly good. So good I just might orgasm from him touching my back. How pathetic is that? I *am* the office slut.

I say, "I like the words, and Ricky's voice when it goes up real high in that one part? You know the part? It sounds real gospel, almost churchy? Then it comes down all flamenco? You know what part I mean?"

"Uh, yeah, I think so," says Matthew. He snorts so loud it scares me. Is the snort supposed to be sarcasm? Why does he sound like that?

"You don't like that song?" I ask. No matter how much I like

Matthew, I can't really *ever* be a friend of his if he doesn't like that song. That song is about me. If he doesn't understand that song, he'll never stand a chance of understanding me.

"It's a fine song," says Matthew. "If you like that sort of thing." He laughs to himself. I feel him scoot up against me as his hands move lower, to my middle back. "Tell me more. What else do you like about it?"

"That feels really nice," I say. "But maybe you're a little too close, huh?"

He scoots back. "Sorry." Keeps massaging. I close my eyes. David Bisbal. He's fantastic, too. But he needs a haircut. His hair looks like corkscrew noodles. What's up with women in Spain that they actually *like* the wet Pauly Shore look?

"What *else* do you like about that Ricky song?" asks Matthew. I feel his breath on my neck and it sets off a train of goose bumps down my back, around my middle, up my front. I shudder with the surprising chill of it. Office slut, I think. I am the office slut. I blame my upbringing. I'm not supposed to be sexual. So I'm getting revenge on someone. I don't know who. I can't think about that right now because of the goose bumps, the breath. Jesus.

"I don't know," I say. Why is he asking me so many questions about that song? And Ricky? It's weird. "I just like it."

"Did you, like, pretend he was singing it to you?" Matthew whispers this part. He is seriously freaking me out.

"You are seriously freaking me out," I say. I hear a wet sound, like he's opened his mouth but doesn't speak. He says nothing. Freaky. Why is he so into this song? I mean, I know he's the producer. But he shouldn't, like, get turned on about it, no? Freaky-deaky dude. "Why do you . . ."

"Shh," he says. "No more questions."

I worry for a moment that maybe, you know, maybe Matthew has his *own* thing for Ricky. An unhealthy kind of thing.

"Do you have a thing for Ricky?" I blurt. He laughs very loud, in my ear. I slap a hand over my ear and scream in pain. "Ow!" I say. I hate that. Why don't people remember that ears are very sensitive up close like that? "God."

"Oh, Milan, I'm sorry," he says. He's still laughing. "I didn't mean to. Oh boy. You okay?" He puts his hand on top of mine, on top of my ear.

"I'll live." I shoo him away, and he starts massaging me again. "So, did you pretend Ricky was singing to you?"

"Kind of."

"Good." Matthew's hands move to my lower back, and then slowly, ever so slowly, they move around my sides, to my belly.

"Uh, Matthew?"

"Yes?"

"What are you doing?"

"Holding you."

"Why?" Matthew is pressed up against my back. I feel his lips on my neck. I want to protest, but I'm horny from thinking about Ricky and his music, and, who knows. Maybe this is just what Ricky needs to get a little jealous and make me his once and for all.

"Because you pretend Ricky sings that song to you," he says.

Eew? I would push him away, but I am paralyzed by freakness. *His* freakness. I wish I didn't like freakness, but I do. I'm a freaky girl, I suppose. But this is a bit *too* freaky. He likes that I love Ricky? People are so complicated it's not even worth trying to figure them out. I suppose it's better than, say, liking monkeys. Something like that. At least Matthew is still in the human species with his weird fantasies. He bites my earlobe, an earlobe that apparently has a direct connection to my clitoral region, my Kegels of steel. Boing! Maybe I should have skipped the beer. Right. "Can you keep a secret, Milan?"

"Yes," I say. I feel shivers everywhere. He releases me, and then, there he is, in front of me. He grabs my hands and looks me in the eye. He looks a little crazy and I have to confess I kind of like it. "I have to tell you something very important, Milan, before this goes any further."

"Who said I was going to let it go any further?" I say. Might as well pretend. After I say it I realize my hand is on my breast, fondling it a little. Oops. I'm so used to being alone I sometimes forget I'm not.

"Well . . ." He grins, noting my hand. "You *are* the office slut."

"Hey!"

He looks at me with a perfect mixture of humor, hornball, and kindness. His face is flushed. "I'm just quoting *you*. To *me*, you're the office babe. And the office intellect. The office Rick-o-phile." I'd reply, but I am still paralyzed by freakness. His face darkens and he frowns. "Now, let's get serious for a second."

Uh-oh. Matthew leans in and kisses me, gently at first, just the tiniest brushing of lips, and then harder. He has amazing lips and he's as good a kisser as Ricky. Better, actually, except that Ricky is *Ricky* and so Ricky's mediocre kisses are better than any mere mortal's fabulous ones. I don't know why I'm letting him do this to me, except that it feels really right, in a freaky metaphysical sense. That might just be beer talking. I hate when beer talks. Beer is so inarticulate. People talk about how white guys have no lips, but Matthew has beautiful, full lips.

"There," he says when we come up for air. "Okay. Milan. That song you like of Ricky's?"

"God, Matthew," I say. "Forget about it. Let it go." *Do* me, I want to say. *Please stop talking. I have a girlie hard-on.* Why is he bringing it up now? He is a freak, that's why. He needs to think of it to get going. Whatever. I'll let him talk, as long as he eventually eats me alive. That's all. Is that too much to ask?

"I wrote it," he says. He smiles, a little triumphant, like I'm going to like him better now or something.

I stare at him. "That's not funny," I say. "Please don't play games right now, Matthew."

"No. I did. I wrote it. Start to finish. Everything. It's my song."

"Whatever you say, Matthew." I have memorized the CD jacket, and it clearly states that Ricky wrote the song. This guy is freakier than I'd thought. He's a foreplay plagiarist.

"And that's not all." He looks at me as if he is revealing something of tremendous importance. I listen. I don't want to listen. I want to kiss again.

"I sang it, too, Milan."

"Backgrounds, I know. I saw the CD liner notes." Actually, it's tacked to my wall, but he doesn't have to know that.

"No. I sang *everything*. The whole song. The leads. All of it."

"What?"

"Ricky was too high."

"High? Please. No way. High on what? Ricky doesn't do drugs."

"Yes *way*. Ricky was too high that day. So I did it."

Puh-lease! How desperate is this guy? I push away from him and search for my purse. I see what's happening here. And while I'm all for being the office slut, I'm not about to be the office slut for the office *psycho*.

"What are you doing?" Matthew cries. "Where are you going?" He reaches for my arm.

I hiss, "Don't. Touch. Me."

"What? Why? What's wrong?"

"You are so sad," I tell him.

"Me? Sad? Why?"

Hmm. Where to begin? Bad apartment. Liar. I open the front door. "I would have done it with you without the lying," I say.

"Lying?"

"Lying. That's the only thing in the world I hate, Matthew. I'm easygoing, I like men, but I don't suffer liars. How stupid are you to try to take credit for something Ricky did?" Suffer liars? Did I just say something that stupid? "I would have slept with you if you were just, like, the office freak. But I'm not about to be the office slut for the office *liar*."

"You have me confused with Ricky," he says with a smirk. That damn smirk.

"Uh, no," I say. "*You* have *yourself* confused with Ricky."

"I wasn't lying, Milan," he says. He's still talking, but I don't know what he's saying because I've closed the door in his face and I'm racing back to my car. I hope I'm not too drunk to drive. I should call a cab, or Geneva. But I'll be okay.

That was close, I think, taking one last look at the little apartment door. Loser. Matthew Baker is a loser after all. And I almost just had sex with him. Is my self-esteem that low? That I'd have sex with a loser from the office?

Dad's right. I'm *not* me anymore.

monday, july 22

Ricky, high on coke and seated cross-legged on the floor of the control booth with Matthew, listens to the song and thinks of the Seven Dwarfs dancing a jig. Hilarious. He's not sure why he thinks of this, but it makes him laugh. He can't remember all the dwarfs' names, though, and this pisses him off.

"Was Gimpy a dwarf, *cabrón?*" asks Ricky. He scratches himself through his nylon athletic shorts.

Matthew, wearing cargo shorts and a Boston Red Sox T-shirt, ignores him and adjusts the levels. They both hear the front door to the office open, and both turn to see Milan enter in form-fitting black crop pants and a banana-yellow lacy shirt that plays up her tiny waist.

"Yeah, boy, that's what I'm talkin' 'bout," says Ricky. He's been horny as hell since Jill called a few minutes ago and told him she wants him to do her up the *culo.* Her words, not his. *Por detrás.* She knows how to press his buttons, that woman. She's vulgar, and insatiable.

Matthew looks at Milan, waves. She doesn't wave back, just gives him a steamed, hateful stare.

"Oh no," says Matthew under his breath. "I was afraid of that." Ricky looks at him, then at her, then back at him.

"Afraid of what?"

"Nothing," says Matthew, but Ricky knows him well enough to know that face.

"You slept with her," says Ricky as a corner of his mouth rises.

"Nah, man," says Matthew.

"She's *mine*. You know that," says Ricky. "But you can do her if you want." He holds his fist up for dap, but Matthew disses him, and doesn't respond.

"Whatever, dude."

"Every chick in this building is mine. Those are the rules."

Matthew pretends Ricky has not spoken. Who cares.

Ricky smiles. He likes a challenge. Competition. It's healthy to compete. "Be right back," he tells Matthew, and he quietly follows Milan down the hall to her office, watching her very round bottom pendulum back and forth as she walks. Damn Jill for mentioning the whole *"rómpeme por detrás"* ass-fucking thing. Ricky is not normally the kind of guy who wants to screw women in that particular hole, but Jill has changed him. He likes asses now, and Milan's is good. Real good. Pretty little thing. She enters the office without seeing him, and turns around to find him nearly on top of her in the doorway. She jumps, startled.

"Sorry," he says with a big grin. Without missing a beat, he reaches behind him and eases her office door shut. Locks it with a little click, grins. "Have you missed me, baby?" She looks pained as he does this, conflicted, but thrilled. He likes the way he seems to thrill her. "So," he says. "How was he?"

"Who?" she asks. Even through her confusion and pain, she wants him. Look at the way she's leaning against her desk and trying to arrange all of her parts to be in just the right place for him. She's self-conscious and she loves him. It's so great when chicks love you like this, he thinks. They'll do anything. And he's ready to graduate to something bigger with Milan. Something that will prove how much she is willing to suffer to please him, something about the size of her pretty little bottom.

"Matthew," says Ricky.

Milan's mouth drops open. A sweet little mouth. She's very good at the sucking thing. Very. He moves closer. "Yeah," he says, stroking her cheek and kissing her lightly. "Matthew. Was it good?"

"What did he tell you about me?" she asks.

Ricky pushes against her and feels her arms wrap around him. She can't help it, he thinks. "He told me he nailed you last night."

"I swear that's not true," says Milan, a look of panic in her eyes. "I went to his house and we watched part of a movie and had a beer and he gave me a massage and that was *it*."

"How do I know you're telling me the truth?" he asks. She looks guilty and afraid. "You know I want you for myself."

"Isn't that a little hypocritical?" she asks.

"I'm working on the marriage. I'll get out of it, and it will just be us, me and you. My heart is completely yours." As he says it, he has the same feeling of déjà vu an actor has doing the same play night after night.

"Ricky, I swear there's nothing with Matthew. He tried to tell me he wrote and sang 'Not Complicated,' like that was gonna help him score or something, and then . . ."

"He what?" The playfulness escapes Ricky now, and he feels his adrenaline pumping. That little fucking weasel Matthew. *Fuck* him.

"He was trying to get me to have sex with him," says Milan.

"What bullshit. You didn't believe him, did you?"

"No," says Milan. "I think he said it because he's insecure and he wanted me to like him the way I like you. *Love* you."

Ricky does his best to look artistic and tortured. "I wrote that song from the bottom of my heart. Matthew knows that. How can I trust him anymore?" Milan's eyes grow soft and she looks like she wants to rescue him. He loves when woman get that look because it means you can do anything—*anything*—to them. Even conquer them in that littlest of holes, the one that makes them cry out with pain.

"That hurts," says Ricky. "You work really hard at something and your producer tries to take credit for it, just to get with a beautiful woman?"

She smiles, shy. "You think I'm beautiful?"

"Of course, baby." He kisses her neck and rubs against her. She smells like the ocean. "God, you smell good. *Te quiero mamar la chocha.*"

"Ricky," she groans. He hears her voice choked with emotion. "I don't know what to do."

He looks at her. "About what, baby?"

"Us. It's not right. I feel bad about all this. It's not good for me, all this."

Ricky kisses her on the mouth, and tells her the usual song and dance between kisses. She melts into him, pushes against him, grinds her hips toward him. She groans and says she wants him, that she's finally ready to give it all to him, and says she's even accepted that she might have to share him with his wife for now, until the baby's born.

"Are you wearing underwear?" he asks her.

"Yes," she says. "Why do you ask?"

"I'll show you." Ricky turns her around and bends her over the desk. That's it. She just goes where he puts her, like a rag doll. He likes that. He likes that she does what he wants. He pulls down her pants, and there it is, her spectacular, creamy white bottom, round as an apple, with a lacy black thong stuck up the middle.

"Pretty underwear," he says as he loops a finger beneath the fabric and eases it out of the way. "Nice," he says.

"Ricky, I don't think this is right," she says. But her hips start to move anyway.

Ricky unzips his jeans and pulls them down to midthigh. "You know I care about you, Milan," he says. "*Vamos a echar un casquete.*" He positions himself, and eases right in. She's flexing, he can feel it. Powerful girl. He begins to pump and she begins to moan. Yeah, baby. He likes the look of her reddening face as it slides back and forth across the papers on the desktop.

"I don't know," she says, pulling away from him and turning around. "We shouldn't do this anymore."

"Do you love me?" he asks.

"I love you, Ricky. That's not it."

"I have strong feelings for you, too," he says. "You don't love what we were doing?"

"I do, but I have to respect myself."

It's so hard to keep these chicks sane sometimes. "I respect you, baby," he says. "Just be with me. *Chiiiinga.*"

"But I don't want to share you anymore," she says. They all say it, sooner or later.

"I know, baby, I know," he says. "Just wait a little longer. That's all I ask."

"Whatever you want, Ricky," she says. With a conflicted look on her face, she allows him to put her back where she was, and he resumes. She says, "I love you." He does not answer.

Why must they always love him? It would be so much *foquin* easier if they didn't.

So, yeah. Pretty much, yeah. I am *officially* the office slut. I can't even believe what I just did. My black pants feel wet and moldy with guilt, and I wonder if everyone can smell Ricky on my yellow lace top. I should know better than to get myself into a situation like this. God, how stupid *am* I? How in *love* with this man? Here's how much I love Ricky. I'm watching his wife for him. That's right. Watching her, like a guard. He asked me to keep an eye on her because he thinks she's cheating. Don't ask. The irony of it all, eh? I'm a loser. I feel like a loser, but a hopeful loser because part of me believes everything he tells me, and it's his music, I swear it is. When he sings, "She walks alone among many, twisting in her own defeat, they don't appreciate her, never understanding that I see the truth of what she can be, beautiful, the woman that hides behind the sad eyes, walking alone among the many, simple love is all she needs, respect and justice, why can't she just, let me fall into her grace and there forever fly high, high . . ." That's what makes me do these things. Ricky's music is in my soul. He asked me to wait, and I will, even though it erodes me every single second.

I watch as Jasminka, in a colorful rainbow of a sundress and flat brown sandals, wanders from one fruit stall to another, touching the bright mangoes and papayas as if they are jewels. She's been bugging Ricky all day about shakes. Shakes, shakes, shakes. That's all she can think about, he tells me. He asked if I knew anywhere that she could go for a great coconut shake, just what she says her baby is wanting. Of course I know just the place, on Calle Ocho. And here we are. It's a real Cuban-style market, with every kind of shake you could imagine, and a collection of old Cuban guys playing dominoes outside.

"The colors they are *so* bright," says Jasminka to the fruit, with her strange, awkward English. I want to hate her, but I can't. She's sort of an innocent. She holds a huge Mexican papaya to her nose and sniffs it. Men stare at the tall, astonishingly symmetrical and obviously pregnant woman in the sunglasses, her shiny tresses tumbling over her shoulders. I watch as they try to place where they might have seen her before. In a city full of beautiful women, Jasminka is a beauty of a different sort. Most of Miami's beauties have dark eyes and obvious Latin American or Spanish heritage. Jasminka's is altogether a different kind of face.

We go to the counter and order shakes from the bored-looking women who work here. They don't make eye contact. I try to ignore the flies. It's an outdoor market, the flies can't be helped. The shakes are good, flies and all.

We take our drinks in their white Styrofoam cups and sit on picnic benches next to the parking lot. My feet hurt from the fancy shoes. I'm sick of fancy shoes. It's hot. The coolness of the drink feels good on my throat. Jasminka takes off her sunglasses and smiles at me. "Tell me," she said. "Why you are so much glowing, Miss Milan?"

"Me?" Uh-oh.

"You."

"Shimmer?" I put a hand to my cheek and smile with a demure shrug. "You know, the stuff you put on your skin?" Probably not the best time to tell her I just made love to her husband.

"No, is something else. You look like a woman in love."

"Me?" Oh no. Scramble. Think of something. Quick. Don't lie. Lying is obvious. "I am," I say. "I'm in love. Or infatuation."

Scramble, think. Who? Who can I say who won't seem weird? I'm so on the spot here. Matthew? Jasminka claps her hands together. "Tell me about him." She's so sweet.

"I can't," I say. Matthew? Nah. I don't know. Can I make up some dude right now? Jasminka smiles sweetly. She is so nice. Nice. That's the word. I say, "Oh, okay. It's Matthew."

Jasminka's eyes light up. "Really?"

"Yeah. But I don't know if he likes me." Oh, please!

"Aww," she says, turning her head to the side like she's looking at a puppy. "I am sure he likes you." Then, as quickly as she was cute and sweet, her face turns worried. Uh-oh. Did she just figure me out? What do I do? I'm a horrible person. I really am a horrible office slut.

She says, "Milan, I have to ask you to do me a favor."

Please don't ask me if I screwed your man. I blink as innocently as I can and say, "Sure, what is it?"

Jasminka removes a binder from her Louis Vuitton bag and hands it to me. I open it and find a photocopy of what appears to be a hand-written letter. Beneath it are dozens of others.

"What is this?" I ask.

"Read this. Start there, go through all. I am going to get a cookie. Do you want anything?"

"No, thanks," I say. I start to read the first paper on the stack. It's a beautiful letter written by a lovelorn teenage boy named Ricardo Batista. Ricky? Ricky wrote this? More than ten years ago? Why is Jasminka showing me this?

I read the rest.

An hour later, I look up from the notebook of love letters between a young Ricky Biscayne and a young Irene Gallagher with tears in my eyes, and find Jasminka sipping her way through her third shake.

"Do you realize I just worked harder than I have in my life, all to try to ruin that woman's life?" I ask, noting as I say it that there is some bit of literal meaning here.

Jasminka nods. "I know this. We all do this to her. This is why I ask you to bring me here. This is the favor. I need you to show this to the press. We need to save this woman from being stuffed through the mud."

"Dragged through the mud?"

She blushes. She is so pretty and sweet. I can't imagine what Ricky sees in me when he can have this angel. Speaking of Ricky, I'm getting a very sick feeling about him. Very. "Yes. Dragged. But Ricky cannot know I show this to you. You cannot tell him."

"Why are you doing it, then?" I ask.

"It is right thing to do. And . . ." She pauses with a worried face. "And he cheats on me. I know this. I feel it."

"You think?" I ask.

"I know who it is," she says. "I have friend of mine follow him."

Oh no.

She smiles sadly. "Jill Sanchez, can you believe this?"

What? "Really?" I ask, and gulp. "Jill Sanchez?"

Jasminka nods. "He never gets over this woman. Is okay. I am okay with this. After the baby, I will leave him." She looks at me. "I need you to help me on this."

"But I'll lose my job," I say, thinking to myself that I would like to lose my job very much right about now. Jill *Sanchez?*

"You have a job before this?"

"I was a laxative publicist before," I say. Jill Sanchez? *Jill Sanchez?*

"You can do that again, no?" I suspect from her blank expression that Jasminka doesn't know what a laxative publicist is.

I shrug. "I could go back to it," I say. Jill Sanchez? I am dizzy with betrayal. Ricky is cheating on us? Us. I know, it's ridiculous. I shouldn't be surprised. But he said so many beautiful things to me. Jill Sanchez? Talk about competition. What a fool I am.

Jasminka reaches out to touch my hand. "You find other job," she says. She must think my sad face is job related, rather than Ricky related. I look at her arm and see raw red scratches all over it.

"What is all that?" I ask.

Jasminka pulls her arm back quickly. "It is something I do," she says. When Jasminka folds her arms her shawl falls away for a brief moment, and I note a darker mark, a bruise, on her upper arm.

"What is that?"

She covers herself again, and tries to smile. "Is from Ricky. He squeeze me really hard. This is what he did there."

"Why?"

"He says I am too fat." I am more shocked by this than I was by Ricky cheating with Jill Sanchez.

"You're not fat!"

"I know this. He likes me skinny."

Jesus. If Ricky thinks Jasminka's fat, he must think I'm *obese*. I don't know what to say. But in one sobering moment, it hits me that Jasminka's life is not what it seems. Ricky's life is not what it seems. Irene Gallagher's life is not what it seems. What about me? Is my life what it seems? I have the new car, the nice clothes, the high-powered job, the famous boyfriend; but what am I actually doing? Making Ricky look good? At what cost?

"I'll help you," I say, suddenly resenting Ricky in a way I would never have thought possible. Not because of Jasminka. Not really even because of Irene Gallagher. It's because of Jill Sanchez, and because Ricky thinks Jasminka is fat. "Even if I have to go back to my old job."

Violeta, finished with the script for her show the next day, on the topic of genital warts, cervical cancer, and the new HPV vaccine, sits in the peace of her nighttime study and sips her Red Zinger iced tea. She wears a black Donna Karan sleep ensemble, made to look like yoga pants and a tank top, and a thick layer of Orlane

Vitamin C wrinkle cream on her face and neck. Eliseo is sleeping. She plans to wake him gently, later, and make love to him. She ordered nipple clips from an online sex-toy shop, and they arrived today. She wants to see how he'll respond to them. She knows her lover in Fort Lauderdale likes kinky things, but she wants to try it on Eliseo. Her husband isn't interested in sex anymore. It has been too long since they were last intimate. More than a month. His lack of sex drive makes it easier for her to justify her lovers. Besides, in her opinion, the lovers had improved her sex life and feelings for Eliseo. It is too complicated for her simple, domineering husband to understand, so she will keep it secret, forever. They both get so into their lives and routines that they end up exhausted. But a woman has to continue to make an effort to keep those fires burning with her husband, even at this age, with so many years together. No, *especially* at this age, and with so many years together.

Violeta likes to think that she is psychic. It is among her many talents. It helps her, this sixth sense, in relating to the guests on her radio show. All evening she's had a mother's sense that something is wrong with one of her children. Or both. She trains her ears on the sounds in the rest of the house. Refrigerator hum, birds fluttering on their perches. In her parents' bedroom, El General and Maria Katarina snore in concert with each other as they have done for decades, like two rusty gears of a cranky old engine. And in Milan's room—what is that? Laughing? No. Crying?

Violeta sits forward and cocks her head, listening. Why on earth is her daughter crying in the middle of the night? She's worried about Milan. She gets up, walks down the hall to investigate. She stands outside Milan's room, listening.

Violeta opens the door without knocking. It has been years since she's taken that liberty with her child, but this is an unusual situation. Plus, since her daughter shows no desire to move out or go on a simple date, she wonders if there isn't something seriously wrong, worries that one day she'll find a suicide note filled with dark secrets about her daughter she could only imagine.

She finds Milan in her bunny slippers and long prairie-girl cotton nightgown, her hair in double ponytails, sitting on her bed surrounded by Ricky Biscayne paraphernalia. Posters, trading cards, T-shirts, all the garbage she has been collecting about the singer over the years, all of it heaped together like a landfill.

"Mom!" Milan cries upon seeing Violeta scowling at the scene. She scrambles to hide the Ricky Biscayne mess, but without success. "Haven't you ever heard of knocking?"

"What's wrong, *hija*?" asks Violeta. She sweeps toward the bed, arms outstretched to hug her daughter. "Why are you crying in here all alone? Why are you staring at all those pictures of Ricky Biscayne?"

Milan says nothing, but Violeta knows the answer. She was afraid this would happen. She even thought of warning her daughter about falling in love with her employer, but she stepped back and trusted Milan to be sensible enough to do the right thing. Ricky Biscayne is married, and famous; he is not likely to fall for someone like Milan. As much as Violeta loves her daughter, she knows this is true.

"I knew this would happen," says Violeta before her daughter has time to answer. "You should never have taken that job. It was a disaster waiting to happen. Only a balanced woman could take a job like that, not some boy-crazy woman who acts like a little girl."

"Mom! How can you say that?"

"Are you having sex with him? Milan? Ricky Biscayne?"

"No!"

Violeta goes to sit next to Milan on the bed, leaving the door to her room open. She knows when her daughter is lying. Now is one of those times. "Mom, close the door!"

"Why? What do you have to hide? Anything we talk about here can be heard by the other people in the house, is that it?"

"Mom!"

"What, you don't want Daddy and Grandma to know you're in love with Ricky Biscayne? That you're sleeping with a pregnant woman's *husband*?"

"What?"

"Look at you. I can't believe you're doing this to yourself. It's very sad."

"In love with Ricky Biscayne?" Milan's face twists with disgust. "Mom, what are you talking about?"

"Boo hoo hoo, crying over a *married* man. Haven't you listened to anything I've taught you?" Violeta knocks on her daughter's forehead as if it were an impenetrable door. "Hello? Do you ever listen to the people who call in to your mom's show?"

"Mom, you don't understand—"

"You should know better than that. You should—"

"Mom, hold on."

"You should take your job seriously, Milan. Keep your personal feelings out of it. Did he make you do it? Is that it? Say he'd fire you unless you had sex with him? Is that what this is all about?"

"Let me *talk*. Jesus."

Violeta looks at her daughter as if she is bored and has already heard whatever Milan is about to say. "So talk. Go ahead."

"I am *not* in love with Ricky Biscayne, Mom." Softly, she adds, "Anymore."

Violeta looks at Milan as if her daughter has just told her that Cuba is better off since Castro. "Please," she says. "Don't lie to me. I know you better than you know yourself. You've loved that man for years. Look at all of this."

"No, Mom. That's just it. I *thought* I did. I was in love with a man who doesn't exist. That's why I'm crying. I feel like Ricky Biscayne died, and part of me died, too."

Violeta finds this last bit trite and immature, but looks at her daughter with new interest. This isn't what she had expected. "Died? Died how?"

Milan sniffles and yanks a pink tissue from the box on her night-stand. "He's not like I thought."

"What do you mean? He was a bad lover?"

"Mom! I'm not some guest on your show. Now *stop* it! I am entitled to some modicum of privacy in my life."

"Fine. But don't use those book words with me."

"Now, let me tell you why I'm crying. Okay?"

Violeta listens in disbelief as Milan tells her about the letters and Ricky's wife, who he doesn't let leave the house without a chaperone. That the wife thinks he's sleeping with Jill Sanchez, a vulgar woman who Violeta detests. She listens as Milan weeps over having placed stories in the press that discredited Irene Gallagher, at her shame for having done so. She says she believes she has ruined a woman's life, and not just a woman but a woman and her daughter.

"I feel like the worst sinner in the world," says Milan, her eyes straying from her mother's face to the statue of La Caridad on the dresser. "I read that Irene Gallagher might lose her job."

"So? How is that your fault?"

"Mom, it's terrible. Her coworkers ran her off the road and threatened her child. That's what the stories in the paper say, and they always make reference to that stupid Lilia story saying Irene Gallagher is unhinged, which was the exact word I used in the interview, 'unhinged.' I thought about it for a long time before the interview, and created this whole story to make Ricky look good, and now it's out of control and this woman's life is ruined, Mom, because of me."

"You were just doing your job at the time, no?"

"It doesn't make it any better. Not when I really think about the fact that there are these people and they have this shit to deal with now."

Violeta smiles at her daughter's curse word. That's more like it, she thinks. She likes to see Milan thinking for herself, asserting herself, having strong opinions and strong words. Come to think of it, she likes to see Milan in trendy yoga pants and mascara, too. Her daughter is pretty. She has always thought so.

"Well, then you know what you have to do," says Violeta.

Milan nods. "I think so."

"Two things." Violeta holds up two fingers. "One, you tell the truth and apologize to that mother and her poor daughter."

"But my job."

Violeta gives her daughter a silencing stare for having interrupted her. "And two, we go to the chapel of La Caridad and pray Tío Jesús will forgive you for leaving the company."

wednesday, july 24

C lub G is officially here.

I'm standing with the designer, Sara, in the middle of the completed space, and I can hardly breathe. It's gorgeous, sparkling with glitter like the promised land. Everything I wanted. The pointy tents with the shimmering pomegranate fabrics and golden flags, the red silk draped along the walls in great, vulvic O'Keeffian folds. Perfect.

"You're a magician," I tell Sara. She smiles and we watch the photographer from *Architectural Digest* snap pictures for a big spread the magazine has planned for October, on the hippest new club in town. What a coup!

"It's perfect," I say. I hug Sara and she hugs me back.

"Geneva?" Sara places her hands on my arms and smiles. "I have a suggestion I wanted to run by you."

"Sure."

"It's not from me, actually. But my best friend, Elizabeth. She's a producer on my show?"

"Uh-huh."

"Well, she's a lesbian. And she's always complaining about how, you know, even though Miami has this reputation for being a great party place for the gay community, there's really not a lot for lesbians here. It's mostly for boys, you know?"

That's so true. I'm embarrassed I never thought of it. There's a big gap in the entertainment offerings for homosexual men and women in town. Like the women are an afterthought. I look at Sara and wonder if she is a lesbian. Seems unlikely, but you never know around here. Some of the most beautiful women in Miami are lesbians.

"So, I was telling her about this project, and she suggested that you could make a night for lesbians only, and it could be the most amazing thing in town. Because right now all the women really have is Sax on the Beach, and it's kind of corny, the name and all. This could be amazing, the whole G part, which I know is your name, but it could have G-spot connotations, so I don't know if you like that idea, but it would make a lot of money."

"Wow," I say. "You're a hundred percent right."

Sara shrugs. "Just a thought."

"No, I like it. I really like it. I'll do it."

"There's something else," says Sara. "I have to ask you to call Jill Sanchez and have her stop coming in here and bothering me."

Jill Sanchez? "What's she doing?"

"She wants to change everything to her tastes," says Sara, with a roll of the eyes. "And I'm not particularly fond of that woman's tastes."

"She's coming *here*?"

"Every day."

"What? That's not in the investor contract. She's not supposed to do that."

"Well, she does. She calls it 'her club.' She wants it her way. She's making me insane."

"Okay, I'll call her." I probably won't do it until after the opening. But I don't mention this. I really do need the moody, controlling actress to be part of the celebrations and press. I can't afford to alienate her.

My phone rings. I fish it out of my handbag. Milan's number. "Hey. What's up?"

"Geneva, I have to talk to you," she says. She sounds serious, urgent. "It's about Ricky. Can you meet me and Jasminka later?"

"Jasminka?"

"Ricky's wife?"

"Why her?"

Milan pauses and I can hear her taking a deep breath. "I kind of told her she could move in with me and Mom and Dad."

"What? Why?" This is the oddest thing I've heard in a while.

"She can't stay with Ricky anymore. It's too dangerous."

"Dangerous?"

"Look, I'll tell you the whole thing later. Do you know where Vizcaya Gardens are? The museum? In Coconut Grove?"

"Of course," I say. Who doesn't? "I've been there with *you*, Milan."

"You have? Sorry. Okay. I'm a little spacey right now. Meet us there in an hour. We'll get dinner later."

"Why there?"

"Not Ricky's kind of place. If he finds out about this, he'll kill us. All of us."

"You're so melodramatic."

"Just come? Please?"

"Okay," I say. She's lucky I'm not busy.

Sophia and David walk past the park, on their way to the convenience store to get some chips for her grandma, doing their best to look like they don't care because a group of popular kids from their school is there. But they do care. And they know what's coming.

"Just ignore them, sweetie," says David. "Keep walking."

Every time Sophia sees them it gets worse. The group of popular kids sits and stands around the picnic table they have claimed with their markers and their bodies, and she feels their eyes on her.

"Hey, Sophia," one calls. "Talk to your 'dad' lately?"

Sophia tries to ignore them as they laugh, but the jabs keep coming.

"What are you looking at, faggot?" one of them says to David.

"Sorry to hear about your mom's job," says another kid, to Sophia.

"Yeah," says another. "Maybe you can sue the park here."

"Or me. You haven't sued me yet."

The kids laugh wickedly. Sophia stiffens her back and lifts her chin as David puts a protective arm around her, and they duck inside the market.

"What a bunch of hillbillies," says David. "And, trust me, girlfriend, I know from hillbillies."

But as Sophia walks the length of the aisle toward the chips, the sorrow of her life becomes too great to bear. She doesn't want to be here. She needs to get out.

"Let's go," she says to David.

"What about Granny Alice's Pringles?"

"Granny Alice is getting fat. She doesn't need them."

Sophia turns and runs back outside, bumping into some of her tormenters on the way. They laugh at the pain on her face, at her running, but she doesn't care. She doesn't care about anything anymore. David chases after her, catching her a block later.

"Hey," he says. "What the hell's wrong with you, sunshine?"

"I don't want to be here anymore," she says.

"Where?"

"Here. Homestead. I hate it here."

"You and me both, girlfriend."

"Let's go somewhere else," she says.

"Where?"

"I don't know."

"Let's go throw eggs at your dad's house," suggests David.

"Fine with me," says Sophia.

Sophia and David once again take the bus north. Sophia wants never to go back home, and tells David. The only thing she'll find at home is her mom and grandmother sifting through "evidence" and plotting the legal battle that Sophia thinks they are bound to lose. Her mom has been placed "on leave" and never works.

Sophia pays her fare and takes a seat next to a used newspaper. She picks the paper up and sees yet another story on Ricky Biscayne: RICKY GETS TRICKY?

"Don't read that," says David as he tries to swipe it from her. "It's not good for you." She pulls it away.

"Let me," she says. And he does.

Her mother has stopped getting the paper, and Sophia has stopped reading it. All the papers talk about is how great Ricky is and how she and her mom are these scummy people that they aren't.

The story this time is about some new nightclub Ricky is opening with Jill Sanchez and some other people.

"Here's where we're going," she says once she finishes the article. "We'll go trash the club." She hands the paper to David. He reads it, and agrees it's a better plan because maybe there won't be guards.

"This is getting to be a habit with us," says David. "Stalking Ricky Biscayne in SoBe. I like it. Very faggy."

Sophia looks at her best friend and thanks God for him. No one understands her except him. And no one knows how to cheer her up better. She decides to call her mom to tell her she'll be home late, but can't find her phone.

"Where is it?" she asks David. They search the bus, and decide she must have left it at the bus stop.

"You'll get a new one," says David. "Ricky Biscayne will buy you your own cell-phone company."

"I love you, David," she says, putting her head on his shoulder.

"I love you too, crazy girl," he says, planting a wholly platonic, wonderful kiss right on the top of her head. "Let's go teach these obtuse city-folk how awesome Little Miss Sophia from the boonies is."

I hang up the phone in my office and start to pack up for the day. It's so quiet I can hear the ceiling fan buzzing and clicking in circles.

Suddenly, I miss my old life. I miss my old clothes, and my old friends. I'm wearing more fancy nonsense, this time a crocheted blue halter top by Milly, and a blue and white flouncy full skirt. A pair of Prada shoes that are too narrow and tight. The skirt itches. I want sweats and a big T-shirt. I want to dress like Matthew Baker now and then. Maybe I'm just feeling depressed, but I want to lie in bed with a book, for days, and a big chocolate bar for company.

I'm going to have to do something to stop the downward—albeit fashionable—slip of my life, and quick.

But even as I know I have to distance myself from Ricky, I can't stop wanting him. In fact, knowing that he's seeing Jill on the side, and that he might have a kid, has done nothing to squelch my lust for the boy. These facts have oddly increased my desire for him, and I don't have the psychological energy to figure out why. Even as I think to myself that I have to get my act together, I fantasize as I walk down the hall that I can take Ricky into my office for a wild quickie right now, just one last time. One last, delicious time, because of his music and his voice and all that it has spoken to me over the years. He might be troubled, and damaged, but he is still a brilliant artist with a body to die for.

I hear music coming from the recording studio and decide to indulge my fantasy, just to see what happens. Can't hurt. Or, rather, can't hurt any more than I'm already hurt. The door to the recording studio is closed, and I stand outside with my heart breaking, listening as Ricky sings with force and virility. I can almost picture his hips thrusting to the beat. He is so proficient I can hardly breathe. So sexy. I still love him. I love that voice and the emotion he pours into every note, on a new song in Spanish. It's so beautiful, a ballad, and I actually start to cry like a total dweeb as I listen to it. I hate myself for still loving him. But how can I stop loving a man with a voice and a gift like this? Tell me. How is it possible? It's not. That's how. I don't. Can't. Won't.

I turn the knob of the door very slowly. I know Ricky doesn't like to be interrupted when he's laying down tracks. You like how I say that? Laying down tracks. It's part of the cool music-publicist lingo I've picked up along the way. I may be the office slut, but at least I've come away with some useful jargon.

I ease the door open, hoping for one last look at my dream man singing the most beautiful song I've ever heard, before I totally turn around and betray him. I feel like a woman on death row who has chosen Cheetos and Fresca for her last meal. It's not good for me, but I fucking want it. I need to see him, to feel him inside me again. I have loved him for so many years that I fear it's going to take me years to wean myself as well.

I poke my head in, expecting to find Matthew at the control panel and Ricky in the booth. Instead, I find a man I've never seen before at the control panel, headphones on his ears, and Matthew. In the booth. With his eyes closed. Standing in front of the microphone. Singing. No Ricky. Anywhere.

Matthew is *singing*?

Neither man notices me, because they are too absorbed in the song. I watch as Matthew's face tenses with emotion, as he belts out the high notes, and the gospel riffs, and all the other things Ricky Biscayne is famous for.

Only it's not Ricky. Shit.

In this moment, as the notes and words rise out of his lovely mouth, I am struck, dumbstruck really, by the beauty of Matthew Baker. It finally makes sense. I've always known there was something special about him, but until now I assumed that his specialness was, like, *Jerry's*-kids special. That he was somehow sick, or pitiable. But it's not. It's genius. He is beautiful. And sexy. And real. He was telling me the truth that night, the night of the massage and bitten lobe.

I feel sick.

At that moment, Matthew finishes the line and opens his small, shiny brown eyes. They focus instantly on me, almost as if he has sensed me there. He smiles gently and waves with an embarrassed blush. The other man, who looks like Fat Albert, turns to see me and whips off his headphones.

"Hey, what's up," he says. "I'm Rory Clooney." The producer. I know the name. Famous guy. Ugly as hell, with a big, wet tooth-gap like a small river.

Matthew takes off his headphones and opens the door from the recording booth to the mixing studio. "Hi, Milan," he says. "Been here long?" He has a strange, sarcastic look on his face. I realize now that the sarcasm and the smirking are defense mechanisms for a man with a very gentle and sensitive soul. Why didn't I notice that before?

"I just got here," I say. "I thought I heard Ricky in here."

The two men look at each other, and Rory says, "You did. Basically."

Matthew shrugs. "I tried to tell you."

"Oh my God," I say. And it hits me. I mean, *really* hits me. "You were telling the truth?"

Matthew smiles, and there is no bitterness to him. "Ricky hasn't recorded his own leads in more than two years."

"You wrote the song I love?"

"Pretty much all of them," he says.

I can't breathe. I'm blushing. "Oh my God," I say again. If it hasn't been Ricky, then who on earth have I been screwing around with? A liar? An egomaniac? A drug addict? A wife beater? A cheater? "OhmyGodOhmyGod." I hope to God Jill Sanchez doesn't have hepatitis or something.

Matthew puts a gentle arm over my shoulders. "So, now you know. I'm not a liar. And I am definitely not the office psycho."

"No," I say in a whisper. "That would be *me*."

D ay after day, they come to her, seeking guidance. They throw their pennies into the water, and come in with their whispered sins, begging to be forgiven. She knows them all quite well by now, and, in general, nothing they do or say can surprise her. She has been listening to the same lists of sins and virtues, hopes and vengeances, for many thousands of years.

But today is something new. Milan Gotay, with conflict and torture marring her pleasant face. What can she possibly have to share that bothers her this much? Is it that her initial prayer to meet Ricky Biscayne did not bring her what she had hoped for? Human beings are so fragile. La Caridad del Cobre smiles to herself. Sometimes you just have to let people figure things out for themselves. Sometimes, you can't warn them with feelings of trepidation, because they have had lives too sheltered to allow them to be cautious at the right times.

In truth, La Caridad del Cobre has been expecting Milan. She is surprised that it has taken this long. She is also surprised by the new clothes, as she has not taken Milan for the vain type. The young woman kneels before her and speaks the problem. La Caridad del Cobre listens. Ah, yes. Ricky Biscayne. The superstar. She's been hearing about him from his grieving mother for years. And from various unsavory cocaine dealers who see the error of their ways only too late. And from Jasminka. There are so many people who come to whisper their secrets about Ricky, to ask for peace and rest in the face of his tempestuous habits. The loudest of the voices comes from a long, long distance, from a child who has not been raised to know La Caridad del Cobre, but who has the blood of the virgin's people flowing strongly through her veins. Sophia's spectacular and solitary sadness has touched La Caridad, curling up through the night over South Florida, and washing out to sea. La Caridad knows that when she feels that child's pain, she has to do something. Something. Something.

La Caridad has been plotting to help Ricky. Help him? Yes. Help him to change. You try. It does not always work. People are not always ready to hear what she has to say. They ignore La Caridad del Cobre more often than they listen to her these days. But that doesn't make her powerless. She knows that there will be a resolution to his behavior. She has not bargained precisely on the solution involving the quiet young woman from Coral Gables, whose mission thus far has been mostly the care of her ailing grandfather, eating cookies, and pretending not to have womanly desires that threaten to overtake her life. She had imagined that by bringing Ricky and Milan together, the main outcome would be that Milan would realize there was a Milan, and that she was real, and that real people ought to live real lives and not waste their youth and energy pining for a fantasy that not only would never be theirs, but that wasn't anyone's. That had been the goal of La Caridad del Cobre, who despises commercialism and false idols.

But as Milan speaks, the force of her words surprises the virgin. Milan has found more than reality. She has found torture. She has made love to Ricky as he fucked her. Yes, La Caridad can say words like that. She knows more about human nature than anyone in the universe. And now Milan is here, realizing that she has fallen in love but has directed it to the wrong man. Milan has learned. She has learned the lesson, but almost too late.

"Help me, blessed virgin, to do the right thing and to know what that is."

La Caridad thinks, and thinks. There will be a way to resolve this thing. There will. And then it comes to her, and La Caridad del Cobre knows what has to happen. There are many lessons to be learned here, by many people. The delight of being a goddess is in weaving the paths so that the synchronicities occur, so that they are surprising to the people on those paths, surprising enough to make them realize in the gentlest and most ironic of ways that there is someone looking out for them, and that there is purpose and meaning to all of it.

So she calculates. This is what goddesses do best. And, she realizes with the delight of a mathematician who finally figures out a complex equation, there is a way to fix everything at one moment in time. Mortals call it a miracle. But La Caridad knows that miracles happen with the help of human beings who want to help others. Those are the best kinds of miracles. And there will be a miracle.

Soon.

Ricky paces the empty bedroom with the phone in his hand, wearing Paul Smith striped cotton pajama pants and nothing else, not even underwear. His hair stands on end from having been pulled by his own hands. Hating himself. Blaming himself. For what? For fucking up his entire life. For being a *huelebicho*. For losing everyone and everything that has ever meant anything, really anything, to him. Jasminka. His mother. His father. He is at fault. Never good enough.

Ricky falls to his knees on the floor, finds himself pathetically melodramatic, gets himself up, and falls again. He doesn't know what to do with his feet, his hands, his body. His mind. It goes too fast. It has always gone too fast and fucked him up. He gets bored easily, loses interest too quickly. Moves on when he shouldn't, pushes people away just to see if they'll come back. He is an ass. A *bollo*. He hates himself. This house. He hates it. He doesn't want it anymore. What is the point without her? He bought the house with the idea of finding a wife to go with it. Jasminka? He loved her. He *loves* her. He never loves women more than when they are unattainable, as she now makes herself. That is the curse of Ricky. He likes it when women hurt, because he can rescue them. Jasminka is hurt now, and he hurt her. How could he do that? Who did that? Hurt a woman like that? Just to rescue her? She is frail. She is injured at the most profound of levels, like a limping seagull with broken wings. How could this have happened? How has his life come to this? He has screwed up everything with his selfish ways. Drugs. That is the most selfish shit he does. He is terrible, a terrible person, and everything is his fault. It always has been. He is unlovable, born that way, flawed, to blame, always to blame. A *foquin pendejo*.

He feels a hole open in his belly, and there is nothing beyond but emptiness, and silence, and cold. He will never be full, because no one will ever love him enough. Why is he never good enough for people to love him forever? What does he do wrong? He tries to be the best. He practices, and he dances. He performs. But no one really knows him. They don't care. And it is his own fucking fault. He stands and walks to the mirror and looks at his face. He isn't beautiful, as they all say. He is ugly. Hideous. A beautiful person does not hurt other people like this. A beautiful person doesn't need coke to feel confident, to forget. Beautiful people don't have so many things to forget, so many ghosts, so much that crushes from the inside out, until you can't fucking *breathe*.

He calls Jasminka's cell phone again, and still she doesn't answer. He's left messages. Lots of them. And she doesn't answer. Where the fuck did she go? Doesn't she know how dangerous it is in the world? She is carrying his child, and no matter what he says, he does want this baby, he does love them. He wants to cry, but it has been years since he's been able to. It is like his body doesn't know, doesn't remember how. There was crying early in his life, and it didn't help. You don't keep doing things that don't work, if you want to progress, and that has been Ricky's singular goal from the time he was aware that he could formulate goals. To escape. To excel. To succeed. To own, to consume, to persuade, to be the fucking king of the fucking world. To marry her, the model everyone else wanted. So that they'd look at him when he showed up for Grammy parties and motherfuckers would be, like, Look at that. He's got a beautiful wife. But models are people, too. That's the part he didn't understand. That Jasminka isn't a picture in a magazine. That her breath stinks in the morning, and she cries, and she has a story, a history so big, and so dark, so much worse than his, that he can't imagine it, and now that he thinks about it, he has no idea how the fuck he's been such a fucking bastard to her when she needed, cried out for, someone to fucking *protect* her.

"Fuck!" He kicks the pillow he kicked moments before. Where *is* she? Why is she doing this to him? Why doesn't he love people better? What is wrong with him? Why has God put him on earth so broken? Jasminka is the best thing that ever happened to him, a soft, gentle soul, and here he is, ruining everything, pushing her away. He clenches a fist and draws his arm back, ready to strike the wall. But even as he does it, he realizes that this is exactly what is wrong with him. He is weak. He is violent. He hates the look of himself right now. This isn't how his mother raised him. This isn't who he believes he really is.

Ricky pulls his arms in and hugs himself. He feels like his head is going to split open. He dials Jasminka's number again. "Answer the phone," he chants to himself. "Answer the phone. Answer the phone." He looks at the crucifix on the wall, the wooden one his mother gave him when he got his first recording contract, and promises God, Jesus, anyone who is listening, that he will change this time. If only they will give him the strength. Then, the unexpected strikes.

"Hello?" It is Jasminka, answering her phone after hours of not. She sniffles as if she's been crying, her voice hollow and nasal the way it gets when you have a cold or heartbreak.

"Jasminka, thank God you're okay," says Ricky. He tells her he loves her. He falls into the soft beige carpet of the room and begs her to forgive him for hitting her. He was never that rough with her before, and even he can't believe he could do such a thing to the most wonderful and amazing woman in the world, the woman who has saved him from addictions and bad friends, the woman he wants to love for the rest of his life, the woman who will soon bear his child.

"I messed up," he says. "But I'll get help. I swear I will. I'll go to anger management. I'll do anything. Whatever it takes. *Te lo juro, mamita*. If you'll just come back."

Jasminka remains silent for a few moments, then asks him if he means it. He says yes, and asks her where she is.

"I'm sorry," she says. "No."

"I'll never do it again. I can learn from my mistakes. I *can*." He means it. Fuck but Jesus fucking Christ he means it.

"No, Ricky."

No? *No?* "Fuck that," he says. No one says no to Ricky. He has come too far, worked too hard, for that.

"Don't speak to me in this way," says Jasminka. "I do not take this anymore, Ricky. I'm not."

Suddenly, all of the warm and charitable feelings Ricky has, and all the remorse, disappear as he imagines Jasminka with another man. Is that why she's acting this way? Because she's already on to the next guy? Because she is trying to hide something? She wouldn't do that to him, would she? Not in her condition? Unless the condition was the result of sex with someone other than Ricky. As the thoughts bubble through his mind, a part of Ricky stands off to the side, watching, aware of the absurdity of his behavior. He is irrational. How is he supposed to act? He thinks about it, and decides to control himself. Don't get angry, he tells himself.

"Please come home, baby," he says, knowing the moment he says it that it will be really fucking hard not to hit her again when she gets back.

"You are angry at me?" she asks quietly, reeled in, coming back, convinced. Ricky feels the rush of victory. He did it. He got through to her. Even after what he's done. He convinced her. He is the fucking *man*.

"No, baby," he says with a gentleness that has nothing whatsoever to do with the churning fury in his gut. "I'm angry at myself. And I'll never do it again."

The bells in the first-class cabin chime to indicate that the airplane has reached ten thousand feet, and the flight attendant gets on the intercom to tell the passengers it is now okay to use "portable electronic devices." Jack wonders if that includes jackrabbit vibrators, and considers asking the flight attendant, who isn't ugly. He realizes that the very fact that he is noticing pretty flight attendants is a sign that he is losing interest in his fiancée. When he first hooked up with Jill Sanchez, he thought of her in much the same way as most of the men in the world think of her—as the sexiest woman on earth, an alluring creature without rival, exotic, passionate, seemingly insatiable. The truth of Jill Sanchez is so far removed from her public persona that Jack laughs out loud as he recalls his illusions about what she'd be like. He thought she would be wild in bed, twisty and turny like she was in her videos. That she would behave beneath him in the same sultry way she behaved in front of the camera. Not. He laughs harder, drawing stares from his fellow passengers.

"It's the drugs," he jokes to them. He realizes as he says it that there is a very good chance he will see a news item on his supposed drug addiction in the *Los Angeles Times* the next day. That's where he is headed, Los Angeles, to spend a few days at his own comfortable pigpen of a house in Encino, and to sign a new movie deal.

Jack pulls his laptop out from beneath the seat and starts to type a letter to the editor of *Vanity Fair* regarding a recent article they ran on the suicide of Hunter S. Thompson. He'd complained about the article last night to Jill, but she hadn't even known who Thompson was.

In all, he spent two hours crafting the letter, and another two hours reading *Manufacturing Consent: The Political Economy of the Mass Media,* by Noam Chomsky and others.

Hours later, with the taste of disgust for his nation and its media machine like metal in his mouth, Jack holds on to the armrests with tense hands as the plane lands at LAX, uncharacteristically coming in from the east, in a pounding rainstorm.

Jack goes straight from the plane to the baggage claim area, even though he has no bags. He has everything he needs at home, and left his other clothes and things at Jill's. He despises himself for being so bourgeois, but what could he do, walk around with hideous suitcases full of shit he doesn't need?

The driver from the studio waits for him with a sign reading PIPER, the code name they've given him for the day. It is stupid, because everyone who sees him knows exactly who he is—that stupid asshole with the goatee, engaged to Jill Sanchez. People, especially those who hate their lives, are weird about celebrities. They point at him and talk about him as if he isn't there. Like he is still stuck in the television or on the movie screen or magazine pages, wherever the last place the gawkers in question had seen him. He hates the entire concept of celebrity. If he had it to do over again, he would never choose this life. He wasn't made for the attention and stupidity of the thing. If he had it to do over again, he would try to be a writer, or a philosopher. But he is thirty-four, recognizable in most parts of the world, and basically does *not* have it to do over again. All he has, he figures, is a bogus, overrated career that he intends to milk for what it's worth before he fades into that oblivion twilight from which vile, small-dick producers pluck victims for their "where are they now" cable shows.

Jack allows the driver to open the door for him and steps in without his usual litany of protests in defense of the proletariat. He doesn't have the energy to get to know the driver this time. This time, he keeps his sunglasses on, and his mouth shut. He is tired, and when you're tired, it's easiest to just act like a fucking celebrity.

Jack's various agents, managers, handlers, and other assorted maggots wait for him in the office of the studio president, wearing their usual black and trendy outfits that try to look like they aren't trying to look too good. The signing is a formality. He has already agreed to the project. This is just a meeting to introduce him to Lara Bryant, the muscular, fresh-faced, big-toothed young TV star, originally from Idaho, who will play his love interest. He's seen her show a few times and has always thought she has a comforting look to her, like a dimpled, bright young college student who's just scrubbed her face in the dorm bathroom. She looks like the kind of girl who flosses her teeth twice a day.

Lara enters the office a few minutes after Jack, soaking wet from the rain. She wears jeans and a sweatshirt, and duck boots, and looks like a model from the L.L.Bean catalog who has accidentally gotten stuck in a storm. He hasn't seen duck boots since New England, and the sight of them makes him nostalgic. She wears no makeup, and her short, possibly bitten nails are bare of paint, polish, or any of the other toxic waste Jill never leaves home without. Lara smiles as she shakes his hand, and her teeth look naturally white, like she's grown up eating fruits and vegetables and drinking lots of water. He can't see a single pore on her glowing face. Her eyes are what strike him hardest. Brown, with long lashes, they broadcast an intense intelligence that appears to be utterly clear of cynicism. She is smart, and kind. That's what her eyes tell him. Most interesting of all, Jack notices that she carries a book in her other hand. *The Impossible Will Take a Little While: A Citizen's Guide to Hope in a Time of Fear*, by Paul Loeb. Wow. Was there a God after all?

"Jack Ingroff. I've wanted to meet you for a long time," she says, her eyes sparkling with a secret Jack suddenly feels compelled to learn. "This is going to be fun."

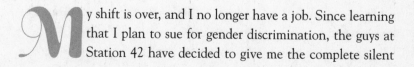

y shift is over, and I no longer have a job. Since learning that I plan to sue for gender discrimination, the guys at Station 42 have decided to give me the complete silent treatment and to put me on indefinite leave. Right. Like I'm invisible. It's worse to be ignored like this than to be made fun of openly. But it's okay. I'm at the point where I'm starting to feel unsafe with them on fires. And, as Captain Sullivan himself once told me, as soon as a firefighter starts to feel unsafe in a team, it's time to request a transfer, or time to quit. You can't leave your safety in the hands of men who despise you.

Nestor comes into the bunk room, tall, clean, with his hard body, and smiles at me the way people smile at someone they've just noticed has a cast on their arm. "You okay?" he asks. Pity. Just what I need.

I shrug and stuff a bottle of Pantene shampoo into my duffel bag. "Oh, yeah," I say. "I'm great. Nothing like getting ignored for two straight days, then hearing you don't have a job just because you want to have the same chances as everyone else."

He sits on the bench and sighs. "I wanted to tell you, I support you."

"Yeah, thanks." I sigh. "I'm burnt out, man. I need to go for a jog or something. I need to mow the lawn."

"Let's talk about all this over dinner."

I feel a warm chill run through my body as I remember the night talking at his house. "You're crazy, you know that?" I say.

"That's what our boss just told me when I told him I thought you were brave, so I figure it can't be true."

I try not to smile, just as my cell phone rings. Mom, daughter, or reporter. Take your pick. No one else ever really calls me. I check the phone screen. Mom.

"Sophia with you?" Alice asks, even before I've had a chance to say hello. My mother is such a charmer.

"No," I say. "Why would she be?"

"I sent her out for chips this morning and she ain't come back."

"Hasn't." I always correct her, but she never learns. "Did you call her phone?"

"I did. A man answered who didn't speak no English, and he laughed and hung up," says my mother.

"Jesus, Alice, why didn't you tell me this first?"

That flutter of womanly lust I felt, the wanting of Nestor, hardens instantly into a knot of motherly dread.

The young pop producer Rory Clooney sits in the control booth of his Miami recording studio with a few of his fellow producers and tries not to cringe in a way that might be visible to Jill Sanchez.

Superstar Jill, wearing low-rise jeans with a white turtleneck that has long sleeves but a bra-short torso section, stands before the microphone in the recording studio on the other side of the large Plexiglas window. Her abdominal muscles ripple and sparkle. Is she wearing glitter? Who wears glitter to a recording session? Headphones perched on her head, on top of a white glistening baseball cap that Rory has asked her to remove because it refracts her voice in a way he doesn't like, making it smaller and more metallic. When your voice is small and metallic to begin with, you don't want to do anything to exacerbate the problem. This is Rory's educated musical opinion. But, as is the usual drill, his opinion comes second to Jill's as long as she is in the building. Jill Sanchez does not want to remove the hat, which she claims to have designed, even though Rory and everyone else in Jill's employ knows that Jill's designs were in fact the creations of a team of talented designers who hid in her shadows and let her take the glory. Much as did Rory himself.

The purpose of the session is for Jill to correct some of the vocals she laid down months ago on the tracks for her upcoming album, *Born Again*. The final version of the album is due to the record label at the end of the week, and will hit stores a few weeks after that. Rory did Jill's first two albums, and this, like those, cries out for corrections like a room full of murderers.

"Okay," he says into his microphone, holding down the red button that enables Jill to hear him through her headphones. "That was better. But let's try it a couple more times, just to be sure we get the right take."

He releases the button, so Jill can no longer hear what is said in the control booth. Next to him, one of the assistants speaks under his breath: "'Better.' That's a subjective term, my brother, wouldn't you say? Better, as in better than a plate of steaming shit." The other assistant chimes in, "Better than a battery-acid enema." The first assistant volleys back, "Better than a paper cut on your eyeball."

In the studio, Jill furrows her brow, and clears her throat, standing straighter and doing her very best to act like a professional singer getting ready to lay down some kick-ass tracks. It is a performance worthy of an Oscar. Rory steels his face and does not let Jill Sanchez see the way the comments of his colleagues create bubbles of laughter in his ample gut. Because he can't control the impulse altogether, he pretends to cough, hand over mouth.

"You guys are cold," he says.

"Cold," says the first assistant. "Let's see. Better than a cold stick up your rectum?"

"Oh, shit," says Rory, continuing to "cough."

"Hello? Time is money. You guys ready?" calls Jill into the microphone. She sounds like Mickey Mouse. She affects a superior attitude in these sessions, as if she thinks she is a fabulous singer. Maybe she *does* think she's a fabulous singer. If she knows how truly terrible her voice and abilities are, she never lets on. But the truth is that the woman is stone-cold tone deaf. He knows it, and every other musician, songwriter, and producer who works on her albums knows it. But after they stay up late into the night, working their computerized magic with the pitch adjuster and the paid studio singers who do "backup" vocals for her, Jill Sanchez has albums with phat hooks that sell into the millions. She looks good in her videos, and these days, that counts for a lot. Rory himself is a phenomenal singer and songwriter, but he is bulky and ugly and therefore condemned forever to the background of the modern music industry. He longs for the days of Fats Domino. But they can't afford to fuck with their paychecks, no matter how much working with Jill reminds them of fingernails scraped across a chalkboard. Most of her producers live in mansions and drive luxury cars now, and they are used to them and don't want to go back. Rory knows for a fact he'd never give up his Pinecrest crib with the fountains and the outdoor poolside kitchen if he didn't have to. He doesn't want to give up his Range Rover, either.

"Ready, sweetie," says Rory. "I'll punch you in on the chorus. Really reach on those high notes, Jill, okay? Lots of support in the diaphragm. Don't be afraid to belt them out."

Jill cocks her head and plants a furious hand on her hip. "You don't fucking tell me how to sing," she snaps. "I have Balthazar to tell me how to sing, okay? You I have to punch *buttons*."

Rory nods, but what he really wants to do is remind Jill of how, just last week, Balthazar, the finest vocal coach in the industry, refused in an *Entertainment Weekly* article to take credit for Jill Sanchez's singing, even though she has employed him full-time for the past five years.

"Better than having your dick cut off with a soup-can lid," says the second assistant producer, with a shrug meant to express how reasonable he is.

"And flushed down the toilet," suggests the first assistant. The assistants exchange shrugs of agreement and vicious grins.

"Fuck," says Rory, feeling a very real pain between his legs. Then, he presses the button, and like everyone else getting paid to be in Jill Sanchez's orbit, he lies to her. "You're right, baby. You sound great. Let's hit it."

In the booth, Jill tells Rory he has three more takes to get it right.

As Ricky lights up a postcoital afternoon cigarette and settles back on Jill's bed to watch MTV en Español, Jill shrugs back into her nightgown. She burrows under the soft, cool sheets and opens the latest issue of *Star* magazine, which one of her assistants picked up for her and left downstairs. There is Jack, on the cover, in a photo that looks like he's walking out of an Encino Coffee Bean & Tea Leaf holding hands with that girl-next-door–looking actress, Lara something or other. Bryant. Like Anita. Her teeth are huge.

"No, he *didn't*," fumes Jill. Ricky, eyes squinted against the smoke curling up out of his mouth, is engrossed in the latest Kumbia Kings video and doesn't pay attention. Sex with Jill wears him out.

Jill flips to the cover story inside the magazine, finding several more photos of Jack with Lara. In one photo, they appear to be kissing. Jill feels a shock of emotion. It isn't jealousy, or even hurt. She doesn't care who he messes around with, ultimately, as long as no one else knows and the public believes that she and Jack are happy together. What pisses her off is how *sloppy* Jack has been about it. Doesn't he know the press is following him? Is he that naïve? Does he not *understand* how important it is for fans to think of him as being attached to her, Jill Sanchez, and not to some nothing wannabe TV actress who wears black leather and a pink wig on a nothing network? Is he stupid?

The story reports that Jack and Lara met at a contract signing for the new movie they are set to star in together, and that sparks flew as soon as Jack saw that Lara shared his interest in "liberal lefty screeding material." How ridiculous, thinks Jill Sanchez. Do neither of these people realize that the political climate of the mainstream is solidly leaning toward the right? Even though Jill's personal politics tend toward the liberal side, she knows better than to flap it around in the air for everyone to see, especially now. Wasn't she, Jill Sanchez, the one who had gotten Jack the stint consoling soldiers in the Middle East a while back, hoping to win him fans among conservatives? Now he is ruining everything. Honestly, she is starting to wonder whether Jack Ingroff is worth the time and energy. She had hoped to hold off on dumping him until their movie came out in a few weeks. The last thing Jill Sanchez needs right now is to have Jack actually fall in love with that skinny little white girl and leave her, Jill Sanchez. It is unthinkable that any man on earth might find that weed of a woman more interesting and fascinating than the exotic and multitalented Jill. The emotion—confusion—overwhelms her. She simply doesn't understand how Jack could make such a bad, career-slaying decision.

"I can't believe he'd do this to me," she wails.

Ricky stubs his cigarette out in the Jill Sanchez–shaped ashtray on the bedside table and rolls toward Jill. He kisses her hand, wrist, arm, shoulder, neck, and lips. "Do what, *mamita?*"

Jill shoves the magazine at Ricky, who reads it with a grin. Jill crosses her arms and shakes her head. "He should know better," she says with a wagging finger. "He's playing with fire."

Ricky feels an emotion, too, but unlike Jill's emotion, his *is* truly jealousy. He loves this woman to the point of worship, and even though she tells him she loves him and will be with him, she still seems to care about her stupid-ass fiancé. He hates her for it.

"You're a bitch, you know that?"

Jill Sanchez snaps her head around to look at him, and her beautiful eyes close to snakelike slits. "What did you just say?"

"I said you're a bitch."

Jill, stung by Jack's careless infidelity and Ricky's insult, slaps him on the cheek. Ricky responds with a gorgeous, furious grin. He grabs her hands, pins them behind her head against the soft pink-fur-upholstered headboard. Jill squirms, angry as a cat in a trap, but gives up a minute later. Ricky lowers his face to hers, and speaks in a soft, intense voice.

"The problem with Jack Ingroff," he says, "is that he don't know how to keep you in check. He don't know that Jill Sanchez is just a woman and like all women likes to be put in her place now and then. He don't get it that you want me to say *mámame el bicho*, eh?"

Jill hears Ricky but doesn't find his predictable faux ghetto swagger all that impressive. She knows that if she demands he back the fuck off her, he will; that's what Ricky is best at, jumping when she says jump. Jill Sanchez has that sort of power over people. But she is thinking, strategizing, and it is best to pretend to listen to him so that she can have some time alone in her head.

"Does he do you like I do you?" asks Ricky, all hot and bothered. Jill does not reply. She looks into Ricky's gorgeous light brown, almost yellow, eyes and considers the situation. It would actually work to her advantage to be the poor dear sweet Latina who got left by the big, mean, overly intellectual gringo. She could cry to Barbara Walters or Diane Sawyer—or, better yet, Oprah!—about her heartache, in perfect timing with her new movie and album. Her handlers have gently hinted to Jill that the public is growing weary of her unstoppable successes, and this might just be the perfect solution. If she looks like a lovelorn innocent, if she could paint Jack as the bad guy, America will love her, Jill Sanchez, more than ever. And if America loves Jill Sanchez more than ever, they'll pay more money than ever for her products. Jill smiles as she feels excitement bubble through her body, and she spreads her legs.

"No, baby," she says to Ricky. "Jack doesn't do me like you do." Silently, she adds, *His dick is bigger and he pretends I'm a Japanese boy.*

Ricky smiles and presses his entire body against hers. *"Trágate la leche, mamita."*

"Put me in my place, Ricky," she challenges him, suppressing a yawn. "Drop it on me."

D oes your mother know where you are?" My mom is scowling at Sophia.

Yep. That's right. Geneva just showed up with Sophia, Ricky's illegitimate daughter, in tow. Oh, and Sophia's little gay friend, David. Don't ask. Okay, go ahead. Ask. I'll tell you.

The girl and her friend here both showed up at Club G and started pelting the door with eggs. Geneva was inside with her designer and they heard the sound and went out, and Geneva had to beg the designer not to call the police. I guess Geneva feels sorry for the girl, and I do, too, but still. You don't egg my sister's nightclub. That's just wrong. And now Geneva has brought them here for dinner, like waifs she picked up on the street.

Weird. Just when you decide to think Geneva's heartless, she goes and does something like this. Almost as weird as the fact that I have replaced my Ricky obsession with a new Matthew obsession, only I am pretty sure Matthew hates me for not believing him in the first place and I don't stand a chance in hell with him now.

Jasminka comes out of the bathroom, her hands on her lower back. She's still skinny as a deer, but with a big beach-ball belly. She looks like a beautiful, pregnant alien. Oh. Have I mentioned that she lives here now? Looks like we're taking in all of Ricky's refugees.

"My mom doesn't need to know where I am," huffs the girl. She is taller than my mom, and her eyes shine with indignation. Thirteen these days looks a lot like fifteen a generation ago. "My mom doesn't care about me."

My mother gives Sophia a wicked stare. "Of course your mommy cares about you," she says. Her pal, David, shakes his head in Sophia's defense. My mother gives him the stare now, and he backs down. He says he thinks we have a "fabulous" home. Jasminka silently stands against a wall, eating a pear. "All mommies care about their babies," hisses Mom. "Where is your mommy?"

"Homestead," Sophia says, it as if the very word sickens her.

"Sunny D capital of South Florida," adds David.

"*Pero Dios mío!*" cries Violeta, clapping her hands together in a way that scares the kids, raising her voice the way Cubans do, looking at Geneva in consternation. "How did they get all the way to Miami Beach?"

"Bus," says Sophia.

Geneva shrugs, out of her comfort zone. "Bus?" she tells Mom weakly. Mom gives Geneva the stare now. God, I hope I'm not next. Says Mom, "Let's give your mommy a call and tell her you're okay. She's got to be worried sick about you."

"All she worries about is herself," says Sophia.

"That can't be true," says Jasminka, finally speaking through her mouthful of fruit.

"What do you know about it?" snaps Sophia. "You wouldn't even admit Ricky was my dad."

"I'm sorry about that," says Jasminka. "I didn't know what I know now."

"Come, let's call your mommy," says my mom.

"No! She hates me," Sophia tells her.

"Nonsense," says Violeta, over the top of Sophia's comments. She orders me to bring her the phone, as if she herself is incapable of fetching it. Fine. They all still think I'm the dutiful daughter. Let them. I don't care. It sure beats the truth. Says Mom, "We are calling her mother."

"I don't know her number," says Sophia. Yeah, right! What a stupid thing to say. I come back with the phone (it was, you know, all the way across the room, God forbid), and I see my mom scrutinizing poor Sophia's face. Mom looks like a predator.

"You," she says, pointing to the girl. "You remind me," she looks at Geneva, "of a very difficult girl I used to know."

Ha! I win. I win. Geneva was the difficult girl.

Ha.

Yes, I'm mature.

Mom takes the phone and weighs it in her hands, savoring the young girl's discomfort.

"Please don't call her," says Sophia.

Mom squints, and says, "You look hungry."

"I'm starving," says Jasminka.

"Not you," my mother tells Jasminka. "With you, hunger is a given."

"Please don't call my mom." Sophia looks at Geneva this time. "She'll kill me."

"She'll kill her," Geneva says to Mom, with a look of contrition.

"I raised two girls and I know your mommy is worried about you," says my mother. Okay. Now I'm a little annoyed with the whole "mommy" thing. She's talking to a teenager who's taller than she is. She should say "mom" instead. But maybe she's saying it in Spanish, like "*mami*," and it comes across as "mommy"? Who the fuck knows. Who the fuck cares.

"Please," says Sophia. "She probably hasn't even noticed I'm gone."

"Probably not," says David. "Her mom doesn't notice anything. She's ADD."

"David!" says Sophia. "She is not."

"Is too."

"Is not."

At that moment, my Hello Kitty phone rings in my bedroom. Great. I'm trying to be an adult, and I have to deal with a Hello Kitty phone.

"Excuse me," I say.

I run to see who is calling me, with a sick feeling that it just might be Ricky. I look at the caller ID, and, sure enough, it says RICKY BIS-CAYNE PRODUCTIONS. I pick it up.

"Hi, Ricky."

There's a pause. And then I hear Ricky's voice, only it says, "Mi-lan? It's Matthew."

Matthew? "Uh, hi."

I hear him laugh, and can't believe I never before noticed that his voice, even his speaking voice, sounds like the voice I've loved for years. I still love those songs. I feel my heartbeat accelerate, thinking that the man responsible for them is single, kind, and *calling me.*

"Um," he says. "I was wondering if you wanted to try to watch that movie again sometime."

I smile to myself and feel butterflies. "But we've both seen it," I say.

"Even better," he says. "Because that way, I can focus on the mas-sage."

"How about tonight?" I blurt.

He pauses. "Okay."

"ey, wait. I'm coming with you," calls Nestor, chasing me through the fire station parking lot. I don't have time to say the whole final good-bye to my colleagues. I doubt they'll notice I'm gone. I dial Sophia's cell number and now it goes straight to voicemail.

"No," I say. I drop my keys to the blacktop. My hands tremble. "I have to handle this alone."

Nestor jogs to my side and picks up my keys. He puts a hand on my arm, looks into my eyes. "Irene, I know you're tough. You are. Look at you. You've done so much by yourself. I'm impressed. But you shouldn't be alone right now," he says.

"I won't be alone," I snap. "I'm going to the police. I'll have *them*."

"*They're* not friends," he says. "You need a friend."

He's right. Anyway, I haven't allowed myself the time to even think about friends since Sophia was born. I've been running ever since, and never thought there'd be anyone in the world who'd want to run alongside me. I don't want to be alone anymore. I don't. I fight the tears, fumble with the lock on the car, say, "Why is she doing this to me?" It comes out like a lament.

"Hey." Nestor puts his hand over mine and eases the key into the lock. Turns it. Calm. Helpful. Loving. "Sophia might not have done anything. We just have to do our best to find her. No blame, okay?"

He opens my door for me, helps me in. I reach over to unlock the passenger door. He opens it, folds himself into the car. Such a tall man, so strong, and so kind. I can hardly believe it. As I start the engine, I feel my throat close off in a swallowed cry. I feel his eyes on me. I don't want to cry in front of him. I don't want to fall apart now. Sophia needs me.

"She's fine, Irene, okay?" says Nestor. So he's a mind reader, too? "I'm sure she's fine. She's just a teenager. And she's going through a hard time. Let's just try to think of the places she might go."

I pull the car onto the street and bite my lower lip. "I don't know," I say. "Other than soccer camp, school, and her friends' houses, I don't know."

"Let's start by calling her friends," suggests Nestor. He is so calm, rational. Of course. Sophia is at a friend's house. Why didn't I think of that? Why is my impulse always to assume the negative, to prepare for the worst of the worst in life?

Nestor takes out his cell phone and opens it. "Do you know the numbers, or the names? I'll call while you drive."

"Where am I driving again?" I ask. I am blank, overwhelmed, collapsing under the weight of my soul.

"Police station."

"Thank you."

I rattle off the number for David's house. Nestor calls, and David's mother says she doesn't know where her son is, either, but that she isn't all that worried. We press her for David's cell number. We call but get no answer. I tell Nestor I don't think Sophia really spends much time with anyone else anymore. They have all turned on Sophia, her friends. They believe what they read in the newspaper about us.

"Let's think for a minute," he says, steady, as I drive. "Do you think she might have gone to Ricky's house again?"

My blood runs cold. Ricky's. Of course. "She better not have," I say. "I told her she'd be in big trouble if she pulled that again. We had a very good talk about that."

Nestor laughs.

"What's so funny? This isn't funny!"

"You told her she'd be in trouble?"

"Yeah, so?"

"And Sophia's how old?"

"Thirteen." He grins at me and says nothing. I look at him. "What?" I ask. "Why are you looking at me like that?"

"You do realize, Irene, that your daughter is now at an age where the thought of getting into trouble is a motivation rather than a deterrent?"

I pull into the police station parking lot, feeling a little more hopeful. He's right. Again. Nestor is sensible. Sophia *wants* to upset me.

"Let's check Ricky's first," I say.

"Okay," says Nestor. "Probably a good idea. You don't need anything with the police right now."

I turn out of the lot, and almost crash into an oncoming car. Nestor offers to drive. "I remember the way," he says. "Let me help."

An hour later, as Nestor drives through Miami Beach, my cell rings. Not Mom. Not Sophia. Not David's cell. I answer. "Hello?"

The woman speaks with a distinct Spanish accent. "Miss Gallagher? This is Violeta Gotay. I have your daughter here in my living room, and I wanted you to know she's fine. I had a girl like this myself once, and I know you must have been worried sick. So no need to worry, Mami, she's fine."

"Who is this?"

"I'm Ricky Biscayne's publicist's mother, and your daughter just had dinner with my family and now she's ready for you to come get her."

Thank God. She's okay. But, Ricky's publicist? Wait. That can't be good. "Violeta, may I talk to her please?"

om, Dad, I have to go back to work to take care of some forms I forgot about," I say. My mother and father sit at the little homemade bar on the back patio, with their friends and my grandparents, sipping cognac and talking about—what else?—the good old days in Cuba. It's a lie I'm telling them. My mother seems to suspect it, and narrows her eyes at me.

"Work, work, work," my father says to his friends, in Spanish. He's been drinking and is unusually loud. "These girls have been ruined by America. They work like men."

I wave to Jasminka and Sophia, who are looking through *Living in Cuba*, a gorgeous coffee-table photo book in the living room, and duck down the hall. I lock myself in my bedroom and open the closet door. What to wear to Matthew's? It's evening, but Matthew isn't exactly the smoking-jacket, dress-for-success type. I'm sick of dressing up all the time, but I want to look good. I want to make a good impression. I wish I could take a shower without raising my father's suspicions. You know, I'm thinking it's finally time to move out of here. Soon.

I toss skirts, pants, and tops onto the bed, and dig through my dresser for more. The virgin watches me with her porcelain eyes. She looks amused. "What?" I ask her. "I should have known Ricky was a liar? How could I have known that? I'm sorry I asked to meet him. You happy now? Be careful what you wish for. I know, I know."

I turn to the clothes. I choose a hippie-girl outfit, an Anna Sui mesh top, white, that gathers in the front like a peasant blouse, and a moss-green tiered skirt, with a white eyelet slip underneath, slightly longer than the skirt. I finish the outfit off with ballet flats, Marc Jacobs, in blue. I'm getting more experimental with color. Either that, or I'm getting too lazy to try to match everything all the time. I put the most thought into my underwear, because I want to be prepared for Matthew to *see* my underwear. I pick a slightly padded Body by Victoria bra from Victoria's Secret—far and away the best bra ever made—and matching thong panties. Men like thongs. I probably shouldn't think like this. I should learn from my mistakes and take this slowly. But now that I know he's the voice and the talent behind the songs that have changed my life, the songs that have driven me to tears and laughter, I am fully prepared to give myself to him. He is the most attractive man on earth.

I sneak out of the house, and drive to Miami Beach listening to Matthew's songs, and I feel dizzy with excitement. Matthew is the talent, and Matthew is available. He's humble, and funny. It makes so much sense. Now that I think about it, Ricky's personality never seemed to match the songs. Matthew *is* the songs.

I park along the street, even though it's permit-only, and hope I don't get a ticket. I hurry up the stairs to Matthew's front door, and knock. I hear music coming from inside, something that sounds African, like drums and singing. I hear stumbling, and then the door opens. Matthew smiles at me. He's wearing baggy cargo shorts again, this time with a faded green T-shirt that says YOU BET YOUR ASS I LOVE BLUEGRASS, with a picture of a banjo on it.

"Hi!" he says. He stands out of the way for me to come in.

"We're both wearing green," I say. It's not a smart thing to say. But it's what comes out.

"Indeed," says Matthew.

The apartment looks significantly better than it did the last time I was here, like Matthew has straightened up the mess a little bit. Two unopened beers, Red Stripe brand, sit on the coffee table next to a large blue plastic bowl full of popcorn. We exchange the usual small talk, about work, the weather, the state of the apartment, how pretty he thinks I look, and then we sit on the sofa. I'm surprised he finds me attractive.

"So," he says as he lowers the music on the stereo. "We've got some choices for the movie. I got *Ocean's Twelve*, still haven't watched it, but I don't think I want to compete with Brad Pitt and George Clooney tonight. There's *Spanglish*, but I watched it already and, trust me, you don't need to watch that imperialist, colonialist bit of stereotyped crap, seriously, all about the noble poor Latina and the benevolent rich white guy. Total shit. And I'm, like, an Adam Sandler and James Brooks *freak*. But whatever. They blew it with this one. Okay. What else? I got *In the Bedroom* because I thought it was porn, but it ended up being something with Sissy Spacek."

"Grim," I say.

"Indeed. No one wants a porn with Sissy Spacek."

"Any other choices?"

"Yeah. *Hero*. That's it, though."

"That's good."

Matthew gets up and I watch him walk across the room. Again I am struck by his comfort in his own body. His legs are strong from riding his bike so much, and I want to touch the curly reddish hair on them. He's very manly, in a way that I don't see much in Miami. He looks like he could climb a mountain, and pitch a tent.

"What?" Matthew notices me staring at him. "Do I have something stuck to my ass?"

"No. You have a cute ass, actually."

"Really?"

"Yeah."

He grins and puts the DVD into the machine, turns off the overhead light, switches on a lamp on the desk in the corner, and joins me on the sofa again.

"Funny, I think the same of yours," he says. I nibble absently at the popcorn as he comes to the coffee table, pops the tops of the beer bottles, and hands one to me. "Cheers," he says. "To the truth."

"To the truth," I say.

"I hear it sets you free."

"Yeah, so I've heard."

He sits back, comfortable in his skin, and pulls the popcorn onto his lap. "Come here," he says.

"Where? I'm right here."

"No. Closer. Share this with me."

I scoot closer, and feel the warmth of him from inches away. He takes the remote and flips past the credits. I try to watch the movie as it begins, but I can't stop feeling drawn to him. I can hardly breathe. The realization that I am next to the talent behind my life's obsession is stronger now than it was even with Ricky, because the truth is here. I believe in Matthew. With Ricky, something was always a little off.

"What about that massage you promised me?" I ask.

Matthew sets the popcorn on the table again, and his beer, and smiles at me. "Thought you'd never ask."

I chug my beer, set the bottle down, and turn my back to Matthew. As before, he begins to rub my neck and shoulders, with warm, strong fingers that seem to know exactly where and how I need to be touched. It feels so good I close my eyes and pray this will never end. Matthew moves closer to me and presses his body into mine as he rubs and kneads all the tension out of my body. I feel his lips on the back of my neck, small, tender kisses.

"You smell so good," he says in that voice. That amazing, sexy voice. That beautiful voice. I can't speak. He kisses me again, and his hands continue on my back, and then slowly, gently, his hands slide under my shirt and around my sides. He holds me around the waist, my back to his chest. He kisses my ear, tenderly, gently, and I feel his breath. Goose bumps everywhere. "I love your smell," he says.

"I'm so sorry," I say. I fall against him, limp, relaxed.

"For what?"

"The whole thing with Ricky."

"Let's not talk about him," says Matthew. "Let's just be together now."

I arch my neck and turn my head to see his face. "Okay," I say. I kiss his mouth, softly, gently, a healing kiss. I feel a heat inside me I've never felt before, a connection that I can only describe as being of the soul. I have wanted men in the past, but never like this, never where our souls collided and the sparks rained down over our bodies. Electricity in every pore.

I turn to face him, and we kiss, a long, passionate, searching kiss where we explore, taste, nibble, and press. Over and over. Matthew's kisses are not the trigger-fast, aggressive kisses Ricky gave me. They are tender, filled with humor and kindness, and reverence. That's what it is. He seems to feel a respect and reverence for me that were missing totally in my lovemaking with Ricky.

"You are so beautiful," he tells me. His hands roam, gently, barely touching the skin of my hands, my arms, my shoulders, neck. In the background, the movie plays. Now my hands search along his body, testing, touching, holding. I want to own him. I want so much to be a part of this man. I want to eat him. I want to be consumed by him. I wish us to both be one body.

"Do you want to take this to the bedroom?" he asks.

"Is Sissy Spacek in there?"

"I think she's gone now."

"Okay."

Matthew twines my hand in his, and I follow him to his bedroom. It is simple, and very clean compared to the living room, uncluttered, just a bed with a modern black metal frame, a dresser, and a chair. The bed is made, with gray sheets only. He takes my hands, pulls me in, and kisses me, standing up. I feel a jolt in my center, and it's as if our life forces meet between us, magnets pulling us together. We tumble to the bed in a fit of kisses. The sheets are very soft, the kind of sheets that feel like T-shirts, jersey sheets.

I lie on one of my arms, on my side, and Matthew does the same, facing me, and we kiss. With his top arm he pulls me in, close to his body, and for a moment we simply hold each other. I feel his heart beating through his chest. My arm is getting numb. I roll over and straddle him. He grins up at me with a hint of surprise.

"You're a little bit wild, eh?" he asks.

"Don't move," I say. I lean down and brush my lips against his. I feel his hands pull me closer, and he kisses me passionately, and for a long time. My right hand slides down his chest to his belly, and lower. He's hard, and thick. Thick is good. A good size, very good.

"Oh, God," he says, pushing his hips up toward my hand as I squeeze. I look into his eyes and see a smile there. There is none of the distance and aggression I felt with other men. Matthew is present, as a person, and the Matthew in this moment is no different from the Matthew at other times. He's just Matthew, plain and simple—and after so many complications, plain and simple is good.

I release my grip and lower myself to sit on him, both of us still fully clothed. I smile back at him as I remove my white mesh top and my bra. He looks at me. "Wow," he says. "You're amazing."

I blush. Matthew sits up slightly and wriggles out of his T-shirt. He, too, is amazing. I love the way he looks, smells, is. He is so here, so open, so present with me, it's like I'm with a friend. I don't think that in my limited experience with men I was ever with one where it didn't feel like I was performing, or where there wasn't some kind of distance or nastiness between us.

I lie on him again, and feel the hairs of his chest against my breasts. His warmth. I kiss him, and he kisses back. He ducks his head and kisses my breasts, tracing my nipples with his tongue, then taking them into his mouth. God, it's divine.

Matthew lifts me up and rolls me over so that I am now on the bottom, and he continues to kiss my breasts, and then lower, and lower. He gets to my skirt and gently slides it off me. Then the slip. Then my thong. He kisses my hip bones, my belly button, my belly, lower, and lower. My legs part, and my back arches, all against my will. I am help-less under his touch. And then, there. He is kissing me there, softly, expertly, gently, as if he knows exactly what I need. And then his fin-gers enter me, and I feel a sensation I have never, in my life, experi-enced. It's almost as if I have to pee, but I don't. I gasp. His tongue to my clitoris, his fingers from one hand inside, the fingers from the other hand on my breast. Again, an overwhelming sensation from deep inside me, pleasurable beyond belief. I have never felt this be-fore. Ever.

"What are you doing?" I ask, rising onto my elbows.

"G-spot," he says with a glistening grin. "Did I get it?"

I flop back down on the bed, weak and squirming in his clutches, filled with a pleasure and love I did not know was possible.

"Yes!" I cry. I have found the perfect man. "Yes! Yes! Yes!"

monday, july 29

I sit at my my desk, listening to the drum roll of steady rain out-side. The plan is in motion. The plans. In my grape-colored David Meister sundress from Neiman Marcus. I look so sweet, too. In my sundress, which I bought only because Jasminka looked so cute in hers. You would never suspect a woman in a sundress of doing something as evil as I'm about to do to Ricky.

It isn't wrong, is it? To frame a man? To frame a man in a dress like this, a dress that makes you want to skip along the hillsides singing to the sheep? Still. What is wrong is that he's harmed people. Karma. That's what I say. I am no longer the office slut. I am the of-fice equalizer.

I sit up straight, do my best to seem like an ignorant and happy em-ployee of Ricky Biscayne Entertainment. I should add "actress" to my list of talents. Remember how I used to say I'd have a life one of these days? Something with meaning? Well, I think I may have found it. My life is all about setting the record straight now. All about exposing liars and cheats. I guess it's all about revenge, too, on Ricky, but that's not exactly noble so we don't have to discuss it. I pick up the phone and call the Red Cross public relations office, offering up Ricky as a spokesperson if they are interested. Phase one.

After fifteen minutes of jolly discussion of Ricky's rising-star status, the agency, or the people who work there, think me a genius. An agency can't think. But I can. And have. I arrange for Ricky do a public service announcement in which he fearlessly agrees to have his blood drawn for donation to the needy. We agree that it will motivate the notoriously squeamish population of Miami and Latinos around the nation to do likewise. I ask them to send me a formal letter of request so Ricky can see that this very good idea came from them. They are flattered to take credit for my idea.

An hour later, the letter from the Red Cross arrives by messenger, and I take it into the studio to show Ricky and ask his opinion. Ricky is listening to a song that I now know is Matthew's composition, sung by Matthew. A choreographer shows Ricky some new shimmies for the guitar flutter parts. Ricky moves beautifully as always, but his eyes are bloodshot and sunken; he looks like he's spent the last few nights awake. Knowing that Ricky is a disgusting control freak who likes to do things his own way, I pretend to think it might not be a great idea to do the Red Cross thing. I approach it the same way people reason with toddlers and teenagers.

"I hate getting my blood drawn," I say. "I mean, it's a weird thing to do. Well, not that weird. I mean, some big stars have done it before. The good news is they only ask people who are big mainstream stars, so that means we're getting you there! And, you know, you wouldn't want to do it if, like, you had something you didn't want people to see in your blood. Not that I'm saying you do."

Ricky adjusts his sweatpants, grins at me like he thinks he's gonna get nookie again. Poor bastard. He sips a bottle of water and shakes his head.

"You're wrong, Milan," he says. "I think it's a good idea, actually. There are lots of people who need blood, and it's a way to get my name out. I just, you know, I might have alcohol or something in there."

"Think about it, Ricky. They're not screening you." I do my best to look doubtful and afraid.

"I don't need to think," he says. "Sign me up."

I go back to my office and call the Red Cross. I say, "There's just one request. Ricky wants to have a vial or two of his blood saved for himself. I don't know why. I think it's like that thing Angelina Jolie did, where he wants to put it on a necklace or something. And he doesn't want the rest really used for anything, I'm sure you understand we'd like this to be discreet. He, just between us, he takes some growth hormones for his muscles. That's all. But he doesn't really want, you know, the public and everything."

Amazingly, they agree.

I see motion out of the corner of my eye, look up, and see Ricky walking into the office. He shuts the door. Uh-oh.

"What's up, Ricky? You sound amazing on that new track."

"Yeah, huh?"

"Uhm-hmm."

He takes one of my hands and looks me straight in the eye. "I have to ask you something, Milan."

"Uh, I'm on my period."

He ignores my comment. "Do you know where my wife is?"

My heart knocks to get out of my chest and run the hell out of the room. Lie. Lie to the bastard. Like I have never lied before. "Jasminka?" I ask. Stalling for time. He stares at me with wet, drugged eyes. Cold. I say, "Sorry. I have no idea."

Ricky takes my hand to his lips and plants small kisses across my knuckles. He licks my skin lightly. "*Déjame mamarte la chocha, mamita.*"

"Uh, Ricky, I can't. Not right now. I'm really busy."

He takes one of my fingers into his mouth and sucks it. I feel the shock through my entire body. But instead of a shock of lust, like before, it's a shock of disgust. I want him gone, okay?

"I hear you're seeing Matthew," he says, moving from the desk to the floor between me and the desk. He kneels down in front of me and pushes my knees apart, placing his hands on my thighs.

"We've gone out a couple of times," I say. "I like him." I try to push away from him, but he holds me down and keeps me pinned to the chair.

"I don't mind my employees messing around," he says, moving his fingers closer to the apex of my legs. "As long as it's with me. You are mine. Not his. Remember that, Milan."

"Ricky, don't," I say.

"What, baby? What's wrong? Don't want Matthew to see us?"

"No," I stammer. "Yes. I mean, I don't want to do this anymore."

"Or maybe," says Ricky as he slithers up between my legs and plants a light kiss on my cheek. He grabs my crotch, hard. "You know where Jasminka is?"

I try to push Ricky off, but he persists, forcing a kiss on my lips.

"What are you doing?" I squirm away. His eyes are hollow. Frozen. Why didn't I notice this before?

"Most women would die to be in your shoes right now," he says.

"I know," I say. Don't reveal too much, not yet, not before the plan is in motion. At that moment, I hear a light knock on her door. I look up, past Ricky between my legs, and see Matthew standing in the door to the office with take-out menus.

"Matthew," I cry, as Ricky's mouth closes over mine.

Matthew says nothing, just stares with pain in his eyes. He turns, and leaves.

"No!" I scream. I kick Ricky off me. "Matthew!"

I push past Ricky and chase after Matthew, but he's nowhere to be found. The front door to the offices is open. He's run into the rain.

Ricky strolls past as if nothing has happened.

"So," he says. "Now you know how it feels to lose someone you love. If you hear from Jasminka, you know, let me know."

I flee to my office, lock the door, and call Matthew's cell phone. No answer. I see the filing cabinets. I raid them, looking for contracts. I find them.

I read for two hours, and I cannot believe what I'm seeing. Ricky has robbed Matthew savagely, for years.

Then I call him again, and speak to his machine.

"Matthew. It wasn't what you thought. I'm coming over," I say, tears choking my voice. "And I'm bringing your contracts. We're calling a lawyer."

Nestor pops the top on the can of food for Chester, washes his hands, and retrieves his own microwave dinner—Annie's Organic—from the white radioactive box on which he has come to rely too much for sustenance.

He sits on his favorite chair and rereads the acceptance letter to the law school at Florida International University. They are willing to accept almost all of his credits from CUNY, and within the year he'll have his law degree. He isn't cut out for fighting fires, he decides. Not the kind that you normally think of. He is meant for fighting of a different nature.

He picks the phone up from the coffee table and dials Irene's lawyer, Sy Berman, just to check in. Irene is so busy trying to keep her daughter at home and away from trouble, and trying to get her mom on antidepressants, that the last thing on her mind is this lawsuit. It actually seems like Irene is sick of fighting, sick of the press, and doesn't want to deal with it anymore. The last time he talked to her, on the phone earlier today, she sounded resigned to finding work as a waitress and "lying low for a while." That is unacceptable. Irene is smart, capable, and one of the best firefighters South Florida has ever seen, in Nestor's opinion. And Nestor isn't going to let her go down without a fight.

The lawyer assures Nestor he is doing all that he can, but says that with the negative press about Irene and Ricky Biscayne it is going to be very difficult to find a jury willing to take her side. Nestor tells the lawyer to call a woman named Milan Gotay, who might have some information that will change his mind about the case. "Just a hunch," he says. The lawyer thanks Nestor and says he'll call him later.

Nestor flips on the television, to try to distract himself from the ghosts. They don't come as often anymore, but they still come. He settles on an entertainment talk show, something cheesy and glossy, colorful and cheerful enough to take his mind off his own life for a minute.

On the screen, a tearful Jill Sanchez sits next to Oprah Winfrey, talking about how Jack Ingroff has fallen in love with someone else and left her. "I did everything for him," weeps the actress and singer. "I cooked, I cleaned. I became a real homebody. But I guess that wasn't what he was looking for. I guess I'm just, deep down inside, too traditional for him. I still love him and I always will." Jill wears a high turtleneck dress like a schoolteacher from an old Western movie. Oprah grabs her hand, and then the camera goes to the audience. Women openly weep in sympathy with Jill Sanchez, as a sad bolero song plays in the background.

"Ugh," says Nestor, flipping to dirt-bike racing on ESPN. He finds Jill Sanchez and her vanity disturbing. He doesn't understand why anyone finds that woman attractive.

Compared to the self-sacrifice and dedication to family of a woman like Irene, or to the artistic vision of a woman like his deceased wife, the public prattling of Jill Sanchez, a multimillionaire with no talent that he can see, comes up woefully short.

The Third
Trimester

monday, august 5

ang, bang, bang. Come on, Matthew. Open the door. I know he's home. I've been knocking for six minutes. I'm sure he's there. His bike is locked up downstairs and I hear music playing beyond the door. I have with me a collection of the crappy contracts Ricky somehow managed to talk Matthew into signing, and I need to talk to him. I need to explain it all to him, and the kiss with Ricky, how he forced it on me. I have to talk to him, because I think I'm in love with him.

I knock again. And again. Finally, I scream, "Open the door, Matthew! It's me, Milan. I have to talk to you!"

He finally gives in. "What," he says, voice flat, through the tiniest crack in the door. He looks messy, like he's been sleeping. Like he needs a shower. I remember the good old days when I used to look like that.

"It wasn't what it looked like, Matthew," I say. "With Ricky."

He nods solemnly, sarcastically. "Right. Ricky, between your legs, with his tongue in your mouth. Easily misunderstood." He blows his nose.

"He forced himself on me, Matthew."

Matthew snorts a laugh. "Please don't come here anymore," he says. "I don't need this. I truly don't."

"I want you to know I'm taking your contracts to a lawyer, and they'll find out if they're legal," I say.

"What?" He opens the door a little wider and stares at me in horror. "Why would you do that? To put a nail in the coffin, Milan? Are you insane?"

"Because he should pay you what you're worth."

"I don't *want* his money."

"And people need to know how talented you are."

"So I can get a record deal and then you'll have sex with me, too? Oh, wait. You *do* fuck me. Anyone else I should add to that list?"

"That's not fair," I say. "What happened with us was magical."

Matthew's face screws up in torture. "Jesus, Milan. I never wanted to share a hole with that guy."

He slams the door, and I try to hold back the tears. A hole? Ouch. That hurts. I don't like to think of myself as a hole. A 'ho maybe, but not a hole. I knock again, and again. No answer. I resort to kicking the door. He finally opens it.

"Go away," he says. "You don't want to wear your hand out for when you give Ricky a hand job later."

"Stop it! You don't have to be so mean!"

"Is that why you came here? To tell me how mean I am? That's ironic, don't you think?"

"Look," I say. "I know it looked bad. I don't blame you. But I love you, Matthew, and I'm not having sex with Ricky. He was trying to scare me."

Matthew laughs again. "I missed 'making out with a superstud' under 'scare' in the dictionary."

"I don't think of him like that."

"Yeah, right."

"I used to. But not anymore."

"You know, ever since college, Ricky has taken everything from me," says Matthew. His voice is almost too controlled. It scares me.

"He didn't take me," I say. "I'm yours if you want me."

"Everything I've worked for or cared about, he took. And now you."

"No. Matthew. It's not like that."

"Then quit. Prove it. Get another gig."

"I can't."

"Of course not."

"Not now. I can't quit for a little while."

"Leave," says Matthew.

"You don't have to talk to me ever again, Matthew, but just do me a favor. Come to the opening of Club G, so you can see why I'm still working for Ricky. I have a plan. Please."

"What?"

I start to cry. I can't believe this is happening. I hate Ricky right now. I really do. "Just be there. Then you'll know what I'm all about, okay? Please?"

"See you at the office," Matthew says. He looks me in the eye for a quick moment. I think it he's surprised to see me crying. "Bye, Milan," he says. "I'm sorry it turned out this way." He shuts, but does not slam, the door.

friday, august 9

Wearing a baggy diamond-studded paperboy cap and sunglasses with shiny peach satin short shorts, white patent leather thigh-high boots, and a sheer silvery top with a Barely There bra, Jill leans back on one of the elegant, modern chaise longues at the sleek club Rain, surrounded by an army of handlers, bodyguards, and cute but not-too-cute female actresses she's hired to play her friends for the evening. She used to have friends. She just doesn't know their phone numbers anymore.

She needs to get out and mingle with the masses to keep up appearances, and what better place? Once, she spotted Jose Canseco here. She doesn't care what the press say about him, that man is irresistible. Besides, Jill Sanchez does not see herself, Jill Sanchez, as the kind of woman who gets pushed around by men. At least not unless she wants to.

She sips a bottle of water and gloats for a moment in the looks of pity and the smiles she gets from the people who pass by. They feel sorry for her, and she is aiming to give the impression that in spite of her horrific heartbreak, she is forcing herself to get out with friends and have a good time. People seem to *feel* for her. Perfect. Her idea to play the poor little abandoned woman has been a resounding success. All the major gossip magazines are piled in the center of the table, each with some sort of story about how heartbroken she is. The stories all say that she has learned a lesson about love, and quote her as saying she will not let Jack's cruelty ruin her, but neither will she ever rush into love again.

At the bar, a young Puerto Rican woman named Lisette is celebrating her twenty-first birthday with a group of friends. She has just lost twenty pounds and is happily wearing a size-eight little black dress from Caché. She feels amazingly beautiful and happy. When the group of young women look up from their flirtinis and see none other than Jill Sanchez among the clubgoers, they can't believe their luck. The birthday girl, Lisette, is a huge Jill Sanchez fan. Her friends always complain that she *dresses* like Jill Sanchez, sings along to her *songs,* and someday hopes to be as successful in acting and music as Jill Sanchez. She is even wearing Jill Sanchez perfume and earrings right now!

With her friends encouraging her, the shy young woman gets up and cautiously approaches Jill and her group of friends. The young woman's sister, a social worker in Hialeah, has told her that Jill Sanchez is very important to the young women in the poor, underserved communities where she works, because Jill Sanchez is the only Latina they have to look up to sometimes. The young woman has read about Jill's recent heartbreak over Jack Ingroff, and she thinks Jill

Sanchez needs cheering up and would like to hear this kind of news. She decides this is an opportunity not to be passed up.

The young woman manages to slip past Jill's bodyguards, who are momentarily distracted by the appearance of Christina Milian on the other side of the room. Jill Sanchez would not be pleased to know that La Milian is here, usurping her visibility. The bodyguards are trying to figure out a way to keep Jill from spotting Christina because they knew that once she does, they'll have to work overtime harassing the younger star out of the room.

"Excuse me," says the young woman celebrating her birthday as she taps Jill on the arm. Lisette can't believe how good Jill Sanchez smells. She is so beautiful, too, more beautiful than she'd imagined, and tiny. In photos, Jill looks like she is the same size as many other women, but now that Lisette sees her in person, she thinks Jill is a miniature version of herself, a tight-bodied, unreal creature who almost reminds her of a gazelle.

ill turns her head slowly toward the annoying pecking on her arm, and catches sight of a fat girl in a frumpy black frock, with cheeks red from drinking too much or exercising too little. What's up with her hair? And hasn't she heard of tweezers?

"What do you want?" Jill snaps. "I don't sign autographs at clubs."

"Gosh," says Lisette. "Miss Sanchez, I just wanted to tell you how much you mean to me, and to my community. I'm, like, so nervous! You—"

"Bruno?" Jill tugs on her bodyguard's jacket. "What are you doing?" She points a gleaming fingernail at the interloper.

Lisette stares up at Bruno, all six-foot-six of him, with a look of surprise.

"Sorry, miss," says Bruno. "You have to go."

"But I was just telling Jill how important my sister thinks she is to young girls, especially young Puerto Rican girls like me . . ."

Bruno lifts Lisette off the floor and begins to walk across the room with her. "Jill," calls Lisette. "I only wanted to talk to you to thank you!"

"Please," says Jill Sanchez with amusement as she watches the girl's skirt rise. "Can't you see I'm busy, ho?"

Bruno dumps Lisette in front of her group of friends with a warning. "If you come near her again, I'll knock your fucking teeth out."

Bruno returns, saying that the fan has wished her well with her heartbreak.

"They're such suckers," Jill says to Bruno. "It's almost funny. But you know what? As long as they're talking about me, I'm happy."

Jill's manager asks her if she is ready for next week. "It's going to be a hell of a week. Your movie hits, the record hits, and what was the other thing?"

"Club G," she says. "We better get some chaise longues like this in there. Make sure Geneva knows I want chaise longues."

"Right. Miami's newest hotspot."

"Did you hear me?" she snaps.

"About what?"

"Chaise longues."

"Right. Okay. Chaise longues."

"I think that's going to be the right time and place to let everyone start to think that there might be something new between me and Ricky Biscayne," she says.

"Now, Jill, you know you can't just go around making up huge lies. Little ones are okay. But that?"

Jill smiles. "Who said it's a lie?"

"Get *out*," says her manager. "You and Ricky? Again?"

Jill pretends to be holding a key, which she uses to lock her lips, both sets. "If you want to know the real deal, you'll have to be at the grand opening of Club G. Ricky and I will be there, and who knows? We might have some big news for everybody."

Then, to keep her management on their toes, and to foment the media speculation that she might be with child (she isn't, but God knows her handlers like to gossip about her with reporters behind her back), Jill giggles and places her perfectly manicured hands over her flat slab of lower belly, implying a pregnancy that she is nowhere near. In truth, she is having her period and stuffed with a deodorant tampon.

"Get *out*," says her manager.

Jill giggles with unbridled aggression. "You know, I've always wanted babies. I just *love* love," she says with fast-blinking eyes. "Don't you?"

saturday, august 10

These people look like they want to kill me right here in the middle of Starbucks, which, given my addictions, would be not only the perfect place to die but the perfect place to bury me. All except the girl, Sophia, the only one of the bunch whose arms aren't crossed over her body. She is nice, or at least she smiles. But her mom and the mom's really hot-looking friend sit with their arms crossed, scowling at me over their frozen lattes. They remind me of those old photos of Native American leaders at "treaty" signings with the men who had come to take their land. They glower that deeply.

"I really *am* on your side," I repeat. I've worn jeans and a T-shirt, with jogging shoes. My mom smiled when she saw me leave the house like this, and I think part of her was relieved that I feel comfortable with myself again. But these people hate me.

"Talk," says the man, still scowling. "You got us here, now tell us what it is you want."

Well, no. I can't do that. What I want is for Matthew to love me again. To be my boyfriend. To marry me someday. To bear my children. Oh, wait. Oops.

"Look," I say. "I know I'm the one that messed things up for you. I honestly didn't know anything. I was new at the job, and I was starstruck by my boss." It sounds lame coming out of my mouth.

Irene looks out the window and says nothing. She's so pretty, even without makeup, in simple jeans. She looks like one of those statuesque women athletes.

"Mom, she wants to help us," says Sophia, who is also strong as an athlete and has a pretty face. The girl is obviously Ricky's with that wavy dark hair and those beautiful light brown eyes. She reminds me of the actress Sonia Braga, but very much younger. "Give her a chance?"

Irene returns her gaze to her daughter, a tired, worn-out look on her face. She sighs. "If I *do* give Milan a chance, it's only because you asked me to."

Sophia smiles at her mother. "Good," she says.

Now Irene looks at me. Same tired expression. I feel bad for her. "How exactly do you plan to help us, Miss Gotay?"

I explain to her that we've gotten a couple of vials of Ricky's dragon blood, and that I've gotten him to sign some papers allowing a laboratory to do a full DNA workup on it. I don't mention he was high at the time. "Now all we have to do is get Sophia there and have them draw some blood and see if they match."

"They'll match," says Irene.

"I don't doubt that," I tell her. "They could be twins."

"I need you to sign the forms, Mom," says Sophia. "I'd have gone by now, but they won't let minors have tests like that without parental consent."

"Why do you even want to prove you're related to him?" asks Irene. "Hasn't he shown you yet how irresponsible he is, Sophia?" Good point.

"But he's my dad, Mom. Can't you understand that?" Another good point.

"Can I say something?" I ask.

Irene looks at me with hatred. Why? What did I ever do to her? Oh, wait. That's right. I ruined her life.

"I think there's a benefit to Sophia getting the test. For one, it will settle things for her in her own heart and mind about who her dad is.

Two, it will mean Ricky will have to pay you guys something in child support."

"I don't want his filthy money. I have a job."

Sophia gapes at her mother. "*Child* support. Not *mom* support. It's not for you!" she says. And yet another good point from the younger generation. "It's for me! And maybe I'd like some new clothes, or money for college! I think I deserve that, Mom!"

I interrupt. "But there's another thing. I already talked to your lawyer about this."

"You talked to my lawyer?"

"Yes. He called me. Your man here told him to."

Irene glares at the man.

"What I'm getting at," I continue, "is that the lawyer said that if you can show the public that you guys were telling the truth about Ricky, then the reporters and everybody are going to be forced to take another look at your claims against the fire department."

Irene shrugs. "Look, I don't care about that anymore, either."

The man finally speaks. "It's actually a pretty good plan," he says. He looks at Irene with a gentle respect and love that I envy. I wish a man looked at me like that. What would that be like? I've never known a man like that.

"Maybe it's a good plan," says Irene. "If I cared. But I don't. I really don't, Nestor. I'm so sick of all this."

Sophia looks pained. "Mom! Don't say that!"

I take a risk and touch Irene's hand. "Irene. I don't know you. I just met you. But I can tell you one thing. You *do* care. You care about your career and your job. You care about your child. You deserve to win."

"Milan, right?" says the man. "What's in it for you? Why are you doing this?"

I blush. I decide I've lied enough. "I'd like to say it's all just professional," I say. "That I'm tired of doing the wrong things, that I don't care if I lose my job because I know that in the end it will be worth it for the truth to be out. But . . ." I pause. "It's personal. For me, it's very personal. I have some very good reasons to dislike Ricky Biscayne. Reasons of my own."

The man grins. "You too?" he asks.

Irene looks at me like she's seeing me for the first time. She smiles and I can see that she actually has a sense of humor. That's good. "That's sort of vindictive, isn't it?"

"Yes," I say.

"But it should make us listen to you more," says Sophia. To her mother she adds, "See? I told you."

Irene shrugs. "I don't know," she says. "I'm sick of fighting. I just want to move away, where no one knows me, and rest."

I say, "You don't have to fight anymore. I'll do the fighting for you now. I'm a very good publicist." And then I say something that makes no sense to anyone who has ever really *known* a publicist: "Trust me." And then, because I have a meeting, I excuse myself and walk away.

So this is Club G, eh? Pretty snazzy. I'm sitting with Geneva, my apparently genius club-owner sister, at the bar, as she downs Fiji water and checks her BlackBerry. The dark red wooden bar has intricate hennaesque scrawling across it in dark brown, beneath a layer of shiny lacquer. The bar is well designed. The rest of the club is draped on every surface with velvets and silks, with the aura of a decadent, women-friendly harem. Even the support columns in the club have been sculpted to resemble, if you look hard enough, a man's most private appendage. Racy. I don't think Dad would like this place. Mom, though? Yeah, well, we know all about *her*.

Geneva, as we know, is as bold and elegant as her club, with her hair up in a high, *I Dream of Jeannie* ponytail, a billowy bohemian blouse, and jeans. My sister can work some jeans, man. She looks better in jeans than most people look in the finest of couture. I used to hate her for all that, but now I'm realizing that I don't have to be like her to be attractive. Ricky found me attractive, I think. Maybe not. But Matthew does. Or at least he used to before I fucked it up.

It is the middle of the day. We sip herbal iced tea and wait for a meeting with a very famous person who I have unfavorable feelings for at the moment. We don't have to wait long. Geneva grabs my arm and says, "Look what the cat dragged in."

I look up and see Jill Sanchez and her army of handlers march in the front door. The superstar wears low-rise dark blue jeans with a transparent tank top and short mink minijacket. She can work jeans even better than Geneva, no easy feat.

"God, she's stunning," I say. "It's not fair."

"Until you talk to her for five minutes," whispers Geneva.

I blink innocently and say, "Aw, come on. She can't be that bad. I've read that she's really a nice person."

Geneva looks at me like I've suggested she eat the contents of a used airline sick bag. I smile and punch her playfully on the arm. "Gotcha."

Jill waits for her bodyguards to pull out a seat at one of the tables before she sits down. Another assistant removes and begins to brush her coat like a pet groomer, while yet another places a notebook and diamond-encrusted pen on the table in front of her. Then, Jill's manager approaches Geneva and me.

"Miss Sanchez would like me to tell you she is ready to take the meeting."

Uh, hello? I can *see* her? I could blow real hard and move her hair? The star is not ten feet away, yet she sends her errand boy to share this news with Geneva? How pompous! Geneva looks at her watch. Jill is ten minutes early. "We're still waiting on Ricky Biscayne," she says, standing. "I'll just tell her it'll be another couple of minutes."

"No," says the manager, putting up his hand to stop Geneva. "*You* are not to approach Miss Sanchez until it's time for the meeting, per her request."

Excuse me? This isn't Geneva's club anymore? This is Jill's club now, is that it? It's so weird it's funny. I want to laugh. I do. I laugh, and listen as the manager says, "She values her privacy and needs this time to meditate and gather her thoughts."

The manager walks away and Geneva raises her eyebrows in triumph at me, as if this proves that Jill Sanchez is a lunatic nightmare, which I already sort of knew.

"Oh my God," I say under my breath. "That's unbelievable."

Geneva pretends to drink her tea, but mumbles to me, "Gather her thoughts. Yeah, right. She hasn't had an original thought in her entire life!"

Another handler scurries over to Jill Sanchez and hands her a white paper bag that appears to be from a deli. She wants for an assistant to remove a bundle wrapped in aluminum foil. The assistant unwraps it, and places what appears to be a sandwich on the table. Everyone in Jill's camp stands back, waiting to see what she will do. My guess? She'll . . . eat it?

Nope. My guess is wrong. She picks up the sandwich and sniffs it. She makes a face that makes me think the sandwich is made of pure excrement.

"Hey," Jill calls to her manager. "This smells like *crica*."

Whoa! I grab Geneva's arm and we exchange looks of disbelief. Jill was gathering her thoughts, and this was her thought? For the record, *crica* is a very vulgar slang word for a woman's crotch region.

Jill's manager rushes to her side. "I'm so sorry," he says, trying to rewrap the sandwich to dispose of it. Jill stops him, and lifts the sandwich toward his nose.

"Smell it," she orders. He looks at her in a weirdly neutral way. "It smells like *crica*."

"Yes, I heard you the first time," he says. She shoves the sandwich at him, and, true to his job as her slave, he sniffs.

"*Crica*, right?" asks Jill. Her manager nods solemnly.

"Absolutely," he says. "Absolutely . . . what you said."

Mercifully for him, the front door flies open and in saunters Ricky Biscayne and his by comparison limited entourage of two people— compared to Jill's ten. Jill looks up and calls out, "Hey, Gordito. Come here. This sandwich. What does it smell like to you?" Gordito? Fatty? She has a cute nickname for him?

Ricky joins her at the table and takes a whiff. "Tuna fish?" he asks. "No, *crica*," she says.

"How would you know?" asks Ricky.

"Can we get started now?" calls Geneva. "And can we please stop discussing your sandwich?"

"You," says Jill's manager, pointing at Geneva. "No direct talking until Miss Sanchez says so."

Jill says so two minutes later. She makes all of us sign a statement agreeing to keep everything discussed in the meeting confidential and leak nothing to the press without Jill's permission or face a one-million-dollar fine. Unbelievable. We all gather around Jill's table, the sandwich sitting like a stink bomb in the middle, and begin to discuss the details of tomorrow's opening-night performance, a duet between Jill and Ricky that is a preview of the single Jill's record company has rushed onto *Born Again* in anticipation of her big announcement of a rekindled romance between the two.

Jill does most of the talking. She has designed a set, she says, made to look like a luxurious bedroom. She wants a "Spanish novela" feel, she says, with "big drama and big emotion." Now that Jasminka has officially left Ricky, she says, grabbing "Gordito's" hand, there will be no problem from a publicity point of view in telling the public that the two have reignited their romance. I try to make eye contact with Ricky, but he doesn't look at me. I can't believe I believed all the lies. It makes me sick.

"We put it this way," says Jill, her hands flying across the air as if she were tracing a gigantic headline. "The two biggest crossover stars in American pop culture find solace in each other's arms after being coldly abandoned by the loves of their lives."

Abandoned by Jasminka? That's rich. Hilarious, even. I hate them both so much, but I hide it and say, instead, "Brilliant." No one notices me. Oh well. Jill goes on to say that at the opening, the club will give everyone a free copy of Jill's new CD, and after showing a clip from Jill's new movie, they will talk about the club itself. I look at Geneva and she looks ready to spit.

"After that, we sing our duet," says Jill.

"Are you singing live, or to a click track?" Ricky asks Jill.

"Live, of course," she says.

Ricky fidgets, then leans across the table toward her. "Are you sure that's a good idea, beautiful?"

"Absolutely, Gordito," she says with supreme confidence. Then, Jill turns to me. "You. In the . . . shirt. What's your name?"

"Milan."

"Okay, Marian. Ricky tells me you've handled the publicity end of this for him?" I nod, thinking of how good it would feel to poke her with a pitchfork. "Who all is coming of our delightful friends in the media?"

I rattle off a list of media outlets that includes everyone who is anyone locally, and an impressive representation of national media as well.

"Best of all," I say, "it's going to be aired live on MTV, all over the world."

"Good," says Jill with a feline smile. "Thanks, Milton."

"Milan," I say weakly.

"Whatever," says Jill Sanchez.

monday, august 12

Sophia flinches in the orange fiberglass chair and lets the nurse roll up her sleeve. The chair is like a school desk, only the desk part is really small and meant to hold your arm while the nurse sticks a needle in you. A huge needle! Look at the size of that thing, she thinks, as the nurse swabs her arm with an alcohol pad.

"I don't want to," Sophia whines to her mother, who stands at her side.

"It won't hurt," says the nurse.

"It probably will hurt," says Irene. "But only a little."

Sophia looks away as the nurse stabs her on the inside of her elbow.

"Got a good vein there!" says the nurse. Sophia sneaks a look, and sees bright red blood spurting into a glass vial. It occurs to her that the nurse could tie her down and continue to let the blood flow out until she is dead. The medical establishment has entirely too much control over our lives, she thinks. "Almost done," says the nurse.

"Hurry, hurry," says Sophia, wishing to be anywhere but here.

"There," says the nurse. "All done." Sophia looks at her arm and sees only a white square of gauze, held tightly against her by the nurse's fingers. "That wasn't so bad, was it?"

"I guess not," says Sophia, thinking that it patently *sucked*.

C hester watches Nestor sort through the clothes in his closet, dancing a little and singing "Isn't She Lovely," and feels as sorry for him as is possible for a cat to feel sorry for a human being.

Chester appreciates Nestor. But he doesn't understand him. He loves him the way a kitten loves its mother, with privilege and with confidence that Nestor will always be there to serve him, no matter what, even though Chester has no idea what Nestor is saying most of the time.

The woman and the girl, though? He understands *them* perfectly. They speak cat, for some reason. It also seems that Chester is the only one in the apartment who can see them. Nestor walks right through them sometimes, while Chester watches. This does not seem creepy or odd to the cat, of course, because, as is the case with all cats, Chester has lived in the company of ghosts since he was born.

"Just look at him," says the woman of Nestor. Chester looks. He is able to speak with her in the same way he speaks to other cats—silently, through telepathy.

"Why is he so nervous?" asks the cat.

The woman strokes his shiny black fur. "He's going on a date," she says.

Chester doesn't know what a date is, and says so.

"He's found a woman he really likes," says the woman. "They're having dinner tonight, alone."

"We're glad," says the little girl.

"Why are you glad?" asks Chester. He remembers his days of tom-catting, and the many scars he has suffered to ensure that no other males encroached on his territory or females. "Shouldn't you be spitting mad?"

"Oh, Chester," says the woman. "We have places to go. And we haven't been able to go yet because Nestor has needed us."

"Nestor needed you?" Chester is perplexed. He has not been aware that Nestor needed anyone. Nestor is the one who opens the cans, opens the doors, turns on the lights. Nestor made the decision to neuter him. Nestor seems to be in complete control.

"He hasn't been able to let us go," the little girl says with a pout. "And so we haven't gone."

"Gone?" Chester looks at the girl. She plays happily with a doll on the floor by her mother's feet. "Gone where?"

"Heaven," the girl says simply.

"What's that?" asks Chester.

"It's a wonderful place," says the woman.

"Are there cats there?" asks Chester.

"Lots of cats!" cries the girl.

"More cats than people," says the woman.

Nestor stands in front of the full-length mirror that was left in the apartment by the previous renter. It would never have occurred to him to get a full-length mirror on his own. What a handy thing it is. "Blue?" he asks his reflection, holding up a shirt. "Or red." Chester puzzles over the differences between the shirts; being color-blind, he doesn't understand what all the fuss is about.

"Can we go now, Mommy?" asks the little girl. "Great-grandma's waiting for us. I keep hearing her calling us."

"I know," says the woman. "I'll know in a moment."

Chester and the ghosts watch Nestor dress himself in one of the shirts and a pair of jeans. He begins to whistle, and smiles to himself, and looks for all the world like a happy man. Then, he catches sight of the framed photo on his dresser.

"Oh no," says the woman. "Don't. Don't, Nestor."

Chester recognizes the people in the picture as the woman and the little girl, with Nestor, all of them smiling.

"Let it go, Nestor," says the woman, but it seems that Nestor has not heard her. He picks the photo up, dusts it gently with his finger-tips, and kisses it.

"I love you guys," he says. "I hope you know that, wherever you are."

"We *know*, Daddy," says the little girl, frustrated and bored and ready to leave. She is tired of waiting. Chester knows how she feels. There are nights when Nestor forgets to let him out and he has to watch the bugs and night birds from the apartment window, wedged between the glass and the rattling plastic window shade. It sucks, waiting for Nestor to set you free.

"Let us go," says the woman.

Nestor turns his head to one side, as if he's heard something. He looks around, as if suddenly spooked. People think cats are skittish, but Chester knows that people are worse. Nestor gets creeped out all the time.

That can't be, Nestor says to himself. I'm going crazy.

"Let us go," repeats the woman.

Nestor shakes his head. "Let you go? Baby? Is that *you*?"

The woman says nothing, and holds her finger to her lips to silence the little girl.

"Mmmrrreow," says Chester, out loud, sensing that he can help ease the situation.

"Chester," says Nestor, relieved, as if this explained something. "I forgot you were here."

"Mmmmreeeoow," says Chester.

"You want to go out?" asks Nestor. Chester hops off the bed and rubs Nestor's ankles. "Okay, buddy. I'll let you out. Just one sec."

Chester waits patiently as Nestor takes the photo that has sat on the dresser and, after some hesitation, tucks it neatly into the top drawer.

"Good-bye, my loves," he says to the photo as he shuts the drawer.

He begins to hum the tune to "Isn't She Lovely." Chester is not a fan of the original song. Too heavy on the harmonica. Cats, for what it is worth, detest the harmonica.

The woman stands and takes the girl's hand. The girl smiles and hops up and down with excitement.

"Are we going now, Mama?" she asks. The woman nods and looks at Nestor.

"Good-bye, my love," she whispers with a smile, disappearing into the air as Chester waits for Nestor to open the front door and set him free, too.

I stand next to Milan at kitchen counter in the Gotay house and try to memorize steps for making a Cuban-style *sofrito*. Green peppers, onions, garlic, oil, annatto seed. Once you let food into your life, particularly if you are pregnant, your life changes. I am obsessed with food. Ricky has been calling my cell phone all day, and finally I just turned it off and stuffed it in drawer—a drawer—in the Gotays' small, homey spare bedroom. Milan looks up at me and smiles. Sophia sits at table, flipping through today's *Herald* and talking now and then about how happy she is that her mother is finally seeing a man she likes.

"She always dated these uptight loser cop types," says Sophia. "But now she's got a lawyer."

"You want to try?" Milan asks me, holding out the garlic press and two peeled cloves. I take them.

"Okay," I say. "But I don't want mess it up."

"Woo-hoo!" exclaims Sophia, clapping her hands and slamming the newspaper closed. "No mention of me!"

"That's great," says Milan to Sophia. "I don't usually tell people I'm happy they're not in the paper, either. It's my job to do the opposite." To me she says, "Okay, just stuff them in there, like this, and then squeeze the two sides together like that."

I follow her instructions, and soon a mass of mashed garlic spews out of the little holes in the device. I laugh out loud. It feels so good to be here, in a kitchen with other women, cooking, living, being. I've gained sixty pounds so far. I'm alive.

"Good job, Jasminka!" says Milan.

From the living room comes loud voice of Milan's mother, asking how long until dinner. Milan shouts back that it will be another half hour or so. After that, doorbell rings, and then Milan's mother shouts something in Spanish that I don't quite understand.

Milan translates, "She just said we better make extra because some family friends from down the street just came by."

Moments later, two men and woman enter the kitchen with Milan's mother and father, everyone laughing and chatting. The woman offers a bottle of wine to Milan, and gives everyone, even me, a kiss on both cheeks. I realize that these people have stopped by uninvited, and unannounced. In most of America, this is considered ill manners, but in my own culture, and Milan's family's, too, it is normal. People are always welcome. I feel warmth and joy in my belly, and then girl's eyes on me. "What are you so happy about?" asks Sophia. She comes to inspect my work.

"I like it here," I say.

"Me too," says the girl.

I feel sharp jab as the baby kicks me in the ribs, awakened by all the noise and commotion, and by scent of garlic frying. I set the garlic press on the counter and place my hands on belly, wincing.

"She's kicking," I tell Sophia and Milan.

"Can I feel?" asks Sophia.

"Sure," I say. I take girl's hand and place it on my belly. "There. You feel that?" I asked Ricky to feel kicking baby many times, but he always acted bored by this idea, or pretended he was going to kick back.

Sophia laughs as the baby kicks, and it seems as if girl shares my love and awe for life.

"Wow," she says. "My sister has some strong legs, eh?"

I feel time stop.

Her sister?

I cried myself to sleep for days, ever since moving in here and leaving Ricky, thinking that I would be having this baby alone in the world, that I would raise child by myself. I assumed that baby and I would be a family isolated. But there is Sophia. Of course there is. A blood relative for my child. My daughter's sister.

Standing here, with the scent and sizzle of garlic frying and noise of people talking and laughing, holding this girl's hand, I feel something I have not felt in many, many years: I am among family. I can't speak. I simply squeeze Sophia's hand, and Sophia squeezes back.

opening night: friday, august 23

Lilia opens her mouth and gives her tongue a shot or two of Binaca. Not everyone uses the stuff anymore, and that's too damn bad, in her opinion. Binaca is the best thing for bad breath, hands down.

Convinced that her breath is fresh enough to take on whatever the night has to offer, Lilia adjusts the lapels on her women's tux and struts across the street from the parking lot toward the former hotel now known as Club G. From this distance she can already feel the bass of dance music thrumming through her solar plexus. She knows this isn't a *real* club night, but something about the warm moisture of the air and the sea of bodies walking toward Club G makes Lilia feel hopeful, and alive. Love could find her here. You just never know.

Geneva Gotay waits at the door in a sleek, simple black dress, her shiny dark hair pulled back in a high ponytail with a red scarf tied in a bow around it. She has her makeup done like a genie or something, and gold bangles almost all the way up her arms from wrist to elbow. Appetizing, but definitely straight, thinks Lilia. Nothing like her sister, the closet dyke. Lilia will draw that delectable little Milan out of her shell one of these days. You can bet on it.

"Hi, Lilia," says Geneva, with that insincere straight-girl smile Lilia hates. "Welcome to Club G!"

Geneva marks Lilia's name off the VIP list on her clipboard and steps back to let her in.

The usual assortment of competitors are here. Lilia detests most of them but does her best to seem friendly. The last people in the world you want to alienate are journalists. They are gossipy, vindictive egomaniacs who pretend to be objective while shoving their personal agendas and psychological problems down the public's throat. Lilia should know. She is one of them. She's wanted to leave this business for years, and even tried to flee a few years back when a dot-com came calling, only to be cast aside when the dot-com-bubble burst. Most amazing of all, she has no idea just how many clichés it took her to even have this memory.

Sexy men and women, half-dressed of course, skim the rooms carrying trays of Champagne and appetizers. Lilia doesn't drink on the job, though plenty of her colleagues do. She refuses the Champagne again and again, but when she sees Milan sitting at the bar with a pretty, short-haired white woman who looks like Kate Hudson but whose face she can't place, chatting as if she were in love, she grows thirsty. Unable to find water, she grabs a flute of Champagne and chugs it down, and approaches Milan.

"Hey," says Lilia, leaning on the bar.

"Uh, Lilia. Hi."

Lilia gives the short-haired blond woman a dirty look. "Lilia, this is my friend Irene Gallagher."

Now Lilia remembers. The woman from Homestead. "You two are friends?" she asks, suddenly feeling uneasy.

"You're the *Herald* reporter?" asks Irene, and a huge, buff man who looks like the Rock approaches and sits next to her.

"Yes," says Lilia. She looks at Milan. "But I don't understand. I thought you two wouldn't, I mean . . ." She can't think of anything to say. Irene Gallagher isn't what she imagined when she wrote that the woman was crazy and a gold digger. She looks wholesome.

"You will," says Milan. "Just stay through the night and you'll understand."

"Oh," says Lilia, with a wiggled brow at Milan. "I'll stay all night. I'm not leaving until you're leaving, and then, I hope, we're leaving together."

Milan chokes on her drink, and Lilia sees Irene and the man next to her hold back a laugh. "What?" asks Lilia. She could take him in a fight. Both of them. She really could.

"Nothing," says Irene. "Good to meet you." Irene gets up. "Milan, I think we're going to go into one of the tents now, lay low for a while."

"Good idea," says Milan.

Lilia winks at her, and moves on, watching Irene and the big dude as they enter a tent that appears to already have a young girl in it. Probably *the* girl, Ricky's so-called illegitimate daughter.

As soon as all the press members have arrived, the music is turned down and Jill Sanchez, dressed in a tiger-print Versace gown with a plunging neckline, takes her place behind a podium on the stage. She giggles as usual, welcoming everyone to the event. Lilia believes Jill Sanchez is one of the tastiest women to walk the face of the earth, and she listens, enraptured and entranced by Jill's easy manner and giggle. She is so darn gorgeous. Too cute for words, almost. Jill apologizes for having to take a moment to talk about her movie and album, "but you know," she says, "they both come out tomorrow, and the business side wanted me to say a few words. You guys know how it is with publicists." Jill giggles. Lilia knows how it is with publicists, all right. She stares across the room at Milan, but fails to make eye contact.

After Jill talks about her projects, the lights go down and a clip from Jill's upcoming movie plays on a large screen at the end of the room. Everyone watches, and claps when it is over. The movie looks great. Jill plays an Italian personal shopper who falls in love with the husband of one of her top clients. The client is a raging bitch, and the husband comes to see that he really loves Jill, and they live, Lilia assumes, happily ever after. She likes the general idea, but wonders, and not for the first time, why Jill always has to play Italians when she isn't playing a maid.

She raises her hand as soon as the lights came up. Jill sees her, and points. "Yes, Lilia?"

"Does Hollywood force you to refute your Latin roots in order to portray characters nonstereotypical in nature?"

Jill screws up her face and giggles. "Sorry?" she says. "I didn't understand the question. Next question?"

After ten minutes of insipid back and forth between Jill and the media—mostly concerning how she and Ricky Biscayne, after coming together for the opening of this club, have fallen into each other's arms after both of their relationships fell apart through no fault of their own—Jill announces a special surprise.

"Ricky and I," she pauses to giggle and look down at her pointy Dior crocodile skin boots. "Gosh, it's so embarrassing!"

"Go on, Jill, tell us!" calls a male reporter, gaga over her sweet little cleavage.

"Well," says Jill. "Geneva, who is the G in Club G, asked us to sing a duet."

Everyone claps. Lilia looks for Geneva, and spots her sitting near her closet-case sister, her mouth open in shock. Lilia guesses that Geneva has not requested any such thing.

"And even though I'm still a little stage-shy about singing in front of people, we agreed," says Jill, with another giggle. "So, here goes!"

A small curtain rises and a band appears behind Jill. The music shifts to a slow, sappy Spanish-language ballad, and Jill allows herself to be whisked off stage by several men. She returns moments later in a long, flowing green gown, her hair in a romantic bun on top her of head, with tendrils of hair curling at the sides of her face. She looks like Venus.

Soon, the voice of Ricky Biscayne booms through the speakers, and the crowd begins to clap. They are supposed to be journalists, thinks Lilia. They should be observing impartially, not applauding. But there aren't many real journalists left anymore, and certainly few in the world of entertainment.

Ricky, in a gray men's suit with a completely open white shirt under the jacket, sits next to Jill on a large, round bed on the stage. The bed is draped in sparkly silks and satins. Ricky sings a pretty good verse, even though he sounds weaker than on his records, and then Jill joins him for the chorus. Her singing is horrendously bad. She sounds like a dying sea bird. Even Lilia recognizes this. Lilia has all of Jill Sanchez's albums at home, and she has sort of suspected that a little doctoring was done on them. But she likes them just fine. This, though? This sounds like something only dogs can hear, slowed down to human range. A collective groan rises through in the crowd. Ricky notices, and seems ashamed, but Jill pretends that everything is fine. She continues to sing even as the reporters boo and laugh. She sings an entire verse totally off pitch. And as the next chorus begins, it seems as if Jill completely loses her place in the song. Ricky keeps trying to get her back on track, but she drifts off, furiously singing and insisting with her facial expression that he come along with her, and acting like she is a great singer and assuming no one will notice otherwise. When Ricky gives up and stops singing, she slaps his arm.

Finally, mercifully, the performance ends. No one claps. The MTV cameras pan across the astonished faces, and a reporter from the music network starts to ask the assembled journalists what they thought of the performance.

"It freakin' sucked," Lilia says with a smile, thinking that maybe, just maybe, there is a beautiful lesbian watching out there who, once she lays eyes on Lilia, will seek her out.

Jill tries to thank the crowd, but Ricky grabs her hard around the wrist, as though catching a child who is running into traffic, and escorts her off the stage.

After the band clears out, Geneva and Milan take the stage.

"That stank," Geneva says to Milan, into the microphone. "Wouldn't you say?"

"Yes," says Milan. "It pretty much flat sucked, Geneva."

The gathered journalists look at one another in confusion.

"But," says Milan, turning to face the reporters. "It didn't stink nearly as much as the latest news we got on my employer, and, I'm pretty sure, my soon-to-be former employer."

Geneva explains to the crowd that her sister is Ricky's personal publicist and has some important information to present. She asks a doctor to join them on stage. After the doctor, they ask the young girl from the tent, and her mother, Irene, to join them, too. Lilia, previously bored to the point that she hasn't even really considered taking out her notebook to write anything down, starts to pay attention.

"Many of you know that Sophia here, a thirteen-year-old from Homestead, has claimed to be Ricky's daughter," says Milan. "And many of you interviewed me about it and I told you it wasn't true. Well, I want to apologize for that, to you, and to Ricky's daughter, Sophia Gallagher, and to her mother, Irene."

She turns to Sophia and takes her hands. "I'm sorry, sweetie. I truly am." Next, Milan embraces Irene. Lilia feels jealousy well up in her throat, but lets it go in the name of a good story.

Suddenly, the reporters gasp, as the lights dim once more and the recognizable slashes of DNA imprints appear on the screen, followed by beautiful photographs of Sophia Gallagher.

"The doctor can explain more about what you're looking at," says Milan.

The doctor goes on to say that blood drawn from Ricky and Sophia shows with more than a 99.9 percent certainty that he is her biological father. Then, a copy of a love letter from Ricky to Irene is displayed on the screen, and Irene takes the microphone.

"He was my first love," she says, her voice trembling with nervousness. "And for a long time I thought he'd be my last. He never helped out, or acknowledged us at all."

A new woman takes the stage, and Irene and Sophia look surprised. "Everyone, this is Alma Batista, Ricky's mother, and she has some things she'd like to say, too."

The older woman takes the microphone, and Lilia wonders if she is a lesbian, too. "I'm ashamed to be here," says Alma. She looks at Irene and Sophia. "Most of this is my fault. I was a very close-minded woman, and I encouraged Ricky to ignore Irene because of her family background." Alma looks ashamed and says, "Irene came from poor white trash, that's what I mean. It was a stupid, ignorant thing to do." Alma begins to cry. "And I've regretted it. I wanted to get in touch with you but I didn't know how, and I didn't know if you'd want me."

Alma hands the microphone to Milan, and Irene stares with loathing at the older woman. Sophia, however, does not. The girl approaches Alma and gingerly hugs her. Alma, realizing what is happening, wraps her arms around the child and squeezes her as if she were a raft on a choppy sea.

When the house lights come back on, arms zoom up, microphones are thrust forward, and everyone seems to want to know the same thing: *Why did Milan decide to share this information tonight? What was in it for Ricky, a key investor in the club?*

"We, my sister and I, decided tonight was the best time to get the news out because you all were going to be here, and a little girl in Homestead needs your support instead of your cynicism. As for my job? I think I just kissed it good-bye. But I have a new job I want to tell you about."

Geneva chimes in, saying, "We fully expect both Jill and Ricky to withdraw their support from Club G after this evening, and we are fine with that. In fact, we have reason to believe the two of them have been cheating on their respective significant others with each other for a long time. They've been lying to you, to us, to everyone, and expecting the rest of us would play along, and we're tired of it."

Several men bring a large neon sign up to the stage and plug it in. It reads CLUB SOPHIA.

"We've renamed the club in honor of Sophia, who shares Ricky's looks and talent, but none of his denial. She's an amazing girl! You'll be hearing lots about her in the future."

Lilia feels someone bump into her, and turns to see the balding little guy who rode his bike up to Milan at Lady Luck. He looks worried, and doesn't notice that he's bumped her. Lilia watches as he makes eye contact with Milan, and Milan smiles. He smiles back, and waves, and there is something secret in their communication that Lilia hates. She raises her hand. "But how will you fund the club if Ricky and Jill pull out?"

"That's where you guys come in," says Geneva. "We're hoping you'll get the word out, and we'll find some new investors."

Lilia shouts out another question: "What's this new job, Milan?"

Milan smiles, and music begins to play. "I thought you'd never ask," she says. She motions to Matthew to come to the stage. He shakes his head. "Come on," she says into the microphone. "Please, Matthew."

Matthew Baker steps up to the stage, and Milan tells the crowd that she is going to manage him from now on, if he lets her. Then she says that she wants everyone to close their eyes and listen to Matthew sing. The guy looks shy, but she hands him the microphone and he begins. Lilia doesn't like being told what to do, so she does not close her eyes. Even so, she could have sworn the voice was Ricky Biscayne's.

When the song is over, Geneva says, "As you can see, this is a night about secrets."

"And that voice you just heard, while familiar, is not the voice of Ricky Biscayne, though that's what this stack of illegal contracts would like you to believe," Milan chimes in. She takes a stack of papers out of a box on the floor of the stage. "They're available to all reporters to look at. We have a lawyer looking into them, as well."

"It's the voice of my sister's boyfriend," says Geneva. "San Francisco's own Matthew Baker."

sunday, august 25

In the Los Angeles home belonging to Lara Bryant, the only woman Jack has ever met whose brains and humor allowed him to forget his hunger for transvestite prostitutes, Jack Ingroff reads the Sunday morning paper with a glass of fresh-squeezed orange juice and feels like a normal man. Lara and her golden retriever have just come back from jogging, and she sits next to him at the edge of the swimming pool. Lara also likes hiking, skiing, and New Mexico.

"What's new?" asks Lara, leaning over to kiss him. She smells sweet, even though she's just done her daily six miles in the Hollywood Hills.

"Look at this," he says with a grin, sliding the paper to her. She takes it and begins to read the section he pointed out. When she is finished, she stares at him with an open mouth.

"Incredible," he says.

"How did you put up with her?" asks Lara.

"I didn't know you yet," says Jack.

They kiss, and Jack's body and soul flood with desire for her. "Hold on," he says. "Hold that thought." He pulls away and walks toward the house.

"Where are you going?" Lara asks.

"I'll be right back," says Jack. "I just have to call my banker and tell him to write a check to Geneva Gotay."

"Who?"

"Keep reading," he says. "You'll see."

monday, august 26

*J*ill soaks in a warm bubble bath, in her $70,000 Medicis by Herbeau handmade polished-nickel tub as her personal masseuse stifles a yawn and rubs her shoulders. She calls her manager to tell him to cancel her promotional appearances for the next two weeks, her eyes steady on the TV in the wall above her feet.

"But you have an album and a movie out in two days, you can't just do that," he protests.

"Do it or lose your job," says Jill Sanchez. "We have to tell everyone I'm sick with the flu, or maybe strep throat, and that I had swollen glands when I sang at the opening of Club G." She coughs for effect.

"They know you didn't have the flu," says the manager.

"You are now officially fired," says Jill Sanchez. "Have a nice life."

She hangs up the phone and flips through the cable stations, amazed at how many of them carry stories about her, Jill Sanchez. And while they aren't the sort of stories she hoped for, she is a firm believer that "all news is good news" in the world of stardom. Publicity is publicity, end of story, even if they keep playing the same four particularly questionable notes over and over again, like they did with Ashlee Simpson's lip-synch disaster years before.

Jill removes herself from the tub, but leaves the water for one of her housekeepers to drain. She doesn't like bending over to pull up the plug. She has other things to worry about. Her masseuse hands her a thick D. Porthault scalloped-edge towel and quietly leaves the room. Jill dries off with the world's most expensive towel, slathers her entire body in Crème de la Mer, the world's most expensive face cream—if it is good enough for a face, she figures, it is good enough for her body—and wraps herself in one of the world's most expensive silk robes, as no fewer than twenty of the world's most expensive candles—Jo Malone—burn around the room.

Jill settles on her fifteen-thousand-dollar Hypnos bed with a script, and starts to read. This one calls for her to play another maid. A maid with a conscience. A maid who falls in love with her employer and teaches him, through her earthy Latin value system, that dignity is more important than money. What a sack of crap, Jill thinks. She considers dumping the script in the trash, then reconsiders it carefully. Playing an earthy maid, as opposed to the "sexy" and "vengeful" maids she has played in the past, might be just what the public wants from her right now. Like it or not, the public in this stupid country wants Latinas to still be oppressed like that, or they want her to play an Italian. Whatever. But she knows that if she doesn't take it, someone else will. Someone like Christina Milian. Jill decides to take the role.

Jill hears a toilet flush, and soon Ricky shuffles into the room in the cashmere Daniel Hanson robe she bought him, depressed and with eyes sunken from crying and who knows what else. Last week he got a letter from a judge saying he had to pay more than a million dollars in back child support to Irene and Sophia Gallagher, equal to about eighty thousand a year for the kid's life so far. The judge has also ordered him to cough up eleven thousand dollars a month in child support from now until Sophia turns eighteen. From a different judge, he got the details of Jasminka's divorce requests. She wants the house in Miami Beach, six thousand a month in alimony, and eleven thousand a month in child support. Ricky cried when he read those letters and told Jill he'd snorted most of his money and didn't know where he was going to come up with the cash for all this child nonsense. Jill has money, but he won't be getting any of it. He knows that, and her lack of generosity (robe aside) makes him depressed. He needs her so much, and with such droopy desperation, that it makes her want to throw up.

"How are you holding up, baby?" he asks. "You okay?"

"Of course I'm okay," she snaps. "Why *wouldn't* I be okay?"

"Well," he says. "No offense, but your album didn't even make the Hot 100, and it doesn't look like anyone's going to see the movie. The news is already saying it's a stinker."

"What the hell do they know?" she rages. "It will earn back with DVD sales."

"I don't know," says Ricky. He tries to ease into bed next to her, but she kicks him away. "I just want you to know that no matter what happens, I'm here for you."

"I have guest rooms," she says, realizing that she will probably never find Ricky as exciting as she did when he was unavailably married. "Use them."

"Jill," he whines. "Don't do this."

Jill observes him for a moment. "Okay," she says. "Here's what I think. You have one sure route to getting your career back."

"I do?" Ricky shuffles to the puffy pink chair in the corner and sits down.

"You find religion."

He looks confused. "I'm not religious."

Jill sighs impatiently. "You know that, and I know that. But the idiot masses don't know that."

"What are you getting at?"

"You *find* religion. It's the only way I can think of that America will forgive you for the sin of leaving your pregnant wife and abandoning your first daughter."

"I didn't abandon her."

"Ricky?"

"Yes?"

"Shut up until I'm finished."

"Sorry."

"You find religion, like a real Jesus freak, okay? You go on all those networks and talk to the preachers and their crazy-ass wives about how sorry you are. You say you found Jesus and he forgave you for your sins. Then, when all those yokel Christians decide to embrace you, you release a religious album and get Jaci Velasquez or somebody like that to guest star on a duet."

"Why would I want to do that?"

"Because, genius," she hisses, her eyes closing to mere slits, "if Jesus forgives you, who in the rest of America is going to argue with *him?*"

"That's never going to work," Ricky moans. *"Estoy jodido."*

"One word," says Jill, counting on her perfectly pretty little fingers. "Hammer."

"Hammer?"

"M.C. Hammer. So what do you think?"

Ricky brightens. He looks at her as if seeing her for the first time, and he smiles. Jill hasn't seen him smile like this in a long time. She likes Ricky when he has confidence and balls. *"¡Mamabicho!* You rotten, evil, conniving, brilliant little *bollo!"* he says.

"Say that to my face, *mamagüebo,"* says Jill, offering up her cheek for a kiss from Ricky. He trots over, kisses her cheek, and tries again to get in bed with her. She pushes him away.

"You have two months," she says. "Two months to get saved, and save your sorry-ass career. Save your career, you get some of this." She slaps her rump.

"Okay," says Ricky. "Can I fuck you now?"

"Guest room," says Jill Sanchez, turning back to her script. "There are six. Take your pick."

wednesday, august 28

I sit with Nestor in the bleachers at the park, eating raw almonds from a Baggie and watching Sophia chase the ball around the field like a true pro among all the other soccer-camp girls. Eleven thousand dollars a month. That's what we'll get, on top of a million-plus payout from Ricky. I can't get my mind around it. I can't even begin to understand what that kind of money means, what it can buy, how it might change our lives. I'm pretty sure it's going to mean my dream house in Coral Gables, better schools for Sophia, and an apartment for my mother where she can live on her own. I am still fighting the fire department, but now there's not the desperate sense that I need to fight for money. I don't. I need to fight to prevent this kind of gender discrimination against other women in the future. I can take my time, get out the word, do it right. And now that they know I have money, their defense—that I'm trying to sue for bucks—has no merit.

Sophia has become the star of the team in no time at all. She has even gained the attention of scouts from a couple of prep schools in South Florida. She's asked me to start looking for a house close to the school she likes best, in Coral Gables, and I can hardly believe that we can actually do that now. Pride makes me want to find a job. I don't want to live on Ricky's money. I want to take care of things on my own. Out on the field, Sophia does a quick dancelike move around two girls, and kicks, and scores.

"She's incredible," says Nestor, and we both stand and cheer.

"Yes, she is, isn't she?"

My eyes stray across the field to the parking lot, where a car pulling in catches my attention. It is a familiar gray Infiniti sedan. My lawyer's sedan. I've been spending so much time with him lately, he's come to feel more like a friend. The thought scares me, actually.

"Uh-oh," I say. I jut my chin toward the car. "It's Sy. This is either really good, or really bad."

Nestor quietly grabs my hand and holds tight to it. Of the many things to love about Nestor, this is the one I like most—his ability to comfort me without trying to tell me what to do. Rare is the man who doesn't feel the need to fix the world.

I watch Sy Berman get out of his car and walk across the edges of the soccer field, keeping his face down and out of view. My heart rate increases as I see that he holds a file folder in one hand.

He looks up, sees us, and waves. We wave back, and I call out to ask what he's doing here. He hurries to us, grinning.

"Good news," he says with a smile. I feel my shoulders relax as Nestor places a magic hand between my shoulder blades and rubs softly.

We scoot down to make room for Sy. He hands me the folder. I take it and look inside. It is a letter from the fire department's legal department, offering to settle out of court for eight hundred thousand dollars. I blink. I could buy a house in cash. I could invest and never work again.

"Wow," I say. "Why did they do that?"

Sy sits down and speaks in a hushed voice. "They saw all the good press you've been getting lately, and didn't see how the hell they'd ever win this fucking thing. That's all."

"You think we should take it?" I ask.

"Nope," says Sy. "Not unless they pay a lot more than that."

We all stop to cheer as Sophia kicks her third goal of the game.

"You think they will?"

Sy smiles and nods. "I got something else for you, too."

He flips through the folder and pulls out another sheet of paper. It is a letter from a fire department up in the Surfside area, which has a female fire chief, inviting me to come join their team. "We would be proud to have such an outstanding firefighter on our staff," says the letter, "and we have a lieutenant opening we'd like you to try out for, if you are ever in the market for a new job."

saturday, september 7

I am now seven months pregnant. This is the stage where everyone smiles at you and puts their hands on your belly. I'm feeling good, though, very good. Strong.

I drive my new Volvo station wagon through Fort Lauderdale, to Alma's house. I traded in the Escalade, which was much more Ricky's style than my own. I see Alma kneeling in the front yard as I pull up. She's wearing creased jeans and a denim button-down shirt, and looks as neat and put together as Martha Stewart. She looks up and smiles as I park the car, and removes her gardening gloves. She's been pruning rose bushes.

She joins me and helps heave me out of the driver's seat. Ugh. You take so many motions for granted until you are pregnant. "How are you?" she asks me. She looks peaceful, and I know it has something to do with Sophia, her granddaughter, who has been visiting her every weekend. They get along so well, and I'm so happy for everyone.

"I am fine," I say as we walk up the sidewalk to Alma's front porch.

"What have you been up to?" she asks.

"Looking for house," I say. "I cannot stay with the Gotays forever. Ricky pays me now, I can find a place. But I don't know Ricky will pay. He has no money."

Alma looks into my eyes with a thought I can't decipher, and helps me through the front door. She sits me in the living room. "You look so beautiful, Jasminka," she says. She gets ice water for us both and offers me a bowl of fruit. I take an apple.

"What did you want to talk to me about?" I ask. She called a couple of hours ago to ask me to come see her as soon as I could.

"Come with me. I want your opinion on something." Alma leads me to a back bedroom, Ricky's old bedroom, and opens door. It has been totally redone in solid furniture.

"Very pretty, Alma," I say. "I am glad you finally got rid of all things that make you so sad."

Alma takes my hand and leads me to the second spare room. She opens the door. It is painted in the palest of pinks, with baby furniture and a rocking chair.

"I do not understand," I say. Alma continues to hold my hand, and this time takes me to the garage. She opens the door, and we walk in.

I take it in slowly. The large counter space. The buckets. The supplies for making soaps. The molds and tools. It's a soapmaking workshop. Alma doesn't make soap. I do.

"You know the saying," says Alma. "When you marry off your son, you gain a daughter. And when they divorce, you keep the daughter." She smiles. "I made up that last part."

"Oh, Alma," I say. I blink back the tears. "You do not have to do this."

"It's here if you want it," she says with a a shrug that underplays the importance of her offer. "For the two of you."

atthew wears ripped jeans that fit just right, and a Mötley Crüe shirt that is all about satire. I stand at the top of the stairway up behind Club Sophia and watch as he carries up a large box of my papers and books.

"Easy there," I say.

"Yeah, you too," he calls, straining. "Don't hurt yourself standing there, Milan." He smiles up at me.

"I'm waiting for the pizza guy," I remind him. "I can't carry anything right now. Gotta keep the hands free for pizza."

He gets to the top of the steps and leans past the box in his arms to kiss me. "Pizza is an important calling," he says. "I agree. Now please get out of the way."

I step to the side and he stumbles in with the box and dumps it on the floor of my new office. I'm renting the space above Club Sophia from Geneva. It's smaller than the office I had at Ricky's, but it has a huge window that overlooks a palm tree, and it is mine, and only mine. I thought about going back to work for Tío Jesús but decided that this was the perfect time to try to make it on my own—as an artist's manager and as Matthew's manager in particular. I'm looking for a condo, too. It won't be in the Portofino, like Geneva's, but it will be in Miami Beach, and it will be mine. I have this idea that one day I'll marry Matthew, but I'm not in a hurry. As I've learned the hard way, it sometimes takes a long time to really get to know someone. Maybe I need to take that Rebuilding Trust Cruise again.

I shouldn't say I'm entirely on my own. I'm actually on Geneva's payroll as a publicist and talent booker, which will support me just fine, but Matthew and I have other plans, too. In a perfect world, mainstream American record labels would have responded as enthusiastically to Matthew Baker as the public did. I have boxes full of letters and e-mails from people who heard Matthew sing on MTV the night of the opening and want to know where they can buy his albums. We've set up a Matthew Baker Web site, which gets thousands of hits a day. Matthew's original songs are among the top-selling downloads for unsigned artists at MP3 and Imusic.

But the fact is, no major label is very excited about either Matthew or me at the moment. We are both seen as risky. Matthew is thought of as risky because, even though he obviously has the talent and "chops," as he calls his skills, to create beautiful songs, he is all wrong for other reasons. First, the label executives I've talked to say they think he's the wrong ethnicity; he was right in assuming they'd be wary of a "gringo salsero." Second, they think he is too chubby and bald. But the biggest problem they seem to have is that he has been so "disloyal" to Ricky Biscayne and his contracts, meaning that Matthew is risky because he finally knows what he is really worth; if Matthew is capable of screwing Ricky, the labels seem to say, why wouldn't he screw them, too?

The same is true of me, in their view. If I was conniving enough to frame my employer when he did me wrong, what might I be able to do to them? In reality, entertainment is a vile industry, full of vile people, and we are no match for it. We've sent out CDs of Matthew, and letters, and we've only heard back from a few labels, all of them in Europe. There's a great little indie label in Barcelona, and we're heading there in a few days to see what might be worked out.

With all of this in mind, it has been my idea to add a café to Club Sophia, where Matthew can perform at brunch on the weekends. The kitchen is being built as we speak. It is Matthew's idea to call some of his old buddies from his days at Berklee, to see if they'd be interested in slumming it in Miami for a while, playing in the house band and recording a Latin-pop album on their own. Geneva and I are working on a business plan to come up with some money to eventually start our own record label, Matt-Mil Records, dedicated to good music in any language, by people of any background and any physical description, with the credo that language and culture, like music and soul, are not genetic, they are learned. A few promising singers have already contacted Matthew about producing for them, and the idea is to start a whole new label that will cater to the public's need for good music without slick imagery, without interference from the fearful executives at existing labels. No bean counters, in other words.

In the past, I might have thought a dream like this was impossible. But watching Geneva succeed with her club, and seeing Jasminka start a soap business in her last month of pregnancy—and land a deal with Burdines-Macy's to actually sell her stuff—has given me hope. Even seeing that Jill Sanchez's career has astoundingly rebounded from the disaster of an opening, and that the star is in production on a new movie with an aging female star who was a hippie icon, and that she is now (cough, gag) engaged to marry Ricky Biscayne, proves that in Miami, a city filled with people from somewhere else who are trying to start anew, with the right people behind you, anything—truly anything—is possible.

monday, october 7, columbus day

Pop.

I wake early in the morning in my cozy new bed at Alma's house. I could have gotten my own place, but with the baby coming I decided to stay with Alma for now. And now, apparently, is when the baby has decided to come. She's coming!

Pop. There is no pain. Not yet. I just felt the most peculiar hollow *pop* in my lower abdomen. I get up and walk to the bathroom. I sit on the toilet and feel the whoosh of hot water flood out of my body. It keeps going, and going, like the world's longest pee. It doesn't stop. Why am I peeing so much? Then it hits me. My water is breaking! Gushing, actually.

"Alma!" I cry. The silence of the house shatters like glass. I hear a rustle, the sound of something falling in a distant room, hurried footsteps, and a gentle knock on the bathroom door.

"Are you okay?" she calls.

"My water broke!"

"Can I open the door?"

"Yes!"

I squat over the toilet and bend over to see the water spilling out from between my legs. I remind myself of a waterfall from back home. "Oh my God. What do I do, Alma?"

Alma opens the cabinet under the sink and starts to toss out rolls of toilet paper and bottles of cleaner. "Please don't let me have thrown them all away," she says. Then she pulls out an old, mashed-up plastic package of sanitary napkins. "Yes! I had menopause two years ago, but I just couldn't throw them all away."

She helps me place a pad on my underpants and gets me dressed. Alma helps me pack an overnight bag with some clothes for me and baby, and then drives me to the hospital in my Volvo. I sit in the passenger seat and watch the dark early-morning sky. My uterus has begun to contract, very slightly, just a crampy feeling to go along with the liquid flowing out of me. I place my hands over my lower belly and rub, gently, trying to stay calm. Is it going to hurt? I know that it will. Am I going to survive the pain? Will baby feel pain on the way out, too? I feel oddly calm, and excited at the same time, a peaceful sort of excitement and resignation for things to come.

We arrive at Memorial Regional West hospital as dawn breaks, and Alma helps me across the parking lot. I hear birds calling to each other in trees. I smell motor oil from the cars, but also the peppery scent of banyan trees in the morning moisture. All of my senses are sharp, alive. I feel excitement in every cell. Is coming. My baby is on the way. This time tomorrow, I will have seen my baby's face. People look at us and smile at the sight of me hobbling in pajamas, knowing exactly why I'm here. The birth of child—a child—is one of the few happy reasons people have for going to a hospital. The only one, I think.

I registered in advance, and we called en route, so there is little waiting. I am ushered right into my private room, with the private bath. My doctor checks my vital signs and sticks sensors on my belly to measure my contractions. I've got a way to go, she tells me. I might as well try to get comfortable, she says. I spend time soaking in jetted tub, a long time. Hours. And the cramping gets more and more intense. I dress in pretty nightgown and walk the corridors as much as I can, as Alma and my doula massage my back and try to keep me hopeful. The contractions grow closer, and the pain begins. What was uncomfortable cramping grows in intensity, and even though I hoped to avoid drugs, I ask for them now. I have endured a lot of pain in my life, but this is almost too much for me. They give me an epidural, and the pain calms a bit. And then, twelve hours after my water broke in her grandmother's bathroom, she is born, quiet, breathing calmly, and with her eyes wide open. Her lungs are fine, and no one tries to make her cry. She is wrapped in a blanket and placed on my chest. She looks up at me with milky gray eyes and blinks wetly. We stare at each other.

"Hi there," I say to her in Serbian, kissing her softly on the head and breathing her in. She smells of the soft, wet earth in Slunj, of blood, of woman, of life. She smells of my history, come back to find me in the form of a brand-new soul. "Welcome to the world."

I name her Danijela, after my mother, and promise her I will always protect her.

While the baby sleeps and I doze, I hear Alma in the reclining chair across room, phoning everyone she can think of to tell them the good news. Again and again she says the same thing: "Imagine, a Mexican, Cuban, Serbian girl, how beautiful, no? She looks just like her mother."

She calls my model friends, and Sophia and Irene, Geneva and Milan, and their parents. Everyone. And she invites them all to come to the hospital later, to share Mexican take-out food, and Champagne in celebration of the baby's arrival. I let the baby sleep in her bassinet, and take a shower, inhaling deeply of the soap I made myself especially for this moment, a soap of sweet almond oil, milk, and helichrysum, a healing soap for injured flesh. I am sore, and bleeding from between legs like something ripped open and near death, but I feel alive and beautiful. I blow-dry my hair and put little bit of makeup on. I dress in a long-sleeved satin nursing nightgown, with slits over the breasts for me to feed my daughter. I am still here, I think. I am here. I survived Ricky, and I survived childbirth. I didn't die.

By six o'clock, the following people have all crammed themselves into my maternity suite: Sophia, Irene, Irene's boyfriend Nestor, Geneva, Milan and Matthew, Violeta and Eliseo, El General and Maria Katarina. I am so hungry, very very much so. The Mexican food arrives as everyone coos over my daughter. Enchiladas in red sauce, refried beans, tamales, red rice, fried potatoes, chips and salsa. Eliseo, Milan's father, looks uncomfortable in the company of so many women talking about so many things to do with birthing babies. He finds the remote control for the television, and he and the other men gather at one end of the room to flip through the stations in search of sports or news. What he finds, however, is unexpected. On one of the religious stations, a priest with a pompadour sits on an ornate and gilded stage interviewing none other than my ex-husband, Ricky Biscayne. My jaw drops as I hold my plate of food, and I simply stare.

"Dad," shouts Geneva. "Leave that there a sec."

"Oh my God," I say. "I do not believe this sight."

All eyes go to the television as the camera does a close-up on Ricky's face. I recognize the phony expression as the same one he uses when he tries to act in movies.

"So, Ricky," says the preacher, with thick Texan accent. "Tell us all about how you were saved."

As violin music plays in background, Ricky speaks about finding Jesus. He talks about how great Jesus is, and everyone in the crowded auditorium where he is being interviewed cries out and waves their hands over their heads. A camera pan of the audience shows thousands of men and women with eyes tightly closed, many of them crying, listening to every word he says.

"I have done a lot of bad things in my life," says Ricky, with a sniffle and a scratch at his nose. "The worst thing of all was letting my children down. But I repented, and I changed my ways. As soon as I found our Lord Jesus Christ, I fell down on my knees and I begged him to forgive me for going ashtray. I mean, astray."

"Amen," says preacher.

"And Jesus forgave me," says Ricky, a phony tear shining at edge of his eye.

"Amen," says the crowd.

"That is the wonderful thing about our Lord," Ricky continues. He sounds like a politician. "That no matter how badly you mess up, no matter how much evil you do, it is never too late to ask him for forgiveness." Ricky looks at the floor modestly and sniffles.

"Amen," says the host, handing him a tissue.

"It is never too late to pray to Jesus to bring you back to the fold," says Ricky.

"Now, you have a new Christian-music album coming out, Ricky, is that right?" asks the preacher.

"That's not the only thing," says Ricky. "Jill and I are trying to have a baby."

"A baby? Really?"

Ricky smiles. "Since I found God, I realized I really *was* cut out to be a father," he says. "I love children."

Danijela chooses this as the first moment of her life to cry out loud. She opens her mouth in wet circle, and screams for me. I rush to her, and pick her up, soothing her at my breast. Everyone in the room stares at us, as Ricky keeps talking on the screen. Milan makes sickened face, and says, sarcastically, "Gosh, you guys. Do you think he means it?"

I look at Alma. Alma looks at Irene. Irene looks at Sophia. Sophia looks at Milan. Milan looks at Matthew. Matthew looks at Geneva. Geneva looks at Violeta. And then, as everyone looks at everyone else, and as if guided by spirit greater than ourselves, we all begin to laugh.

saturday, october 12

Geneva stands in the doorway to my little office, in her True Religion jeans and yet another black tank top, this one decorated with a sparkly jeweled flag of Cuba above a peace symbol. Dad would hate it. Matthew and I cuddle in a beanbag in the corner (his contribution to my office space) and listen to a demo tape from a metal-rock singer in Peru. We are dressed alike, as the people in couples tend to be, in Gap jeans, T-shirts, and flat, square sandals. I have not given up on clothes, but I now know that they really don't matter. At least they really don't matter to me. Geneva isn't even disappointed. She says it's a relief not to have to help me get dressed anymore. Sometimes, I realize, you just have to be yourself, even in Miami. Sometimes, being yourself is the one thing that will rocket you toward your destiny.

"You guys ready?" she asks. I hear heavy feet on the stairs outside, and soon enough see Ignacio's handsome face peeking at us over Geneva's shoulder. He's a god, and he's wearing a pink polo shirt. My sister has found a god who looks good in pink. Amazing.

"We're ready," I say, pushing up from the beanbag with a little help from my man. "Are you?"

Geneva and Ignacio share a look of bravery and concern. "I think so," says Geneva. She lifts her left hand and looks at the diamond. Ignacio takes the hand and kisses it softly.

We are headed to La Carreta for our weekly dinner with our parents, but this will be a weekly dinner with two big differences.

Difference one: Geneva is bringing Ignacio, who our parents have never met, with the plan to tell them that she is going to marry him "even though he is black" (this matters to our parents, sadly); that he's Cuban might win her points, we have no idea.

Difference two: I am bringing Matthew, with the intention of telling my parents that I am moving out in a month, unmarried and scandalous, into my own condo mere blocks from Matthew. I will also break it to them that I have a boyfriend, a boyfriend who is not even Cuban. I can hear them now: "Well, at least he's not black."

"Ignacio, dude," says Matthew, as he gets up from the beanbag and reaches out to shake the other man's hand. "You ready for this?"

Ignacio shrugs, and grins with the grace and peace of the ballet dancer he is. "I don't know," he says. "But we're about to find out."

We lock up, head down the stairs, and pile into Geneva's BMW for the trek to Coral Gables, all four of us a mess of nerves, but feeling very much like the budding family that we are. The guys take the backseat, and Geneva and I sit side by side in front.

"You think Mom and Dad will be okay with this?" I ask Geneva, "this" referring to the men, and to our own ambitions.

"If they're not," she says with a pat to my knee, "just know I've got your back, girlie."

I smile at her, and hold her hand for a moment, as goose bumps creep up my arms. I realize that I was never *really* a slacker. I was a slightly sloppy, basically independent woman, stuck in a family and town that didn't quite accept me that way. I now realize, at last, that no matter what happens tonight, one thing is certain: We, the crazy, excellent Gotay daughters of Coral Gables, will always have an easier time breaking from tradition, and moving forward in the direction of our dreams, if we do it as a team.

"I love you, G," I tell my sister. She grins, and cranks up the reggaeton rap song in her car stereo.

"I love you too, *loca*," she says. "Let's hit it."

1. Milan was waiting for her life to happen to her. Do you think she would have changed if she hadn't met Ricky?

2. What do you make of the contrast between many of the characters' public images and their real selves?

3. Geneva doesn't believe in luck or failure. Which characters would identify with her? Do you?

4. Jasminka hates that Ricky uses people to do his dirty work for him. Why do you think people let Ricky use them?

5. How much of a role does image-conscious, style-obsessed Miami play in the story? If you have read Alisa Valdes-Rodriguez's previous books, how does this setting differ?

6. Geneva's family regards itself as "white" and judges her for dating a "black" boyfriend. Are you surprised that his family judges Geneva too?

7. Milan says she's more in love with Ricky's music than with his body. Do you think that's true? Why or why not?

8. What motivates Geneva's efforts to help Milan: guilt, love, or something else? Does Geneva see more potential in Milan than Milan sees in herself?

9. How does the Gotays' dysfunctional marriage affect Geneva's and Milan's romantic relationships?

10. Do you know any families with sisters as different from one another as Milan and Geneva? Does the dynamic between them ring true to you?

A Reading Group Guide

For more reading group suggestions, visit www.readinggroupgold.com

St. Martin's
Griffin